ITALIAN STORIES/ NOVELLE ITALIANE

A DUAL-LANGUAGE BOOK

Edited by

Robert A. Hall, Jr.

Professor Emeritus of Linguistics and Italian
Cornell University

DOVER PUBLICATIONS, INC.
NEW YORK

Published in Canada by General Publishing Company, Ltd., 30 Lesmill Road, Don Mills, Toronto, Ontario.

This Dover edition, first published in 1989, is an unabridged, slightly corrected republication of the work originally published by Bantam Books, Inc., in 1961.

Manufactured in the United States of America
Dover Publications, Inc., 31 East 2nd Street, Mineola, N.Y. 11501

Library of Congress Cataloging-in-Publication Data

Italian stories.

Reprint. Originally published: New York : Bantam Books, 1961.
 1. Short stories, Italian—Translations into English.
2. Short stories, English—Translations from Italian.
I. Hall, Robert Anderson, 1911–
PQ4254.I8   1989   853'.0108   89-23477
ISBN 0-486-26180-8

CONTENTS

CONTENTS

For those who are interested in this book primarily as a
linguistical tool, it is suggested that the stories be read in the
following order of difficulty: Moravia, Alvaro, Fucini, Palazzeschi, Pirandello, Verga, Fogazzaro, Bandello, Machiavelli, Boccaccio, d'Annunzio.

Foreword

SINCE TIME immemorial, in Italy as elsewhere, people have told each other stories about things which were new, different or interesting; hence the Italian name for such a story, *novella*, derived from the adjective *nuovo*, "new." At the outset, the *novella* was simply a brief anecdote, told with no more artistic pretensions than the little tales which pass from one person to another by word of mouth, and depend for their effect on a brief build-up and a single concluding twist or punch-line. In medieval Europe, numerous such stories were circulating; in addition to contemporary events and personages, their subjects might include folk-tales, animal fables, and other material derived either from ancient sources or from the East, particularly the Indian story collections entitled the *Panchatantra* and the *Hitopadeśa.* Likewise of ultimately Indian origin was the frequently used device—familiar to most of us through the *Arabian Nights*—of unifying a collection of otherwise unrelated stories by incorporating them in the *cornice* or "framework" of still another story.

The first step towards developing the unadorned anecdote into an artistic form was taken in Italy with the two collections known as the *Libro de' Sette Savî* ("Book of the Seven Sages") and the *Novellino,* both of which date from the thirteenth century. The stories contained in these collections range from the brief anecdote of a single paragraph, to the more extended story. In the *Libro de' Sette*

Savî, the stories, set in a framework, are traditional in subject-matter; in the *Novellino,* on the other hand, the tales are derived from many different sources—classical, Biblical, Oriental, and contemporary literature (especially the French *Matière de Bretagne* or Breton cycle of romances). Even in the longer stories, the narrative technique of these two collections is primitive and naïve, with relatively little artistic pretensions, and represents only the first step in the development of the *novella* as a literary genre.

In the fourteenth century, Italy had three men who, each in a particular field of literature, created such masterpieces as to set an example for later generations and thereby exert lasting influence on literary development: Dante Alighieri (1265–1321) in epico-didactic poetry, Petrarch (Francesco Petrarca, 1304–1374) in lyric poetry, and Giovanni Boccaccio (1313–1375) in prose narration. Boccaccio, in his *Decameron* (probably written in the early 1350's), at one stroke carried the medieval *novella* to its furthest development as a form of art. He accomplished this by careful observation and analysis of character, especially as revealed in dialogue; and elaboration of narrative style, by imitation of Latin prose models. To his contemporaries, Boccaccio's Latinizing manner seemed highly ornamental and meritorious, but to moderns it seems heavy and often excessively grandiose for his subject-matter, which is frequently light and humorous. Everyone is still agreed, however, in prizing Boccaccio's insight into human character and his skill in revealing it through realistic and sparkling dialogue.

After Boccaccio's time, a number of relatively minor authors continued the tradition of story-telling in collections of *novelle.* The most important of these writers in the fourteenth century was Franco Sacchetti (ca. 1330–1400), whose collection of three hundred stories (*Il Trecentonovelle*) affords us a reflection of bourgeois life of the time. In comparison with Boccaccio, Sacchetti is unpretentious in his choice of subject-matter and in his narrative technique, but pleasant and amusing in his own right.

Of the story-tellers of the fifteenth century, the most important was a Neapolitan, Masuccio Salernitano (i.e., of Salerno), the author of a collection entitled the *Novellino* (1476), notable especially for his moralistic aim and his strong anticlerical feeling. Although influenced stylistically by Boccaccio, Masuccio writes in a language which is markedly Neapolitan in flavor. Another late fifteenth-century writer of *novelle*, Giovanni Sabbadino degli Arienti (ca. 1450–1510), in his collection *Le Porrettane* ("Tales Told at the Baths of Porretta," 1478, pub. 1483), also writes in heavily dialectal Italian, this time strongly tinged with Bolognese.

The development of printing at the end of the fifteenth and the beginning of the sixteenth century brought with it a renewed surge of story-telling, to supply the newly created popular demand for reading-matter. From this period date two individual *novelle* which deserve mention: the *Giulietta e Romeo* ("Romeo and Juliet") of Luigi da Porto (1486–1519), which is unfortunately too long for inclusion in this collection, and the *Novella di Belfagor arcidiàvolo* ("Story of Belphagor, the Arch-Demon") by the Florentine statesman and political scientist, Niccolò Machiavelli (1469–1527). Among the authors of collections, the most outstanding was Matteo Bandello (ca. 1485–1561), whose stories, in general extremely licentious, reflect the corruption prevalent in the first part of the sixteenth century. Bandello's narrative skill, although not pretentious in the manner of Boccaccio, is sufficient to recount striking and romantic happenings in such a way as to arouse our interest, if not our tragic or comic sense. Other sixteenth-century writers of *novelle* were Agnolo Firenzuola (1493–1549); Anton Francesco Grazzini (1503–1584) with his *Le Cene* ("The Suppers," 1540–1547); and G. B. Giraldi Cinzio (1504–1573), from whose *Ecatommiti* ("Hundred Tales," 1565) a great many Elizabethan dramatists, including Shakespeare, drew their subject-matter. Almost all of these sixteenth-century tellers of tales give their readers accounts of illicit love or of brutal, horrible and revolting crimes; however, they remain essentially within the Boccaccesque tradition of the *novella*, in

that their stories are expansions of the indigenous oral type
of tale, with little or no background (of landscape or cultural setting) and with attention focused almost wholly on
the characters' actions and sayings rather than on presentation or extensive analysis of their inner feelings.

In the seventeenth century, there was only one notable
continuator of the medieval and Renaissance tradition of
short-story narration, the Neapolitan G. B. Basile, whose
collection of *novelle* in Neapolitan, *Lu Cuntu de li Cunti*
("The Tale of Tales") was published in 1634–1636. Basile's
framework and stories are fanciful and folkloristic in character, told with a baroque freedom of imagination and
style; they are extremely valuable as a source for Neapolitan
popular traditions, since Basile gathered his material from
the living speech of the people. By the eighteenth century,
the old tradition of the *novella* in the fashion of Boccaccio,
Sacchetti and Bandello had completely died out, due at
least in part to the moralistically repressive attitudes of
ecclesiastical censorship; even editions of Boccaccio were
expurgated and bowdlerized in this period for popular
consumption.

When the short story revived as a type of literary com-
position, in the latter part of the nineteenth century, it went
by the same name, the *novella,* but it was historically and
artistically a totally new and different genre. The new
novella derived, in style and content, from international,
pan-European literary currents, especially the movement of
realism or, as it was known in Italy, *verismo.* This approach
to literature aimed at representing life (usually modern,
and often that of the lower classes) in its true colors, not
seen through the distorting spectacles of any set of literary
principles, whether neo-classic or romantic. At its best,
realism led to careful, detailed description of external reality
and, at the same time, good analysis of the characters' psychology and motives, but presented especially as seen in
their behavior. At its worst, it covered up a basically romantic predilection for the disagreeable, the repulsive and
the base, and a naïvely behavioristic psychology which assumed that infinite description of external detail could take

the place of psychological penetration and analysis. The outstanding Italian representative of realism as such was Luigi Capuana (1839–1915), in his novels and short stories.

In general, Italian *verismo* combined the principles of realism with another interest of the time, regionalism—the effort to portray life in a given province or city, with an accent on its local peculiarities in customs and psychology— a particularly rich field in a country so diverse as Italy. The leaders in this field were the Sicilian Giovanni Verga (1840–1922), who gave a detailed, accurate, objective portrayal of middle- and lower-class life in Sicily, and the North Italian Antonio Fogazzaro (1842–1911), also a realist and regionalist, but with a stronger Romantic heritage, influenced especially by Sir Walter Scott. Other realist-regionalist writers of this period were the Tuscan humorist Renato Fucini (1843–1921); the Neapolitan journalist and novelist Matilde Serao (1856–1927); and the Sardinian Nobel Prize winner Grazia Deledda (1875–1936). All of these wrote both novels and short stories; for the modern author, the *novella* differs from the novel simply in being shorter and in concentrating on a single event or aspect of character. Somewhat apart from these writers stands Gabriele d'Annunzio (1863–1938), because of his strong interest in depravity, especially (in his regionalistic works) as revealed in the least admirable aspects of peasant life; this interest, which rendered him exceptionally popular during his lifetime and caused the Fascists to make him into a national hero, links him with the French naturalists like Zola rather than with the earlier realists.

In more recent times, Italian prose authors have kept the essential techniques of realism in narration, while extending their interest to the revelation of personality in the inner thoughts and feelings of their characters, as well as in external behavior. The leader in this direction, in the first part of the twentieth century, was Luigi Pirandello (1867–1936). Other modern authors of *novelle* include Italo Svevo (the Triestine Èttore Schmitz, 1861–1928), who has often been compared to Proust and Joyce because of his stream-

of-consciousness technique and his extremely detailed psychological analysis of ordinary people in their everyday lives; Ignàzio Silone (b. 1900), whose novels and short stories reveal an intense, passionate human sympathy for the downtrodden Italian lower classes; and Aldo Palazzeschi (b. 1885), an author with an especial interest in quirks and oddities of human character. Of authors who have come to the fore in the middle of the twentieth century, one of the most outstanding was Corrado Alvaro (1895–1956), whose understanding of character and sympathy for the human race considerably surpassed that of his more internationally famous junior Alberto Moravia (b. 1907). At present, Italian short-story writing, like modern Italian literature in general, follows over-all European trends, and forms part of the modern "concert of nations" in literary matters.

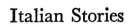
Italian Stories

Giovanni Boccaccio

(1313–1375)

ALTHOUGH BOCCACCIO wrote, in his youth, a number of works of fiction in prose and poetry, and, in his old age, collectanea of classical erudition, he is universally remembered for only one work: his *Decameron*. This collection of tales was given its definitive form at some time after 1348, probably in the early 1350's; however, he may well have been gathering material for the *Decameron* for a considerable time previously.

The *Decameron* takes its name from the framework in which the tales are set: a house-party lasting ten days (Greek *deka* "ten" + *hemera* "day") at a country house in the hills near Florence, during the plague of 1348. A group of seven young ladies and three young men have gone there to escape the plague; to while away the time the ten of them organize games and dances, and on each day each of them tells a story, thus making a hundred tales in all. Boccaccio's young people are of the same level of fourteenth-century Florentine society to which he belonged, the well-to-do bourgeoisie, and they share its rather self-centered, materialistic, skeptical and amoral outlook. A few of his tales are obscene, but the majority, although they reflect a free-and-easy attitude in sexual matters, are not immoral. The major themes of his stories are love and wit, and their opposites, hate and stupidity.

2

GIOVANNI BOCCACCIO

The tale of Calandrino, Bruno and Buffalmacco reproduced here (the third *novella* of the eighth day) exemplifies Boccaccio's humorous narration at its best. These characters recur in other stories of the *Decameron;* Calandrino is the type of the naïve, credulous fool who is easily duped by others for their profit or amusement. He is guilty of one of the cardinal sins in medieval and modern Italian culture—he does not "know the score," does not have a clear picture of his own actions and their relations to others'—and hence is regarded as legitimate game. In telling the story, Boccaccio is especially skillful in analyzing his characters' psychology and making their actions seem plausible and likely. His style is rather heavily Latinizing, except in the dialogue, which he makes especially lively and realistic.

IL DECAMERONE
GIORNATA OTTAVA, NOVELLA TERZA
di Giovanni Boccaccio

CALANDRINO, BRUNO e Buffalmacco giù per lo Mugnone vanno cercando di trovar l'elitropia, e Calandrino la si crede aver trovata; tornasi a casa carico di pietre; la moglie il proverbia ed egli turbato la batte, ed a' suoi compagni racconta ciò che essi sanno meglio di lui.

Finita la novella di Panfilo,[1] della quale le donne avevan tanto riso che ancora ridono, la reina[2] ad Elissa[3] commise che seguitasse; la quale, ancora ridendo, incominciò:

Io non so, piacevoli donne, se egli mi se verrà fatto di farvi con una mia novelletta non men vera che piacevole tanto ridere quanto ha fatto Panfilo con la sua, ma me ne 'ngegnerò.[4]

Nella nostra città, la qual sempre di varie maniere e di nuove genti è stata abbondevole, fu, ancora non è gran tempo, un dipintore chiamato Calandrino, uom[5] semplice e di nuovi costumi, il quale il più del tempo con due altri dipintori usava, chiamati l'un Bruno e l'altro Buffalmacco, uomini sollazzevoli molto, ma per altro avveduti e sagaci, li quali con Calandrino usavan per ciò che de' modi suoi e della sua simplicità sovente gran festa prendevano. Era

4

THE DECAMERON
EIGHTH DAY, THIRD STORY

by Giovanni Boccaccio

CALANDRINO, BRUNO and Buffalmacco go down the
Mugnone looking for the helitropia stone, and Calandrino
thinks he has found it; he goes back home laden down
with stones; his wife scolds him and he, being angered,
beats her, and tells his companions what they know better
than he does.

When Panfilo's story was finished (at which the ladies
had laughed so hard that they are still laughing), the queen
commanded Elissa to continue; the latter, still laughing,
began:

I do not know, charming ladies, whether I shall be able,
with a little story of mine, no less true than pleasing, to
make you laugh as much as Panfilo has with his, but I
shall try.

In our city, which has always been well supplied with
sundry customs and strange people, there was, not long ago,
a painter named Calandrino, a man of simple and naïve
behavior, who for the greater part of the time kept company with two other painters; one of these was named
Bruno and the other Buffalmacco—men who were very
humorous, but also shrewd and clever—who kept company
with Calandrino because they often made very merry over

similmente allora in Firenze un giovane di maravigliosa piacevolezza, in ciascuna cosa che far voleva astuto ed avvenevole, chiamato Maso del Saggio,[6] il quale, udendo alcune cose della semplicità di Calandrino, propose di voler prender diletto de' fatti suoi col fargli alcuna beffa o fargli credere alcuna nuova cosa. Per ventura trovandolo un dì nella chiesa di San Giovanni e veggendolo[7] stare attento a riguardare le dipinture e gl'intagli del tabernaculo il quale è sopra l'altare della detta chiesa, non molto tempo davanti postovi,[8] pensò essergli dato luogo e tempo alla sua intenzione. Ed informato un suo compagno di ciò che fare intendeva, insieme s'accostarono là dove Calandrino solo si sedeva. Faccendo vista[9] di non vederlo, insieme incominciarono a ragionare delle vertù di diverse pietre, delle quali Maso così efficacemente parlava come se stato fosse un solenne e gran lapidario; a' quali ragionamenti Calandrino posto orecchi, e dopo alquanto levatosi in piè, sentendo che non era credenza, si congiunse con loro, il che forte piacque a Maso. Il quale, seguendo le sue parole, fu da Calandrin domandato dove queste pietre così virtuose si trovassero.

Maso rispose che le più si trovavano in Berlinzone,[10] terra de' baschi, in una contrada che si chiamava Bengodi,[11] nella quale si legano le vigne con le salsicce, ed avevavisi una oca a denaio[12] ed un papero giunta, ed eravi una montagna tutta di formaggio parmigiano grattugiato sopra la quale stavan genti che niuna altra cosa facevano che far maccheroni e raviuoli e cuocergli in brodo di capponi, e poi gli gittavan quindi giù, e chi più ne pigliava più se n'aveva;[13] ed ivi presso correva un fiumicel di vernaccia, della migliore che mai si bevve, senza avervi entro gocciola d'acqua.

— Oh!—disse Calandrino—cotesto è buon paese; ma dimmi, che si fa de' capponi che cuocon coloro?

Rispose Maso:
— Mangianglisi i baschi tutti.
Disse allora Calandrino:

his ways and his naïveté. There was also in Florence at that time a young man of remarkable cheerfulness, and clever and graceful in everything he wished to do, named Maso del Saggio, who, on hearing something about Calandrino's naïveté, resolved to make merry at his expense by playing some joke on him or persuading him of some strange thing; and finding him one day by chance in the church of St. John and seeing him intent on looking at the paintings and the carvings of the tabernacle which is on the altar of the aforesaid church, standing in front of it for a short time, he decided that the time and place for his intention had come. And, having told a friend of his what he intended to do, together they approached where Calandrino was sitting alone. Pretending not to see him, they started to talk to each other about the magic powers of various stones, about which Maso talked as knowingly as if he had been a great and impressive lapidary. Calandrino, on hearing this discussion, and standing up after a while, hearing that it was not confidential, joined them, which pleased Maso greatly. The latter, continuing to talk, was asked by Calandrino where stones with such powerful magic as these were to be found.

Maso answered that most of them were to be found in Berlinzone, the country of the Basques, in a region called Bengodi, in which the vines are tied up with sausages, and there was a goose that lays money and a gander too, and there was a mountain made wholly of grated Parmesan cheese on which were people who did nothing but make macaroni and ravioli, and boil them in chicken broth and throw them down, and everyone took as much as he could; and nearby there ran a stream of white wine, of the best that was ever drunk, without a drop of water in it.

"Oh!" said Calandrino, "that is a good country; but tell me, what do they do with the chickens that those people cook?"

Maso answered:

"The Basques eat them all up."

Calandrino then said:

7

— Fostivi tu mai?

A cui Maso rispose:

— Di' tu se io vi fu' mai? Sí, vi sono stato cosí una volta come mille!

Disse allora Calandrino:

— E quante miglia ci ha?

Maso rispose:

— Haccene [14] piú di millanta, che tutta notte canta.[15]

Disse Calandrino:

— Adunque dee [16] egli essere piú là che Abruzzi.

— Sí bene,—rispose Maso—si è cavelle.[17]

Calandrino semplice, veggendo Maso dir queste parole con un viso fermo e senza ridere, quella fede vi dava che dar si può a qualunque verità è piú manifesta, e cosí l'aveva per vere; e disse:

— Troppo c'è di lungi a' fatti miei; ma se piú presso ci fosse, ben ti dico che io vi verrei una volta con essoteco [18] pur per veder fare il tomo [19] a que' maccheroni e tôrmene una satolla.[20] Ma dimmi, che lieto sii tu: in queste contrade non se ne truova [21] niuna di queste pietre sí virtuose?

A cui Maso rispose:

— Sí, due maniere di pietre ci si truovano di grandissima vertú. L'una sono i macigni da Settignano e da Montisci,[22] per vertú de' quali, quando son macine fatti, se ne fa la farina, e per ciò si dice egli in que' paesi di là che da Dio vengon le grazie e da Montisci le macine; ma ècci [23] di questi macigni sí gran quantità, che appo noi è poco prezzata, come appo loro gli smeraldi, de' quali v'ha maggior montagne che Montemorello,[24] che rilucon di mezzanotte vatti con Dio; [25] e sappi che chi facesse le macine belle e fatte legare in anella prima che elle si forassero, e portassele al soldano, n'avrebbe ciò che volesse. L'altra maniera si è [26] una pietra, la quale noi altri lapidari appelliamo elitropia, pietra di troppo gran vertú, per ciò che qualunque persona la porta sopra di sé, mentre la tiene, non è da alcuna altra persona veduto dove non è.[27]

Allora Calandrin disse:

— Gran vertú son queste; ma questa seconda dove si truova?

8

"Were you ever there?"

To which Maso answered: "Do you ask if I was ever there? Yes, if I've been there once I've been there a thousand times!"

Then Calandrino said:

"And how many miles away is it?"

Maso answered:

"Thousands and thousands of miles."

Calandrino said: "Then it must be farther away than the Abruzzi."

"Yes indeed," answered Maso, "it is quite a bit."

Calandrino, the naïve man, seeing that Maso said these words with a straight face and without laughing, believed them as one believes the most obvious truth, and therefore considered them true; and said:

"It is too far off for my means; but if it were nearer, I can tell you that I would go there once with you just to see those macaroni tumble down and to eat my fill of them. But tell me, bless you: in these parts are there none of these stones which are so powerful?"

To which Maso answered: "Yes, there are two kinds of stones of very great power. One kind is the boulders of Settignano and of Montisci, by means of which, when they are made into millstones, flour is made, and therefore in those countries out there it is said that blessings come from God and millstones from Montisci. But there is such a great quantity of those boulders that they are, with us, held in low esteem, just as emeralds are with them, of which there are greater mountains than Montemorello, which shine brightly at midnight. And know you, that anyone who would have millstones in finished shape tied up in rings before they were pierced, and took them to the Sultan, could get anything he wanted for them. The other kind is a stone, which we lapidaries call helitropia—a stone of very great power, because anyone who has it on his person, while he has it, is not seen by anyone where he is not."

Then Calandrino said:

"These are great powers; but where is this second kind of stone to be found?"

A cui Maso rispose che nel Mugnone [28] se ne solevan trovare.

Disse Calandrino:

— Di che grossezza è questa pietra o che colore è il suo?

Rispose Maso:

— Ella è di varie grossezze, ché alcuna n'è più, alcuna meno; ma tutte son di colore quasi come nero.

Calandrino, avendo tutte queste cose seco notate, fatto sembianti d'avere altro a fare, si partì da Maso, e seco propose di volere cercare di questa pietra; ma diliberò di non volerlo fare senza saputa di Bruno e di Buffalmacco, li quali spezialissimamente amava. Diessi [29] adunque a cercar di costoro, acciò che senza indugio e prima che alcuno altro n'andassero a cercare, e tutto il rimanente di quella mattina consumò in cercargli. Ultimamente, essendo già l'ora della nona passata, ricordandosi egli che essi lavoravano nel monistero delle donne [30] di Faenza, quantunque il caldo fosse grandissimo, lasciata ogni altra sua faccenda, quasi correndo n'andò a costoro, e chiamatigli, così disse loro:

— Compagni, quando voi vogliate credermi, noi possiamo divenire i più ricchi uomini di Firenze, per ciò che io ho inteso da uomo degno di fede che in Mugnone si truova una pietra, la qual chi la porta sopra non è veduto da niuna altra persona; per che a me parrebbe che noi senza alcuno indugio, prima che altra persona v'andasse, v'andassimo a cercare. Noi la troverem [31] per certo, per ciò che io la conosco; e trovata che noi l'avremo, che avrem noi a fare altro se non mettercela nella scarsella ed andare alle tavole de' cambiatori, le quali sapete che stanno sempre cariche di grossi [32] e di fiorini, e tôrcene quanti noi ne vorremo? Niuno ci vedrà; e così potremo arricchire subitamente, senza avere tuttodì a schiccherare le mura a modo che fa la lumaca.

Bruno e Buffalmacco, udendo costui, fra sé medesimi cominciarono a ridere; e guatando l'un verso l'altro, fecer sembianti di maravigliarsi forte e lodarono il consiglio di Calandrino; ma domandò Buffalmacco come questa pietra avesse nome. A Calandrino, che era di grossa pasta,[33] era già il nome uscito di mente; per che egli rispose:

To which Maso answered that they were usually found in the Mugnone.

Calandrino said:

"Of what size is this stone and of what color?"

Maso answered:

"It is of various sizes, some larger, some smaller; but all are of a color almost like black."

Calandrino, taking note of all these things, and making believe that he had other matters to tend to, took leave of Maso, and decided to go and look for this stone; but he resolved not to do it without the knowledge of Bruno and Buffalmacco, of whom he was particularly fond. He therefore started to look for them, so that they could go searching without further ado and before anyone else, and he used up all the rest of that morning in looking for them. Finally, when it was after three P.M., remembering that they were working at the Faenza convent, although the heat was very great, leaving all other tasks aside, he went to them almost on the run, and calling them, said to them:

"Friends, if you will believe me, we can become the richest men in Florence, because I have heard from a trustworthy man that in the Mugnone there is a stone whose bearer is not seen by any other person; for which reason it would seem to me that we should go to look for it without any delay, before anyone else goes. We shall certainly find it, because I know it; and when we have found it, what else need we do but put it in our pocket and go to the money-changers' tables, which you know are always laden with 'grossi' and florins, and take as many as we want of them? No one will see us; and thus we can get rich quickly, without having to make tracks on walls like snails all day long."

Bruno and Buffalmacco, on hearing him, started to laugh to themselves; and looking the one at the other, they made as if they were greatly amazed and praised Calandrino's plan; but Buffalmacco asked what was the name of this stone. Calandrino, who was slow on the uptake, had already forgotten the name; wherefore he answered, "What do we

— Che abbiam noi a far del nome, poi che noi sappiamo la vertù? A me parrebbe che noi andassimo a cercare senza star più.

— Or ben,—disse Bruno—come è ella fatta?

Calandrino disse:

— Egli ne son d'ogni fatta, ma tutte son quasi nere; per che a me pare che noi abbiamo a ricogliere tutte quelle che noi vedrem nere, tanto che noi ci abbattiamo ad essa; e per ciò non perdiam tempo, andiamo.

A cui Bruno disse:

— Or t'aspetta.

E vòlto a Buffalmacco, disse:

— A me pare che Calandrino dica bene; ma non mi pare che questa sia ora da ciò, per ciò che il sole è alto e dà per lo Mugnone entro ed ha tutte le pietre rasciutte;[34] per che tali paion testé bianche, delle pietre che vi sono, che la mattina, anzi che il sole l'abbia rasciutte, paion nere. Ed oltre a ciò, molta gente per diverse cagioni è oggi, che è dì da lavorare, per lo Mugnone, li quali, veggendoci, si potrebbono indovinare quello che noi andassimo faccendo e forse farlo essi altressì; e potrebbe venire alle mani a loro, e noi avremmo perduto il trotto per l'ambiadura.[35] A me pare, se pare a voi, che questa sia opera da dover far da mattina, che si conoscon meglio le nere dalle bianche, ed in dì di festa, che non vi sarà persona che ci veggia.[36]

Buffalmacco lodò il consiglio di Bruno, e Calandrino vi s'accordò, ed ordinarono che la domenica mattina vegnente[37] tutti e tre fossero insieme a cercar di questa pietra; ma sopra ogni altra cosa gli pregò Calandrino che essi non dovesser questa cosa con persona del mondo ragionare, per ciò che a lui era stata posta in credenza. E ragionato questo, disse loro ciò che udito avea della contrada di Bengodi, con saramenti affermando che così era. Partito Calandrino da loro, essi quello che intorno a questo avessero a fare ordinarono fra sé medesimi.

Calandrino con disidèro aspettò la domenica mattina; la qual venuta, in sul far del dì[38] si levò, e chiamati i com-

care about the name, since we know its power? To me it would seem that we ought to go and look without waiting any longer."

"Well," said Bruno, "what is it like?"

Calandrino said:

"There are all kinds of them, but all are almost black; therefore it seems to me that we ought to collect all those which we see are black, until we come upon it; and therefore let's not lose any time, let's go."

To which Bruno said:

"Now wait."

And turning to Buffalmacco, he said: "It seems to me that Calandrino speaks well; but it does not seem to me that this is the time for it now, because the sun is high and is shining on the Mugnone and has dried out all the stones, so that some of the stones which are there will now seem white, whereas in the morning, before the sun has dried them, they seem black. And furthermore, there are many people out today along the Mugnone—for various reasons, because today is a working day—who, on seeing us, might guess what we were about and might perhaps do likewise; and it might fall into their hands, and we would have lost out through being in too much of a hurry. It seems to me, if you agree, that this is a job to be done in the morning, when the black stones can be distinguished more easily from the white ones, and on a holiday, when there will be no one to see us."

Buffalmacco praised Bruno's opinion, and Calandrino agreed, and they arranged that on the following Sunday morning, all three together would go to look for this stone; but Calandrino begged them above all else not to speak of this to anyone in the world, because it had been given to him in confidence. And having said this, he told them what he had heard about the region of Bengodi, swearing with oaths that it was so. When Calandrino had left them, they arranged between them what was to be done in this matter.

Calandrino waited eagerly for the Sunday morning; when it had come, he arose at dawn and, calling his companions,

pagni, per la porta a San Gallo usciti e nel Mugnon discesi, cominciarono ad andare ingiù, della pietra cercando. Calandrino andava, come più volenteroso, avanti, e prestamente or qua ed or là saltando, dovunque alcuna pietra nera vedeva, si gittava, e quella ricogliendo si metteva in seno. I compagni andavano appresso, e quando una e quando un'altra ne ricoglievano; ma Calandrino non fu guari di via andato, che egli il seno se n'ebbe pieno; per che, alzandosi i gheroni della gonnella (che all'analda non era), e faccendo di quegli ampio grembo, bene avendogli alla coreggia attaccati d'ogni parte, non dopo molto gli empiè, e similmente, dopo alquanto spazio, fatto del mantello grembo, quello di pietre empiè. Per che, veggendo Buffalmacco e Bruno che Calandrino era carico e l'ora del mangiare s'avvicinava, secondo l'ordine da sé posto, disse Bruno a Buffalmacco:

— Calandrino dov'è?
Buffalmacco, che ivi presso sel [39] vedea, volgendosi intorno ed or qua ed or là riguardando, rispose:
— Io non so, ma egli era pur poco fa qui dinanzi da noi.

Disse Bruno:
— Benché fa poco, a me pare egli esser certo che egli è ora a casa a desinare, e noi ha lasciati nel farnetico d'andar cercando le pietre nere giù per lo Mugnone.
— Deh! come egli ha ben fatto—disse allor Buffalmacco—d'averci beffati e lasciati qui, poscia che noi fummo sì sciocchi che noi gli credemmo. Sappi, chi sarebbe stato sì stolto che avesse creduto che in Mugnone si dovesse trovare una così virtuosa pietra, altri che noi?!
Calandrino, queste parole udendo, imaginò che quella pietra alle mani gli fosse venuta e che per la vertù d'essa coloro, ancor che loro fosse presente, nol [40] vedessero. Lieto adunque oltre modo di tal ventura, senza dir loro alcuna cosa, pensò di tornarsi a casa; e vòlti i passi indietro, se ne cominciò a venire. Veggendo ciò Buffalmacco, disse a Bruno:
— Noi che faremo? Ché non ce n'andiam noi?

after they had gone out together by the San Gallo gate and descended to the Mugnone, they started to go downstream, looking for the stone. Calandrino, as the most eager, went ahead, and jumping vigorously now hither and now yon, leaped wherever he saw some black stone, and collecting it put it in his bosom. His companions followed after, and gathered sometimes one and sometimes another. But Calandrino had scarcely gone very far, before he had his bosom full of them; wherefore, raising the gussets of his robe (which was not hemmed up), and making a broad apron of them, and having attached them firmly to the belt on all sides, he soon filled them; and likewise, after a short time, making an apron of his cloak, he filled that with stones. Wherefore, when Buffalmacco and Bruno saw that Calandrino was loaded down and that the dinner hour was approaching, according to the plan they had made, Bruno said to Buffalmacco:

"Where is Calandrino?"

Buffalmacco, who saw him there near himself, turning around and looking now here and now there, answered: "I do not know, but he was here in front of us only a short while ago."

Bruno said: "Although it was a short time, it seems to me certain that he is at home now eating, and has left us in the mad activity of going down the Mugnone looking for black stones."

"Oh! How well he did," said Buffalmacco then, "to have tricked us and left us here, since we were so foolish as to have believed him. Do you know, who would have been so foolish as to have believed that such a powerful stone was to be found in the Mugnone, except us!"

Calandrino, hearing these words, imagined that *that* stone had come into his hands and that through its power they, although he was in their presence, did not see him. Being, therefore, very glad at such good luck, without saying anything to them, he decided to go back home; and, turning back, started to go away. Buffalmacco, on seeing this, said to Bruno:

"What shall we do? Why don't we go away?"

A cui Bruno rispose:

— Andianne; [41] ma io giuro a Dio che mai Calandrino non me ne farà più niuna; e se io gli fossi presso come stato sono tutta mattina, io gli darei tale di questo ciotto nelle calcagna, che egli si ricorderebbe forse un mese di questa beffa!

Ed il dir le parole e l'aprirsi [42] ed il dar del ciotto nel calcagno a Calandrino fu tutto uno. [43] Calandrino, sentendo il duolo, levò alto il piè e cominciò a soffiare, ma pur si tacque ed andò oltre. Buffalmacco, recatosi in mano un de' codoli che raccolti avea, disse a Bruno:

— Deh! vedi bel codolo: così giugnesse egli testé nelle reni a Calandrino!

E lasciato andare, gli diè con esso nelle reni una gran percossa; ed in brieve, in cotal guisa, or con una parola ed or con un'altra, su per lo Mugnone infino alla porta a San Gallo il vennero lapidando. Quindi, in terra gittate le pietre che ricolte aveano, alquanto con le guardie de' gabellieri si ristettero, le quali, prima da loro informate, faccendo vista di non vedere, lasciarono andar Calandrino con le maggior risa del mondo. Il quale senza arrestarsi ne venne a casa sua, la quale era vicina al Canto alla Macina; ed in tanto fu la fortuna piacevole alla beffa, che, mentre Calandrino per lo fiume ne venne e poi per la città, niuna persona gli fece motto, come che pochi ne scontrasse, per ciò che quasi a desinare era ciascuno.

Entrossene adunque Calandrino così carico in casa sua. Era per ventura la moglie di lui, la quale ebbe nome monna [44] Tessa, bella e valente donna, in capo della scala; ed alquanto turbata della sua lunga dimora, veggendol [45] venire, cominciò proverbiando a dire:

— Mai, frate, il diavol ti ci reca! Ogni gente ha già desinato quando tu torni a desinare.

Il che udendo Calandrino e veggendo che veduto era, pieno di cruccio e di dolore cominciò a gridare:

— Oimè! malvagia femmina, o eri tu costì? Tu m'hai diserto; [46] ma in fè di Dio io te ne pagherò!

To which Bruno answered:

"Let us go; but I swear to God that Calandrino will never play another trick on us; and if I were as near to him as I have been all morning, I would give him such a one of these rocks on the heels, that he would remember this trick for perhaps a month!"

And no sooner did he say the words than he hauled off and hurled a rock at Calandrino's heel. Calandrino, feeling the pain, lifted up his foot and started to puff, but nevertheless kept quiet and went ahead. Buffalmacco, taking in his hand one of the stones which they had picked up, said to Bruno:

"Oh! Look what a fine stone! I wish it would hit Calandrino in the back right now!"

And, letting it fly, he gave him a tremendous blow with it in the back; and in short, in this way, now saying one thing and now another, they kept stoning him along the Mugnone as far as the San Gallo gate. Thereupon, throwing to the ground the stones which they had collected, they stayed for a while with the customs guards, whom they had informed beforehand, and who, pretending not to see, let Calandrino go through with the greatest laughter in the world. He went on without stopping to his house, which was near the Canto della Macina; and Fortune was so favorable to the jest, that, while Calandrino went up along the river and then through the city, no person spoke to him, since he met but few, because almost everyone was at lunch.

And so Calandrino, thus loaded down, went into his house. By chance his wife, monna Tessa, a beautiful and clever woman, was at the head of the stairs; and, being somewhat worried at his long absence, when she saw him coming, she started to say, scolding him:

"Now, brother, the devil brings you! Everyone has already eaten when you come back to eat."

Calandrino, hearing this and perceiving that he was seen, full of rage and sorrow began to shout:

"Alas! wicked woman, were you there? You have ruined me; but, by the faith of God, I will repay you for it!"

E salito in una sua saletta e quivi scaricate le molte pietre che recate avea, niquitoso corse verso la moglie, e presala per le trecce, la si gittò a' piedi, e quivi, quanto egli potè mener le braccia ed i piedi, tanto le die' per tutta la persona pugna e calci, senza lasciarle in capo capello o osso addosso che macero non fosse, niuna cosa valendole il chieder mercè con le mani in croce.

Buffalmacco e Bruno, poi che co' guardiani della porta ebbero alquanto riso, con lento passo cominciarono alquanto lontani a seguitar Calandrino; e giunti a piè dell'uscio di lui, sentirono la fiera battitura la quale alla moglie dava, e faccendo vista di giugnere pure allora, il chiamarono. Calandrino tutto sudato, rosso ed affannato si fece alla finestra e pregògli che suso a lui dovessero andare. Essi, mostrandosi alquanto turbati, andaron suso e videro la sala piena di pietre, e nell'un de' canti la donna scapigliata, stracciata, tutta livida e rotta nel viso, dolorosamente piagnere; e d'altra parte, Calandrino, scinto ed ansando a guisa d'uom lasso, sedersi. Dove come alquanto ebbero riguardato, dissero:

— Che è questo, Calandrino? Vuoi tu murare, che noi veggiamo qui tante pietre?
Ed oltre a questo, soggiunsero:
— E monna Tessa che ha? El par [47] che tu l'abbi battuta; che novelle son queste?
Calandrino, faticato dal peso delle pietre e dalla rabbia con la quale la donna aveva battuta e dal dolore della ventura la quale perduta gli pareva avere, non poteva raccoglier lo spirito a formare intera la parola alla risposta; per che soprastando, Buffalmacco ricominciò:

— Calandrino, se tu avevi altra ira, tu non ci dovevi per ciò straziare come fatto hai; ché, poi sodotti ci avesti a cercar teco della pietra preziosa, senza dirci né a Dio né a diavolo,[48] a guisa di due becconi nel Mugnon ci lasciasti e venistitene,[49] il che noi abbiamo forte per male; ma per certo questa fia la sezzaia che tu ci farai mai.

And going up into a little room and unloading there the quantity of stones which he had brought, he ran in fury towards his wife, and grasping her by the hair, he hurled her down at his feet, and there, as hard as he could strike with hands and feet, he gave her kicks and blows over all her body, without leaving a single hair on her head or bone in her body that was not bruised; and it did her no good to beg for mercy with her hands crossed.

Buffalmacco and Bruno, after they had laughed a while with the guardians of the gate, with slow steps started to follow Calandrino at some distance; and when they arrived at the foot of his door, they heard the savage beating that he was giving his wife; and pretending to be arriving just then, they called him. Calandrino, all sweating, red in the face and panting, appeared at the window and asked them to come up to where he was. They, behaving somewhat alarmed, went up and saw the room full of stones, and in one of the corners the woman disheveled, in tatters, all black-and-blue and lacerated in the face, weeping bitterly; and on the other side, Calandrino, ungirded and panting like a weary man, sitting down. Whereupon, when they had looked for a while, they said:

"What is this, Calandrino? Do you want to build a wall, that we see so many stones here?"

And in addition to this, they added:

"And what is the matter with monna Tessa? It seems that you have beaten her; what strange thing is this?"

Calandrino, worn out by the weight of the stones and by the rage with which he had beaten the woman and by sorrow at the luck which he thought he had lost, was not able to gather his wits together to form words to answer coherently; since he was not speaking, Buffalmacco began again:

"Calandrino, if you had some other cause for anger, you should not have tormented us as you have, for that reason; for, after you had persuaded us to look for the precious stone with you, without saying a word of farewell you left us in the Mugnone like two boobies and came away, at which we are greatly offended; but certainly this will be the last trick

A queste parole Calandrino, sforzandosi, rispose:

— Compagni, non vi turbate: l'opera sta altrimenti che voi non pensate. Io, sventurato, aveva quella pietra trovata: e volete udire se io dico il vero? Quando voi primieramente di me domandaste l'un l'altro, io v'era presso a men di diece braccia, e veggendo che voi ve ne venivate e non mi vedevate, v'entrai innanzi, e continuamente poco innanzi a voi me ne son venuto.

E cominciandosi dall'un de' capi, infino alla fine raccontò loro ciò che essi fatto e detto aveano, e mostrò loro il dosso e le calcagna come i ciotti conci[50] gliel'avessero, e poi seguitò:

— E dicovi che, entrando alla porta con tutte queste pietre in seno che voi vedete qui, niuna cosa mi fu detta, ché sapete quanto esser sogliano spiacevoli e noiosi que' guardiani a volere ogni cosa vedere; ed oltre a questo, ho trovati per la via più miei compari ed amici, li quali sempre mi soglion far motto ed invitarmi a bere, né alcun fu che parola mi dicesse né mezza, sì come quegli che non mi vedeano. Alla fine, giunto qui a casa, questo diavolo di questa femina maladetta mi si parò dinanzi ed ebbemi veduto, per ciò che, come voi sapete, le femine fanno perder la vertù ad ogni cosa; di che io, che mi poteva dire il più avventurato uom di Firenze, sono rimaso il più sventurato; e per questo l'ho tanto battuta quanto io ho potuto menar le mani, e non so a quello che io mi tengo che io non le sego le veni, che maladetta sia l'ora che io prima la vidi e quando ella mai venne in questa casa! E raccesosi nell'ira, si voleva levare per tornare a batterla da capo.

Buffalmacco e Bruno, queste cose udendo, facevan vista di maravigliarsi forte e spesso affermavano quello che Calandrino diceva, ed avevano sì gran voglia di ridere che quasi scoppiavano; ma veggendolo furioso levare per battere un'altra volta la moglie, levatiglisi allo 'ncontro, il ritennero, dicendo, di queste cose niuna colpa aver la donna ma egli, che sapeva che le femine facevano perdere la vertù alle cose, e non l'aveva detto che ella si guardasse

you will ever play on us."

At these words Calandrino, making an effort, answered:
"Friends, do not be upset; the matter stands otherwise
than you think. I, unlucky man, had found that stone; and
will you listen if I tell the truth? When you first asked each
other about me, I was near you, less than ten arm's lengths
away, and seeing that you were going away and did not see
me, I went in front of you, and went along continually a
little in front of you."

And starting at the beginning, he told them up to the
end what they had said and done, and showed them how
the rocks had bruised his heels and his back, and then
continued:

"And I tell you that, when I came in through the gate
with all these rocks that you see here in my bosom, nothing
was said to me—and you know how nasty and disagreeable
those guards usually are in insisting on seeing everything—
and in addition to this, I met along the way several of my
cronies and friends, who are always in the habit of speaking
to me and inviting me to drink, but here was not a one who
said a word or even half a word to me, just like people who
did not see me. Finally, when I got back home here, this
cursed devil of a woman planted herself in front of me and
saw me, because, as you know, women make all magic lose its
power; whereby I, who might have been called the luckiest
man in Florence, ended up as the unluckiest; and therefore
I have beaten her as hard as I could hit with my hands, and
I don't know why I refrain from cutting her veins; curses
on the hour when I first saw her and when she ever came
into this house!" And, getting angry again, he was going to
get up and start beating her again.

Buffalmacco and Bruno, on hearing these things, pretended to be very much astounded and often confirmed
what Calandrino was saying, and felt so much like laughing
that they were almost bursting; but seeing him get up in rage
in order to beat his wife again, they got up and went
towards him and restrained him, saying that the woman
was not to blame for these things but that he was, because
he knew that women make things lose their magic power,

d'apparirgli innanzi quel giorno; il quale avvedimento Iddio gli aveva tolto o per ciò che la ventura non doveva esser sua o perché egli aveva in animo d'ingannare i suoi compagni, a' quali, come s'avvedeva d'averla trovata, il dovea palesare. E dopo molte parole, non senza gran fatica la dolente donna riconciliata con essolui,[51] e lasciandol malinconoso con la casa piena di pietre, si partirono.

and had not told her to avoid appearing in his presence that day; and that God had deprived him of this foresight, either because good fortune was not to be his, or because he was intending to cheat his companions, whom he should have informed as soon as he realized that he had found the stone. And after much talk, reconciling the woman with him (though not without great difficulty) and leaving him in gloom with his house full of stones, they took their departure.

Niccolò Machiavelli

(1469–1527)

THE FLORENTINE Niccolò Machiavelli is best known for a short treatise on applied political science, *Il Prìncipe* ("The Prince," ca. 1515), an analysis of the technique to be used by a monarchical ruler to gain and keep control of a state. In addition to *The Prince,* Machiavelli wrote a series of *Discorsi sulla prima deca di Tito Livio* ("Reflections on the First Ten Books of Livy"), containing analogous reflections on the relation of the state to its citizens under a republican government; the *Istorie fiorentine* ("History of Florence") and a semi-fictionalized biography of a four-teenth-century Lucchese tyrant, Castruccio Castracane. His fictional production was much smaller, and consists prin-cipally of two plays, *La Mandràgola* ("The Mandrake") and *Clizia,* plus the short story of Belfagor the Arch-Devil, re-produced here.

In *The Prince,* Machiavelli analyzed the procedures to be followed by a ruler, solely from the point of view of their effectiveness, and without regard to traditional ethics. From this apparent neglect of morality, many readers of Machia-velli have concluded that he was favorable to dishonesty and deceit; especially in Elizabethan times, he was regarded as a base scoundrel who counseled the vilest treachery and the blackest wickedness. In actuality, Machiavelli's analysis of statecraft, both under a monarch in *The Prince* and

24

under a republic in the *Discourses on Livy*, was based on dispassionate, scientific analysis of the facts as they exist, not as they are supposed to be according to the prescriptions of moralists. Something of this same objectivity appears in his treatment of a traditional, folkloristic theme in the tale of Belfagor. In narrating Belfagor-Roderick's marital adventures and ultimate discomfiture, Machiavelli does not take sides, but simply presents events as they happen. Thus, the character of the demon when he assumes the shape of a man is shown to be inevitably conditioned by the innate drives and passions of the human race.

BELFAGOR;
NOVELLA DEL DEMONIO
CHE PRESE MOGLIE
di Niccolò Machiavelli

Leggesi nelle antiche memorie delle fiorentine cose, come già s'intese per relazione di alcuno santissimo uomo la cui vita appresso qualunque in quelli tempi vivea era celebrata, che standosi astratto nelle sue orazioni, vide, mediante quelle, come andando infinite anime di quelli miseri mortali che nella disgrazia di Dio morivano all'inferno, tutte o la maggior parte si dolevano non per altro che per avere preso moglie essersi a tanta infelicità condotte. Donde che Minos [1] e Radamanto,[2] insieme con gli altri infernali giudici, ne avevano maraviglia grandissima; e non potendo credere queste calunnie che costoro al sesso femmineo davano essere vere, e crescendo ogni giorno le querele, e avendo di tutto fatto a Plutone [3] conveniente rapporto, fu deliberato per lui di avere sopra questo caso con tutti gl'infernali prìncipi maturo esàmine, e pigliarne dipoi quel partito che fusse [4] giudicato migliore per scoprire questa fallacia e conoscerne in tutto la verità. Chiamatoli adunque a concilio, parlò Plutone in questa sentenza:

— Ancora che io, dilettissimi miei, per celeste disposizione e fatale sorte al tutto irrevocabile, possegga questo regno, e che per questo io non possa essere obligato ad alcuno iudizio o celeste o mondano, nondimeno—perché gli è maggiore prudenza di quelli che possono più sottomettersi più alle

BELFAGOR;
STORY OF THE DEVIL
WHO TOOK A WIFE

by Niccolò Machiavelli

WE READ in ancient histories of Florentine affairs, that once it was heard, from the narration of a certain most holy man whose life was well known to anyone who lived in those times, that, when he was absorbed in his prayers, he saw, by means of them, that, whereas an infinite number of souls of those unfortunate mortals who died in the disfavor of God were going to Hell, all or the greater part of them complained that they had been brought to such unhappiness only because they had taken wives. At this Minos and Rhadamanthos, together with the other judges of Hell, were greatly amazed. Since they could not believe that these accusations made by those souls against the female sex could be true, and since the complaints grew day by day, they had made a suitable report about the whole matter to Pluto. He then decided to make a thorough study of this matter with all the princes of Hell, and to take whatever action might be considered best to discover this fallacy and to know completely how true it was. When, therefore, he had called them to a council, Pluto spoke to this effect:

"Although I, my dear friends, am the owner of this kingdom by the order of Heaven and by completely irrevocable decision of Fate, and can therefore not be subject to any judgment, heavenly or earthly, nevertheless—since it is greater wisdom on the part of those who have the most

27

leggi e più stimare l'altrui iudizio—ho deliberato esser consigliato da voi come, in uno caso il quale potrebbe seguire con qualche infamia del nostro imperio, io mi debba governare. Perché dicendo tutte l'anime degli uomini che vengono nel nostro regno esserne stata cagione la moglie, e parendoci questo impossibile, dubitiamo che, dando iudizio sopra questa relazione, ne possiamo essere calunniati come troppo creduli, e non ne dando, come manco severi e poco amatori della iustizia. E perché l'uno peccato è da uomini leggieri e l'altro da ingiusti, e volendo fuggire quegli carichi che da l'uno e l'altro potrebbono dependere, e non trovandone il modo, vi abbiamo chiamati acciò che consigliandone ci aiutiate, e siate cagione che questo regno, come per lo passato è vivuto sanza infamia, così per lo avvenire viva.

Parve a ciascheduno di quegli prìncipi il caso importantissimo e di molta considerazione; e concludendo tutti come egli era necessario scoprirne la verità, erano discrepanti del modo. Perché a chi pareva che si mandasse uno, a chi più, nel mondo, che sotto forma di uomo conoscesse personalmente questo vero. A molti altri occorreva potersi fare sanza tanto disagio, costringendo varie anime con vari tormenti a scoprirlo. Pure la maggior parte consigliando che si mandasse, s'indirizzorno [5] a questa opinione. E non si trovando alcuno che voluntariamente prendesse questa impresa, deliberorno che la sorte fusse quella che lo dichiarasse. La quale cadde sopra Belfagor, arcidiavolo, ma per lo adietro, avanti che cadesse di cielo, arcangelo. Il quale, ancora che male volentieri pigliasse questo carico, nondimeno constretto da lo imperio di Plutone, si dispose a seguire quanto nel concilio si era determinato, e si obligò a quelle condizioni che infra loro solennemente erano state deliberate. Le quali erano: che subito a colui che fusse a questa commissione deputato, fussino [6] consegnati centomila ducati, con i quali doveva venire nel mondo, e sotto forma di uomo prender moglie, e con quella vivere dieci anni; e dipoi, fingendo di morire, tornarsene, e per isperienza far fede ai suoi superiori quali sieno [7] i carichi e

power, to submit most to law and to set most store by others'
opinion—I have decided to be advised by you as to how,
in a matter which might redound somewhat to the discredit
of our realm, I should proceed. For, since all the souls of
men that come to our kingdom say that their wives were
the cause of this, and since this seems to us impossible, we
fear lest, if we pass judgment on the basis of this story, we
be accused of being too credulous; and, if we do not do so,
we be accused of being insufficiently firm and of not loving
justice. And because the first error is characteristic of irresponsible men, and the second of unjust men, and since
we wish to avoid those charges which might result from the
one and the other, and since we cannot find the way to do
so, we have called you to aid us by your advice, and to
cause this kingdom, just as it has existed in past times without reproach, to continue so in the future."

The matter seemed very important to each of those
princes and deserving of great consideration; and, although
they all agreed that it was necessary to discover how much
truth there was in it, they disagreed as to the means. For
some thought that one person should be sent, and some that
several should be sent, to the world, to find the truth of this
personally, in human shape. Many others thought this could
be done without so much trouble, by forcing a number of
souls to tell the truth by different kinds of torture. However,
since the majority advised that someone be sent, they
adhered to this opinion. And since there was no one willing
to undertake this mission voluntarily, they decided that lots
should be drawn to decide. The lot fell upon Belfagor, an
arch-devil, but formerly, before he fell from Heaven, an
archangel. He, although he did not wish to undertake this
task, was nevertheless forced to do so by Pluto's authority;
he prepared to carry out what had been decided in the
council, and placed himself under those conditions which
had solemnly been decided among them. These were: that,
immediately, the one who was assigned to this undertaking
should receive a hundred thousand ducats; with these he
was to go into the world, and, in human shape, take a wife
and live with her for ten years; and then, pretending to die,

le incommodità del matrimonio. Dichiarossi [8] ancora, che durante detto tempo ei [9] fusse sottoposto a tutti quegli disagi e mali a che sono sottoposti gli uomini, e che si tira dietro la povertà, la carcere, la malattia, e ogni altro infortunio nel quale gli uomini incorrono, eccetto se con inganno o astuzia se ne liberasse.

Prese adunque Belfagor la condizione e i danari, ne venne nel mondo; e ordinato di sua masnada cavagli [10] e compagni, entrò onoratissimamente in Firenze: la quale città innanzi a tutte altre elesse per suo domicilio, come quella che gli pareva più atta a sopportare chi con arti usurarie esercitasse i suoi danari. E fattosi chiamare Roderigo di Castiglia,[11] prese una casa a fitto nel borgo d'Ognissanti; [12] e perché non si potessino [13] rinvenire le sue condizioni, disse essersi da piccolo partito di Spagna e itone [14] in Soria,[15] e avere in Aleppe [16] guadagnato tutte le sue facultà, donde s'era poi partito per venire in Italia, a prender donna in luoghi più umani, e alla vita civile e allo animo suo più conformi.

Era Roderigo bellissimo uomo, e monstrava [17] una età di trenta anni; e avendo in pochi giorni dimostro [18] di quante ricchezze abundasse, e dando esempli di sé di essere umano e liberale, molti nobili cittadini che avevano assai figliole e pochi danari, se gli offerivano. Intra le quali tutte Roderigo scelse una bellissima fanciulla chiamata Onesta, figliuola di Amerigo Donati; [19] il quale ne aveva tre altre quasi che da marito, insieme con tre figliuoli maschi, tutti uomini. E benché fusse d'una nobilissima famiglia, e di lui fusse in Firenze tenuto buono conto, nondimanco [20] era, rispetto alla brigata ch'avea e alla nobilità, poverissimo.

Fece Roderigo magnifiche e splendidissime nozze, né lasciò indietro alcuna di quelle cose che in simili feste si desiderano. Et essendo, per la legge che gli era stata data nello uscire d'inferno, sottoposto a tutte le passioni umane, subito cominciò a pigliare piacere degli onori e delle pompe del mondo, e avere caro di essere laudato intra gli uomini; il

return, and on the basis of his experience give testimony to his superiors as to what are the burdens and inconveniences of marriage. It was decided further that during this time he should be subject to all those discomforts and ills to which men are subject, and that he should be exposed to poverty, imprisonment, sickness, and every other misfortune into which men fall, unless he free himself from them by trickery or cleverness.

Belfagor therefore accepted the condition and the money, and came into the world; and, when he had gathered a retinue of horses and followers, he entered Florence with highest honors. He had chosen this city in preference to all others for his dwelling-place, since it seemed most suited to support one who employed his money in the usurer's arts. He took the name of Roderick of Castile, rented a house in the suburb of Ognissanti, and, so that his origin could not be traced, said that he had left Spain a short while before and gone to Syria, and that he had earned all his wealth in Aleppo, whence he had departed to come to Italy, to take a wife in a region which was more civilized and more suited to urbane living and to his character.

Roderick was a very handsome man, and appeared about thirty years old, and, since in a few days he had shown with how much riches he was endowed and had demonstrated how sociable and generous he was, many noble townsmen, who had many daughters and little money, offered them to him. Among all of these, Roderick chose a very beautiful damsel named Onesta, daughter of Amerigo Donati, who also had three others almost of marriageable age, together with three sons, all grown men. And, although he was from a very noble family, and was esteemed highly in Florence, nevertheless he was, in proportion to the household he maintained and to his nobility, very poor.

Roderick had a magnificent and very splendid wedding, nor did he neglect any of the things that are desirable at such festivities. And, since he was, by the rule that had been imposed on him when he had left Hell, subject to all human emotions, he immediately began to take pleasure in the honors and the display of the world, and to enjoy being praised

che gli arrecava spesa non piccola. Oltra di questo, non fu
dimorato molto con la sua monna Onesta, che se ne innamorò fuori di misura; né poteva vivere qualunque volta la
vedeva stare trista e avere alcuno dispiacere.

Aveva monna Onesta portato in casa di Roderigo, insieme
con la nobilità e con la bellezza, tanta superbia, che non ne
ebbe mai tanta Lucifero; e Roderigo, che aveva provata
l'una e l'altra, giudicava quella della moglie superiore. Ma
diventò di gran lunga maggiore, come prima quella si
accorse dello amore che il marito le portava; e parendole
poterlo da ogni parte signoreggiare, sanza alcuna pietà o
rispetto lo comandava; né dubitava,[21] quando da lui alcuna cosa gli era negata, con parole villane e iniuriose
morderlo: il che era a Roderigo cagione di inestimabile noia.
Pur nondimeno il suocero, i frategli, il parentado, l'obligo
del matrimonio, e sopra tutto il grande amore le portava,
gli faceva avere pazienza. Io voglio lasciare ire [22] le grandi
spese che per contentarla faceva, in vestirla di nuove usanze
e contentarla di nuove fogge, che continuamente la nostra
città per sua naturale consuetudine varia; che fu necessi-
tato, volendo stare in pace con lei, aiutare al suocero mari-
tare l'altre sue figliuole, dove spese grossa somma di danari.
Dopo questo, volendo avere bene con quella, gli convenne
mandare uno de' frategli in Levante [23] con panni, un altro
in Ponente [24] con drappi, all'altro aprire uno battiloro in
Firenze. Nelle quali cose dispensò la maggiore parte delle
sue fortune. Oltre a questo, ne' tempi dei carnasciali e di
San Giovanni—quando tutta la città per antica consuetudine festeggia, e che molti cittadini nobili e ricchi con splen-
didissimi conviti si onorono [25]—per non essere monna
Onesta all'altre donne inferiore, voleva che il suo Roderigo
con simili feste tutti gli altri superasse. Le quali cose tutte
erano da lui per le sopradette cagioni sopportate; né gli
sarebbono, ancora che gravissime, parute [26] gravi a farle,
se da questo ne fusse nata la quiete della casa sua, e s'egli
avesse potuto pacificamente aspettare i tempi della sua
rovina. Ma gl'interveniva l'opposito; perché con le in-
sopportabili spese la insolente natura di lei infinite incommodità gli arrecava. E non erano in casa sua né servi né

among men; and this led him to no small expense. In addition to this, he had not lived long with his monna Onesta before he fell immoderately in love with her; nor could he live whenever he saw her sad or displeased in any way.

Monna Onesta had brought to Roderick's house, together with her nobility and her beauty, so much pride as Lucifer had never had; and Roderick, who had experienced both, considered his wife's greater. But it became very much greater as soon as she became aware of the love which her husband bore her; and, since she thought that she could rule over him in every respect, she dominated him with no pity or restraint; nor did she hesitate, if he denied her anything, to speak sharply to him with discourteous and insulting words; this was, for Roderick, the cause of countless worries. Yet nevertheless his father-in-law, his brothers, his relatives, the obligations of marriage, and above all the great love he bore her, made him be patient. I shall pass over the great expenditures he made to keep her happy, dressing her in new fashions and indulging her in new styles, which our city is continually changing by its innate custom; for he was obliged, if he wanted to remain at peace with her, to help his father-in-law marry off his other daughters, on which he spent a huge sum of money. After this, since he wished to be on good terms with his wife, he had to send one of her brothers to the East with woolen cloths, another to the West with silk goods, and open a goldbeater's shop for the third in Florence. On these things he spent the greater part of his fortune. In addition to this, at the time of the carnival and of St. John's Day—when the whole city, by ancient custom, makes merry and when many noble and wealthy citizens honor each other with very lavish banquets—in order not to lag behind the other ladies, monna Onesta desired her Roderick to surpass all the others with festivities of this kind. He bore all these burdens for the reasons we have already mentioned. Nor would they have seemed burdensome, to say nothing of being difficult, to him, if from them peace had come into his household, and if he had been able to await his downfall in quiet. But the opposite happened to him; for, in addition to the unbear-

serventi che, non che molto tempo, ma brevissimi giorni la
potessino sopportare; donde ne nascevano a Roderigo
disagi gravissimi, per non potere tenere servo fidato che
avesse amore alle cose sue; e non che altri, quegli diavoli i
quali in persona di famigli aveva condotti seco, più tosto
elessono [27] di tornarsene in inferno a stare nel fuoco, che
vivere nel mondo sotto lo imperio di quella.

Standosi adunque Roderigo in questa tumultuosa e in-
quieta vita, e avendo per le disordinate spese già consumato
quanto mobile si aveva riserbato, cominciò a vivere sopra la
speranza de' ritratti che di Ponente e di Levante aspettava.
E avendo ancora buono credito, per non mancar di suo
grado, prese a cambio; e girandogli già molti marchi adosso,
fu presto notato da quegli che in simile esercizio in mercato
si travagliano. Et essendo di già il caso suo tenero, vennero
in un subito di Levante e di Ponente nuove, come l'uno de'
frategli di monna Onesta s'aveva giucato [28] il mobile di
Roderigo, e che l'altro, tornando sopra una nave carica di
sua mercatanzie, sanza [29] essersi altrimenti assicurato,[30] era
insieme con quelle annegato. Né fu prima publicata questa
cosa, che i creditori di Roderigo si ristrinsono insieme, e
giudicando che fosse spacciato, né possendo ancora sco-
pririsi per non essere venuto il tempo de' pagamenti loro,
conclusono che fusse bene osservato così destramente, acciò
che dal detto al fatto [31] di nascoso [32] non se ne fuggisse.
Roderigo da l'altra parte, non veggendo al caso suo remedio, e sapendo a quanto la legge infernale lo costringeva,
pensò di fuggirsi in ogni modo; e montato una mattina a
cavallo, abitando propinquo alla porta al Prato,[33] per
quella se ne uscì. Né prima fu veduta la partita sua, che il
romore si levò fra i creditori; i quali ricorsi ai magistrati,
non solamente con i cursori, ma popularmente si missono [34]
a seguirlo.

Non era Roderigo, quando se gli levò drieto il romore,

able expenses, her haughty nature brought him numberless difficulties. Nor were there in his household either man-servants or maidservants who could stand her even a very few days, to say nothing of a long time; from which cause, very serious difficulties confronted Roderick, since he could not keep a trusted servant who was devoted to his cause; and, to say nothing of others, even those devils whom he had brought along as familiars, chose to return to Hell to be in hell-fire, rather than to live in the world under her rule.

When, therefore, Roderick was in this disorganized and disturbed condition of life, and since he had, because of excessive expenses, already used up all the liquid assets he had set aside, he began to live on the expectations of the profits he anticipated from the West and the East. And since his credit was still good, so as not to live below his station, he borrowed money; and since many of his promissory notes were already circulating, this fact was soon noticed by those who deal on the market in such matters. And when his situation was already shaky, there suddenly came news from both East and West, that one of monna Onesta's brothers had gambled away all Roderick's capital, and that the other, returning on a boat loaded with his wares, without being insured in any way, had been drowned together with them. Scarcely was this news made known, than Roderick's credi-tors got together, and decided that he was done for; but, since they could not yet act because the due dates of their payments had not come, they decided that he should be watched so carefully that he could not suddenly flee in secret. Roderick, on the other hand, seeing no remedy for his situation, and knowing under what obligations he was placed by the decree of Hell, decided to flee in any way possible; and, mounting on horseback one morning, since he lived near the Prato gate, he went out through it. As soon as his departure was observed, his creditors raised a hue and cry; when they had gone to the magistrates, they set out to follow him not only with couriers but also with a mob.

Roderick, when the hue and cry arose behind him, had

dilungato da la città uno miglio; in modo che vedendosi a male partito, deliberò, per fuggire più secreto, uscire di strada, e a traverso per gli campi cercare sua fortuna. Ma sendo [35] a fare questo impedito da le assai fosse che attraversano il paese, non potendo per questo ire a cavallo, si misse a fuggire a piè. Lasciata la cavalcatura in su la strada, attraversando di campo in campo, coperto da le vigne e da' canneti di che quel paese abonda, arrivò sopra Perètola,[36] a casa Gianmatteo del Bricca, lavoratore di Giovanni Del Bene. E a sorte trovò Gianmatteo che arrecava a casa da rodere ai buoi, e se gli raccomandò, promettendogli che se lo salvava da le mani de' suoi nimici, i quali per farlo morire in prigione lo seguitavano, che [37] lo farebbe ricco, e gliene darebbe innanzi alla sua partita tale saggio che gli crederebbe; e quando questo non facesse, era contento che esso proprio lo ponesse in mano ai suoi avversari.

Era Gianmatteo, ancora che contadino, uomo animoso, e giudicando non potere perdere a pigliare partito di salvarlo, gliene promise; e cacciatolo in uno monte di letame quale aveva davanti a la sua casa, lo ricoperse con cannucce e altre mondiglie che per ardere aveva ragunate. Non era Roderigo a pena fornito [38] di nascondersi, che i suoi perseguitatori sopraggiunsono, e per spaventi che facessino a Gianmatteo, non trassono mai da lui che lo avesse visto. Talché passati più innanzi, avendolo invano quel dì e quell'altro cerco,[39] stracchi se ne tornarno a Firenze.

Gianmatteo adunque, cessato il romore e tràttolo del loco ove era, lo richiese della fede data. Al quale Roderigo disse:
— Fratello mio, io ho con teco un grande obligo, e lo voglio in ogni modo sodisfare; e perché tu creda che io possa farlo, ti dirò chi io sono.
E quivi gli narrò di suo essere, e delle leggi avute allo uscire d'inferno, e della moglie tolta; e di più gli disse il modo con il quale lo voleva arricchire; che insumma sarebbe questo, che come ei sentiva che alcuna donna fusse spiritata, credesse lui essere quello che le fusse a dosso, né mai se

not gone a mile from the city; so that, when he saw he was in a bad way, he decided, in order to flee more secretly, to leave the road and to seek his safety by cutting across the fields. But, since he was hindered in doing this by the numerous ditches that cross the region, and since for this reason he could not go on horseback, he began to flee on foot. Having left his mount on the road, and crossing from field to field, protected by the vineyards and canebrakes in which that region abounds, he arrived above Perètola, at the house of Gianmatteo del Bricca, a worker of Giovanni Del Bene. And by chance he found Gianmatteo coming home to feed his oxen, and he begged his help, promising him that if he would save him from the hands of his enemies, who were pursuing him to put him in prison, he would make him rich, and he would give him, before leaving, such proof of this that he would believe him; and if he [Gianmatteo] did not do this, he would be willing for him to hand him over personally to his adversaries.

Gianmatteo, although a peasant, was a man of spirit, and, judging that he could not lose if he decided to save him, promised to do so; and, putting him in a pile of manure which he had in front of his house, he covered him with canes and other rubbish which he had collected to burn. Scarcely had Roderick finished hiding, when his pursuers arrived, and no matter how much they tried to frighten Gianmatteo, they never got him to admit he had seen him. So that going on, and looking for him in vain that day and the next, they went back to Florence dead tired.

Gianmatteo then, when the uproar had died down and he had taken Roderick out of the place where he was, asked him to keep his promise. To which Roderick answered:

"My brother, I am deeply indebted to you, and I wish to repay my debt in every way possible; and, that you may believe I am able to do so, I will tell you who I am."

And then he told him of his true nature, and of the rules imposed on him when he had left Hell, and of the wife he had taken. Moreover, he told him of the manner in which he planned to make him rich; which, in short, was to be this: that when he heard that some woman was possessed by

37

n'uscirebbe s'egli non venisse a trarnelo: donde arebbe occasione di farsi a suo modo pagare dai parenti di quella. E rimasi in questa conclusione, sparì via.

Né passorno molti giorni, che si sparse per tutto Firenze come una figliuola di messer Ambruogio Amidei, la quale aveva maritata a Bonaiuto Tebalducci, era indemoniata; né mancorno i parenti di farvi tutti quegli remedii che in simili accidenti si fanno, ponendole in capo la testa di san Zanobi [40] e il mantello di san Giovanni Gualberto; le quali cose tutte da Roderigo erano uccellate. E per chiarire ciascuno come il male della fanciulla era uno spirito e non altra fantastica imaginazione, parlava in latino, e disputava delle cose di filosofia, e scopriva i peccati di molti: intra i quali scoperse quelli d'uno frate che si aveva tenuta una femmina vestita a uso di fraticino più di quattro anni nella sua cella. Le quali cose facevano maravigliare ciascuno. Viveva pertanto messer Ambruogio mal contento; e avendo invano provati tutti i remedii, aveva perduta ogni speranza di guarirla, quando Gianmatteo venne a trovarlo, e gli promisse la salute de la sua figiuola, quando gli voglia donare cinquecento fiorini per comperare uno podere a Perètola. Accettò messer Ambruogio il partito; donde Gianmatteo, fatte dire prima certe messe e fatte sue cerimonie per abbellire la cosa, si accostò agli orecchi della fanciulla e disse:

— Roderigo, io sono venuto a trovarti perché tu mi osservi la promessa.

Al quale Roderigo rispose:

— Io sono contento. Ma questo non basta a farti ricco; e però, partito che io sarò di qui, entrerò nella figliuola di Carlo re di Napoli,[41] né mai n'uscirò sanza te. Fara'ti [42] allora fare una mancia a tuo modo, né poi mi darai più briga.

E detto questo, s'uscì d'adosso a colei, con piacere e ammirazione di tutta Firenze.

Non passò dipoi molto tempo, che per tutta Italia si

a demon, he should believe that it was he [Roderick] who was possessing her, and that he would not leave her until he [Gianmatteo] came to draw him forth; on which occasion he would have the chance to demand what payment he would from her relatives. And when they had agreed on this, he disappeared.

Not many days passed, before word spread through all Florence that a daughter of Messer Ambrogio Amidei, whom he had married off to Bonaiuto Tebalducci, was possessed of a devil. Nor did her relatives fail to try all the remedies which are tried in such cases—placing on her head the head of St. Zenobius and the cloak of St. Giovanni Gualberto; all of which things were laughed to scorn by Roderick. And to make it clear to everyone that the maiden's trouble was a spirit and not some other imaginary phantasm, he spoke through her in Latin, and discoursed on philosophical topics, and revealed the sins of many, among which he revealed those of a friar who had kept a woman, dressed as a novice, for more than four years in his cell. These things amazed everyone. Messer Ambrogio was, therefore, very unhappy; and, having tried all cures in vain, he had lost all hope of healing her, when Gianmatteo came to see him, and promised to restore his daughter to health if he would give him five hundred florins to buy a farm at Perètola. Messer Ambrogio agreed to the bargain; whereupon Gianmatteo, having first had some masses said and having performed some ceremonies of his own to embellish the procedure, went up to the girl's ear and said:

"Roderick, I have come to see you so that you can keep your promise to me."

To this, Roderick answered:

"I am willing. But this is not enough to make you rich; and therefore, when I leave here, I shall enter into the daughter of Charles, King of Naples, and will never leave her except for you. Then you will ask for a recompense such as you wish, and are never to bother me again."

And, saying this, he left the damsel, to the pleasure and wonder of all Florence.

Not much time passed after this, before the mishap which

sparse l'accidente venuto a la figliuola del re Carlo; né vi si trovando remedio, avuta il Re notizia di Gianmatteo, mandò a Firenze per lui. Il quale arrivato a Napoli, dopo qualche finta cerimonia, la guarì. Ma Roderigo, prima che partisse, disse:

— Tu vedi, Gianmatteo, io ti ho osservato le promesse di averti arricchito; e però sendo disobligo, io non sono più tenuto di cosa alcuna. Pertanto sarai contento non mi capitare più innanzi, perché dove io ti ho fatto bene, ti farei per lo avvenire male.

Tornato adunque a Firenze Gianmatteo ricchissimo, perché aveva avuto dal Re meglio che cinquantamila ducati, pensava di godersi quelle ricchezze pacificamente, non credendo però che Roderigo pensasse di offenderlo. Ma questo suo pensiero fu subito turbato da una nuova che venne, come una figliuola di Lodovico [43] VII re di Francia era spiritata; la quale nuova alterò tutta la mente di Gianmatteo, pensando a l'autorità di quel Re e a le parole che gli aveva Roderigo dette. Non trovando adunque quel Re alla sua figliuola remedio, e intendendo la virtù di Gianmatteo, mandò prima a richiederlo semplicemente per un suo cursore; ma allegando quello certe indisposizioni, fu forzato quel Re a richiederne la Signoria. La quale forzò Gianmatteo a ubbidire. Andato pertanto costui tutto sconsolato a Parigi, mostrò prima al Re come egli era certa cosa che per lo adrieto [44] aveva guarita qualche indemoniata, ma che non era per questo ch'egli sapesse o potesse guarire tutti, perché se ne trovavano [45] di sì perfida natura che non temevano né minacce né incanti né alcuna religione; ma con tutto questo, era per fare suo debito, e non gli riuscendo, ne domandava scusa e perdono. Al quale il Re, turbato, disse che se non la guariva, che lo appenderebbe. Sentì per questo Gianmatteo dolore grande; pure, fatto buono cuore, fece venire la indemoniata, e accostatosi all'orecchio di quella, umilmente si raccomandò a Roderigo, ricordandogli il beneficio fattogli, e di quanta ingratitudine sarebbe esemplo se lo abbandonasse in tanta necessità. Al

had befallen the daughter of King Charles became known throughout Italy; and, when no cure could be found for her, and the King had heard about Gianmatteo, he sent to Florence for him. Gianmatteo, upon arriving at Naples, after a few pretended ceremonies, healed her. But Roderick, before departing, said:

"You see, Gianmatteo, I have kept my promise to make you rich; and therefore, having discharged my debt, I am no longer obliged to you in any respect. Therefore you will be pleased not to appear before me any longer, because, whereas I have done well by you, I should henceforth harm you."

Therefore, when Gianmatteo had returned to Florence a very rich man—for he had received more than fifty thousand ducats from the King—he thought he would enjoy those riches in peace, not thinking that Roderick would trouble him further. But this intention of his was immediately upset by news that came, that a daughter of Louis VII, King of France, was bewitched; this news completely upset Gianmatteo's mind, when he thought of the authority of that King and of the words which Roderick had said to him. When the King found no cure for his daughter, and had heard of Gianmatteo's magic powers, he first simply sent to request him, by means of a courier; but when Gianmatteo gave certain indispositions as an excuse, the King was forced to request him of the Florentine government, and the government forced Gianmatteo to obey. When he, therefore, had gone, all despairing, to Paris, he first told the King that it was true that in the past he had cured a few women possessed by devils, but that this did not mean that he knew how or was able to cure all; for there were some demons of such perfidious character that they feared neither threats nor incantations nor any supernatural power; but that nevertheless, he was ready to do his duty, and, if he did not succeed, he begged the King's forgiveness and pardon. To this the King, disturbed, said that if he did not cure her, he would have him hanged. Gianmatteo was greatly disturbed at this; yet, taking heart, he had the bewitched girl brought, and, going close to her ear, he humbly

quale Roderigo disse:

— Do',[46] villan traditore, sì che tu hai ardire di venirmi inanzi? Credi tu poterti vantare d'essere arricchito per le mie mani? Io voglio mostrare a te e a ciascuno come io so dare e tôrre [47] ogni cosa a mia posta; e innanzi che tu ti parta di qui, io ti farò impiccare in ogni modo.

Donde che Gianmatteo non veggendo per allora remedio, pensò di tentare la sua fortuna per un'altra via. E fatto andar via la spiritata, disse al Re:

— Sire, come io vi ho detto, e' sono di molti spiriti che sono sì maligni che con loro non si ha alcuno buono partito; e questo è uno di quegli. Pertanto io voglio fare una ultima sperienza, la quale se gioverà, la Vostra Maestà e io aremo [48] la intenzione nostra; quando non giovi, io sarò nelle tue forze, e arai di me quella compassione che merita la innocenzia mia. Farai pertanto fare in su la piazza di Nostra Dama [49] un palco grande, e capace di tutti i tuoi baroni e di tutto il clero di questa città; farai parare il palco di drappi di seta e d'oro; fabbricherai nel mezzo di quello uno altare; e voglio che domenica mattina prossima tu con il clero, insieme con tutti i tuoi prìncipi e baroni, con la reale pompa, con splendidi e ricchi abbigliamenti conveniate sopra quello; dove, celebrata prima una solenne messa, farai venire l'indemoniata. Voglio, oltra [50] di questo, che da l'uno canto de la piazza sieno insieme venti persone almeno che abbino [51] trombe, corni, tamburi, cornamuse, cembanelle, cémboli, e d'ogn'altra qualità romori,[52] i quali, quando io alzerò uno cappello, dieno [53] in quegli strumenti, e sonando ne venghino [54] verso il palco. Le quali cose, insieme con certi altri segreti remedii, credo che faranno partire questo spirito.

Fu subito dal Re ordinato tutto. E venuta la domenica mattina, e ripieno il palco di personaggi e la piazza di populo,[55] celebrata la messa, venne la spiritata condutta [56] in sul palco per le mani di due vescovi e molti signori.

begged Roderick's aid, reminding him of the good turn he had done him, and what an example of ingratitude it would be if he were to desert him in such dire straits. To this, Roderick answered:

"How is it, base traitor, that you dare to come into my presence? Do you think you can boast that you became rich by my handiwork? I shall show you and everyone how I can give and take away everything according to my will; and before you leave here, I shall certainly have you hanged."

Wherefore Gianmatteo, seeing no way out for the time being, decided to try his fortune in another way. And, having the bewitched girl taken away, he said to the King:

"Sire, as I told you, there are many spirits which are so wicked that one can make no headway with them; and this is one of those. Nevertheless, I want to try one last experiment, and if it succeeds, Your Majesty and I will succeed in our aim; if it does not do any good, I shall be in your power, and shall have on me such pity as my innocence deserves. Therefore, please have built on the square in front of Notre Dame a great stand, large enough to hold all your nobles and all the clergy of this city; have the stand decorated with cloth of silk and gold; have an altar built in the middle of it; and I want you and the clergy, with all your princes and nobles, with royal pomp and with splendid and rich garb, to assemble on it; and there, after a solemn mass has been celebrated, you will have the bewitched girl brought forth. In addition to this, I want stationed together on one side of the square at least twenty persons with trumpets, horns, drums, bagpipes, clarinets, cymbals, and every other kind of noise-maker; when I raise my hat, they are to play on those instruments and, as they play, come towards the stand. These things, together with certain other secret remedies, I believe will make this spirit depart."

Everything was immediately ordered by the King. And when Sunday morning had come, and the stand was full of important personages and the square was full of people, and the mass had been celebrated, the bewitched girl was

Quando Roderigo vide tanto populo insieme e tanto apparato, rimase quasi che stupido, e fra sè disse:

— Che cosa ha pensato di fare questo poltrone di questo villano? Crede egli sbigottirmi con questa pompa? Non sa egli che io sono uso a vedere le pompe del cielo e le furie dello inferno? Io lo gastigherò in ogni modo.

E accostandosegli Gianmatteo, e pregandolo che dovesse uscire, gli disse:

— Oh tu hai fatto il bel pensiero! Che credi tu fare con questi tuoi apparati? Credi tu fuggire per questo la potenza mia e l'ira del Re? Villano ribaldo, io ti farò impiccare in ogni modo!

E così, ripregandolo quello e quell'altro dicendogli villania, non parve a Gianmatteo di perdere più tempo; e fatto il cenno col cappello, tutti quegli ch'erano a romoreggiare diputati, dettono [57] in quegli suoni, e con romori che andavono al cielo ne vennono verso il palco. Al quale romore alzò Roderigo gli orecchi, e non sappiendo [58] che cosa fusse e stando forte maravigliato, tutto stupido domandò Gianmatteo che cosa quella fusse. Al quale Gianmatteo tutto turbato disse:

— Oimé, Roderigo mio, quella è mógliata tua,[59] che ti viene a ritrovare!

Fu cosa maravigliosa a pensare [60] quanta alterazione di mente recasse a Roderigo sentire ricordato il nome della moglie. La quale fu tanta, che non pensando s'egli era possibile o ragionevole se la fusse dessa,[61] senza replicare altro, tutto spaventato se ne fuggì, lasciando la fanciulla libera; e volse [62] più tosto tornarsene in inferno a rendere ragione delle sue azioni, che di nuovo, con tanti fastidii dispetti e periculo, sottoporsi al giogo matrimoniale.

E così Belfagor, tornato in inferno, fece fede de' mali che conduceva in una casa la moglie; e Gianmatteo, che ne seppe più che il diavolo, se ne ritornò tutto lieto a casa.

brought onto the stand by the hands of two bishops and a number of lords. When Roderick saw so many people gathered together, and so many preparations, he was almost stupefied, and said to himself:

"What has this cowardly knave tried to do? Does he think he can frighten me with this display? Does he not know that I am accustomed to see the pomp of heaven and the furies of Hell? I shall punish him, come what may."

And when Gianmatteo went up close to him and begged him to depart, he said:

"That is a wonderful idea of yours! What do you think you are doing with these preparations of yours? Do you think that you can dispel my magic power and the wrath of the King by these? Base knave, I shall have you hanged, no matter what happens."

And so, while the one pleaded and the other uttered insults, it seemed to Gianmatteo that he should lose no more time; and when he had given the signal with his hat, all those who had been assigned to make a noise, began to play, and with an uproar which arose to heaven they came towards the stand. At this din, Roderick pricked up his ears, and not knowing what this was and being very much amazed, in a daze he asked Gianmatteo what this was. To this, Gianmatteo replied, very much worried:

"Alas, my dear Roderick, that is your wife who has come to get you!"

It was a wonderful thing to imagine, what a change of mind it caused in Roderick, just to hear his wife's name mentioned. It was so great that, not stopping to think whether it was possible or reasonable that it should be his wife, without making any further answer, he fled in complete dismay, leaving the girl free; and he preferred to return to Hell to give an account of his actions, rather than, with so much annoyance, spitefulness and danger, to submit to the yoke of matrimony.

And thus Belfagor, returning to Hell, attested to the evils which a wife brings into a home; and Gianmatteo, who was cleverer than the devil, went back home in complete happiness.

Matteo Bandello

(ca. 1485–1561)

MATTEO BANDELLO, a Dominican monk, spent most of his life in various Italian courts and high society rather than in a monastery. The later years of his life were spent in southern France, where he died in 1561. In his earlier years, he made a collection of short stories, which was destroyed in the Spanish sack of Milan in 1526; later, he collected them anew and put them in final form, publishing them in three volumes in 1554, with a posthumous fourth part in 1573. They are two hundred and fourteen in all, not incorporated in a framework, but tied together by dedicatory letters, each of which accompanies one of the *novelle* and dedicates it to some outstanding contemporary.

Bandello's stories are in general extremely licentious; in this, they reflect the corrupt and dissolute condition of the Italian aristocracy in the first part of the sixteenth century. The story of Madonna Zilia and Monsignor Filiberto, reproduced here, is somewhat atypical in this respect; it is, however, quite representative of Bandello's portrayal of the manners of his time, and of his reflection of everyday speech in his style. The especial interest of this *novella* lies in its presentation of two psychological types which were in conflict at the time, even in Italy: the Puritan, exemplified in Madonna Zilia, and the libertine, in Filiberto. Madonna Zilia wishes to live quietly and devote herself to her son's upbringing, not even yielding to the local custom of casual

osculation by way of greeting; her mistakes are those of an honest but naïve person. Filiberto, on the other hand, regards the satisfaction of his masculine desires as his natural right, as do Italian men in general; inner moral compulsion is absent from his character, and when he decides to observe the promise he has made to Zilia, it is because of the external obligation laid on him by his vow. He misinterprets Zilia's actions because he conceives her as having acted out of selfishness. Yet it is clear that Bandello's and his audience's sympathies lay with Filiberto rather than with Zilia. It is the former who has success and reward in the end, and the latter who loses the honor that she had tried to keep and returns home in shame.

MADONNA ZILIA
di Matteo Bandello

IL SIGNOR FILIBERTO s'innamora di madonna Zilia che per
un bacio lo fa star lungo tempo mutolo, e la vendetta
ch'egli altamente ne prese.

In Moncalieri,[1] castello non molto lontano da Turino,
fu una vedova chiamata madonna Zilia Duca, a cui poco
innanzi era morto il marito, ed ella era giovane di venti-
quattro anni,[2] assai bella, ma di costumi ruvidi e che più
tosto [3] tenevano del contadinesco [4] che del civile. Onde
avendo deliberato di più non maritarsi, attendeva a far de
la roba ad un figliuoletto che aveva, senza più, che era di
tre in quattro anni. Viveva in casa non da gentildonna par
sua ma da povera femina, e faceva tutti gli uffici vili di casa
per risparmiare e tener meno fantesche che poteva. Ella di
rado si lasciava vedere, e le feste la mattina a buon'ora
andava a la prima messa ad una chiesetta a la casa sua
vicina, e subito ritornava a la sua stanza.[5] General costume
è di tutte le donne del paese di basciare tutti i forastieri
che in casa loro vengono o da chi sono visitate, e domesticamente con ciascuno intertenersi; ma ella tutte queste
pratiche fuggiva e sola se ne viveva.

Ora avvenne che essendo venuto in Moncalieri messer
Filiberto da Virle,[6] gentiluomo del paese, ch'era soldato
molto valente e prode de la sua persona, egli, volendo ri-

MADONNA ZILIA

by Matteo Bandello

Signor Filiberto falls in love with Madonna Zilia, who makes him remain mute for a long time in exchange for a kiss, and the proud vengeance which he took for this.

In Moncalieri, a town not far from Turin, there was a widow called Madonna Zilia Duca, whose husband had died not long previously; she was twenty-four years old, and quite beautiful, but her manners were rough and closer to those of a peasant than of a civilized person. Therefore, having determined not to marry again, she devoted herself to caring for an only son she had, who was three or four years old. She lived at home in a style suitable, not to a noble lady of her standing, but to a poor woman; and she performed all the menial tasks of her household so as to save and have as few maids as possible. She rarely appeared in public, and on feast-days went to early morning mass in a little church near her house, and immediately returned to her dwelling. It is a general custom of all the women of the town to kiss all the strangers who come to their homes or by whom they are visited, and to entertain everyone in a familiar way; but she shunned all these practices and lived to herself.

Now it happened that when Messer Filiberto of Virle—a nobleman of the region, who was a very brave soldier and of great personal valor—had come to Moncalieri; when he

tornar a Virle, andò a messa a la chiesa ove era madonna
Zilia, la quale veduta e parutagli bella e molto avvenente,
domandò chi ella fosse, sentendosi di dentro tutto acceso del
suo amore. Ed intendendo i modi che ella teneva, ancora
che gli dispiacessero, non poteva perciò fare che non
l'amasse. Egli andò quel giorno a Virle, ove ordinate alcune
sue cose, deliberò di tornarsene a Moncalieri che molto non
era distante, ed ivi più che poteva dimorarsi e tentar con
ogni industria se poteva acquistar l'amor de la donna. Onde,
trovate alcune sue occasioni, condusse una casa in Moncalieri e quivi abitava, usando ogni diligenza per veder spesse
volte la donna. Ma egli le feste a pena la poteva vedere, e
volendo con lei parlare ed entrar in lunghi ragionamenti, ella
a le due parole prendeva congedo e casa se n'andava; del che
egli viveva molto mal contento e non si poteva in modo
veruno [7] da questo suo amore ritrarre. Ebbe mezzo d'altre
donne che le parlarono, le scrisse ed usò il tutto che possibile fosse; ma il tutto era indarno, imperciò che ella stava
più dura che uno scoglio in mare, nè mai degnò di fargli
buona risposta.

Il misero amante, non ritrovando compenso alcuno in
questo suo amore, nè sapendosi da questa impresa levare,
e di già perdutone il sonno e appresso il mangiare, infermò
assai gravemente. E non conoscendo i medici il suo male,
non gli sapevano che rimedio dare; di maniera che il povero
giovine correva a lunghi passi a la morte senza ritrovar aita.[8]
Venne, mentre era in letto, a vederlo un uomo d'arme, che
seco aveva gran domestichezza, ed era da Spoleto. A costui
narrò messer Filiberto tutto il suo amore e la fiera rigidezza
de la sua dura e crudelissima donna, conchiudendogli che
non ritrovando altro rimedio egli di doglia e soverchia pena
se ne moriva. Lo spoletino, udendo la cagione del male di
messer Filiberto, a cui egli voleva un grandissimo bene, gli
disse:

— Filiberto, lascia far a me, ch'io troverò modo che tu
parlerai a costei a tuo agio.
— Io non vo'[9] altro—rispose l'infermo—ché se io ho

was about to return to Virle, he attended mass at the church where Madonna Zilia was. When he saw her, he thought her beautiful and very charming; he asked who she was, feeling inwardly all aflame with his love. On hearing of the modes of life she kept, although he did not like them, he was nevertheless unable to keep from loving her. He went to Virle that day, where he put some of his affairs in order and decided to return to Moncalieri (which was not very far away) and to stay there as long as possible, and to try with all his diligence to gain the lady's love. Whereupon, finding the opportunity, he set up a household in Moncalieri and lived there, devoting all his attention to seeing the lady often. But even on feast days he was scarcely able to see her, and when he tried to speak with her and enter into long conversations, she took her leave after two words and went off home. As a consequence, he lived very unhappily and was in no wise able to profit by this love of his. He made use of other women who spoke to her, he wrote to her and used every possible device; but it was all in vain, because she was harder than a rock in the sea, nor did she ever deign to give him a favorable reply.

The wretched lover, although he gained no reward from this love of his, was not able to desist from this undertaking. He had already lost his sleep over it, and then lost his appetite, and fell quite seriously ill. Since the doctors did not know his malady, they did not know what remedy to prescribe for him, so that the poor young man was hastening towards death with long strides, without finding any help. While he was abed, there came to see him a soldier, who was a great friend of his, and who was from Spoleto. To him Messer Filiberto told all about his love and the unyielding pride of his harsh and most cruel lady, concluding that, since he found no other remedy, he was dying of sorrow and excessive distress. The man from Spoleto, on hearing the reason for the sickness of Messer Filiberto, of whom he was very fond, said to him:

"Filiberto, leave it to me, and I will find a way for you to speak with her at your leisure."

"I wish nothing more," said the sick man, "for if I have

questo, e' [10] mi dà l'animo d'indurla che di me ella averà [11] pietà. Ma come farai? ch'io ci ho speso gran fatica, l'ho mandati messi, ricchi doni, promesse grandissime, e nulla mai ho potuto ottenere.

— Attendi pur—soggiunse lo spoletino—a guarire, e del rimanente a me la cura lascierai.

Con questa promessa Filiberto se ne rimase tanto contento che in breve si sentì meravigliosamente megliorare e indi a pochi giorni se n'uscì del letto.

Sono tutti gli spoletini, come sapete, grandissimi cicalatori, e vanno per tutta Italia quasi ordinariamente cogliendo l'elemosine del barone messer santo Antonio, ché sono onnipotenti nel favellare, audaci e pronti, e mai non si lasciano mancar soggetto di ragionare, e sono mirabilissimi persuasori di tutto quello che loro entra in capo di voler suadere. La maggior parte anco di quelli che vanno ciurmando i semplici uomini—dando loro la grazia di San Paolo, e portando bisce, serpentelli ed aspidi sordi, e facendo simil mestiero, e cantando su per le piazze—sono spoletini. Era adunque l'amico di messer Filiberto di questa nazione, e forse a' giorni suoi s'era trovato su tre paia di piazze a vender polve di fava per unguento da rogna. Egli veggendo messer Filiberto guarito, non si scordando la promessa che fatta gli aveva, ebbe modo di trovar uno di quelli che, con una cesta legata al collo e pendente sotto il braccio sinistro, vanno per la contrada gridando e vendendo nastri, ditali, spilletti, cordoni, bindelli, corone di paternostri e altre simili cosette da donne.

Convenutosi adunque con costui e fattolo restar contento, prese i panni di lui ed il canestro, e vestitosi in abito di tal venditore se n'andò ne la contrada ove era la casa di madonna Zilia, e quivi cominciò, passeggiando, a gridare come si suole. Madonna Zilia, udendo la voce e bisognandole alcuni veli, lo fece chiamare in casa. Egli, veggendo che il suo avviso gli riusciva, entrò in casa animosamente e salutò la donna con amorevoli e belle parole, come se egli fosse stato gran domestico. Ella, mettendo la mano dentro la cesta, cominciò a pigliar in mano questa e quella cosa; ed egli, del tutto compiacendole, dispiegava ora nastri ora veli.

this, it will give me courage to persuade her to have pity on me. But what will you do? for I have put in great efforts on it—I have sent messengers to her, rich gifts, very great promises, and have never been able to obtain anything."

"Just devote your attention," said the man from Spoleto, "to getting well, and leave the rest to me."

Filiberto was so happy over this promise that in a short time he felt he was recovering marvellously, and within a few days he got up from bed.

All the Spoletines, as you know, have a tremendous gift of gab, and go around through all Italy almost regularly collecting alms under false pretenses. They are all-powerful in talking, daring and quick-witted; they never lack for a topic to speak on, and are wonderful persuaders for anything that they take it into their heads to persuade people about. Also, the majority of those men who go around swindling dull-witted people—giving them false blessings, and carrying snakes, little serpents and deaf adders, and plying similar trades, and singing in the public squares—are from Spoleto. Now Messer Filiberto's friend was of this race, and perhaps in his day had been in not a few public squares, selling bean powder for mange ointment. When he saw that Messer Filiberto had gotten well, not forgetting the promise he had made him, he found a way to seek out one of those men who, with a basket tied around their neck and hanging under their left arm, go through the country calling their wares and selling ribbons, thimbles, pins, strings, bands, rosaries and other feminine trinkets of that kind.

When he had made an agreement with the man and paid him well, he took his clothes and basket, and, dressing himself in the garb of such a vendor, he went off to the part of town where Madonna Zilia's house was, and there began, as he walked along, to shout as is the custom. Madonna Zilia, hearing the voice, and being in need of some cloth, had him called into the house. He, seeing that his plan was succeeding, went boldly into the house and greeted the lady with kindly and fine words, as if he had been on very familiar terms with her. She, putting her hand into the basket, began to take in her hand one thing and another; and

Onde ella, veggendo certi veli di che aveva bisogno e che gli [12] parevano molto belli, disse:

— Buon uomo, che vendete voi il braccio di cotesti veli? Se me ne fate buon mercato, io ne piglierò fin a trentacinque braccia.

— Madonna—rispose lo spoletino,—se i veli vi piaceno,[13] pigliateli e non ricercate ciò che si vendano, perché il pagamento è fatto. E non solo i veli ma tutto ciò che ho qui è vostro senz'altro pagamento, pur che degnate pigliarlo.

— Oh io non vo' questo—disse la donna,—che non è onesto. Io vi ringrazio de le vostre offerte. Ditemi pur ciò che volete dei veli e io vi sodisfarò, ché non istà [14] bene che voi, che guadagnate in queste fatiche il viver vostro, ci perdiate così grossamente. Fatemi onesto mercato e vi darò i vostri danari.

— Io non perdo, anzi acquisto assai quando qui ci sia cosa che vi aggradi—rispose lo spoletino;—e se voi avete l'animo così gentile come l'aspetto vostro ci dimostra, voi accettarete in dono questi veli e anco [15] de l'altre cose, quando vi piacciano, con ciò sia cosa che [16] che uno ve gli dona che per voi non solo la roba ma la vita per compiacervi spenderebbe.

La donna, udendo questo, divenne colorita come una vermiglia rosa quando di maggio ne l'apparir del sole comincia a spiegar le sue novelle foglie; e guardato fisamente nel viso a lo spoletino, gli disse:

— Voi mi fate molto meravigliare di tal vostro ragionamento, onde saperei [17] volentieri chi voi sète [18] e a che fine m'avete detto queste parole, perciò che penso che m'abbiate presa in fallo, non essendo io tale quale voi forse v'imaginate.

Egli alora,[19] punto non si sgomentando, con accomodate parole, ché era, come ho detto, da Spoleto, le narrò e in quanta pena per amor di lei messer Filiberto vivesse e quanto l'era fedel servidore, e che non aveva persona al mondo de la quale più potesse disporre che di lui e di quanto al mondo possedeva; che era pur ricco e dei signori di

he, pleasing her in everything, unfolded now ribbons and now cloth. Whereupon she, seeing certain pieces of cloth which she needed and which seemed to her very fine, said:

"My good man, how much do you charge for an ell of this cloth? If you make me a good bargain on it, I will take up to thirty-five ells."

"My lady," answered the Spoletine, "if you like the cloth, take it and do not ask how much it costs, because the payment is already made. And not only the cloth but everything I have here is yours without payment, provided only that you deign to take it."

"Oh, I do not want that," said the lady, "for it is not honest. I thank you for your offer, but simply tell me what you charge for the cloth and I will pay you; for it is not right that you, who earn your living by this work, should lose so heavily by it. Strike an honest bargain with me and I will give you your money."

"I do not lose, on the contrary I gain a great deal if there is anything here which pleases you," answered the Spoletine; "and if you have a disposition as noble as your appearance shows, you will accept as a gift this cloth and other things too, if you like them, because they are given to you by someone who would gladly sacrifice not only his substance but his life for you."

The lady, on hearing this, became as scarlet as a red rose when it begins to unfold its new leaves in May at the appearance of the sun; and looking the Spoletine straight in the face, she said to him:

"You amaze me greatly with this speech of yours, and I should like very much to know who you are and for what purpose you have said these words to me, because I imagine that you have selected me by mistake, since I am not such as you perhaps think I am."

He then, in no wise dismayed, with suitable words (for he was, as I have said, from Spoleto), told her both in how much distress Messer Filiberto was living on her account, and how faithful a servant of hers he was; that there was no one in the world whom she could have more at her disposal than Messer Filiberto and all his worldly pos-

Virle, e galantissimo compagno. Ed insomma egli seppe sì ben dire e tanto persuaderla, che ella fu contenta che il suo amante segretamente le venisse a parlare, e gli assegnò il tempo e il luogo.

Messer Filiberto, avuta questa buona nuova, si tenne ottimamente sodisfatto da lo spoletino. E secondo l'ordine posto, si condusse a parlare con madonna Zilia in una camera terrena de la casa di lei. Quivi giunto, ritrovò la donna che l'attendeva e aveva seco una sua fantesca. La camera era assai grande e potevano agiatamente tutti dui [20] ragionare, ché la fante niente averebbe sentito. Onde messer Filiberto cominciò con più accomodate [21] parole che seppe a narrar a la donna le sue amorose passioni e quanto per amor di lei aveva sofferto, pregandola affezionatissimamente che di lui le calesse [22] e ne volesse aver compassione, assicurandola che in eterno le saria [23] servidore. Ma per quanto egli mai le sapesse dire, non puotè[24] altro cavarne se non ch'ella era vedova e che a lei non istava bene andar dietro a queste così fatte cose, e che voleva attender a governare suo figliuolo, e che a lui non mancherebbero de l'altre donne più belle di lei. Ora, dopo molti ragionamenti, veggendo il povero amante che s'affaticava indarno e ch'ella non era disposto in modo alcuno di contentarlo, e sentendosi di gran doglia morire, con le lagrime sugli occhi pietosamente le disse:

— Poi che, signora mia, in tutto mi levate la speranza di volermi per servidore e da voi mi convien partire con tanto mio dispiacere, né forse avverrà più mai ch'io abbia occasione di vosco [25] ragionare, almeno in questa ultima mia partenza datemi in guiderdone [26] di quanto amore vi ho portato, porto e porterò tanto ch'io viva, un solo bacio, che quando venni qui volli da voi secondo la costuma de la patria prendere, e voi contro il lodevole nostro uso mi negaste. E sapete pure che basciarsi ne la via publica non è vergogna, quando gli uomini incontrano le donne.

La donna stette un pochetto sovra sé; [27] poi rispose:

sessions; and that he was also rich and a member of the noble family of Virle, and a most courteous friend. In short, he was able to speak so well that he persuaded her to be willing for her lover to come and speak to her in private, and to set a time and place for the visit.

Messer Filiberto, on receiving this good news, deemed himself excellently served by the Spoletine. According to the procedure agreed upon, he went to speak to Madonna Zilia in a room on the ground floor of her house. When he arrived there, he found the lady awaiting him, accompanied by one of her maids. The room was quite large and they were able to talk together at their ease, for the maid would have heard nothing. Thereupon Messer Filiberto began, with the most suitable expressions he knew, to tell the lady of his sufferings for love and how much he had endured for love of her, begging her most affectionately to care for him and to have pity on him, assuring her that he would be her servant for all eternity. But no matter how much he said to her, all he could get out of her was that she was a widow and that it was not seemly for her to indulge in pursuits of this kind; that she wanted to devote her attention to bringing up her son, and that he would be sure to find other women more beautiful than her. Now, after many speeches, when the poor lover saw that his efforts were all in vain and that she was in no wise disposed to make him happy, and feeling that he was dying of great sorrow, with tears in his eyes he said piteously to her:

"Since, my lady, you wholly deprive me of the hope that you may wish me as your servant, and I must leave you with so great unhappiness—nor will I perhaps ever again have the opportunity of speaking with you—at least, at this last parting, give me as a reward for all the love I have borne, bear and shall bear you as long as I live, a single kiss, which I desired to have from you when I came here, according to the custom of the country, and you denied me, contrary to our admirable usage. And you should know that to kiss in the public street is not shameful, when men meet women."

The lady remained sunk in thought for a moment, and

— Io vo', monsignor [28] Filiberto, vedere se il vostro amore è così fervente come predicate. Voi da me al presente averete il bacio che mi richiedete, se giurate di far una cosa cho io vi chiederò, e servando il giuramento vostro, io potrò assicurarmi esser tanto da voi amata quanto detto m'avete.

Giurò l'incauto amante che farebbe ogni cosa a lui possibile di fare. E dicendole che comandasse quanto voleva, stava attendendo il comandamento de la donna. Ella alora, avvinchiategli al collo le braccia, in bocca lo basciò e, basciato che l'ebbe, gli disse:

— Monsignor Filiberto, io vi ho dato un bacio che chiesto m'avete, con speranza che farete quando vi commetterò. Onde vi dico che io voglio in essecuzione de la fede vostra che voi, da questa ora fin che siano passati tre anni intieri, non parliate mai con persona del mondo, uomo né femina, sia chi si voglia, di modo che per tre anni continovi restiate mutolo.

Stette non molto messer Filiberto tutto ammirativo, e quantunque questo comandamento gli paresse indiscreto, senza ragione e difficillimo da esser integralmente osservato, nondimeno egli con mano le accennò che faria quanto ella gli comandava. E dinanzi a lei inchinatosi, se ne partì e al suo albergo ritornò. Quivi pensando a' casi suoi e per la mente ravvolgendo l'aspro giuramento che fatto aveva, deliberò, se leggermente s'era con fede di sacramento obligato, di volerlo con saldo proponimento e intera osservanza mantenere.

Fingendo dunque casualmente aver perduta la favella, partitosi da Moncalieri, andò a Virle e, vivendo da mutolo, con cenni e con iscritti [29] si faceva intendere. La compassione che tutti gli avevano era grande, e meravigliosa cosa pareva a ciascuno che senza accidente d'infermità egli avesse la loquela perduta. Ordinò messer Filiberto tutto il governo de le cose sue, facendo suo procuratore un suo cugino germano; e postosi in assetto di buone cavalcature e dato ordine come danari a certi tempi gli fossero mandati, si partì di Piemonte e passò a Lioni di Francia. Egli era

then answered:

"I wish, Monsignor Filiberto, to see whether your love is as fervent as you proclaim. You will have from me, at present, the kiss which you ask of me, if you swear to do something which I shall request of you; and if you keep your oath, I can be sure that I am as much beloved by you as you have said to me."

The incautious lover swore that he would do everything within his power. After telling her to command whatever she wished, he stood waiting for her command. She then, throwing her arms around his neck, kissed him on the mouth and, after kissing him, said:

"Monsignor Filiberto, I have given you the kiss for which you asked me, expecting that you will do what I command you. Therefore I tell you that I wish you to keep your faith, for three full years from this hour, by never speaking with any person in the world, man or woman, whoever it may be, so that you remain mute for three years on end."

Messer Filiberto stood in complete amazement for a short time, and, although this command seemed to him unwise, unreasonable and extremely difficult to be observed completely, nevertheless he made her a sign with his hand that he would do what she commanded him. Bowing to her, he went away and returned to his house. There, thinking upon his situation and revolving in his mind the cruel oath which he had taken, he decided, even though he had committed himself irresponsibly by a solemn oath, to keep it with firm intent and complete observance.

He therefore pretended that he had lost his power of speech by chance; leaving Moncalieri, he went to Virle and, living as a mute person, communicated by signs and by writing. The compassion that all felt for him was great, and it seemed to all a marvellous thing that he had lost his speech without any sickness having befallen him. Messer Filiberto arranged for the management of his affairs, naming a cousin of his as administrator; and, providing himself with good horses and ordering that money be remitted to him at certain times, left Piedmont and went to Lyons, in

bellissimo de la persona, ben membruto e gentile ne lo aspetto, di modo che ovunque andava e sapevasi la sua disaventura, aveva ciascuno di lui pietà.

Aveva in quei tempi Carlo settimo re di Francia avuta crudelissima guerra con gli inglesi e tuttavia gli combatteva, ricuperando per forza d'arme quanto eglino per molti anni innanzi agli altri re di Francia avevano occupato. E cacciandogli di Guascogna e d'altre bande, attendeva a finire di levargli la Normandia. Udendo questo, messer Filiberto si deliberò andar a la corte del re Carlo, che alora era in Normandia. Arrivato che ci fu, vi ritrovò alcuni baroni suoi amici dai quali fu benignamente raccolto. Ed inteso il caso suo—che era per accidente incognito fatto mutolo—gli ebbero compassione. Egli a costoro fece cenno che là era venuto per far il mestiero de l'arme in servigio del re. Il che a loro fu molto caro, conoscendolo per innanzi uomo di grandissimo animo e molto prode de la sua persona. Onde messosi in arnese[30] d'arme e di cavalli, avvenne che si deveva[31] dar l'assalto a Roano,[32] città principale di Normandia. In questo assalto messer Filiberto si diportò tanto valorosamente quanto altro che ci fosse, e fu dal re Carlo veduto più volte far opera di fortissimo e prudente soldato, di modo che fu cagione che, rinovato l'assalto, Roano si prese.

Avuto che si fu Roano, il re si fece chiamar messer Filiberto e volle saper chi fosse, per darli convenevole guiderdone del suo valore. Ed inteso che era dei signori di Virle in Piemonte e che era poco tempo innanzi restato mutolo non si sapendo in che modo, lo ritenne per gentiluomo de la sua camera con la solita pensione, e gli fece pagare alora duo mila franchi, essortandolo a servire come aveva cominciato e promettendogli far ogni cosa per farlo guarire. Egli con cenni umilissimamente ringraziò del tutto il re e, alzata la mano, accennò che egli non mancheria di servire fedelmente. Occorse un dì che al passare di certo ponte

France. He was very handsome in his person, well-proportioned and noble in his appearance, so that wherever he went and his misfortune was known, everyone felt pity for him.

In those times, Charles VII, King of France, had been waging a very savage war against the English, and was still fighting them, regaining through force of arms the land that they had occupied for many years previously at the expense of the previous kings of France. Expelling them from Gascony and other regions, he was now finishing the task of taking Normany from them. On hearing this, Messer Filiberto decided to go to the court of King Charles, who was at that time in Normandy. On arriving there, he found some barons who were friends of his, by whom he was kindly received. On hearing of his case—that he had been struck dumb by an unknown mishap—they had compassion on him. He made signs to them that he had come there to serve under arms in the service of the king. This was very pleasing to them, since they knew him from earlier times as a man of great courage and very brave in his person. When he had provided himself with arms and horses, it happened that they were about to attack Rouen, the principal city of Normandy. In this assault Messer Filiberto carried himself as bravely as any man that was present, and he was seen by King Charles several times performing the deeds of a very brave and wise soldier, as a result of which, when the attack was renewed, Rouen was captured.

When Rouen had been taken, the king had Messer Filiberto called and inquired who he was, in order to give him a suitable reward for his bravery. When he heard that he was of the family of the lords of Virle in Piedmont and that he had been struck dumb a short while previously in an unknown way, he retained him as gentleman of his bedchamber with the customary pension, and then had him paid two thousand francs, urging him to keep on serving as he had begun, and promising him that he would do everything to have him cured. He [Messer Filiberto], with signs, humbly thanked the king for everything and, raising his

s'attaccò una grossa scaramuccia tra i francesi e nemici; e dandosi con le trombe—A l'arme! a l'arme!—e tuttavia il romore tra i soldati crescendo, il re per far animo ai suoi v'andò. Guidava Talabotto,[33] capitano degli inglesi, i suoi, ed egli in persona era sovra il ponte e quasi tutto l'aveva preso. Il re animava i suoi e mandava questi e quelli in soccorso, quando ci sopravvenne il prode e valoroso messer Filiberto armato suso un bravo corsiero. Egli a prima giunta con la lancia in resta animosamente investì Talabotto e lui e il cavallo riversò per terra. Presa poi una forte e poderosa mazza in mano, si cacciò tra gli inglesi e fieramente percotendo questi e quelli, mai non dava colpo in fallo e ad ogni bòtta o gettava per terra o ammazzava uno inglese, di modo che i nemici furono sforzati d'abbandonar il ponte e senza ordine fuggirsene. Talabotto, aitato dai suoi a montar a cavallo, ebbe carestia di terreno. Questa vittoria fu cagione che quasi tutta la Normandia venne in potere del re Carlo; onde veggendo il buon re di quanto giovamento gli era stato messer Filiberto, molto onoratamente a la presenza di tutti i baroni di corte lo lodò e gli donò alcune castella con la condutta di cento uomini d'arme, e gli accrebbe grossamente la provigione, facendogli ogni giorno maggiori carezze.

Finita questa guerra, il re in Roano ordinò una solenne giostra, ove intervennero tutti i valenti e primi di Francia, de la quale messer Filiberto n'ebbe l'onore. Il re, che molto l'amava e desiderava sommamente che egli guarisse per aver a ragionar seco, fece bandire per tutte le sue provincie come egli aveva un gentiluomo che era diventato mutolo in una notte, e che se v'era nessuno[34] che lo volesse sanare, che averebbe subito dieci mila franchi. Il bando si publicò per tutta la Francia e anco pervenne in Italia. Onde molti così oltramontani come francesi, tratti da la cupidigia del danaio, si misero a la prova; ma effetto nessuno non riuscì. E certo era la fatica dei medici gettata via, non volendo il

hand, indicated that he would not fail to serve him faith-fully. It happened one day that, as they were passing a certain bridge, a heavy skirmish arose between the French and their enemies; and when, the call "to arms! to arms!" was given by the trumpets, as the noise among the soldiers kept on growing, the king went there to encourage his men. Talbot, the captain of the English, was leading his men, and he was on the bridge in person and had taken it almost completely. The king was encouraging his men and was sending various of them to help, when the able and cour-ageous Messer Filiberto arrived, armed and mounted on a fine warhorse. Immediately on arriving, with his lance in its rest he boldly ran against Talbot and knocked both him and his horse to the ground. Then he took a stout and heavy mace in his hand, rushed in among the English and fiercely struck one after another; he never missed a stroke, and at every blow he either knocked to the ground or killed an Englishman, so that the enemies were forced to abandon the bridge and flee in disorder. Talbot, helped by his men to remount, lost his ground. As a result of this victory, almost all of Normandy came into King Charles's power. When the good king saw how much help Messer Filiberto had been to him, he honored him greatly and praised him in the presence of all the barons of his court; he gave him some castles together with the leadership of a hundred men-at-arms, and greatly increased his stipend, showing him greater favor every day.

When this war was over, the king held a solemn tourna-ment in Rouen, in which all the bravest and most outstand-ing men of France took part, and in which Messer Fili-berto carried off the honors. The king, who was very fond of him and greatly wished him to recover so that he could converse with him, had it proclaimed throughout all his provinces that he had a nobleman who had become mute in a single night, and that if there was anyone who would cure him, this person would immediately receive ten thou-sand francs. The proclamation was made known through-out France and even reached Italy. Thereupon many per-sons, both Italians and French, attracted by the greed of

finto mutolo favellare. Onde il re, sdegnatosi che medico non si trovasse che lo volesse curare, e veggendo che infiniti tutto il dì venivano, così medici solenni [35] come altri, che con loro isperimenti pensavano sanarlo, e giudicando che fossero più tosto tratti da l'ingordigia del guadagno che da sapere o speranza che avessero di poterlo guarire, fece far un bando: che chi voleva guarire messer Filiberto, pigliasse quel termine che gli pareva atto a far tal cura, e curandolo avrebbe i dieci mila franchi con altri doni che a lui donerebbe, nol curando ne perdesse il capo, se modo non aveva di pagare dieci mila franchi. Divolgato questo fiero proclamo, cessò la moltitudine dei medici. E pure ci fu qualcuno che, da vana speranza sostenuto, non dubitò porsi a tanto rischio; di modo che alcuni, non lo potendo curare, erano condannati a pagar i dieci mila franchi o perder la testa, ed alcuni altri furono condannati a perpetua prigione.

Era già la fama di questa cosa venuta in Moncalieri, come monsignor Filiberto da Virle era in grandissimo stato appo il re di Francia e n'era divenuto ricchissimo. Madonna Zilia, udendo questa cosa e sapendo molto bene la cagione perché messer Filiberto non parlava, e veggendo che già erano passati dui anni, pensò che egli non tanto per la riverenza de lo stretto giuramento che fatto aveva non parlasse, quanto per amore di lei, per non le mancar de la promessa. E giudicando che l'amor di lui fosse in quel fervore che era quando partì da Moncalieri, si deliberò andare a Parigi, ove alora era il re, e far che messer Filiberto parlasse e guadagnare i dieci mila franchi, ché non si poteva persuadere che egli, essendo ad instanzia di lei divenuto mutolo, che come la vedesse e fosse da lei pregato a parlare, che non parlasse. Messo dunque quell'ordine a le cose sue che le parve e divolgate certe favole, s'inviò in Francia e pervenne a Parigi; ove arrivata, senza dar indugio

money, made the attempt, but without success. And certainly the healers' efforts were wasted, since the pretended mute was unwilling to speak. At this, the king, angry that there was no doctor who would cure him, and seeing that they came in countless numbers all day long—both serious doctors and others—who expected to cure him with their experiments, judged that they were attracted more by the desire of gain than by knowledge or any hope that they might have of being able to cure him. He therefore sent out a proclamation: that whoever wished to cure Messer Filiberto should take whatever length of time seemed to him necessary to effect this cure, and that if he cured him, he should have the ten thousand francs, with other gifts that he would give him; but if he did not cure him, he should lose his head as a result, if he did not have the ten thousand francs [to pay as a fine]. When this drastic proclamation had been made, the great number of doctors ceased. Yet there were still a few who, sustained by vain hopes, did not hesitate to run such a risk, so that a few, who were not able to cure him, were condemned to pay the ten thousand francs or lose their heads, and some others were condemned to life imprisonment.

The report of this matter had already come to Moncalieri, namely that Monsignor Filiberto of Virle was in very great favor with the king of France and had thereby become very rich. Madonna Zilia, hearing this and knowing very well the reason why Messer Filiberto did not speak, and seeing that two years had already passed, thought that his silence was due, not so much to strict reverence for the oath that he had taken, as to love for her, so as not to fail his promise. Deeming that his love was still as strong as it had been when he left Moncalieri, she decided to go to Paris, where the king was at that time, and cause Messer Filiberto to speak and thereby gain the ten thousand francs; for she could not imagine that (since he had become mute by her insistence) he would not speak when he saw her and was requested by her to speak. She therefore put her affairs in such order as seemed best and gave out certain stories [about her going]; then she set out for France and reached

a la cosa, andò a parlar a quei commissari che la cura di
monsignor Filiberto circa a farlo sanare avevano, e disse
loro:

— Signori, io sono venuta per curare monsignor Filiberto,
avend'io alcuni segreti in questa arte eccellenti, col mezzo
dei quali spero in Dio operare ch'in quindici giorni egli
favellerà benissimo. E se io nol riduco nel termine preso a
perfetta sanità, io ne vo' perdere la testa. Ma io non intendo
che durando [36] la cura ch'io farò, che persona rimanga in
camera con monsignor Filiberto se non io, perché non mi
par convenevole che nessuno impari la medicina che io
intendo adoperare in questa cura: di modo che la notte e
il dì io mi rimarrò seco, perciò che anco di notte a certe
ore mi converrà i miei rimedi usare.

Udendo i signori commissari questa gentildonna parlare
così animosamente in tanto periglioso caso e dove i più dotti
di Francia e d'altri luoghi erano mancati, fecero intendere
a monsignor Filiberto esser venuta una gentildonna del
paese del Piemonte che s'offeriva curarlo. Egli se la fece a
l'albergo condurre e, come la vide, subito la conobbe. Onde
giudicò che ella, non per amor di lui, ma per la gola dei
dieci milia franchi avesse preso la fatica di quel viaggio.
E pensando a la gran durezza di lei e crudeltà che verso lui
aveva ella usato e agli strazi che per lei aveva patito, sentì il
suo fervente amore, che già quasi era intepidito, cangiarsi
in desìo di giusta vendetta. Per questo deliberò di prender
di lei quel piacere che la fortuna gli metteva innanzi e de
la moneta che meritava pagarla. Perciò essendo restati soli
in camera e l'uscio di quella di dentro da lei fermato col
chiavistello, ella gli disse:

— Monsignor mio, non mi conoscete voi? non vedete che
io sono la vostra cara Zilia, che già tanto dicevate amare?

Egli accennò che bene la conosceva; ma toccandosi la
lingua con il dito, mostrava che non poteva parlare e si
stringeva ne le spalle. E dicendoli la donna che l'assolveva
dal giuramento e da la promessa fattale e che era venuta a

Paris. When she had arrived there, without delaying matters, she went to speak to those officials who were entrusted with Messer Filiberto's recovery, and said to them:

"My lords, I have come to cure Monsignor Filiberto, since I have some outstanding secrets in this art, by means of which I hope, God willing, to bring it about that in two weeks he will speak excellently. And if I do not bring him into perfect health in the time agreed upon, I am willing to lose my head for it. But I do not intend that anyone except myself should remain in the room with Monsignor Filiberto during the cure that I shall perform, because it does not seem to me to be fitting that anyone should learn [of] the medicine that I intend to use in this cure; consequently I shall remain with him night and day, because I shall have to apply my remedies also at certain hours of the night."

When the officials heard this gentlewoman speak so boldly in such a perilous matter, in which the most learnèd men of France and of other places had failed, they gave Monsignor Filiberto to understand that a lady had come from the region of Piedmont offering to cure him. He had her brought to his dwelling, and, when he saw her, he recognized her immediately. Thereupon he judged that she had undertaken that trip, not out of love for him, but out of greed for the ten thousand francs. And thinking of her great harshness and of the cruelty which she had shown him, and of the torments which he had endured on her account, he felt his intense love, which had already become almost cold, turn into a desire for a just vengeance. Therefore he decided to have of her such pleasure as fortune might place in his way and to repay her in the coin that she deserved. And so, when they were alone in the room and she had bolted the door from within, she said to him:

"My lord, do you not know me? Do you not see that I am your dear Zilia, whom you used to say you loved so much?"

He made signs that he knew her very well; but touching his tongue with his finger, made signs that he could not talk, and shrugged his shoulders. When the lady told him that she was releasing him from the oath and from the

Parigi per far tutto quello che egli le comandasse, egli altro non faceva se non stringersi ne le spalle e toccarsi la lingua col dito. Madonna Zilia, veggendo questi modi che monsignor Filiberto teneva, era in grandissimo dispiacere; e veggendo che preghiere che facesse nulla giovavano, cominciò amorosamente a basciarlo e fargli tutte le carezze che sapeva, di modo che egli, che era giovine e che pure aveva ardentemente la donna amata, che nel vero era molto bella, si sentì destare il concupiscibile appetito. Il perché, così a la mutola, egli prese quell'amoroso piacere di lei che tanto aveva desiderato. E così molte fiate ne lo spazio di quindici giorni seco si trastullò amorosamente, ove la lingua mai snodare non volle, non gli parendo che un bacio che in Moncalieri dato gli aveva meritasse così lunga e grave penitenza. Onde chi volesse narrare i ragionamenti che la donna gli fece e i caldi prieghi che ella gli sporse e le lagrime che sparse per ottenere da lui che parlasse, non se ne verrebbe a capo in tutto oggi.[37]

Ora, venuto il termine da lei preso e non volendo monsignor Filiberto parlare, ella conobbe la grandissima sua sciochezza e presunzione ed insiememente la crudeltà che al suo amante aveva usata, e si tenne per morta; perciò che, passato il termine prefisso, le fu detto che pagasse i dieci milia franchi o che si confessasse, perché il capo il dì seguente le saria tagliato. Fu dunque levata da la stanza di monsignor Filiberto e condutta a le prigioni. La sua dote non era tanta che potesse pagar la pena, onde si dispose al morire. Il che intendendo monsignor Filiberto e parendogli averla assai straziata ed essersi di lei a bastanza vendicato, andò a trovare il re; e fattagli la debita riverenza, con meravigliosa festa del re e di tutti cominciò a favellare, e a quello narrò tutta l'istoria di questo suo sì lungo silenzio. Poi supplicò umilissimamente al re che a tutti quelli che erano in prigione fosse perdonato e medesimamente a la donna; il che fu dal re fatto essequire. Onde cavata la donna di prigione e a la volta di Piemonte volendo con grandissima vergogna ritornare, monsignor Filiberto volle

promise he had made her, and that she had come to Paris to do everything that he commanded her, he did nothing but shrug his shoulders and touch his tongue with his finger. Madonna Zilia, on seeing the way Monsignor Filiberto behaved, was greatly disappointed; and, seeing that no entreaties on her part were of any avail, she started amorously to kiss him and to caress him; so that he—who was young and had, after all, felt an ardent love for the lady, who was in truth very beautiful—felt his carnal appetites aroused. Therefore, thus in dumb show, he had that amorous pleasure of her which he had so much desired. And thus many times in the course of two weeks he enjoyed himself making love with her, but he was never willing to set free his tongue, since it did not seem to him that a kiss which she had given him in Moncalieri deserved such a long and severe penitence. But if anyone were to attempt to tell the arguments that the lady urged upon him and the intense entreaties that she made to him and the tears that she shed to get him to talk, he would not get through them in a whole day.

Now, when the period which she had set was past and Monsignor Filiberto was unwilling to speak, she recognized how extremely foolish and presumptuous she had been and also how cruel she had been to her lover, and gave herself up as dead; because, when the established period of time was past, she was told that she must pay the ten thousand francs or make her last confession, because on the next day she would be beheaded. She was, therefore, taken away from Monsignor Filiberto's room and put in prison. Her dowry was not large enough to enable her to pay the fine, and so she prepared to die. When Monsignor Filiberto heard this, he considered that he had tormented her enough and avenged himself sufficiently on her. He went to see the king and, after making an appropriate reverence, he began to speak, to the wonder and joy of the king and of everyone; and he told him the whole story of that silence of his which had lasted so long. Then he humbly begged the king to pardon all those who were in prison, and likewise the lady; and the king had this done. Thereupon, when the lady was

che al suo albergo ella e la sua compagnia alloggiassero. Chiamata poi a parte la donna, egli così le disse:

— Madonna, voi sapete come in Moncalieri io molti mesi vi feci il servidore, ché in vero io ardentissimamente v'amava. Sapete poi che per un bacio mi comandaste che io stessi tre anni mutolo. E vi giuro, se voi alora o dapoi che andai a Virle m'aveste assolto dal giuramento, che io vi sarei restato eternamente servidore. Ma la crudeltà vostra m'ha fatto andare ramingo circa tre anni, nel qual tempo, Dio grazia e non la vostra mercè,[38] mi è sì bene avvenuto che io ci sono diventato ricco e mi trovo in buona grazia del mio re. E parendomi aver di voi giusta vendetta presa, voglio esservi di tanto cortese, che, possendovi lasciar troncare il capo, vi pagherò largamente le spese del viaggio che fatto avete e anco per il ritorno. Imparate mo' a governarvi con prudenza e non istraziar i gentiluomini, perciò che, come proverbialmente si dice, "gli uomini s'incontrano e non i monti".

Fecele dunque dar danari a sufficienza e la licenziò. Volle il re che pigliasse moglie e gli diede una ricca giovane che ereditava alcune castella. Mandò poi a chiamar l'amico suo spoletino e lo ritenne seco, dandogli il modo di vivere agiatamente. E così con buona grazia del re sempre se ne visse, e dopo la morte del re Carlo settimo restò anco in favore appo il re Lodovico undecimo.

released from prison and she desired to return to Piedmont in great shame, Monsignor Filiberto insisted that she and her retinue stay at his dwelling. Then, calling the lady aside, he spoke to her in this manner:

"My lady, you know that in Moncalieri I was your servant for many months, because in truth I loved you most ardently. You know, too, that for a kiss you commanded me to remain mute for three years. And I swear to you that if you, at that time or after I went to Virle, had released me from the oath, I would have been your servant forever. But your cruelty has made me rove for three years, and in this time, thanks be to God (but no thanks to you), I have had such good fortune as to have become rich and I am in the good graces of my king. Now it seems to me that I have taken just revenge upon you, and I wish to show you this much courtesy, that, although I could have let your head be cut off, I will generously pay the expenses of the trip you have made and also of your return. Now learn to behave wisely and not put gentlemen to torment, because, as the proverb says, 'men, not mountains, should be met half-way'."

He therefore had her given enough money and sent her away. The king wished him to take a wife, and gave him a rich young lady who was heiress to several castles. Then he [Filiberto] sent for his friend from Spoleto and kept him in his company, giving him the means to live in comfort. And thus he lived ever after in the good graces of the king, and after the death of King Charles VII he was still in favor with King Louis XI.

Giovanni Verga

(1840–1922)

THE MOST important of the Italian "naturalists" of the latter part of the nineteenth century was the Sicilian Giovanni Verga, a native of Catania. Following in the footsteps of the French realist and naturalist school (Daudet, Zola, Maupassant), Verga gave, in his best works, a detailed, accurate picture of lower- and middle-class life in Sicily. It was his original intention to write a series of novels, to be called *I Vinti* ("The Conquered"), which would portray contemporary society from the point of view of those who had struggled to improve their lot and had failed. However, he only finished two novels of the series, *I Malavoglia* ("The Malavoglia Family," also translated as "The House by the Medlar Tree," 1881) and *Mastro Don Gesualdo* (1888). His best short stories, the collection *Vita dei Campi* ("Country Life," 1880), from which *Rosso Malpelo* is taken, and *Cavalleria Rusticana* ("Rustic Chivalry," 1884), also deal with Sicilian life in the same vein.

Although he derived much of his technique from the French naturalists, Verga was not wholly in sympathy with their cold, pseudoscientific approach. His realism is both more selective—in that his material is presented from the viewpoint of his characters and hence involves the reader in a kind of cultural empathy—and more sympathetic. Verga realizes and presents the tragic aspects of his per-

sonages' fate, objectively, it is true, but not without pity and feeling for them. Such a presentation arouses the reader's sympathy, but creates also a feeling of fatalism, such as has been inherent in Sicilian culture for centuries; it has been said that in Sicily, the greatest crime is, not to call attention to human misery, but to attempt to alleviate the situation.

Verga's style, in his most mature works, conforms to the Tuscan base of the standard language in its formal aspects, but reflects Sicilian usage in its syntax and colloquial turn of phrase. Verga made little use of Sicilian dialect, but the entire sentence-structure and rhythm of his prose reflect Sicilian speech.

ROSSO MALPELO

di Giovanni Verga

MALPELO [1] si chiamava così perchè aveva i capelli rossi, ed aveva i capelli rossi perchè era un ragazzo malizioso e cattivo, che prometteva di riescire un fior di birbone.[2] Sicchè tutti alla cava della rena rossa lo chiamavano *Malpelo,* e persino sua madre col sentirgli dir sempre a quel modo aveva quasi dimenticato il suo nome di battesimo.

Del resto, ella lo vedeva soltanto il sabato sera, quando tornava a casa con quei pochi soldi della settimana; e siccome era *Malpelo* c'era anche a temere che ne sottraesse un paio di quei soldi; e nel dubbio, per non sbagliare, la sorella maggiore gli faceva la ricevuta a scapaccioni.

Però il padrone della cava aveva confermato che i soldi erano tanti e non più; e in coscienza erano anche troppi per *Malpelo,* un monellaccio che nessuno avrebbe voluto vedersi davanti, e che tutti schivavano come un can rognoso, e lo accarezzavano coi piedi, allorchè se lo trovavano a tiro.

Egli era davvero un brutto ceffo, torvo, ringhioso e selvatico. Al mezzogiorno, mentre tutti gli altri operai della cava si mangiavano in crocchio la loro minestra, e facevano un po' di ricreazione, egli andava a rincantucciarsi col suo corbello fra le gambe, per rosicchiarsi quel suo pane di otto giorni, come fanno le bestie sue pari; e ciascuno gli

ROSSO MALPELO

by Giovanni Verga

MALPELO WAS called that because he had red hair, and he had red hair because he was a malicious and bad boy who promised to turn out a prize rascal. So that everyone at the red sand mine called him Malpelo, and even his mother, from hearing him called that all the time, had almost forgotten his baptismal name.

For that matter, she saw him only on Saturday evenings, when he came back home with those few pennies earned during the week; and since he was Malpelo there was also reason to fear that he might steal a couple of those pennies; and in that uncertainty, so as to make no mistake, his elder sister would give him the receipt in the form of cuffs.

However, the owner of the mine had confirmed that the pennies were so many and no more; and, in all honesty, they were even too many for Malpelo, a nasty urchin whom nobody cared to see around and whom all avoided like a mangy dog. The caresses they gave him were with their feet, whenever he was in kicking range.

He had in truth an ugly face, sullen, snarling and savage. At midday, while all the other mine workers were eating their soup in a group and were having a little recreation, he would go off into a corner with his basket between his legs, to nibble on his eight-day-old bread, as animals like him do. Everyone would tell him what they thought of him,

diceva la sua motteggiandolo, e gli tiravan dei sassi, finchè il soprastante lo rimandava al lavoro con una pedata. Ei s'ingrassava fra i calci e si lasciava caricare meglio dell'asino grigio, senza osar di lagnarsi. Era sempre cencioso e lordo di rena rossa, chè la sua sorella s'era fatta sposa, e avea altro pel capo: nondimeno era conosciuto come la bettonica [3] per tutto Monserrato [4] e la Carvana,[5] tanto che la cava dove lavorava la chiamavano "la cava di Malpelo," e cotesto al padrone gli seccava assai. Insomma lo tenevano addirittura per carità e perchè mastro [6] Misciu, suo padre, era morto nella cava.

Era morto così, che un sabato aveva voluto terminare certo lavoro preso a cottimo, di un pilastro lasciato altra volta per sostegno nella cava, e che ora non serviva più, e s'era calcolato così ad occhio [7] col padrone per 35 o 40 carra di rena. Invece mastro Misciu sterrava da tre giorni e ne avanzava ancora per la mezza giornata del lunedì. Era stato un magro affare e solo un minchione come mastro Misciu aveva potuto lasciarsi gabbare a questo modo dal padrone; perciò appunto lo chiamavano mastro Misciu Bestia,[8] ed era l'asino da basto di tutta la cava. Ei, povero diavolaccio, lasciava dire e si contentava di buscarsi il pane colle sue braccia, invece di menarle addosso ai compagni, e attaccar brighe. *Malpelo* faceva un visaccio come se quelle soperchierie cascassero sulle sue spalle, e così piccolo com'era aveva di quelle occhiate che facevano dire agli altri:—Va' là, che tu non ci morrai nel tuo letto, come tuo padre.—

Invece nemmen suo padre ci morì nel suo letto, tuttochè fosse una buona bestia. Zio Mommu lo sciancato, aveva detto che quel pilastro lì ei non l'avrebbe tolto per venti onze,[9] tanto era pericoloso; ma d'altra parte tutto è pericoloso nelle cave, e se si sta a badare al pericolo, è meglio andare a fare l'avvocato.

Adunque il sabato sera mastro Misciu raschiava ancora il suo pilastro che l'avemmaria era suonata da un pezzo,[10] e tutti i suoi compagni avevano accesa la pipa e se n'erano

making fun of him, and they would throw rocks at him, until the supervisor sent him back to work with a kick. He got fat on the kicks and let himself be loaded more than the gray donkey, without daring to complain. He was always in rags and filthy with red sand, for his sister had gotten engaged and had other things to think about. Nevertheless he was known to everyone throughout Monserrato and the Carvana, so much so that the mine in which he worked was called "Malpelo's mine," much to the annoyance of its owner. In short, they kept him purely out of charity and because his father, Mastro Misciu, had died in the mine.

He had died in this way: one Saturday he had insisted on finishing a certain job (which he had taken on a piece-work basis) on a pillar which had formerly been left as a prop in the mine, and which was not needed any longer; at a rough estimate, he and the owner had figured it would make 35 or 40 carts of sand. Instead, Mastro Misciu had been digging for three days and there was still some left over for the half-day on Monday. It had been a poor bargain, and only a simpleton like Mastro Misciu could have let himself be cheated in this way by the owner. It was just for this reason that they called him Master Misciu the Beast, for he was the pack-horse of the whole mine. He, poor devil, let them have their say and was content to eke out his bread with his arms, instead of hitting his companions with them and starting fights. Malpelo would make a nasty face as if those insults were falling on his own shoulders, and, small as he was, he would dart such glances as to make the others say: "Go on, you won't die in your bed like your father."

On the contrary, not even his father died in his bed, even though he was a good beast. Uncle Mommu, the cripple, had said that he wouldn't have taken out that pillar for twenty *onze*, it was so dangerous; but on the other hand, everything is dangerous in mines, and if you start worrying about danger, you had better go and be a lawyer.

That Saturday evening, therefore, Mastro Misciu was still scratching at his pillar, although the Ave Maria had already sounded a while back, and all his fellow-workers

77

andati dicendogli di divertirsi a grattarsi la pancia per amor del padrone, e raccomandandogli di non fare *la morte del sorcio.* Ei, che c'era avvezzo alle beffe, non dava retta, e rispondeva soltanto cogli ah! ah! dei suoi bei colpi di zappa in pieno; e intanto borbottava:—Questo è per il pane! Questo pel vino! Questo per la gonnella di Nunziata!—e così andava facendo il conto del come avrebbe speso i denari del suo *appalto,* il cottimante!

Fuori della cava il cielo formicolava di stelle, e laggiù, la lanterna fumava e girava al pari di un arcolaio; ed il grosso pilastro rosso, sventrato a colpi di zappa, contorcevasi e si piegava in arco come se avesse il mal di pancia, e dicesse: *ohi, ohi!* anch'esso. *Malpelo* andava sgamberando il terreno, e metteva al sicuro il piccone, il sacco vuoto ed il fiasco del vino. Il padre che gli voleva bene, poveretto, andava dicendogli: "Tìrati indietro!" oppure "Sta' attento! Sta' attento se cascano dall'alto dei sassolini o della rena grossa". Tutt'a un tratto non disse più nulla, e *Malpelo,* che si era voltato a riporre i ferri nel corbello, udì un rumore sordo e soffocato, come fa la rena allorchè si rovescia tutta in una volta; ed il lume si spense.

Quella sera in cui vennero a cercare in tutta fretta l'ingegnere che dirigeva i lavori della cava, ei si trovava a teatro, e non avrebbe cambiato la sua poltrona con un trono, perch' era gran dilettante. Rossi rappresentava l'*Amleto,*[11] e c' era un bellissimo teatro. Sulla porta si vide accerchiato da tutte le femminucce di Monserrato, che strillavano e si picchiavano il petto per annunziare la gran disgrazia ch'era toccata a comare [12] Santa, la sola, poveretta, che non dicesse nulla, e sbatteva i denti quasi fosse in gennaio. L'ingegnere, quando gli ebbero detto che il caso era accaduto da circa quattro ore, domandò cosa venissero a fare da lui dopo quattro ore. Nondimeno ci andò con scale e torcie a vento, ma passarono altre due ore, e fecero sei, e lo sciancato disse che a sgomberare il sotterraneo dal materiale caduto ci voleva una settimana.

had lit their pipes and had left, telling him to have a good time scratching his belly out of love for the owner, and advising him not to die like a rat. He, who was accustomed to jests, paid no attention, and answered only with the "ah! ah!" of his fine, full mattock blows; and meanwhile he muttered: "This one is for the bread! This one is for the wine! This one is for Nunziata's skirt!" In this way he was figuring up how he was going to spend the reward for his "contract"—the piece-worker!

Outside the mine the sky was teeming with stars, and down there the lantern was smoking and turning like a skein-winder; and the big red pillar, disemboweled by the blows of the mattock, was twisting and bending in an arch as if it too had a belly-ache and were saying "Ohi, ohi!" Malpelo was occupied in clearing the ground and putting the pick-axe, the empty sack and the wine-flask out of harm's way. His father, who was fond of him, poor man, kept telling him: "Get back!" or "Look out! Look out! Take care that stones or chunks of sand don't fall on you from above!" All of a sudden he didn't say anything more, and Malpelo, who had turned away to put the irons back in the basket, heard a dull, stifled noise, such as the sand makes when it falls in all at once; and the light went out.

That night, when they came in a tremendous hurry to get the engineer who was in charge of the mine works, he was at the theater, and would not have exchanged his orchestra seat for a throne, because he was a great music-lover. Rossi was playing Hamlet, and there was a very good house. At the door, he was surrounded by all the silly women of Monserrato, who were shrieking and beating their breasts to proclaim the great misfortune that had befallen comare Santa. She, poor thing, was the only one who was not saying anything, and her teeth were chattering as if it were January. The engineer, when they told him that the mishap had occurred about four hours previously, asked why they were coming to him after four hours. Nevertheless he went out there, with ladders and wind torches, but two more hours passed (that made six), and the cripple said it would take a week to rid the underground area of the ma-

Altro che quaranta carra di rena! Della rena ne era caduta una montagna, tutta fina e ben bruciata dalla lava che si sarebbe impastata colle mani e doveva prendere il doppio di calce. Ce n'era da riempire delle carra per delle settimane. Il bell'affare di mastro Bestia! [13]

L'ingegnere se ne tornò a veder seppellire Ofelia; [14] e gli altri minatori si strinsero nelle spalle, e se ne tornarono a casa ad uno ad uno. Nella ressa e nel gran chiacchierìo non badarono a una voce di fanciullo, la quale non aveva più nulla di umano, e strillava:

— Scavate! scavate qui! presto!

— To'!—disse lo sciancato—è *Malpelo!*—Da dove è venuto fuori *Malpelo?* Se tu non fossi stato *Malpelo,* non te la saresti scappata,[15] no!—

Gli altri si misero a ridere e chi diceva che *Malpelo* avea il diavolo dalla sua,[16] un altro che avea il cuoio duro a mo' dei gatti. *Malpelo* non rispondeva nulla, non piangeva nemmeno, scavava colle unghie colà nella rena, dentro la buca, sicchè nessuno s'era accorto di lui; e quando si accostarono col lume gli videro tal viso stravolto, e tali occhiacci invetrati, e tale schiuma alla bocca da far paura; le unghie gli si erano strappate e gli pendevano dalle mani tutte in sangue. Poi quando vollero toglierlo di là fu un affar serio; non potendo più graffiare, mordeva come un cane arrabbiato e dovettero afferrarlo pei capelli, per tirarlo via a viva forza.

Però infine tornò alla cava dopo qualche giorno, quando sua madre, piagnucolando, ve lo condusse per mano; giacchè, alle volte il pane che si mangia non si può andare a cercarlo di qua e di là. Anzi non volle più allontanarsi da quella galleria, e sterrava con accanimento, quasi ogni corbello di rena lo levasse di sul petto a suo padre. Alle volte, mentre zappava, si fermava bruscamente, colla zappa in aria, il viso torvo e gli occhi stralunati, e sembrava che stesse ad ascoltare qualche cosa che il suo diavolo gli sussurrava negli orecchi, dall'altra parte della montagna di

terial that had fallen on it.

Anything but forty cart-loads of sand! A mountain of sand had fallen, all fine and thoroughly burned by the lava, so that it could have been kneaded with one's hands and would take a double amount of lime. There was enough to fill carts for weeks on end. A fine bargain Mastro Bestia had made!

The engineer went back to see Ophelia buried; the other miners shrugged their shoulders and went back home one by one. In the crowd and the constant chattering, they paid no attention to a boy's voice, which had nothing human left in it, and which was screaming:

"Dig! Dig here! Quickly!"

"Hello!" said the cripple, "it's Malpelo! Where did Malpelo come out from? If you hadn't been Malpelo, you wouldn't have escaped, you wouldn't!"

The others began to laugh; some said that Malpelo had the devil on his side, others that he had a tough hide like cats'. Malpelo answered nothing, and did not even weep; he was digging with his fingernails in the sand, inside the hole, so that no one had noticed him. When they approached with a light, they saw that he had such a distorted face, and such glazed eyes, and such foam on his mouth as to be frightening; his fingernails had been torn off and were hanging from his hands all covered with blood. Then, when they tried to take him away from there, it was a serious business; since he could no longer scratch, he bit like a mad dog and they had to seize him by the hair, to pull him away by sheer force.

However, he finally came back to the mine a few days later, when his mother, whimpering, brought him there leading him by the hand, since, at times, one's daily bread can't be gotten hither and yon. In fact, he was no longer willing to leave that gallery, and excavated furiously, as if every basketful of sand were being lifted off the chest of his father. At times, while he was hacking away, he would stop suddenly, with his mattock in the air, his face sullen and his eyes vacant, and it seemed as if he were hearkening to something that his demon was whispering into his ears,

rena caduta. In quei giorni era più tristo e cattivo del solito, talmente che non mangiava quasi, e il pane lo buttava al cane, come se non fosse *grazia di Dio*. Il cane gli voleva bene, perchè i cani non guardano altro che la mano la quale dà loro il pane. Ma l'asino grigio, povera bestia, sbilenca e macilenta, sopportava tutto lo sfogo della cattiveria di *Malpelo,* ei lo picchiava senza pietà, col manico della zappa, e borbottava:—Così creperai più presto!—

Dopo la morte del babbo pareva che gli fosse entrato il diavolo in corpo, e lavorava al pari di quei bufali feroci che si tengono coll'anello di ferro al naso. Sapendo che era *Malpelo,* ei si acconciava ad esserlo il peggio che fosse possibile, e se accadeva una disgrazia, o che un operaio smarriva i ferri, o che un asino si rompeva una gamba, o che crollava un pezzo di galleria, si sapeva sempre che era stato lui; e infatti ei si pigliava le busse senza protestare, proprio come se le pigliano gli asini che curvano la schiena, ma seguitano a fare a modo loro. Cogli altri ragazzi poi era addirittura crudele, e sembrava che si volesse vendicare sui deboli di tutto il male che s'immaginava gli avessero fatto, a lui e al suo babbo. Certo ei provava uno strano diletto a rammentare ad uno ad uno tutti i maltrattamenti ed i soprusi che avevano fatto subire a suo padre, e del modo in cui l'avevano lasciato crepare. E quando era solo borbottava: "Anche con me fanno così! e a mio padre gli dicevano Bestia, perchè ei non faceva così!" E una volta che passava il padrone, accompagnandolo con un' occhiata torva: "È stato lui, per trentacinque tarì!" E un'altra volta, dietro allo sciancato: "E anche lui! e si metteva a ridere! Io l'ho udito, quella sera!"

Per un raffinamento di malignità sembrava aver preso a proteggere un povero ragazzetto, venuto a lavorare da poco tempo nella casa, il quale per una caduta da un ponte s'era lussato il femore, e non poteva far più il manovale. Il poveretto, quando portava il suo corbello di rena in spalla, arrancava in modo che sembrava ballasse la tarantella, e aveva fatto ridere tutti quelli della cava, così che gli

from the other side of the mountain of fallen sand. In those days he was more perverse and mean than usual, so much so that he almost did not eat, and would throw his bread to the dog, as if it were not a gift of God. The dog loved him, because dogs heed only the hand which feeds them. But the gray donkey, poor beast, bandy-legged and emaciated, bore the brunt of all the expression of Malpelo's malice; he beat it pitilessly, with the handle of the mattock, and muttered: "This way you'll croak sooner!"

After the death of his father, it seemed as if a devil had taken possession of him, and he worked like those ferocious buffaloes which are held by an iron ring in their noses. Knowing that he was *Malpelo,* he resigned himself to being so in the worst way possible. If a mishap occurred, or if a workman lost his tools, or if a donkey broke its leg, or if a part of a gallery fell in, they always knew that it was his fault. In fact, he took the blows without protesting, just as donkeys take them when they bow their backs but continue to do as they please. To the other boys he was downright cruel, and it seemed as if he were trying to avenge himself on the weak for all the harm that he imagined they had done to him and to his father. Certainly he took a strange delight in calling to mind, one after another, all the mal-treatments and impositions they had made his father undergo, and the way in which they had let him die. And when he was alone, he would mumble: "They treat me the same way! and they used to call my father Beast, because he didn't act like they do!" And once, when the owner was passing by, following him with a sullen gaze: "He was the one, for just thirty-five *tarì!*" And another time, following the cripple: "He too! and he began to laugh! I heard him, that evening!"

Through a refinement of malignity, he seemed to have taken under his protection a poor little boy who had come to work in the establishment a short while previously. The boy had dislocated his thigh through falling from a bridge, and was no longer able to be a day-laborer. The poor fel-low, when he carried his basket of sand on his shoulder, jerked along in such a way that he seemed to be dancing

avevano messo nome *Ranocchio;* [17] ma lavorando sotterra, così ranocchio com'era, il suo pane se lo buscava; e *Malpelo* gliene dava anche del suo, per prendersi il gusto di tiranneggiarlo, dicevano.

Infatti egli lo tormentava in cento modi. Ora lo batteva senza un motivo e senza misericordia, e se *Ranocchio* non si difendeva, lo picchiava più forte, con maggiore accanimento, e gli diceva:—To'! Bestia! Bestia sei! Se non ti senti l'animo di difenderti da me che non ti voglio male, vuol dire che ti lascerai pestare il viso da questo e da quello!—

O se *Ranocchio* si asciugava il sangue che gli usciva dalla bocca o dalle narici.—Così come ti cuocerà il dolore delle busse, imparerai a darne anche tu!—Quando cacciava un asino carico per la ripida salita del soterraneo, e lo vedeva puntare gli zoccoli, rifinito, curvo sotto il peso, ansante e coll'occhio spento, ei lo batteva senza misericordia, col manico della zappa, e i colpi suonavano secchi sugli stinchi e sulle costole scoperte. Alle volte la bestia si piegava in due per le battiture, ma stremo di forze non poteva fare un passo, e cadeva sui ginocchi, e ce n'era uno il quale era caduto tante volte, che ci aveva due piaghe alle gambe; e *Malpelo* allora confidava a *Ranocchio:*—L'asino va picchiato, perchè non può picchiar lui; e s'ei potesse picchiare, ci pesterebbe sotto i piedi e ci strapperebbe la carne a morsi.—Oppure:—Se ti accade di dar delle busse, procura di darle più forte che puoi; così coloro su cui cadranno ti terranno per da più di loro, [18] e ne avrai tanti di meno addosso.—

Lavorando di piccone o di zappa poi menava le mani con accanimento, a mo' di uno che l'avesse con la rena, e batteva e ribatteva coi denti stretti, e con quegli *ah! ah!* che aveva suo padre.—La rena è traditora;—diceva a *Ranacchio* sottovoce—somiglia a tutti gli altri, che se sei più debole ti pestano la faccia, e se sei più forte, o siete in

the tarantella, and he had made all the miners laugh, so that they had nicknamed him *Ranocchio* (frog); but working underground, frog-like as he was, he earned his bread; and Malpelo gave him some of his own too, so as to have the pleasure of tyrannizing over him, so they said.

In fact he tormented him in a hundred ways. On occasion he would beat him without reason and without pity, and if Ranocchio did not defend himself, he would hit him harder, with greater fury, and would say to him: "There! Take that! Beast! You're a beast! If you don't have enough courage to defend yourself against me, who wish you no harm, it means that you'll let your face be bashed in by anybody!"

Or, if Ranocchio wiped off the blood that poured from his mouth and nostrils: "As the pain of the blows sears you, so will you learn to hand them out too!" When he was driving a loaded donkey up the steep slope of the underground passage, and he saw it pointing its hoofs, exhausted, bent under its burden, panting and with its eyes lifeless, he would beat it without pity, with the handle of the mattock, and the blows would resound drily on the animal's shins and exposed ribs. On occasion the animal would bend in two because of the beatings, but, exhausted in strength, would be unable to take a single step and would fall on its knees. There was one of them that had fallen so many times that it had two sores on its legs. Malpelo would then unbosom himself to Ranocchio: "The donkey ought to be beaten, because he can't do any hitting himself; and if he could hit, he would trample us under his feet and tear off our flesh in bites." Or: "If you happen to give blows, try to give them as hard as you can; in that way, the ones on whom they fall will consider you their better, and you will have that many less on your neck."

When he worked with pick-axe and mattock, then, he used to use his hands furiously, like someone who had a grudge against the sand, and he would strike and strike again with clenched teeth, with those same "ah! ah!"'s that his father used to utter. "The sand is treacherous," he used to say to Ranocchio in a low voice, "it's like all the

molti, come fa lo sciancato, allora si lascia vincere.[19] Mio padre la batteva sempre, ed egli non batteva altro che la rena, perciò lo chiamavano Bestia, e la rena se lo mangiò a tradimento, perchè era più forte di lui.—

Ogni volta che a *Ranocchio* toccava un lavoro pesante, e *Ranocchio* piagnucolava a guisa di una femminuccia, *Malpelo* lo picchiava sul dorso, e lo sgridava:—Taci pulcino!— e se *Ranocchio* non la finiva più, ei gli dava una mano, dicendo con un certo orgoglio:—Lasciami fare; io sono più forte di te.—Oppure gli dava la sua mezza cipolla, e si contentava di mangiarsi il pane asciutto, e si stringeva nelle spalle, aggiungendo:—Io ci sono avvezzo.—

Era avvezzo a tutto lui, agli scapaccioni, alle pedate, ai colpi di manico di badile, o di cinghia da basto, a vedersi ingiuriato e beffato da tutti, a dormire sui sassi, colle braccia e la schiena rotta da quattordici ore di lavoro; anche a digiunare era avvezzo, allorchè il padrone lo puniva levandogli il pane o la minestra. Ei diceva che la razione di busse non gliela aveva levata mai il padrone; ma le busse non costavano nulla. Non si lamentava però, e si vendicava di soppiatto, a tradimento, con qualche tiro di quelli che sembrava ci avesse messo la coda il diavolo: [20] perciò ei si pigliava sempre i castighi anche quando il colpevole non era stato lui; già se non era stato lui sarebbe stato capace di esserlo, e non si giustificava mai: per altro sarebbe stato inutile. E qualche volta come *Ranocchio* spaventato lo scongiurava piangendo di dire la verità e di scolparsi, ei ripeteva:—A che giova? Sono *Malpelo!*—e nessuno avrebbe potuto dire se quel curvare il capo e le spalle sempre fosse effetto di bieco orgoglio o di disperata rassegnazione, e non si sapeva nemmeno se la sua fosse salvatichezza o timidità. Il certo era che nemmeno sua madre aveva avuta mai una carezza da lui, e quindi non gliene faceva mai.

others. If you're weaker than they are, they'll bash in your face, and if you're stronger, or if there are a lot of you, as the cripple does, then it gives in. My father always used to beat at it, and he never beat at anything but the sand, that's why they called him Beast, and the sand devoured him by treachery, because it was stronger than he was."

Every time that Ranocchio had to do a heavy job, and whimpered like a feeble little woman, Malpelo would whack him on the back and scold him, saying: "Shut up, you chicken!"; and if Ranocchio could not finish the job, he would give him a hand, saying with a certain pride: "Leave it to me; I'm stronger than you." Or he would give him his half onion, and would be content with eating his dry bread, shrugging his shoulders and adding: "I'm used to it."

He was accustomed to everything—slaps, kicks, blows with mattock handles or with pack-saddle straps, being insulted and mocked by everybody, sleeping on the rocks with his arms and his back broken by fourteen hours' work. He was also accustomed to going without food, when the owner punished him by depriving him of bread or soup. He used to say that the owner had never deprived him of his ration of hard knocks; but hard knocks didn't cost anything. He didn't complain, however, and he would take his revenge on the sly, by treachery, with one of those tricks that seemed to have been inspired by the devil. For this reason he always got the punishment, even when he had not been the guilty one; in any case, if he hadn't done the misdeed, he would have been capable of doing it, and he never tried to defend himself; for that matter, it would have been useless. And sometimes, when Ranocchio, in a fright, urged him, weeping, to tell the truth and defend himself, he would repeat: "What's the use? I'm Malpelo!" And no one could have told whether that bending of his head and shoulders was always the result of grim pride or of desperate resignation, and no one knew either whether his behavior was wildness or timidity. What was certain was that not even his mother had ever had a caress from him, and therefore never gave him any.

ROSSO MALPELO

Il sabato sera, appena arrivava a casa con quel suo visaccio imbrattato di lentiggini e di rena rossa, e quei cenci che gli piangevano addosso [21] da ogni parte, la sorella afferrava il manico della scopa se si metteva sull'uscio in quell' arnese, chè avrebbe fatto scappare il suo damo se avesse visto che razza di cognato gli toccava sorbirsi; la madre era sempre da questa o da quella vicina, e quindi egli andava a rannicchiarsi sul suo saccone come un cane malato. Adunque, la domenica, in cui tutti gli altri ragazzi del vicinato si mettevano la camicia pulita per andare a messa o per ruzzare nel cortile, ei sembrava non avesse altro spasso che di andar randagio per le vie degli orti, a dar la caccia a sassate alle povere lucertole, le quali non gli avevano fatto nulla, oppure a sforacchiare le siepi dei fichidindia. Per altro le beffe e le sassate degli altri fanciulli non gli piacevano.

La vedova di mastro Misciu era disperata di aver per figlio quel malarnese, come dicevano tutti, ed egli era ridotto veramente come quei cani, che a furia di buscarsi dei calci e delle sassate da questo e da quello, finiscono col mettersi la coda fra le gambe e scappare alla prima anima viva che vedono, e diventano affamati, spelati e selvatici come lupi. Almeno sottoterra, nella cava della rena, brutto e cencioso e sbracato com'era, non lo beffavano più, e sembrava fatto apposta per quel mestiere persin nel colore dei capelli, e in quegli occhiacci di gatto che ammiccavano se vedevano il sole. Così ci sono degli asini che lavorano nelle cave per anni ed anni senza uscirne mai più, ed in quei sotterranei, dove il pozzo di ingresso è verticale, ci si calan colle funi, e ci restano finchè vivono. Sono asini vecchi, è vero, comprati a dodici o tredici lire, quando stanno per portarli alla Plaja,[22] a strangolarli; ma pel lavoro che hanno da fare laggiù sono ancora buoni; e *Malpelo,* certo, non valeva di più e se veniva fuori dalla cava il sabato sera, era perchè aveva anche le mani per aiutarsi colla fune, e doveva andare a portare a sua madre la paga della settimana.

Certamente egli avrebbe preferito di fare il manovale,

ROSSO MALPELO

On Saturday evenings, as soon as he arrived home with that nasty face of his smeared with freckles and red sand, and those rags which dripped off him on all sides, his sister would grab the broom-handle; for if he appeared at the door in that rig, it would have frightened away her lover, had he seen what kind of a brother-in-law he had to swallow. His mother was always at one neighbor's or another's, and so he would go and crouch on his pallet like a sick dog. And so, on Sundays, when all the other boys in the neighborhood would put on their clean shirts to go to mass or to romp in the court-yard, he seemed to have no other recreation than wandering aimlessly through the orchard paths, and hunting down with rocks the poor lizards, which had done him no harm, or making holes in the prickly-pear hedges. Besides, he didn't enjoy the jests and the rocks hurled at him by the other boys.

Mastro Misciu's widow was desperate at having that rogue, as they all called him, for a son; and he was really in the same state as those dogs which, as a result of receiving kicks and rocks from everybody, finally put their tails between their legs and run away at the first sight of a living person, and become ravenous, hairless and savage as wolves. At least underground, in the sand mine, ugly and ragged and trouserless as he was, they no longer mocked at him, and he seemed made to order for that job even in the color of his hair and in those cat-like eyes which blinked if they saw the sun. In the same way, there are donkeys that work in the mines for years and years without ever coming out, and in those underground mines where the entrance shaft is vertical they are let down with ropes and stay there as long as they live. They are old donkeys, it is true, bought for twelve or thirteen lire when they are about to be taken out to the Playa and strangled; but for the work they have to do down there, they are still good. Malpelo, certainly, wasn't worth anything more than that, and if he came out of the mine on Saturday evenings, it was because he had hands to help himself up by the rope, and he had to go and take his weekly pay to his mother.

Certainly he would have preferred to be a day-laborer,

come *Ranocchio,* e lavorare cantando sui ponti, in alto, in
mezzo all'azzurro del cielo, col sole sulla schiena—o il carrettiere, come compare [23] Gaspare che veniva a prendersi
la rena della cava, dondolandosi sonnacchioso sulle stanghe,
colla pipa in boca, e andava tutto il giorno per le belle
strade di campagna—o meglio ancora avrebbe voluto fare
il contadino che passa la vita fra i campi, in mezzo al
verde, sotto i folti carrubbi, e il mare turchino là in fondo,
e il canto degli uccelli sulla testa. Ma quello era stato il
mestiere di suo padre, e in quel mestiere era nato lui. E
pensando a tutto ciò, indicava a *Ranocchio* il pilastro che
era caduto addosso al genitore, e dava ancora della rena
fina e bruciata che il carrettiere veniva a caricare colla pipa
in bocca, e dondolandosi sulle stanghe, e gli diceva che
quando avrebbero finito di sterrare si sarebbe trovato il
cadavere di suo padre, il quale doveva avere dei calzoni di
fustagno quasi nuovi. *Ranocchio* aveva paura, ma egli no.
Ei narrava che era stato sempre là, da bambino, e aveva
sempre visto quel buco nero, che si sprofondava sotterra,
dove il padre soleva condurlo per mano. Allora stendeva le
braccia a destra e a sinistra, e descriveva come l'intricato
laberinto delle gallerie si stendesse sotto i loro piedi dappertutto, di qua e di là, sin dove potevano vedere la sciara [24]
nera e desolata, sporca di ginestre riarse, e come degli
uomini ce n'erano rimasti tanti, o schiacciati, o smarriti nel
buio, e che camminano da anni e camminano ancora, senza
poter scorgere lo spiraglio del pozzo pel quale sono entrati,
e senza poter udire le strida disperate dei figli, i quali li
cercano inutilmente.

Ma una volta in cui riempiendo i corbelli si rinvenne una
delle scarpe di mastro Misciu, ei fu colto da tal tremito che
dovettero tirarlo all'aria aperta colle funi, proprio come un
asino che stesse per dar dei calci al vento. Però non si
poterono trovare nè i calzoni quasi nuovi, nè il rimanente
di mastro Misciu; sebbene i pratici asserissero che quello
dovea essere il luogo preciso dove il pilastro gli si era
rovesciato addosso; e qualche operaio, nuovo del mestiere,

like Ranocchio, and sing while he worked on the bridges, up on high, amid the blue of the sky, with the sun on his back; or a carter, like compare Gaspare, who came to get the sand from the cave, rocking sleepily on the shafts, with his pipe in his mouth, and went around all day along the beautiful country roads; or, even better, he would have liked to be a farmer, passing his life in the fields, amid the greenery, under the thick carub trees, with the blue sea off yonder, and the song of the birds over his head. But this had been his father's occupation, and into this occupation he had been born. And, thinking of all that, he showed Ranocchio the pillar which had fallen on his father, and which was still supplying fine, burned sand which the carter came to load with his pipe in his mouth, and rocking on the shafts; and he told him that when they finished digging they would find his father's body, which would be wearing fustian trousers that were almost new. Ranocchio was afraid, but he was not. He would tell him how he had always gone there, as a child, and had always seen that black hole which sank down into the earth, where his father used to lead him by the hand. Then he would stretch out his arms to the right and the left, and would describe how the intricate maze of galleries extended beneath their feet in every direction, this way and that, as far as they could see the *sciara*, black and desolate, filthy with burned-over broom-plant; and he would tell how so many men had remained either crushed or lost in the dark, how they had been walking for years and are still walking, without being able to discover the opening of the shaft through which they entered, and without being able to hear the desperate shouts of their children who are looking for them in vain.

But once, while filling the baskets, they came across one of Mastro Misciu's shoes, and he was seized with such a fit of shivering that they had to pull him up into the open air with ropes, just like a donkey that was about to kick at the air. However, they could find neither the nearly new trousers, nor the remains of Mastro Misciu, although the experts asserted that that must be the exact place where the pillar had fallen on him. Some workers who were new to

osservava curiosamente come fosse capricciosa la rena, che aveva sbatacchiato il Bestia di qua e di là, le scarpe da una parte e i piedi dall'altra.

Dacchè poi fu trovata quella scarpa, *Malpelo* fu colto da tal paura di veder comparire fra la rena anche il piede nudo del babbo, che non volle mai più darvi un colpo di zappa; gliela dessero a lui sul capo, la zappa. Egli andò a lavorare in un altro punto della galleria e non volle più tornare da quelle parti. Due o tre giorni dopo scopersero infatti il cadavere di mastro Misciu, coi calzoni indosso, e steso bocconi che sembrava imbalsamato. Lo zio Mommu osservò che aveva dovuto stentar molto a morire, perchè il pilastro gli si era piegato in arco addosso, e l'aveva seppellito vivo; si poteva persino vedere tuttora che mastro Bestia aveva tentato istintivamente di liberarsi, scavando nella rena, e avea le mani lacerate e le unghie rotte.— Proprio come suo figlio *Malpelo!*—ripeteva lo sciancato— ei scavava di qua, mentre suo figlio scavava di là.—Però non dissero nulla al ragazzo per la ragione che lo sapevano maligno e vendicativo.

Il carrettiere sbarazzò il sotterraneo dal cadavere al modo istesso che lo sbarazzava dalla rena caduta e dagli asini morti, chè stavolta oltre al lezzo del carcame, c'era che il carcame era di *carne battezzata;* e la vedova rimpicciolì i calzoni e la camicia e li adattò a *Malpelo,* il quale così fu vestito quasi a nuovo per la prima volta, e le scarpe furono messe in serbo per quando ei fosse cresciuto, giacchè rimpiccolirsi le scarpe non si potevano, e il fidanzato della sorella non ne aveva volute di scarpe del morto.

Malpelo se li lisciava sulle gambe quei calzoni di fustagno quasi nuovo, gli pareva che fossero dolci e lisci come le mani del babbo che solevano accarezzargli i capelli, così ruvidi e rossi com'erano. Quelle scarpe le teneva appese a un chiodo, sul saccone, quasi fossero state le pantofole del papà, e la domenica se le pigliava in mano, le lustrava e se le provava; poi le metteva per terra. l'una accanto all'altra, e stava a contemplarsele coi gomiti sui ginocchi,

the job remarked with curiosity on how capricious the sand was—that it had knocked the Beast around this way and that, the shoes in this direction and the feet in the other.

After that shoe had been found, Malpelo was seized with such a fear that he might also see his father's bare foot appear in the sand, that he refused to strike even a single mattock-blow more there; he would rather receive a blow with the mattock on his own head. He went off to work at another place in the gallery, and would not return to that part any more. Two or three days later, in fact, they did discover the body of Mastro Misciu, with his trousers on, and flat on his face, seeming as if embalmed. Uncle Mommu remarked that he must have had a hard time dying, because the pillar had fallen curved over him like an arch, and had buried him alive. One could even still see that Mastro Bestia had tried instinctively to free himself, digging in the sand, and his hands were torn and his fingernails broken. "Just like his son Malpelo!" the cripple repeated, "he was digging down here, while his son was digging up there." But they said nothing to the boy, because they knew he was malicious and vindictive.

The carter rid the underground area of the body in the same way that he rid it of fallen sand and of dead donkeys; this time, in addition to the stench of the carcass, there was the fact that the carcass was of baptized flesh. The widow cut down the trousers and the shirt and fitted them to Malpelo, who in this way had nearly new clothes for the first time; the shoes were set aside for the time when he would be big enough for them, since the shoes could not be made any smaller, and his sister's fiancé would have nothing to do with the dead man's shoes.

Malpelo would smooth out on his legs those trousers of nearly new fustian; it seemed to him that they were gentle and smooth like his father's hands as they used to caress his hair, rough and red as it was. The shoes he used to keep hung up on a nail over his pallet, as if they had been his father's slippers, and on Sundays he would take them in his hand, shine them, and try them on. Then he would set them on the ground, side by side, and would contemplate

e il mento nelle palme per delle ore intere, rimugginando chi sa quali idee in quel cervellaccio.

Ei possedeva delle idee strane, *Malpelo!* Siccome aveva ereditato anche il piccone e la zappa del padre, se ne serviva, quantunque fossero troppo pesanti per l'età sua; e quando gli avevano chiesto se voleva venderli, che glieli avrebbero pagati come nuovi, egli aveva risposto di no; suo padre li ha resi così lisci e lucenti nel manico colle sue mani, ed ei non avrebbe potuto farsene degli altri più lisci e lucenti di quelli, se ci avesse lavorato cento e poi cento anni.

In quel tempo era crepato di stenti e di vecchiaia l'asino grigio; e il carrettiere era andato a buttarlo lontano nella sciara.—Così si fa,—brontolava *Malpelo*—gli arnesi che non servono più si buttano lontano.—Ei andava a visitare il carcame del *grigio* in fondo al burrone, e vi conduceva a forza anche *Ranocchio,* il quale non avrebbe voluto andarci; e *Malpelo* gli diceva che a questo mondo bisogna avvezzarsi a vedere in faccia ogni cosa bella o brutta; e stava a considerare con l'avida curiosità di un monellaccio i cani che accorrevano da tutte le fattorie dei dintorni a disputarsi le carni del *grigio*. I cani scappavano guaendo, come comparivano i ragazzi, e si aggiravano ustolando sui greppi di rimpetto, ma il Rosso non lasciava che *Ranocchio* li scacciasse a sassate.—Vedi quella cagna nera,—gli diceva—che non ha paura delle tue sassate; non ha paura perchè ha più fame degli altri. Gliele vedi quelle costole?—Adesso non soffriva più, l'asino grigio, e se ne stava tranquillo colle quattro zampe distese, e lasciava che i cani si divertissero a vuotargli le occhiaie profonde e a spolpargli le ossa bianche e i denti che gli laceravano le viscere non gli avrebbero fatto piegar la schiena come il più semplice colpo di badile che solevano dargli onde mettergli in corpo un po' di vigore quando saliva la ripida viuzza. Ecco come vanno le cose! Anche il grigio ha avuto dei colpi di zappa e delle guidalesche, e anch'esso quando piegava sotto il peso e gli mancava il fiato per andare innanzi, aveva di quelle occhiate, mentre lo battevano, che sembrava dicesse:

them with his elbows on his knees and his chin in his hands for hours on end, turning over Lord only knows what ideas in that crazy brain of his.

He certainly had crazy ideas, Malpelo did! Since he had inherited his father's pick-axe and mattock too, he used them, although they were too heavy for his age. When they asked him if he wanted to sell them, and offered to pay for them as if they were new, he had refused: his father's hands had made them so smooth and shiny on the handles, and he would not have been able to make any others smoother or shinier, if he had worked at it for a hundred and then another hundred years.

Around that time, the gray donkey had died of hard work and old age; and the carter had taken it and thrown it away a long way off in the *sciara*. "That's the way they do," muttered Malpelo, "the tools that aren't any good any more get thrown a long way off." He would go to look at the gray donkey's carcass in the bottom of the ravine, and would drag Ranocchio there too, although the latter would have preferred not to go there. Malpelo would tell him that in this world you have to get accustomed to looking everything straight in the face, be it fair or foul. He would spend his time observing, with the eager curiosity of a young rogue, the dogs that came up from all the farms of the neighborhood to fight over the flesh of the gray donkey. The dogs would run away howling on the appearance of the boys and would hover around whining on the rocky slopes opposite; but Malpelo would not let Ranocchio chase them away by throwing rocks at them. "See that black bitch," he would tell him, "which is not afraid of your rocks. She's not afraid because she's hungrier than the others. Do you see those ribs of hers?" The gray donkey wasn't suffering any more now, and remained quiet with his four legs stuck out and allowed the dogs to have a good time removing the contents of his deep eye-sockets and pulling the flesh off his white bones; and the teeth that were tearing at his vitals would not have made him bend his back like the lightest mattock-blow that they used to give him to infuse a little vigor into his body when he was

Non più! non più! Ma ora gli occhi se li mangiano i cani,
ed esso se ne ride dei colpi e delle guidalesche con quella
bocca spolpata e tutta denti. E se non fosse mai nato sarebbe
stato meglio.

La sciara si stendeva malinconica e deserta fin dove
giungeva la vista, e saliva e scendeva in picchi e burroni, nera
e rugosa, senza un grillo che vi trillasse, o un uccello che vi
volasse su. Non si udiva nulla, nemmeno i colpi di piccone
di coloro che lavoravano sotterra. E ogni volta *Malpelo*
ripeteva che al di sotto era tutta scavata dalle gallerie, per
ogni dove, verso il monte e verso la valle; tanto che una
volta un minatore c'era entrato coi capelli neri, e ne era
uscito coi capelli bianchi, e un altro cui s'era spenta la
torcia aveva invano gridato aiuto ma nessuno poteva
udirlo.—Egli solo ode le sue stesse grida!—diceva, e a
quell'idea, sebbene avesse il cuore più dura della sciara,
trasaliva.

— Il padrone mi manda spesso lontano, dove gli altri
hanno paura d'andare. Ma io sono *Malpelo,* e se io non
torno più, nessuno mi cercherà.—

Pure, durante le belle notti d'estate, le stelle splendevano
lucenti anche sulla sciara, e la campagna circostante era
nera anch'essa, come la sciara, ma *Malpelo* stanco dalla
lunga giornata di lavoro, si sdraiava sul sacco, col viso verso
il cielo, a godersi quella quiete e quella luminaria dell'alto;
perciò odiava le notti di luna, in cui il mare formicola di
scintille, e la campagna si disegna qua e là vagamente:
allora la sciara sembra più brulla e desolata.—Per noi che
siamo fatti per vivere sotterra,—pensava *Malpelo*—ci
dovrebbe essere buio sempre e dappertutto.—La civetta
strideva sulla sciara, e ramingava di qua e di là; ei pensava:—Anche la civetta sente i morti che son qua sotterra
e si dispera perchè non può andare a trovarli.—

going up the steep path. That's how things go! The gray donkey too got mattock-blows and sores, and he too, when he was bending under the weight and didn't have enough breath to keep going, used to cast glances like that, while they beat him, as if to say: "No more! No more!" But now the dogs are eating his eyes, and he laughs at blows and sores with that mouth stripped of flesh and showing all its teeth. And if he had never been born it would have been better.

The *sciara* stretched out, melancholy and deserted, as far as the eye could see, and went up and down in peaks and ravines, black and wrinkled, without a single cricket chirping or a single bird flying over it. Nothing was to be heard, not even the blows of the pick-axes of the men working below the ground. And every time Malpelo would repeat that it was all dug out in tunnels underneath, in every direction, upwards and downwards, to such an extent that once a miner had gone in with his hair black and had come out with it white, and another, whose torch had gone out, had called for help in vain, but no one had been able to hear him. "He is the only one to hear his own cries!", he would say, and at that idea, although his heart was harder than the *sciara,* he would shudder.

"The owner often sends me a long way off, where the others are afraid to go. But I am Malpelo, and if I never come back again, no one will go to look for me."

And yet, during the beautiful summer nights, the stars would shine resplendent on the *sciara* too, and the surrounding countryside was also black like the *sciara,* but Malpelo, tired by the long day's work, would stretch out on his pallet, with his face towards the sky, to enjoy that peace and that illumination from above. For that reason he hated the moonlit nights, when the sea teems with sparks and the countryside is outlined vaguely here and there; then the *sciara* seems more barren and desolate. "For us who are made to live underground," Malpelo would think, "it ought to be dark always and everywhere." The owl would screech over the *sciara,* and would flit here and there, and he would think: "The owl too hears the dead who are underground

Ranocchio aveva paura della civette e dei pipistrelli; ma il Rosso lo sgridava perchè chi è costretto a star solo non deve aver paura di nulla, e nemmeno l'asino grigio aveva paura dei cani che se lo spolpavano, ora che le sue carni non sentivano più il dolore di esser mangiate.

— Tu eri avvezzo a lavorar sui tetti come i gatti—gli diceva—e allora era tutt'altra cosa. Ma adesso che ti tocca a viver sotterra, come i topi, non bisogna più aver paura dei topi, nè pipistrelli, che son topi vecchi con le ali, e i topi ci stanno volentieri in compagnia dei morti.—

Ranocchio invece provava una tale compiacenza a spiegargli quel che ci stessero a far le stelle lassù in alto; e gli raccontava che lassù c'era il paradiso, dove vanno a stare i morti che sono stati buoni e non hanno dato dispiaceri ai loro genitori. "Chi te l'ha detto?" domandava *Malpelo*, e *Ranocchio* rispondeva che glielo aveva detto la mamma.

Allora *Malpelo* si grattava il capo, e sorridendo gli faceva un certo verso da monellaccio malizioso che la sa lunga.— Tua madre ti dice così perchè invece dei calzoni, tu dovresti portar la gonnella.—

E dopo averci pensato su un po':

"Mio padre era buono e non faceva male a nessuno, tanto che gli dicevano Bestia. Invece è là sotto, ed hanno persino trovato i ferri e le scarpe e questi calzoni qui che ho indosso io."

Da lì a poco, *Ranocchio* il quale deperiva da qualche tempo, si ammalò in modo che la sera dovevano portarlo fuori dalla cava sull'asino, disteso fra le corbe, tremante di febbre come un pulcino bagnato. Un operaio disse che quel ragazzo *non ne avrebbe fatto osso duro* [25] a quel mestiere, e che per lavorare in una miniera senza lasciarvi la pelle bisognava nascervi. *Malpelo* allora si sentiva orgoglioso di esserci nato e di mantenersi così sano e vigoroso in quell'aria malsana, e con tutti quegli stenti. Ei si caricava *Ranocchio* sulle spalle, e gli faceva animo alla sua maniera, sgridandolo e picchiandolo. Ma una volta nel picchiarlo

here, and is desperate because she cannot go find them."

Ranocchio was afraid of owls and bats; but Malpelo would scold him because anyone who is forced to be alone should not be afraid of anything, and not even the gray donkey was afraid of the dogs that were stripping the meat off him, now that his flesh no longer felt the pain of being eaten.

"You were accustomed to working on the roofs, like a cat," he would tell him, "and then it was a different matter. But now that you have to live underground, like the rats, you must no longer be afraid of the rats, nor of bats, which are old rats with wings; and rats like to be in the company of the dead."

Ranocchio, instead, took such pleasure in telling him what the stars were doing up there; and he used to tell him that up there was paradise, where the dead go who have been good and have not caused their parents trouble. "Who told you so?" Malpelo would ask, and Ranocchio would answer that his mother had told him so.

Then Malpelo would scratch his head, and, smiling, would talk to him in a certain way like a sly urchin who knows all the answers: "Your mother tells you that because, instead of pants, you ought to wear a skirt."

And, after thinking it over for a little:

"My father was good and harmed no one, so much so that they called him Beast. Instead, he's down there, and they even found his tools and shoes and these pants that I have on."

Shortly afterwards, Ranocchio, whose health had been getting worse for some time, got so sick that in the evening they had to carry him out of the mine on a donkey, stretched out amidst the baskets, trembling with fever like a wet chicken. A workman said that that boy was not strong enough for the job, and that to work in a mine without leaving one's skin there, one had to be born to it. Malpelo then felt proud that he had been born to it and that he kept so healthy and strong in that unhealthy air and with all that toil. He would load Ranocchio onto his shoulders and would encourage him after his fashion, scolding him

sul dorso *Ranocchio* fu colto da uno sbocco di sangue, allora *Malpelo* spaventato si affannò a cercargli nel naso e dentro la bocca cosa gli avesse fatto, e giurava che non avea potuto fargli quel gran male, così come l'aveva battuto, e a dimostrarglielo, si dava dei gran pugni sul petto e sulla schiena con un sasso; anzi un operaio, lì presente, gli sferrò un gran calcio sulle spalle, un calcio che risuonò come su di un tamburo, eppure *Malpelo* non si mosse, e soltanto dopo che l'operaio se ne fu andato, aggiunse:—Lo vedi? Non mi ha fatto nulla! E ha picchiato più forte di me, ti giuro!—

Intanto *Ranocchio* non guariva e seguitava a sputar sangue, e ad aver la febbre tutti i giorni. Allora *Malpelo* rubò dei soldi della paga della settimana, per comperargli del vino e della minestra calda, e gli diede i suoi calzoni quasi nuovi che lo coprivano meglio. Ma *Ranocchio* tossiva sempre e alcune volte sembrava soffocasse, e la sera non c'era modo di vincere il ribrezzo della febbre, nè con sacchi, nè coprendolo di paglia, nè mettendolo dinanzi alla fiammata. *Malpelo* se ne stava zitto ed immobile chino su di lui, colle mani sui ginocchi, fissandolo con quei suoi occhiacci spalancati come se volesse fargli il ritratto, e allorchè lo udiva gemere sottovoce, e gli vedeva il viso trafelato e l'occhio spento, preciso come quello dell'asino grigio allorchè ansava rifinito sotto il carico nel salire la viottola, ei gli borbottava:—È meglio che tu crepi presto! Se devi soffrire in tal modo, è meglio che tu crepi!—E il padrone diceva che *Malpelo* era capace di schiacciargli il capo a quel ragazzo, e bisognava sorvegliarlo.

Finalmente un lunedì *Ranocchio* non venne più alla cava, e il padrone se ne lavò le mani, perchè allo stato in cui era ridotto oramai era più di impiccio che d'altro. *Malpelo* si informò dove stesse di casa, e il sabato andò a trovarlo. Il povero *Ranocchio* era più di là che di qua,[26] e sua madre piangeva e si disperava come se il suo figliolo fosse di quelli che guadagnano dieci lire la settimana.

and hitting him. But once, when he hit him on the back, Ranocchio was seized with blood-spitting. Then Malpelo, frightened, searched anxiously in his nose and throat to see what he had done to him, and swore that he could not have hurt him that badly, the way he had hit him, and, to prove it, gave himself tremendous blows on the chest and the back with a rock. In fact, a workman who was nearby launched a tremendous kick at his shoulders, a kick which resounded like a drum, and yet Malpelo did not move. Only after the workman had gone away, he added: "You see? It did not hurt me at all! And he hit harder than I did, I swear!"

Meanwhile Ranocchio got no better and kept on spitting blood, and running a fever every day. Then Malpelo stole money from his week's pay to buy him wine and hot soup, and gave him his nearly new trousers which covered him better. But Ranocchio kept on coughing, and sometimes it seemed as if he were stifling; in the evenings there was no way to overcome the shivers of fever, either with sacks or by covering him with straw or by putting him in front of the fire. Malpelo remained quiet and motionless bending over him, with his hands on his knees, staring at him with those mean eyes of his opened wide as if he wanted to paint a picture of him. When he heard him groan under his breath, and saw his face worn out and the light of his eyes extinguished, precisely as had happened with the gray donkey when it panted, exhausted, under the load when climbing up the path, he would mutter to him: "It's better for you to croak quickly! If you have to suffer in that way, it's better for you to croak!" And the owner said that Malpelo was capable of crushing the boy's head, and that they ought to keep watch over him.

Finally, one Monday, Ranocchio did not come to the mine any more, and the owner washed his hands of the matter, because in the condition to which he was reduced, he was more in the way than anything else. Malpelo found out where he lived, and on Saturday went to see him. Poor Ranocchio was more in the next world than in this, and his mother was weeping and in despair as if her son were one of

Cotesto non arrivava a comprendere *Malpelo*, e domandò a *Ranocchio* perchè sua madre strillasse a quel modo, mentre che da due mesi ei non guadagnava nemmeno quel che si mangiava. Ma il povero *Ranocchio* non gli dava retta e sembrava che badasse a contare quanti travicelli c'erano sul tetto. Allora il Rosso si diede ad almanaccare che la madre di *Ranocchio* strillasse a quel modo perchè il suo figliuolo era sempre stato debole e malaticcio, e l'aveva tenuto come quei marmocchi che non si slattano mai. Egli invece era stato sano e robusto, ed era *Malpelo*, e sua madre non aveva mai pianto per lui perchè non aveva mai avuto timore di perderlo.

Poco dopo, alla cava dissero che *Ranocchio* era morto, ed ei pensò che la civetta adesso strideva anche per lui nella notte, e tornò a visitare le ossa spolpate del *grigio*, nel burrone dove solevano andare insieme con *Ranocchio*. Ora del *grigio* non rimanevano più che le ossa sgangherate, ed anche di *Ranocchio* sarebbe stato così, e sua madre si sarebbe asciugati gli occhi, poichè anche la madre di *Malpelo* s'era asciugati i suoi dopo che mastro Misciu era morto, e adesso si era maritata un'altra volta, ed era andata a stare a Cifali; [27] anche la sorella si era maritata e avevano chiusa la casa. D'ora in poi, se lo battevano, a loro non importava più nulla, e a lui nemmeno, e quando sarebbe divenuto come il *grigio* o come *Ranocchio* non avrebbe sentito più nulla.

Verso quell'epoca venne a lavorare nella cava uno che non s'era mai visto, e si teneva nascosto il più che poteva; gli altri operai dicevano fra di loro che era scappato dalla prigione, e se lo pigliavano ce lo tornavano a chiudere per degli anni e degli anni. *Malpelo* seppe in quell'occasione che la prigione era un luogo dove si mettevano i ladri, e i malarnesi come lui, e si tenevano sempre chiusi la dentro e guardati a vista.

Da quel momento provò una malsana curiosità per quell'uomo che aveva provata la prigione e n' era scappato.

those who earn ten lire a week.

Malpelo could not manage to understand this, and asked Ranocchio why his mother was shrieking in that way, when for two months he hadn't even earned his keep. But poor Ranocchio paid no attention and seemed to be engaged in counting the number of beams there were on the roof. Then Malpelo started to puzzle it out, and concluded that Ranocchio's mother must be yelling that way because her son had always been weak and sickly and had kept him like those brats that never get weaned. He, on the contrary, had been healthy and strong, and was Malpelo, and his mother had never wept for him because she had never been afraid she would lose him.

Not long afterwards, at the mine, they said that Ranocchio was dead, and Malpelo thought that the owl was screeching for him too at night, and he went back again to see the fleshless bones of the gray donkey in the ravine where he had been accustomed to go with Ranocchio. Now there was nothing left of the gray donkey except his scattered bones, and it would happen the same way with Ranocchio; and his mother would dry her eyes, since Malpelo's mother, too, had dried her eyes after Mastro Misciu had died, and now had gotten re-married and had gone to live at Cifali; his sister, also, had married and they had shut up the house. From now on, if they beat him, they didn't care any more, and neither did he; and when he became like the gray donkey and Ranocchio he wouldn't feel anything any more.

About that time there came to work at the mine a man who had never been seen before, and who kept hidden as much as he could. The other workmen said among themselves that he had escaped from jail, and that if they caught him they would shut him up there again for years and years. Malpelo found out on that occasion that jail was a place where they put thieves and rascals like himself, and where they kept them always shut up inside and under watch.

From that moment on, he felt an unhealthy curiosity about that man who had experienced prison and had

Dopo poche settimane però il fuggitivo dichiarò chiaro e tondo che era stanco di quella vitaccia da talpa e piuttosto si contentava di stare in galera tutta la vita, chè la prigione, in confronto, era un paradiso e preferiva tornarci coi suoi piedi.—Allora perchè tutti quelli che lavorano nella cava non si fanno mettere in prigione?—domandò *Malpelo*.

— Perchè non sono *Malpelo* come te!—rispose lo sciancato.—Ma non temere, che tu ci andrai e ci lascerai le ossa.—

Invece le ossa le lasciò nella cava, *Malpelo*, come suo padre, ma in modo diverso. Una volta si doveva esplorare un passaggio che si riteneva comunicasse col pozzo grande a sinistra, verso la valle, e se la cosa era vera, si sarebbe risparmiata una buona metà di mano d'opera nel cavar fuori la rena. Ma se non era vero, c'era il pericolo di smarrirsi e di non tornare mai più. Sicchè nessun padre di famiglia voleva avventurarvisi, nè avrebbe permesso che ci si arrischiasse il sangue suo per tutto l'oro del mondo.

Ma *Malpelo* non aveva nemmeno chi si prendesse tutto l'oro del mondo per la sua pelle, se pure la sua pelle valeva tutto l'oro del mondo; sua madre si era rimaritata e se n' era andata a stare a Cifali, e sua sorella s'era maritata anch'essa. La porta della casa era chiusa, ed ei non aveva altro che le scarpe di suo padre appese al chiodo; perciò gli commettevano sempre i lavori più pericolosi, e le imprese più arrischiate, e s'ei non si aveva riguardo alcuno, gli altri non ne avevano certamente per lui. Quando lo mandarono per quella esplorazione si risovvenne del minatore, il quale si era smarrito, da anni ed anni, e cammina e cammina ancora al buio gridando aiuto, senza che nessuno possa udirlo; ma non disse nulla. Del resto a che sarebbe giovato? Prese gli arnesi di suo padre, il piccone, la zappa, la lanterna, il sacco col pane, e il fiasco del vino, e se ne andò; nè più si seppe nulla di lui.

Così si persero persin le ossa di *Malpelo*, e i ragazzi della cava abbassano la voce quando parlano di lui nel sotterraneo, chè hanno paura di vederselo comparire dinanzi, coi capelli rossi e gli occhiacci grigi.

escaped. After a few weeks, however, the fugitive declared flat out that he was tired of that horrible mole's life and that he would prefer to stay in prison all his life; that jail, in comparison, was a paradise, and he preferred to go back there on his own feet. "Then why doesn't everybody that works in the mine get himself put in jail?" Malpelo asked.

"Because they're not Malpelo like you!" answered the cripple. "But never fear, you'll go there and leave your bones there."

On the contrary, however, Malpelo left his bones in the mine like his father, but in a different way. Once they had to explore a passageway which was thought to connect with the large shaft to the left, downward; and if it did, they would save fully half their work in getting out the sand. But if it did not, there was the danger of getting lost and never coming back, so that no father of a family was willing to risk it, nor would he have permitted any of his blood to risk it for all the gold in the world.

But Malpelo did not even have anyone to take all the gold in the world for his skin, even if his skin had been worth all the gold in the world: his mother had re-married and had gone to live at Cifali, and his sister too had gotten married. The door of the house was closed, and he had nothing but his father's shoes hanging on the nail. For this reason, they always entrusted to him the most dangerous jobs, and the most risky undertakings; for if he had no care for himself, certainly the others had none for him. When they sent him out on that exploring job, he remembered the miner who had been lost for years and years and was still walking and walking in the dark calling for help without anyone being able to hear him; but he said nothing. For that matter, what good would it have done? He took his father's tools, the pick, the mattock, the lantern, the sack with bread, and the bottle of wine, and went off; and nothing further was ever heard from him.

In this way even Malpelo's bones were lost, and the boys of the mine lower their voices when they talk about him underground, for fear that he may appear before them, with his red hair and his mean gray eyes.

Antonio Fogazzaro

(1842-1911)

THE POET and novelist Antonio Fogazzaro was born in Vicenza in 1842. He lived most of his life in northern Italy—Venetia, Lombardy, Piedmont—and died in his native city in 1911. He began his literary career as a poet, with lyric verse and with a romantic verse novel, *Miranda* (1874); then he passed to prose writing, in a series of stories which established him as the leading Italian novelist of the latter half of the century. He began with a somewhat "Gothic" romance, *Malombra* (1882), followed by a more realistic treatment of the conflict between love and ethics in *Daniele Cortis* (1885). The collection *Fedele,* to which the short story *Un' idea di Ermes Torranza* belongs, dates from this period (1882). Fogazzaro's best work in the novel was done in a series of related stories: *Piccolo mondo antico* ("Little World of Yesteryear," 1896), a story of the Italian Risorgimento; *Piccolo mondo moderno* ("Little World of Nowadays," 1901); *Il Santo* ("The Saint," 1905); and *Leila* (1911). In the three latter, Fogazzaro dealt with problems of the reform of the contemporary Roman Catholic church, in the spirit of the "Modernist" movement, which was at the time much debated and eventually condemned.

In his subject-matter, Fogazzaro was essentially a Late Romantic, with the intensity of feeling and the concern with emotional problems that characterize the Romantics. He

was also profoundly interested in religion and ethics, as they affected human character. He had a strong affinity for music as well as poetry, and, unlike most Italians of his time, had an extensive acquaintance with foreign, especially German, literature and music. At the same time, Fogazzaro was a keen observer of minute detail, with a sharp sense of humor, so that his concern with lofty spiritual matters is paralleled by a remarkable ability to portray lively (and at times strongly satirical) genre scenes.

Fogazzaro's technique of narration is close to that of Scott, whom he greatly admired: extensive background description and detailed analysis of his characters' perceptions and feelings, set forth in an intensely sensitive prose rich in emotional overtones, alternating with realistic dialogue. Almost alone among his contemporaries, Fogazzaro used the local dialect, as Scott had done with "braid Scots," as an element of realism, humor, and (on occasion) emotional intensification.

All of Fogazzaro's novels and many of his short stories are rich in cultural symbolism. His last four novels present, symbolically, the problems facing the devout but forward-looking Christian in adapting him- or herself to the conditions then prevailing in Italy. His short story *An Idea of Hermes Torranza* can be interpreted as representing Fogazzaro's hope that, perhaps, his work might eventually be instrumental in reconciling opposed factions in Italy much as the "old fogey" Torranza brings the estranged couple Bianca and Emilio together after his death.

UN' IDEA DI ERMES TORRANZA

di Antonio Fogazzaro

I

IL PROFESSOR Farsatti di Padova, lo stesso ch'ebbe con M.r Nisard la famosa po¹emica sui *fabulaeque Manes* ¹ di Orazio,² soleva dire di Monte San Donà: "Cossa vorlà? Poesia franzese!" ³ Il solitario palazzo, il vecchio giardino dei San Donà gli erano poco meno antipatici di "monsiù Nisarde" sin dall'autunno del 1846, quando vi era stato invitato dai nobili padroni a mangiare i tordi, e fra questi gli si erano imbanditi degli stornelli. Dal viale d'entrata, con i suoi ippocastani tagliati a dado al laberinto, ai giuochi d'acqua,⁴ alla lunga scalinata che sale il colle; dalla base all'attico pesante del palazzo, l'eccellente professore trovava tutto pretenzioso e meschino, artificioso e prosaico. "Cossa vorlà? Poesia franzese!"

Al tempo degli stornelli, forse, sarà stato così. Il professore non ha più voluto rivedere Monte San Donà e dorme profondamente da parecchi anni nel suo campo di battaglia, come posson ben dirsi:

> . . . Nox fabulaeque Manes
> Et domus exilis Plutonia.

Adesso la famiglia San Donà, che ha vissuto con un certo fasto sino al 1848, pratica rigidamente, sotto l'impero del nobile sior ⁵ Beneto, la economia di cui qualche indizio apparve sino dal 1846. Per il sior Beneto non esiste poesia

AN IDEA OF HERMES TORRANZA

by Antonio Fogazzaro

I

Professor Farsatti of Padua, the same man who had the famous polemic with M. Nisard over the *fabulaeque Manes* of Horace, used to say of Mount San Donà: "What do you expect? French poetry!" The lonely palace and the old garden of the San Donà family had been almost as repulsive to him as "mounseer Nisarde" ever since the autumn of 1846, when he had been invited there by its noble owners to dine on thrushes, and among these latter some starlings had been included. From the avenue at the entrance, with its horse-chestnuts trimmed in the shape of cubes, to the labyrinth, to the fountains, to the long flight of steps going up the hillside; from the foundations to the heavy mansard of the palace, the good professor found everything pretentious and shabby, artificial and prosaic. "What do you expect? French poetry!"

In the days of the thrushes, perhaps, it may have been so. The professor was never willing to return to San Donà, and for many years he has been sleeping profoundly on his battlefield, as may well be said of:

> . . . Night and the storied spirits of the ancestors
> And the narrow house of Pluto.

Now the San Donà family, which up to 1848 lived with a certain amount of ostentation, is rigidly practicing, under the rule of the noble Sior Beneto, that economy of which some signs appeared as early as 1846. For Sior Beneto,

francese né italiana; e, sulla collina, il giardino, lasciato pressoché interamente in balìa delle proprie passioni, ha sciupato le fredde eleganze, ha preso, fra i vigneti blandi degli altri colli, un aspetto selvaggio, vigoroso, che gli sta molto bene in quel seno solitario degli Euganei.[6] Al piano il laberinto fu messo a prato; i tubi dei giuochi d'acqua son tutti guasti; agl'ippocastani il sior Beneto ha sostituito due filari di gelsi. Voleva abbattere con lo stesso scopo scientifico i pioppi secolari del viale pomposo che da Monte San Donà mette ad un'umile stradicciuola comunale; ma la signorina Bianca li difese con passione e lagrime contro l'acuto argomento di papà: "bezzi, bezzi".[7] Quando, nell' aprile del 1875, Bianca sposò il signor Emilio Squarcina di Padova, chiese ed ebbe in dono dal padre la promessa di lasciar in pace i cari pioppi che l'avean tante volte veduta correre e saltare, prima del collegio, con le sue rustiche amiche, e più tardi leggere *Rob Roy, Waverley* e *Ivanhoe,* tre poveri vecchi libri della sottile biblioteca di casa, tre poveri vecchi libri immortali che ora aspettano sul loro scaffale altre cupide mani, altri ardenti cuori inesperti della nostra grande arte moderna.

Ermes Torranza, il poeta, le diceva che ella stessa, a quindici anni, pareva un piccolo pioppo ridente a ogni soffio di vento, e che certo le colossali piante la ricambiavano di tenerezza paterna. Torranza lo diceva sul serio; egli aveva nel sangue questo fantastico sentimento della natura, questi istinti che i nostri freddi critici corretti gli rimproveravano, forse a torto. Infatti, nel settembre del 79 Bianca tornò a Monte San Donà, sola col cuore amaro; e le parve, passando fra i pioppi, che Torranza avesse ragione, che le piante pigliassero con lei la espressione di quel biasimo affettuoso che vien significato con la tristezza e il silenzio. Il piccolo sior Beneto non tenne questo metodo. Lo aveva sempre detto, quel padre sapiente e profetico, che la sarebbe andata a finire così, che troppi libri e troppa musica non conducono a niente di buono, che a forza di volersi raffinare ci si

poetry does not exist, either French or Italian; and, on the hill, the garden, left almost entirely to its uncontrolled desires, has ruined the effect of cold elegance and has taken on, amongst the gentle vineyards of the other hills, a wild and vigorous appearance, which suits it well in that lonely corner of the Euganean Hills. On the plain, the labyrinth has turned into a meadow; the pipes of the fountains are all broken; in place of the horse-chestnuts, Sior Beneto has put two rows of mulberry-trees. He wanted to cut down, for the same scientific purpose, the century-old poplars of the grandiose avenue which leads from Mount San Donà to a humble county road; but Miss Bianca defended them passionately and tearfully against her father's penetrating argument: "money, money!" When, in April of 1875, Bianca married Signor Emilio Squarcina of Padua, she asked and received as a gift from her father the promise that he would not disturb the beloved poplars which had so often seen her run and jump with her country friends before she went off to boarding-school, and had later seen her read *Rob Roy, Waverley* and *Ivanhoe,* three poor old books from the scanty library of her home, three poor old immortal books which are now waiting on their shelf for other eager hands, other ardent hearts unacquainted with our great modern art.

Hermes Torranza, the poet, used to tell her that she herself, at fifteen, seemed like a little poplar smiling at every breath of wind, and that certainly the colossal trees must return her love with fatherly tenderness. Torranza said that in earnest; he had in his blood that imaginative feeling for nature, those instincts which our cold, correct critics condemned in him, perhaps wrongly. In fact, in September of '79 Bianca came back to Mount San Donà, alone and bitter in heart; and she felt, as she passed between the poplars, that Torranza was right, that the trees were assuming towards her that attitude of loving reproof that is expressed by sadness and silence. Little Sior Beneto did not use this technique. He had always said, this wise and prophetic father, that it would end like this, that too many books and too much music would lead to no good end, and that

scavezza. Credeva, la signorina, di esser nata per sposare un principe, un Creso, un chi sa cosa diavolo mai? Eran questi gli esempi avuti dalla santa donna di sua madre? La mansueta signora Giovanna San Donà, una santa per forza, non partecipò alle collere del suo temuto signore, anzi godè segretamente che la ragazza non si fosse lasciata metter i piedi sul collo e santificare come lei. Bianca aveva riamato abbastanza sul serio il bel giovinotto biondo fattosi avanti, dopo un lungo sospirare, per la sua mano; ma i suoceri grossolani, avari, stizzosi, le eran riusciti intollerabili. Il marito, buono ma debole, non osava proteggerla a dovere; indi sdegni e lagrime. Non c'erano figli; e così Bianca aveva potuto, in un impeto di collera, tornarsene al suo solitario angolo degli Euganei, ai suoi pioppi venerabili.

Aveva creduto, sì, a prima giunta, esserne guardata severamente; ma poi raccontò loro tante e tante cose che ogni freddezza fra le vecchie piante e lei ne fu tolta. Due mesi dopo il suo ritorno, quand'ella vide, un lucido giorno di novembre, che le ultime brine e il gran vento del dì innanzi le aveva spogliate di foglie sin quasi alla vetta, quei tremoli pennacchi giallo-rossicci le misero una malinconia da non dire; sentì che i pioppi la salutavano da lontano come amici fedeli, prossimi a venir meno, a perder la parola ed i sensi.

Tutto veniva meno con essi nella gran pace, nella luce limpida del pomeriggio di novembre; tutto, tranne il bruno dorato dei cipressi che dai vigneti deserti presso a Monte San Donà si rizzavano qua e là sul cielo biancastro d'oriente. La giovane signora avea lungamente passeggiato i vigneti, e ora, al cader del sole, scendeva piano piano la costa che ne beve con i suoi cavi sassi e con le quercie inclinate l'ultimo tepore. Ella guardava, distratta, più le foglie dense sul sentiero, più l'erbe grigie e gialliccie del pendìo che il piano e i colli dorati, e il tenero cielo caldo del ponente.

he who tries to be too refined simply breaks his neck. Did the young lady think she was born to marry a prince, a Croesus, or Lord only knows who? Was this the kind of example set her by that saintly woman, her mother? The meek Signora Giovanna San Donà, a saint by compulsion, did not share her dread lord's anger. On the contrary, she was secretly glad that the girl had not bent her neck under the yoke and had not let herself be made a saint as she had. Bianca had quite earnestly returned the love of the handsome blond young man who, after a long period of silent adoration, had come forward to ask her hand; but her parents-in-law—coarse, miserly, irritable—had proven intolerable to her. The husband, a kindly but weak man, had not dared to protect her as he ought; from this, anger and tears had resulted. There were no children; and thus, Bianca had been able, in an outburst of anger, to return to her lonely corner of the Euganean Hills and to her venerable old poplars.

She had indeed believed, at first, that they looked sternly at her; but then she told them so many things that all coolness between her and the old trees disappeared. Two months after her return, when she saw, on a bright November day, that the last frosts and the strong wind of the previous day had robbed them of their leaves almost to their summits, those quivering reddish-yellow tree-tops caused her an inexpressible melancholy. She felt that the poplars were saying farewell to her from afar off like faithful friends who were about to pass away, to lose their power of speech and feeling.

Everything was fading together with them in the great stillness, in the pure light of the November afternoon; everything, except for the golden brown of the cypresses which, from the deserted vineyards near Mount San Donà, stood out here and there against the whitish eastern sky. The young lady had walked for a long time among the vineyards, and now, as the sun was setting, she was slowly descending the hillside, which was drinking in the last warmth of the sun with its hollow rocks and its bent oaks. She was absent-mindedly looking more at the thick carpet

UN' IDEA DI ERMES TORRANZA

Perché mai aveva pensato, la sera precedente, appena spento il lume, a Ermes Torranza? Perché ne aveva sognato tutta la notte? Perché non poteva ancora liberarsi da questa immagine? Eran pur quasi tre mesi che non vedeva il poeta, di cui nessuno a Monte San Donà le parlava mai; ed egli le avea scritto una volta sola in principio d'ottobre per inviarle una romanza da camera. Bianca credeva ai presentimenti, non dubitava che avrebbe presto riveduto l'amico suo; ma pure, come spiegare una impressione così forte? Ella ammirava l'ingegno di Ermes Torranza, gli voleva un gran bene per la squisita nobiltà dell'animo, per la conoscenza che ne aveva sin da bambina; ma il poeta era sui sessant'anni, e benché le portasse un'amicizia più appassionata che paterna, e la sapesse esprimere molto bene in prosa e in versi, con la musica e i fiori, non poteva turbare il cuore della giovine signora; la quale correva con esso il solo pericolo di offenderlo quando bisognava posare una delicata parola fredda sulle sue effervescenze troppo giovanili. Avea ben pensato a lui tante volte con affetto, povero Torranza; non era mai stata assediata come ora dalla sua immagine. Proprio nello spegnere il lume le era venuto in cuore il nome strano *Ermes;* e subito avea veduto l'uomo, la barba bianca, l'abito nero, la gardenia all'occhiello. Si fermò involontariamente per una foglia che cadeva in lenti giri, davanti a lei; e ripensò come lo aveva riveduto in sogno, i versi dolcissimi che le aveva letti, la divina musica che aveva suonato stendendo la mano sul piano senza toccarlo. Venendole meno la vivezza del ricordare, a poco a poco le voci lontane per la pianura, un frequente zittir d'insetti nell'erba la richiamavano al vero. Si ripose in cammino sotto le quercie piene di sole, guardando trasparir dal fogliame secco gli antichi tronchi verdi d'edera che le parlavano, anch'essi! della strofa in cui il Torranza parla a certa gente del proprio ideale:

of leaves on the path, more at the gray and yellow grasses on the slope, than at the plain and the golden hills and the soft, warm sky in the west. Why had she thought of Hermes Torranza on the previous evening, as soon as she had put out the light? Why had she dreamed about him all night? Why could she still not free herself from the vision of him? And yet it was almost three months since she had seen the poet, of whom no one at Mount San Donà ever spoke to her; and he had written her only once, in October, to send her a drawing-room ballad. Bianca believed in presentiments, and did not doubt that she would see her friend again soon; nevertheless, how could one explain such a strong impression? She admired the genius of Hermes Torranza and loved him deeply for the exquisite nobility of his spirit, and for the knowledge that she had had of him since her girlhood. However, the poet was about sixty, and, although he felt for her a friendship more passionate than paternal, and was able to express it very well in prose and verse, with music and flowers, he could not disturb the heart of the young lady. The only danger she ran was that of offending him when she had to dampen, with a delicately cold word, the excessively youthful expressions of his enthusiasm. She had indeed thought of him affectionately many times, poor Torranza; but she had never been assailed as she was now by the vision of him. Just as she had put out the light, the strange name *Hermes* had come to her heart; and immediately she had seen the man, with his white beard, his black suit, and the gardenia in his buttonhole. She stopped involuntarily to look at a leaf circling down slowly in front of her; and thought again of how she had seen him in her dreams, of the intensely sweet verses which he had read to her, and of the divine music which he had played, putting forth his hand over the piano without touching it. As the vividness of her recollections faded away, gradually the distant voices from across the plain and the insistent chirping of insects in the grass brought her back to reality. She started walking again under the sunflooded oaks, noticing how, through the dry foliage, there appeared the old tree-trunks, green with ivy, which re-

Se voi seguite, aride foglie, il vento,
Tutte vi sdegna il mio fedele cor;
Di ruine, com'edera, è contento,
Sul nobil tronco ch'egli ha amato, muor.

Glieli racconterebbe, a Torranza, questi fatti bizzarri. Lui
già metterebbe in campo il suo spiritismo, la occulta influenza di una psiche sopra un'altra. Quest'idea le toccò il
cuore come la sensazione di un mondo strano, forse non
reale ma possibile; e, se reale, anche presente, anche circonfuso a lei; non solamente circonfuso, ma nascosto nel suo
petto, inconscio nei misteri dell'anima.

Una campanellina flebile suonò le ore da lontano, in
mezzo ai campi; una, due, tre e mezzo. Non era più da
credere che Torranza venisse in quel giorno.

Bianca trasalì. Le pareva udire una carrozza sulla strada
di Padova; ma ne passavano tante! Tutti volevano godere
quelle deliziose giornate di novembre. Sì, sì, i cani della
fattoria abbaiavano, le ruote stridevano sulla grossa ghiaia
del viale d'entrata. Bianca affrettò il passo. Per tornare alla
villa doveva scendere, poi risalire.

Presso a casa trovò un ragazzo che veniva in cerca di lei.
Erano arrivati tanti signori in due carrozze e la padrona
gli aveva detto di correre a cercare la padroncina. Non
sapeva il nome di questi signori, né se ci fosse tra loro un
vecchio vestito di nero, con la barba bianca. Gli pareva di
sì, ma non n'era sicuro.

Bianca entrò tutta trafelata nella sala a pian terreno
dove tutti erano ancora in piedi e Beneto distribuiva,
qui i suoi ossequi, lì le sue riverenze, a destra i suoi rispetti,
a sinistra la sua servitù, qualche complementino sotto
voce, qualche risatina cerimoniosa. Bianca si fermò sulla
soglia, raccolse tutta quella gente in un'occhiata: il
poeta non c'era. Erano i Dalla Carretta con i loro ospiti,
un piccolo museo archeologico di lunghi scialli scuri, di

minded her, in their turn, of the stanza in which Torranza speaks to certain people concerning his ideal:

> If you follow, o dry leaves, the wind,
> My faithful heart despises you all;
> It, like ivy, is content with ruins,
> And on the noble trunk which it has loved, it dies.

She would tell Torranza about these strange happenings. He would of course expound his spiritualism, the occult influence of one psyche on another. This idea affected her heart like the sensation of a strange world, perhaps not real but posible; and, if it were real, also present, also surrounding her; not merely surrounding, but hidden in her bosom, unconscious in the mysteries of the soul.

A mournful bell rang the hour from afar off, in the midst of the fields: one, two, three and the half-hour. It was no longer to be expected that Torranza would come that day.

Bianca gave a start. She thought she heard a carriage on the road from Padua; but there were so many of them passing! Everybody wanted to enjoy those delightful November days. Yes, yes, the farm dogs were barking, the wheels were creaking on the coarse gravel of the avenue at the entrance. Bianca hastened her step. To return to the villa she had to descend and then climb again.

Near home she found a boy who was coming to look for her. A lot of ladies and gentlemen had arrived in two carriages, and the lady of the house had told him to run and look for his mistress. He didn't know the people's names, nor whether there was among them an old man dressed in black, with a white beard. He thought there was, but he wasn't sure.

Bianca, all out of breath, entered the ground-floor room where everyone was still standing and where Beneto was distributing, here his regards, there his homage, on the right his respects, on the left his humble service, here a little whispered compliment, there a little ceremonious laugh. Bianca stopped on the threshold and took in the entire group in a single glance: the poet was not there. It was the Dalla Carretta family with their guests, a little archaeological

cappellini barocchi, di calze e nappe canonicali, di facce slavate; gente noiosa che veniva lì una volta l'anno, per convenienza, a sedersi in giro e a guardarsi un tratto in viso senza saper che dire; dopo di che un vecchio servitore in giacchetta bigia entrava molto dignitosamente portando il caffé e i *pandoli* [8] che il cavalleresco Beneto serviva con i suoi scherzetti sempre uguali, di cui la compagnia rideva regolarmente ogni anno sullo stesso tono e sulla stessa misura. Perdere un bel tramonto di novembre per costoro! Bianca non li poteva soffrire, le toglievano il respiro.

— Non so—le disse fra un sorso di caffè e l'altro il canonico Businello—non so se La [9] sappia la brutta notizia . . .

— No. Che notizia? . . . —rispose Bianca a fior di labbro.[10]

— Ah, sicuro—dissero due o tre voci sommesse.—Ah, sicuro.

— Il povero Torranza, poveretto . . . —soggiunse compunto il canonico, intingendo nel caffè l'ultimo pezzetto della sua ciambella.

Bianca si sentì una stretta al cuore, un formicolìo freddo al viso; e non potè articolare parole.

— Pur troppo—disse monsignore agitando la tazza in giro per sciogliere lo zucchero rimasto al fondo.—Mancato, sì, poi . . . —Vuotò la tazza e soggiunse sospirando:—Iersera, alle undici e mezzo.

Bianca perdette un momento la vista, ma oppose alla emozione un voler violento, un impeto, quasi, di collera, e vinse. La signora Giovanna la vide farsi pallida pallida e fu per alzarsi sgomentata; una rapida occhiata dura di sua figlia la fermò sull'atto. Le signore Dalla Carretta, che conoscevano certi maligni epigrammi corsi a Padova sulle fiamme senili di Torranza, si guardarono alla sfuggita e tacquero.

Intanto il canonico raccontava che Torranza s'era posto a letto due o tre giorni prima senza sofferenze gravi, però con tristissimi presentimenti. La catastrofe doveva esser

museum of long black shawls, of over-ornamented bonnets, of ecclesiastical stockings and tassels, of insipid faces: pestiferous people who came once a year, as a matter of propriety, to sit in a circle and look at each other for a while without knowing what to say; after which an old servant in a gray jacket would come in very decorously to bring the coffee and cakes which the gallant Beneto would serve, together with his little jokes which were always the same, and at which the company laughed regularly every year in the same key and rhythm. To miss a beautiful November sunset for those people! Bianca could not stand them; they made it impossible for her to breathe.

"I don't know," Canon Businello said to her between sips of coffee, "I don't know whether you've heard the bad news . . ."

"No. What news . . . ?" Bianca answered in a whisper.

"Ah, to be sure," said two or three low voices. "Ah, yes, to be sure."

"Poor Torranza, poor man . . ." the Canon added mournfully, dipping the last piece of cake in his coffee.

Bianca felt a contraction in her heart and a cold tingling on her face, and could not utter a word.

"Unfortunately," said the monsignore, moving his cup around to dissolve the sugar which had remained at the bottom. "Deceased, yes. . . ." He emptied his cup and added, sighing, "Last night, at half past eleven."

Bianca lost the power of sight for an instant, but she conquered her emotion by a strong effort of will-power, almost a transport of rage. Signora Giovanna saw her grow very pale and was about to rise in alarm; but a quick, firm glance from her daughter stopped her in the act. The Dalla Carretta ladies, who had heard certain malicious epigrams that were circulating in Padua concerning Torranza's senile flame, gave each other a rapid glance and were silent.

Meanwhile the Canon was saying that Torranza had taken to his bed two or three days previously, without great suffering, but with very grave presentiments. The catas-

avvenuta improvvisamente; ma egli non poteva affermarlo. Era partito da Padova poche ore dopo, alle dieci del mattino. La città era già piena della notizia; si sapeva che la Giunta Municipale doveva raccogliersi d'urgenza.

— Le solite commedie—esclamò il sior Beneto.—Beata, quella gente là, di poter far del chiasso e spender dei soldi. Capaci di ringraziar Dio che quel povero infelice sia morto adesso che ci son loro in Comune.[11] E cosa crede, Monsignore, che vogliano onorarlo per quei quattro[12] versi? Ma neanche per idea! È perché era famoso anche lui a spendere e spandere. Basta questo, caro lei.[13] Un uomo grande!

— Papà—disse Bianca agitatissima—se deliberano qualche cosa per Torranza, fanno più onore a sé che a lui.

— Idee tutte vostre, queste—replicò Beneto dispettosamente.—Idee tutte vostre. Non mettetevi mica in mente ch'egli fosse poi questa gran cosa. Non m'intendo di versi, ma siamo stati a scuola insieme, con Torranza, e posso dirlo. Volete metter la testa[14] di Farsatti?

— No, no no—interruppe con certa secchezza molle il canonico.—Per talento, lasciamolo stare, il povero Ermes ne aveva più del bisogno; ma criterio, signora! criterio. La mi scusi proprio, neanche una briciola.

— Egli era de' miei amici, l'avverto, monsignore— rispose Bianca.—A me queste cose non si possono dire.

— Ah, bene!—fece monsignore scuro. I Dalla Carretta si rannuvolarono. Ma Beneto non permise che la[15] finisse così, in un silenzio burrascoso.

— Monsignore parla benissimo—disse egli—e mi meraviglio di voi che non le abbiate mai capite, certe cose.

— Basterebbe l'affare dello spiritismo—osservò a mezza voce il vecchio conte Dalla Carretta, rivolgendosi con un sorrisetto al canonico, per confortarlo.

— Euh![16]—disse questi, alzando gli occhi e le sopracciglia.—Io non parlo.

Una zitellona della compagnia chiese, facendo l'inno-

trophe must have taken place suddenly; but he could not say for certain. He had left Padua a few hours later, at ten in the morning. The news was already all over the city; it was known that the Municipal Council was to hold an emergency meeting.

"The usual fakery," exclaimed Sior Beneto. "They're lucky, those people, that they can make a big fuss and spend money. They're capable of thanking God that that poor unfortunate died at this time, while they are in office. And what do you think, Monsignore—that they want to honor him for those few poems? Not in the slightest! It's because he, too, was a famous spender and squanderer. That's enough, my dear sir. A great man, indeed!"

"Papa," said Bianca in great agitation, "if they decide to do something for Torranza, they are doing more honor to themselves than to him."

"That's just your idea," replied Beneto contemptuously. "Just your idea. Don't get it into your head that he was any great shakes. I don't know anything about poetry, but we were at school together, Torranza and I, and I can talk. Do you want to compare him to Farsatti?"

"No, no, no," the Canon interrupted with a certain weak dryness. "As for talent, there's no question, poor Hermes had more than he needed; but judgment, ma'am, judgment! I'm sorry, but he didn't have a bit."

"He was one of my friends, I warn you, Monsignore," answered Bianca. "In my presence, one may not say such things."

"Oh, very well," said Monsignore, darkly. The Dalla Carretta family's faces clouded over. But Beneto did not let matters end thus, in a stormy silence.

"What Monsignore says is quite right," he said, "and I'm surprised at you that you never understood certain things."

"Just that spiritualism business would be enough," the old Count Dalla Carretta remarked in a low voice, turning to the Canon with a little smile, to comfort him.

"Euh!" said the latter, raising his eyes and his eyebrows. "I have nothing to say."

An old maid in the group asked, pretending innocence,

cente, se Torranza fosse proprio spiritista. Il canonico, che non voleva parlare, si sfogò.—Spiritista fanatico, era. Aveva una biblioteca di pubblicazioni tedesche, francesi, inglesi, americane sullo spiritismo. Stava traducendo un libro di un certo Fechte o Fochte o Fichte, pieno di quelle minchionerie.

— Si capisce che Lei non lo ha letto—interruppe Bianca.

— Sta a vedere [17]—saltò su il sior Beneto—che mi diventate spiritista. Vorrei vedere anche questa.

Bianca fu per dare a suo padre una risposta audace e pungente. Si contenne e rispose solo che non amava i pregiudizi di nessun colore.

— Adesso gli potremo dare la prova, allo spiritismo del povero Torranza—osservò un signore—perché, e questo l'ho udito con le mie orecchie da Pedrocchi,[18] egli diceva che dopo morto si sarebbe fatto sicuramente vedere e intendere da qualcuno.

Beneto nitrì una risata gutturale, a bocca chiusa.

— Gesummaria, papà!—disse la contessina Dalla Carretta al suo genitore.

— Matto, cara, matto!—rispose questi.

— Eh, matto, poveretto; eh, matto.—Ciascuno guardava il suo vicino, gli passava la parola a mezza voce. Bianca si alzò senza dir nulla, spinse via nervosamente la sua sedia e uscì.

Beneto fremeva, la signora Giovanna stava sulle spine. Dopo un breve silenzio, la Dalla Carretta guardò, imbarazzata, suo marito, piegando la persona; in un attimo, tutti furono in piedi, contenti, sollevati da un gran peso. Beneto discese la scalinata a braccio della contessa, che gli espresse, con molta ipocrisia, il suo rincrescimento per i discorsi che si eran fatti prima, per il dispiacere arrecato alla signora Bianca. Beneto protestò. Aveva gusto che sua figlia imparasse a conoscer meglio il mondo; era stato anche lui amico di Torranza, per tradizioni di famiglie; ma pur troppo quel vecchio matto aveva esercitato una pessima influenza in casa Squarcina. Intanto, dietro a loro, scendeva la brigata tutta susurri maligni, interrotti prudentemente da

whether Torranza was really a spiritualist. The Canon, who had nothing to say, let himself go. "A fanatical spiritualist, he was. He had a whole library of German, French, English, American publications on spiritualism. He was translating a book by a certain Fechte or Fochte or Fichte, full of all that nonsense."

"Obviously you have not read it," interrupted Bianca.

"Are we to expect," Sior Beneto leapt into the fray, "that you're going to turn spiritualist on us? I'd just like to see that."

Bianca almost gave her father a sharp and caustic reply. She restrained herself and answered only that she did not like prejudices of any kind.

"Now we can test out poor Torranza's spiritualism," remarked one of the gentlemen, "because, and I heard this with my own ears at Pedrocchi's, he said that after his death he would certainly manifest himself by sight and hearing to someone."

Beneto laughed gutturally, neighing with his mouth closed.

"Good heavens, papa!" said the young Countess Dalla Carretta to her father.

"Crazy, my dear, crazy!" the latter replied.

"Eh, crazy, poor fellow; quite crazy." Everyone looked at his neighbor and passed the word around in a low voice. Bianca got up without saying a word, nervously pushed away her chair and went out.

Beneto was trembling and Signora Giovanna was in torment. After a short silence, the Countess Dalla Carretta leaned forward and cast an embarrassed glance at her husband. In an instant, everyone was on his feet, happy, freed from a great weight. Beneto descended the steps with the Countess on his arm, and she expressed to him, with great hypocrisy, her regrets for the discussion which had occurred and for the offense which had been given to Signora Bianca. Beneto protested. He would have liked for his daughter to become better acquainted with the ways of the world. He too had been a friend of Torranza's, through family tradition; but unfortunately that crazy old man had exercised a very bad influence on the Squarcina family.

qualche osservazione a voce alta sul tramonto vermiglio, sulle campane della parrocchia che suonavano per l'ottavario dei morti,[19] sul nero nebbione che si levava dall'orizzonte, soffiando.

Ecco i due carrozzoni che si fanno avanti: ecco daccapo gli ossequi, i rispetti e i doveri. I lunghi scialli scuri, i cappellini barocchi, le nappe canonicali, le slavate facce noiose si allontanano sotto i pioppi, e il sior Beneto ritorna su, borbottandosi la lettura di un foglio consegnatogli dal cursor comunale che lo segue col berretto in mano. Giunto sulla spianata, trova un servitore uscito ad avertirlo ch'è in tavola;[20] e fa chiamar fuori la padrona.

— Qui c'è l'annuncio di Torranza—diss'egli—e questo galantuomo ha un'altra lettera. Pagate voi?

— Cosa?—diss'ella timidamente.

— Cosa? La multa,[21] cosa! Se vostra figlia si fa scrivere da dei disperati che riempiono Dio sa quanti fogli e poi non sono in caso di metter fuori otto palanche,[22] suo danno! Io non pago sicuro.

La signora Giovanna guardò la lettera.

— Viene da Padova—diss'ella esitando.

— Eh, si sa, cara, che pagate!

— È urgentisima—susurrò la povera donna.

Beneto le domandò qualche cosa con gli occhi e un cenno del capo.

— No—diss'ella.—Mi pare e non mi pare di conoscerlo, il carattere; ma di quella casa là no certo.

— Benone!—esclamò l'ironico marito.—Adesso poi, siccome sarebbe una pazzia, così son sicuro che pagate. Accomodatevi pure.

Ed entrò in casa.

La povera signora non aveva un soldo in tasca, ma fece subito qualche segreta convenzione col cursore, che salutò e sparve nella nebbia, dilagata, in un batter d'occhio, sul piano. Il triste oceano bianco fumava su tutti i pendii,

Meanwhile, behind them, the group came down all whispering maliciously to each other, prudently interspersing a few observations out loud on the vermilion sunset, on the parish bells which were tolling the octave of the dead, and on the black fog which was rising from the horizon in gusts.

Now the two carriages came up, and again there were compliments, respects, regards. The long black shawls, the over-ornamented bonnets and the tedious insipid faces vanished beneath the poplars. Sior Beneto came back up, mumbling as he read to himself a letter which had been handed him by the local mailman, who was following him with his hat in his hand. When he arrived on the esplanade, he found a servant who had come out to tell him that dinner was ready; and he sent for the lady of the house.

"Here's the announcement about Torranza," he said, "and this good man has another letter. Will you pay?"

"What?" she asked timidly.

"What? The excess postage, that's what! If your daughter gets letters from madmen who fill up Lord knows how many pages and then aren't able to shell out eight cents for the postage, that's too bad for her! I won't pay, that's for sure."

Signora Giovanna looked at the letter.

"It comes from Padua," she said hesitantly.

"Eh, they know, my dear, that you will pay!"

"It's marked 'Very Urgent,' " the poor woman whispered.

Beneto asked her something with a glance and a nod of his head.

"No," she said. "I seem to recognize the handwriting and yet again I don't; but it certainly does not come from that house."

"Excellent!" exclaimed her husband, ironically. "So now, since it would be madness, I'm sure that you'll pay. Suit yourself."

And he went into the house.

The signora did not have a penny on her, but she immediately made some kind of secret arrangement with the mailman, who bowed and disappeared into the mist which had suddenly came up on the plain. The sad white ocean of

metteva le prime ondate taciturne sulla spianata di Monte San Donà. Ancora un momento e avrebbe chiusa la casa nel suo vapor denso, avrebbe affacciata a tutte le finestre la sua malinconia stupida.

— Ci vorrà un lume, a tavola—disse al domestico la signora San Donà, rientrando.

— Niente, niente,—gridò Beneto dal salotto—non occorre lume che ci si vede benone. Sbrigatevi e dite alla principessa che si degni, almanco, di non farsi aspettare.

II

L'annuncio così crudo, inatteso, della morte di Torranza era stato per Bianca un colpo di sgomento e di dolore, che volle celare, quanto potè, a quella sciocca compagnia pettegola. Comprimer lo sdegno le riusciva men facile; e, venuti in campo i discorsi di Torranza al caffè Pedrocchi, era uscita per non prorompere contro suo padre che rideva e gli altri che compativano.

Si chiuse in camera. L'immagine di un nuovo Torranza, di un Torranza morto assai più grande e buono che non le fosse mai parso il vivo, le riempiva l'anima; e lo pianse, meravigliata delle proprie lagrime, di sentirsi una tenerezza tanto profonda. Averlo lasciato partire così, senza un addio! Ecco, se non fosse stato quel ch'era stato, ella si sarebbe trovata a Padova, lo avrebbe potuto vedere. Si rimproverò d'aver risposto un po' tardi all'ultima sua lettera, di non averlo ringraziato bene della romanza. Tante altre sue piccole negligenze, tante altre lievi freddezze punto necessarie, che avevan forse rattristato il poeta, le tornavano tutte al cuore, le facevano male. Egli, un potente creatore d'anime e di figure ideali, l'avea cullata, da bambina, sulle sue ginocchia, l'avea consigliata, dopo il collegio, negli studi; sposa, l'aveva condotta alla più squisita intelligenza d'ogni arte; finalmente s'era innamorato di lei come delle creature a cui il suo genio aveva dato vita e passione. Adesso Bianca voleva persuadersi d'essere stata amata così; sentiva più

fog was rising like smoke on all the slopes, and was sending its first silent waves over the esplanade at Mount San Donà. In a moment it would enclose the house in its dense vapor, and would look in at all the windows with its dull melancholy.

"We shall need a light at table," Signora San Donà said to the servant as she came in.

"Not at all, not at all," shouted Beneto from the drawing-room, "we don't need any light, we can see very well. Hurry up and tell the princess to be so kind, at least, as not to keep us waiting."

II

The news, so crude, so unexpected, of Torranza's death had been for Bianca an alarming and painful blow, which she tried to hide, as much as she could, from that silly, gossiping company. It was less easy for her to restrain her contempt; and, when they had started to discuss Torranza's pronouncements at the Caffè Pedrocchi, she had gone out in order not to burst forth against her father when he laughed and against the others when they sympathized.

She shut herself in her room. The vision of a new Torranza, of a dead Torranza who was much greater and kinder than he had seemed to her when alive, filled her soul; and she wept for him, amazed at her own tears, at feeling such a profound tenderness. To have let him depart thus, without farewell! In fact, if it had not been for what had happened, she would have been at Padua and could have seen him. She reproached herself for having been somewhat tardy in answering his last letter, and for not having thanked him sufficiently for the ballad. So many other little acts of negligence on her part, so many other slight expressions of coldness which had been quite unnecessary, which had perhaps saddened the poet, all came back to her mind and hurt her. He, a powerful creator of ideal souls and figures, had dandled her on his knee when she was a little girl, and had advised her in her studies after boarding-school. When she was a bride, he had introduced her to the perceptive understanding of every art. Finally,

alta, in questo concetto, la memoria del poeta, e se più alta, più vicina al paese in cui vivono i sogni dei grandi poeti spiritualisti. Egli l'amava ancora, povero amico; le si era voluto ricordare dal paese dei morti appena giuntovi. Era spirato alle undici e mezzo; e Bianca si era sentito, prima della mezzanotte, il suo nome strano nel cuore.

Si picchiò all'uscio; era la signora Giovanna con una lettera urgentissima. Bianca prese la lettera senza guardarla, pregò sua madre di scendere a pranzo, di lasciarla sola. Non voleva trovarsi con papà prima d'essere un po' più calma; temeva che certi discorsi la irritassero troppo, le facessero dire quello che non avrebbe voluto. La signora Giovanna se n'andò sospirando, mentre sua figlia, chiuso l'uscio, si sorprendeva dell'oscurità sopravvenuta nella camera, del torbido mare che saliva davanti alle finestre. Vide per un momento ancora i fantasmi dei vasi ritti sul muricciolo della spianata, qualche altro spettro di piante vicine; poi niente, neppure un'ombra nel bianco immenso, eguale, impenetrabile. E stette a guardarvi su, attonita, sentendo la voluttuosa dolcezza di trovarsi lì nella sua piccola camera tepida, a pensare, in grembo a quell'oceano silenzioso; sentendo una rispondenza arcana, indefinibile delle cose esterne con i pensieri che le empivano il cuore. Si ricordò a un tratto della lettera che aveva in mano, l'accostò a' vetri per decifrarne il carattere.

"Oh Dio!" diss'ella.
L'aperse in furia con le mani convulse. Vi trovò uno scritto e una fotografia. Ravvisò tosto la barba bianca, l'abito nero, il fiore all'occhiello; lui insomma, Ermes Torranza.
Sentiva di dover leggere subito, non ci vedeva, non sapeva

he had fallen in love with her as he had with the creatures to which his genius had given life and passion. Now Bianca wanted to persuade herself that she had been loved in this way; she felt that, in this conception, the memory of the poet was more lofty, and, being more lofty, was nearer to the land where dwell the dreams of the great spiritualist poets. He still loved her, poor friend; he had wanted to remind her of himself, from the land of the dead, as soon as he had arrived there. He had died at eleven-thirty; and Bianca had felt, before midnight, his strange name in her heart.

There was a knock at the door; it was Signora Giovanna with a very urgent letter. Bianca took the letter without looking at it and begged her mother to go on down to dinner and to leave her alone. She did not want to be with her father until she was somewhat calmer; she was afraid that certain kinds of talk might irritate her and make her say things that she did not want to say. Signora Giovanna went away sighing, while her daughter, on closing the door, was surprised at the darkness which had come over the room and at the sea of fog which was rising in front of the windows. She saw for yet a moment the ghostly shapes of the vases standing upright on the little wall of the esplanade, and the spectral outlines of a few other trees nearby; then nothing, not even a shadow in the immense, even, impenetrable expanse of white. And she remained looking at it, dazed, feeling the voluptuous sweetness of being there in her little warm room, thinking, in the midst of that silent ocean; feeling a hidden, indescribable correspondence between external things and the thoughts that filled her heart. She suddenly remembered the letter which she had in her hand, and put it close to the window-pane to read the handwriting.

"Oh, God!" she said.

She opened it hastily with agitated hands. She found in it a letter and a photograph. She immediately recognized the white beard, the black suit, the flower in the button-hole; in short, it was he, Hermes Torranza.

She felt that she had to read it immediately. She could

che si facesse, andava per la camera con la lettera in mano cercando a tastoni una candela che non v'era. Abbrancò un cerino sul suo tavolino da notte e l'accese. La fiammella mise un picciol lume sul legno lucido e sul crocefisso di bronzo, un gran buio nella camera. Bianca s'inginocchiò, macchinalmente, e lesse, sempre ginocchioni, lo scritto che segue:

Padova, 26 ottobre, 1879.

"Cara, non si turbi, non si sgomenti; legga questa lettera come io la scrivo, con la tranquillità più serena. Non è niente; il vecchio codino Torranza, che cosa strana! se ne va. Mi dia la buona notte, cara Bianca; dispongo perché questa lettera Le sia inviata appena spento il lume.

"Avvertito da una voce interna, ho fatto stamane, spontaneamente, quello che fece, prima di morire, il codino mio padre; adesso mi sento nel cuore qualcosa che si allenta, e insieme un silenzio pieno di riverente aspettazione. Avrò forse ancora quattro, sei, otto giorni; mi basta un'ora, per Lei.

"Bianca, nei nostri passati colloquî Ella mi parve temere, qualche volta, di un'ombra; il suo gentile affetto per me n'era turbato, non sapeva come esprimere un risentimento. Non è vero? Pure vi è solo nel mio cuore una tenerezza che in questo stesso momento solenne non offende i pensieri più alti; tutta la colpa è del vecchio sangue fantastico che lascia sempre un po' di colore sui sentimenti e sulle parole. Mi perdoni e sorridiamone insieme, oramai.

"Ho a farle un'altra preghiera e voglio porvi su il suggello della morte. Mi è amaro non averle dato in addietro più prudenti consigli circa i Suoi dissensi domestici e discender nella tomba con questo pensiero. Bianca, per il bene Suo, per il bene di persone che Le son care e un poco anche per la mia pace nel mondo a cui vado, mi ascolti; non resti a Monte San Donà. Ella, in fondo al cuore, ama certo ancora Suo marito. Questo povero giovane fa pietà.

not see clearly and did not know what to do. She went around the room with the letter in her hand, feeling for a candle which was not there. She seized a taper on her night table and lit it. The little flame sent out a wavering light over the shining wood and the crucifix of bronze, emphasizing the great darkness in the room. Bianca knelt mechanically and read, still on her knees, the following letter:

"Padua, October 26, 1879.

"My dear, do not be upset, do not be alarmed; read this letter just as I am writing it, with the greatest calm. It is nothing; the old reactionary Torranza—how strange!—is departing. Tell me good night, dear Bianca; I am making arrangements for this letter to be sent to you as soon as the light has gone out.

"Warned by an inner voice, I have done this morning, of my own accord, what my reactionary father did before he died; now I feel something slackening in my heart, and at the same time a silence full of reverent expectation. I may have perhaps four or six or eight days yet; all I need is an hour, for you.

"Bianca, in our former conversations it seemed to me that you were afraid, sometimes, of a shadow; your gentle affection for me was disturbed, but you were not able to express resentment. Is this not true? And yet there is in my heart only a tenderness which in this selfsame solemn moment does not offend the most lofty thoughts; it is all the fault of the old imaginative blood which always leaves a little of its color on feelings and words. Forgive me and let us smile together at it, now.

"I have another request to make of you, and I wish to set the seal of death on it. I regret bitterly that I have not previously given you wiser counsels concerning your domestic dissensions, and that I am going down to the tomb with this thought. Bianca, for your own good, and for the good of persons who are dear to you, and somewhat also for my peace in the world to which I am going, give heed to me: do not stay at Mount San Donà. You, in the bottom

L'altro giorno mi ha parlato di Lei per un'ora, con le lagrime agli occhi. Mi disse di averle scritto più volte, mi riferì le Sue risposte che gli tolgono ogni speranza se i vecchi non acconsentono a una separazione, o, almeno, se non promettono mutare contegno con Lei; e coloro non piegano né all'una né all'altra cosa. Bianca, pensi che qualche diritto ceduto in silenzio, qualche torto patito senza sdegno, non per timore, ma per pietà della persone ingiuste che pensano offenderci, leva l'anima nostra al di sopra del loro contatto irritante. Torni con suo marito. Non vi è tanto amore nel mondo da gettar via questo ch'è pur fedele, pur tenero, e non toglie la pace.

"E ora, se si ricorda le nostre conversazioni sul mondo invisibile e sui fenomeni che il secolo nega perché lo umiliano, non troverà strano ch'io desideri manifestarmi a Lei, dopo la mia morte, in qualche modo sensibile. La sera del giorno stesso in cui riceverà questa lettera, si trovi sola, fra le dieci e le dieci e mezzo, nella Sua saletta del piano. Apra la porta che dà sul giardino; le ombre della notte devono poter entrare. Suoni quindi la breve introduzione della romanza che Le ho inviata venti giorni sono. Dopo di questo, se Dio permette ch'io sia presente e possa darne segno, anche lieve, lo darò. Ella non conosce paura e vorrà consentire all'ultima fantasia sentimentale di un vecchio poeta che muore.

"È tempo di dirvi addio, Bianca. Ho qui davanti a me la testina leonardesca [23] che Vi somiglia. Gli occhi dell'incognita sono men grandi, i capelli più chiari; ma l'espressione originale del viso è la stessa. Questo dolce sole d'inverno che passa tra i miei libri chiusi, brilla sul quadretto. Vi vedo viva, depongo la penna. Vi guardo, Vi guardo, un'ultima irragionevole lagrima mi cade e si perde per sempre, come lo merita. Addio, addio!

"Ponete questo ritratto nel vostro salotto di Padova.
"ERMES TORRANZA."

of your heart, certainly still love your husband. This poor young man moves one to pity. The other day, he talked with me about you for an hour, with tears in his eyes. He said that he had written you several times, and told me of your replies which deprive him of all hope if the old people will not agree to living separately, or, at least, if they will not promise to change their behavior towards you; and they will not yield on either point. Bianca, remember that a few rights yielded in silence, a few wrongs suffered without contempt—not through fear but through pity for the unjust persons who think they are hurting us—raise our soul above their irritating contact. Return to your husband. There is not so much love in the world that you can throw away this love, which is, after all, faithful, tender, and does not rob you of peace.

"And now, if you remember our conversations about the invisible world and about the phenomena which the world denies because it is humiliated by them, you will not find it strange that I desire to manifest myself to you, after my death, in some perceptible way. On the evening of the same day you receive this letter, be alone, between ten and ten-thirty, in your music room. Open the door which leads to the garden; the shadows of the night must be able to come in. Then play the brief introduction to the ballad which I sent you three weeks ago. After this, if God permits me to be present and to give a sign, even a slight one, I shall give it. You do not know fear and will be glad to humor the last sentimental fancy of an old poet who is dying.

"It is time to say farewell to you, Bianca. I have here before me the head by Leonardo which looks like you. The eyes of the unknown girl are not as large as yours, and her hair is lighter; but the original expression of the face is the same. This gentle winter sun which enters between my closed books is shining on the little picture. I see you as if alive, and put down my pen. I look at you, I look at you, and one last irrational tear falls from my eye and is lost for ever, as it deserves. Farewell, farewell!

"Put this picture in your drawing-room at Padua.
                                        "HERMES TORRANZA."

— Sì, sì, sì—singhiozzò Bianca appassionatamente.— Tutto!—Si chiuse il viso tra le mani, promise a Torranza, con uno slancio del cuore, che avrebbe appagato tutti i suoi ultimi desiderî e pregò, senza parole, per esso.

Cadendo quell'impeto di fervore, il suo pensiero si assopiva, si perdeva, senz'avvedersene, in un altro campo. Ella non pregava più; aperte le mani, guardava la fiammella del cerino, si sentiva tornar nel cuore le conversazioni avute con Torranza sui misteri d'oltre la tomba. Non cercava né combatteva queste memorie; le lasciava venire, inerte. Ad un tratto spense il cerino, pregò un altro poco e si rizzò. Era notte, il bianco oceano silenzioso empiva sempre le finestre; pareva essere in un'isola. Le venne in mente, malgrado sé stessa, un racconto meraviglioso fattole dal poeta, una camera buia nel vecchio castello reale di Stoccolma,[24] in mezzo al mare; il re Carlo XI che siede taciturno al fuoco ascoltando il dottore Paumgarten parlar della regina morta, poi si alza, va alla finestra e dice al conte Brahe: Chi ha acceso i lumi nella sala degli Stati?

Qui non apparivano lumi; appoggiando il viso ai vetri si vedeva in alto, nella nebbia, un diffuso chiarore lunare. Bianca non potè a meno di pensare alla sala del piano, di vedervisi sola con le candele accese, ad aspettare uno spirito.

Alle sette e mezzo uscì di camera senza lume, discese la scala rischiarata dai quattro finestroni che rompono tutto un fianco del palazzo, dal primo piano alla cornice. Attraverso i due superiori si vedeva la luna mancare e tornare fra le nebbie fumanti; dei vani azzurrognoli si aprivano e si chiudevano nel cielo.

— Sei qua?—disse dal fondo della scala la signora Giovanna.

Subito dopo, la fessa vocina stizzosa di Beneto gridò più da lontano:

— Presto! Oramai, tanto, la poteva anche andare a letto, mi pare. Presto!

"Yes, yes, yes," sobbed Bianca passionately. "Everything!" She closed her hands over her face and promised Torranza, with heartfelt impetuosity, that she would fulfill all his last wishes, and prayed wordlessly for him.

As that outburst of fervor waned, her thoughts became drowsy and were lost, without her realizing it, in another region. She was no longer praying; after opening her hands, she looked at the little flame of the taper, and felt returning to her mind the conversations she had had with Torranza concerning the mysteries of life beyond the tomb. She neither sought nor repelled these memories; she simply let them come, without opposition. Suddenly she extinguished the taper, prayed a little more, and stood up. It was night, and the silent white ocean was still filling the windows; she seemed to be on an island. She remembered, in spite of herself, a tale of wonder which the poet had told her: a dark room in the old royal castle of Stockholm, in the midst of the sea; King Charles XI sitting taciturn by the the fire listening to Doctor Paumgarten speak of the dead queen, and then rising, going to the window and saying to Count Brahe: "Who has lit the lights in the Hall of the Estates?"

Here no lights appeared; on leaning her face against the panes, she could see above, through the mist, the diffuse glow of the moon. Bianca could not help thinking of the music room and seeing herself in it alone, with the candles lit, waiting for a spirit.

At seven-thirty she went out of the room, without a light. She descended the staircase by the light of the four huge windows which broke one whole side of the palace, from the first floor to the eaves. Through the two upper windows she saw the moon vanish and reappear amidst the smoking mists; bluish spaces were opening and closing in the sky.

"Are you there?" asked Signora Giovanna from the bottom of the staircase.

Immediately afterwards, the cracked, irritable voice of Beneto shouted from farther away:

"Hurry! Now, for that matter, you might as well go to bed, I'd think. Hurry!"

Bianca non gli badò. Quel padre amoroso voleva proprio farle costar poco il ritorno in casa Squarcina!

Egli era in salotto, picchiava e ripicchiava sulla tavola un mazzo di carte, impaziente che sua moglie venisse per la solita partita.

— Qua!—diss'egli, brusco.—Qua! Andiamo.

La rassegnata signora prese il suo posto all'angolo della tavola, presso una lucerna a petrolio. Bianca sedette sul canapè, nell'ombra. Povera mamma, pensava, che vita! Emilio era debole, non sapeva proteggerla; ma però, qual differenza da suo padre! Ella era sicura che suo marito, se non ci fossero i vecchi, la farebbe regina in casa propria. Era andato a piangere da Torranza, povero Emilio! Sentiva di volergli bene anche lei; e bisognava pur prenderlo come la natura lo aveva fatto.

— A vu! [25]—brontolava tutti i momenti il sior Beneto.— A vu! Presto!

Egli non rivolse mai una parola a sua figlia, e dopo le otto e mezzo se n'andò, com'era solito, a letto. Allora la signora Giovanna, che prima non aveva mai osato fiatare, si pose attorno a Bianca perché pigliasse qualche cosa, offerse quanto seppe con una premura timida e appassionata nel tempo stesso; ma Bianca non accettò nulla.

— Quella lettera!—disse sua madre.—Era di casa tua?

— No.

— Disgrazie?

— No, mamma.

— Perché ho visto *urgentissima*—rispose l'altra esitante.

Bianca si rizzò e l'abbracciò.

— Mamma—diss'ella sottovoce—se andassi via presto? Se tornassi con Emilio?

— Oh Dio!—rispose la signora Giovanna commossa— cosa vuoi che ti dica? In coscienza non potrei mica dirti di no.

— Forse lo faccio, mamma.

Alla signora Giovanna vennero le lagrime agli occhi.

Bianca paid no attention to him. That loving father really wanted to make it easy for her to go back to the Squarcina household!

He was in the drawing-room, tapping repeatedly on the table with a pack of cards, impatient for his wife to come for their usual game.

"Here!" he said, brusquely. "Here! Let's go."

The signora resignedly took her place at the corner of the table, near an oil lamp. Bianca sat on the sofa, in the shadow. Poor mother, she thought, what a life! Emilio was weak and did not know how to protect her; but still, what a difference from her father! She was sure that her husband, if the old people were not there, would make her queen in her own home. He had gone to weep on Torranza's shoulder, poor Emilio! She felt that she, too, loved him; and she had to take him just as Nature had made him.

"Your turn!" Sior Beneto would grumble every minute. "Your turn! Hurry up!"

He said not a word to his daughter, and after eight-thirty went off, as was his custom, to bed. Then Signora Giovanna, who up to then had not dared to speak, busied herself on Bianca's behalf, begging her to take something, and offering everything she could with a concern that was at the same time timid and passionate; but Bianca accepted nothing.

"That letter!" said her mother. "Was it from your people?"

"No."

"Misfortunes?"

"No, mother."

"Because I saw *very urgent*," the other answered hesitantly.

Bianca got up and embraced her.

"Mother," she said in a low voice, "suppose I were to go away soon? Suppose I were to go back to Emilio?"

"Oh, Heavens!" replied Signora Giovanna, deeply moved, "what can I say? In all conscience I could not say no."

"Perhaps I shall, mother."

Tears came into Signora Giovanna's eyes.

— Ma che ti maltrattino poi, no, sai!—diss'ella con voce soffocata, e soggiunse dopo un breve silenzio:

— Se fosse per il papà, sai bene com'è fatto. Non bisogna mica badare a certe apparenze.

— No, mamma, non è per il papà.

— Bene, cara, cosa vuoi che ti dica?

La povera donna prese la sua calza e si mise a sferruzzare frettolosamente. Dopo le asciutte risposte di Bianca non osava toccar della lettera urgentissima, quantunque comprendesse bene che il segreto di questo probabile ritorno in famiglia doveva trovarsi lì. Lavorava e taceva, sperando ottenere qualche spiegazione col silenzio ch'era come un dignitoso dolersi del riserbo di Bianca, un espresso aspettare che parlasse. Ma Bianca non aperse bocca, per cui, verso le dieci, la buona signora, mortificata e non avendo il coraggio di usare autorità, posò il suo lavoro, chiese alla figlia se volesse andare a letto.

Bianca rispose di non aver sonno. Sarebbe andata volentieri nella saletta del piano a fare un po' di musica. La mamma voleva tenerle compagnia, ma ella protestò tanto nervosamente, che la signora Giovanna le chiese scusa e, accesale una candela, salì le scale con la sua cerea faccia curva sul lumicino a petrolio.

Bianca s'avviò invece per il corridoio che mette alle camere deserte nell'angolo nord-ovest della casa. Entrò in una sala non grande, ma molto alta, tutta istoriata di affreschi mitologici, vuota; e accese con mano ferma le candele del suo piano attraversato a un canto. La lenta luce si allargò, a destra, sopra un tavolino zeppo di musica; a sinistra, sopra una giardiniera; in alto, su per le membra enormi di non so quali Divinità. Non v'erano altri mobili in tutta la sala; i passi della giovine signora vi pigliavano un suono lungo, vibrante.

Ella guardò l'orologio; le dieci erano imminenti. Cercò un pezzo di musica e lo posò sul leggìo del piano. Poi si trasse dal petto il ritratto di Torranza, guardò a lungo la calva testa scultoria del poeta. Oh, voleva bene accontentarne

"But they mustn't maltreat you, you know!" she said with a stifled voice, and added after a brief silence:

"If it's on account of papa, you know how he is. You mustn't pay any attention to certain surface appearances."

"No, mother, it's not on account of papa."

"Well, my dear, what can I say?"

The poor woman took her stocking and set to work hurriedly with her knitting-needles. After Bianca's curt answers she did not dare to touch again on the letter marked "very urgent," although she well understood that the secret of Bianca's probable return to her family must be in that letter. She worked and remained silent, hoping to obtain some explanation by her silence, which was like a dignified complaint at Bianca's reserve, an express expectation that she would speak, but Bianca did not open her mouth. Therefore, towards ten o'clock, the good lady, humiliated and not having the courage to assert her authority, put down her work and asked her daughter if she wanted to go to bed.

Bianca answered that she was not sleepy. She wanted to go to the music room to play a little on the piano. Her mother wanted to keep her company, but she protested so irritably, that Signora Giovanna begged her pardon and, after lighting a candle for her, went up the staircase with her waxen face bent over the oil lamp.

Bianca went through the corridor which led to the unoccupied rooms in the north-west corner of the house. She entered a room which was not large, but which was very high, all painted with mythological frescoes, and empty; and she lit, with a firm hand, the candles on her piano, which was placed across one corner of the room. The dim light extended, on the right, to a little table piled high with music; on the left, to a flower-stand; above, over the enormous limbs of some pagan divinities or other. There was no other furniture in the whole room; the young lady's steps assumed a long, reverberating sound.

She looked at the clock; ten o'clock was imminent. She looked for a piece of music and put it on the music-rack on the piano. Then she took from her bosom the picture of Torranza, and looked for a long time at the bald, finely

l'ultimo desiderio quand'anche fosse una follìa, voleva fedelmente comporgli la scena poetica, cui egli aveva forse pensato con qualche compiacimento prima di morire!

Si giustificava così, con sé stessa, dei suoi preparativi e della sua emozione, senza confessarsi che aspettava davvero, con uno scuro istinto del cuore, qualche cosa di straordinario. Posò il ritratto sul leggìo e stette un momento, involontariamente, in ascolto. Che cosa si muoveva dietro a lei? Niente, un foglio scivolava dalla catasta della musica. Bianca si piegò a leggere i versi riprodotti sulla copertina del pezzo che aveva davanti. Erano stati composti, lo sapeva, fra il contrasto della passione con il sentimento religioso, da un giovane amico di Torranza morto pochi mesi dopo, presso la donna non sua che amava malgrado sé stesso, in silenzio; e dicevano così:

ULTIMO PENSIERO POETICO

Le finestre spalanca a la luna;
T'inginocchia, mi sento morir.
Da i terror de la cieca fortuna,
Da la guerra de i folli desir,

Esco e salgo ne' placidi rai
Lo splendente universo a veder,
A bruciar ne l'amor che bramai,
Che non volli qui impuro goder.

Ma se orribile un ciel senza Dio
Tra le stelle funeree mi appar,
Ricadrò su quel cor ch'era mio,
Disperato m'udrai singhiozzar.

Bianca si coperse il viso con le mani, si rivide dentro alla fronte le sinistre parole:

Ma se orribile un ciel senza Dio
Tra le stelle funeree mi appar.

Immaginava con un brivido quel che proverebbe se udisse

chiselled head of the poet. Oh, she certainly was willing to satisfy his last request, even if it was madness; she was willing to set up for him the poetical tableau of which he had perhaps thought with some pleasure before he died!

She justified herself in this way, in her own eyes, for her preparations and her emotion, without admitting that she was really expecting, with an obscure instinct of her heart, something extraordinary. She set the picture on the music-rack and remained a moment, involuntarily, listening. What was moving behind her? Nothing, a page was sliding down from the heap of music. Bianca leaned forward to read the verses reproduced on the cover of the piece she had in front of her. They had been composed, she knew—in a struggle between passion and religious feeling, by a young friend of Torranza's who had died a few months later— for a woman who was not his but whom he loved in spite of himself, in silence; and they ran thus:

Last Poetical Thought

Open your windows to the moon;
Kneel, for I feel myself dying.
From the fear of blind fortune,
From the attacks of mad desire,

I go out and ascend in the calm rays
To see the resplendent universe,
To burn in the love which I desired,
Which I was not willing to enjoy, impure, here.

But if, horrendous, a Godless sky
Appears to me amidst the funereal stars,
I shall fall back on that heart which was mine,
In desperation you will hear me sob.

Bianca covered her face with her hands, and saw in her mind's eye again the sinister words:

But if, horrendous, a Godless sky
Appears to me amidst the funereal stars.

She imagined with a shudder what she would feel if she

piangere vicino a sé nel vuoto. Aperse la romanza per dar una passata all'introduzione, non troppo facile, che avea letto una volta sola. Ma le pagine non volevano stare aperte, si chiudevano tutti i momenti fastidiosamente. Le fermò col ritrattino di Torranza, e suonò, sotto voce, le quindici o venti battute d'introduzione che ricordano molto, in principio, la *Dernière pensée musicale* di Weber.[26]

Dio, come parlava quella musica! Che amore, che dolore, che sfiduciato pianto! Entrava nel petto come un irresistibile fiume, lo gonfiava, vi metteva il tormento di sentirne la passione sovrumana senza poterla comprendere. Bianca si alzò con gli occhi bagnati di lagrime, andò ad aprir le imposte della porta che mette in giardino. "Le ombre della notte" aveva scritto Torranza "devono poter entrare nella camera".

La notte era chiara. Gli alberi del giardino si vedevano sfumati nella nebbia lattea. Non un susurro, non un soffia; la nebbia, muta e sorda, era immobile.

Bianca tornò con un leggero tremito al piano. Guardò ancora l'orologio; erano le dieci e un quarto. Allora si decise, si raccolse nella musica che aveva davanti, bandì ogni altro pensiero, ogni trepidazione, come se vi fosse dietro a lei un'attenta folla severa, e strappò dal piano, con la sua grazia nervosa, il primo accordo.

Ella suonava ansando, per lo sforzo di metter tutta l'anima nella musica, di non pensare a quel che forse verrebbe dopo. Le fu impossibile eseguire le ultime note smorzate dell'introduzione; il cuore le batteva troppo forte. Passarono dieci, venti, trenta secondi eterni.

Silenzio.

Bianca alzò un poco la testa. In quel momento due colpi sommessi, affrettati, suonarono vicino a lei, che balzò in piedi con un subito ritorno di energia calma, e stette in ascolto.

Altri due colpi affrettati, più forti dei primi; poi un tocco leggero sulla soglia della porta aperta alle ombre della notte. Bianca guardò. Era entrata un'ombra, una figura umana. La giovine signora gittò un grido:

were to hear someone sobbing near her in the void. She opened the ballad to have a try at the introduction, which was not very easy and which she had read only once. But the pages would not stay open, and kept shutting all the time in an irritating way. She held them open with the little picture of Torranza, and she played softly the fifteen or twenty bars of introduction, which were very reminiscent, at the outset, of Weber's *Last Musical Thought*.

Heavens, how that music spoke! What love, what sorrow, what disheartened weeping! It entered her heart like an irresistible river, it filled her to overflowing, it gave her the torment of feeling its superhuman passion without being able to understand it. Bianca got up with her eyes bathed in tears, and went to open the leaves of the door which led to the garden. "The shadows of the night," Torranza had written, "must be able to come into the room."

The night was luminous. The trees of the garden were faintly visible in the milky fog. Not a whisper, not a breath; the mist, mute and deaf, was motionless.

Bianca returned to the piano with a slight shiver. She looked at the clock again; it was ten-fifteen. Then she made up her mind, concentrated on the music in front of her, banished all other thoughts, all fear, as if there were behind her an attentive, critical audience, and tore from the piano, with her nervous grace, the first chord.

She kept playing, breathlessly, in her effort to put all of her heart into the music, and not to think of what might happen afterwards. She was unable to play the last muffled notes of the introduction; her heart was beating too hard. Ten, twenty, thirty eternal seconds passed.

Silence.

Bianca raised her head somewhat. At that moment two low, hasty knocks resounded near her, and she sprang to her feet with a sudden return of calm energy, and remained listening.

Two more hasty knocks, louder than the first; then a light touch on the threshold of the door which was open to the shadows of the night. Bianca looked. A shadow, a human figure had entered. The young lady uttered a cry:

— Emilio!—diss'ella.

Era suo marito.

Egli si fece avanti rosso rosso, a passo incerto e a braccia distese, con la stessa ingenua contraddizione negli occhi, d'imbarazzo e di ardore. Bianca, petrificata, non si muoveva.

— Mi aspettavi bene!—diss'egli supplichevole, fermandosi.

Fu un lampo. Bianca vide confusamente che Torranza, chi sa come, avea combinato questo, e rispose:—sì—buttando le braccia al collo di suo marito con impeto così repentino che il povero giovane, tra la felicità e il non capir niente, perdette addirittura la testa e non sapeva che ripetere, fra un bacio e l'altro: scusa, scusa. Ma ella non lo udiva neppure e piangeva, piangeva, sentendosi una tenera gratitudine per il suo povero amico, una gran consolazione di esser al posto che Dio, finalmente, le aveva dato nel mondo, presso un cuore forse debole, forse male atto a comprenderla, ma buono e fedele.

— Star qui con la porta aperta—susurrò il giovane carezzevolmente—a quest'aria umida, con il dolor di capo che hai! Non voglio mica, io.

Ella passò in un baleno dal pianto al riso, e rise, rise sul suo petto, rise deliziosamente sentendo tornar l'allegria pazza del suo viaggio di nozze. Povero caro Emilio, credere che un doloruccio di capo di due mesi prima le durasse ancora! Egli restò un momento perplesso e poi rise anche lui di tutto cuore.

— Senti—diss'ella a un tratto, facendosi seria:—adesso spiegami bene tutto.

Suo marito parve sorpreso.—Ma se lo sai!—rispose.

— Lo so, ma ho piacere di udirlo da te. Vien qua, conta.

Camminarono su e giù per la sala, cingendosi l'un l'altro la vita con un braccio, parlando piano.

Lui aveva fretta, voleva sbrigarsi in due parole, dir che Torranza gli aveva scritto di venire, e basta. Ma lei non la

"Emilio!" she said.

It was her husband.

He came forward, blushing deeply, with uncertain steps and with outstretched arms, with the same naïve contradiction of embarrassment and ardor in his eyes. Bianca was petrified and did not move.

"You certainly must have been expecting me!" he said, as if in supplication, and stopping.

It happened in a flash. Bianca realized confusedly that Torranza, Lord only knew how, had arranged this, and answered "Yes," throwing her arms around her husband's neck with such sudden impetuosity that the poor young man, out of happiness and incomprehension, completely lost his head and could only repeat, between one kiss and the next, "Excuse me, excuse me!" But she did not even hear him and kept on weeping, feeling a tender gratitude towards her poor friend, a great consolation at being in the place which God, after all, had given her in this world, with a heart which might be weak, which might be inept in understanding her, but which was kind and faithful.

"Standing here with the door open," whispered the young man caressingly, "in this damp air, with the headache you have! Certainly I don't want to."

She passed in a flash from tears to laughter, and laughed long on his breast, laughed deliciously, feeling a return of the mad happiness of her wedding trip. Poor dear Emilio, thinking that a little headache of two months ago would have lasted until now! He remained perplexed for a moment and then he too laughed with all his heart.

"Listen," she said suddenly, becoming serious: "Now explain everything to me."

Her husband seemed surprised. "But you know!" he answered.

"I know, but I want to hear it from you. Come here and tell me."

They walked up and down in the room, with their arms around each other's waists, speaking in low tones.

He was in a hurry and wanted to tell everything in two words, to say that Torranza had written him to come, and

intendeva così! Aveva egli seco la lettera di Torranza? No. Quando gli era pervenuta? Questa mattina stessa, prima di mezzogiorno. E cosa diceva, proprio? Diceva presso a poco: la sera del giorno in cui riceverai questa lettera, trovati fra le dieci e le dieci e mezzo a Monte San Donà. Se vedi lume nella sala del piano, se odi suonare e se la porta è aperta, entra che Bianca ti aspetta, ed è disposta a tornare con te.—Che data aveva la lettera? Anche la data! Egli non volle più rispondere né ascoltare; la sua gioia, la sua passione avevano bene il diritto, oramai, di passare avanti a tutto. E si strinse Bianca tra le braccia, le soffocò nel collo un tal impeto di tenerezza che ne perdette anche lei la parola. Ma, improvvisamente, un lieve suono blando lo scosse.

— Zitto!—diss'ella rialzando il viso. Puntò le mani al petto di suo marito e guardò là ond'era venuto il suono.

Al leggìo del piano la romanza *Ultimo pensiero poetico* si era chiusa sul ritrattino che Bianca, poco prima, vi aveva posato a trattenere le pagine; Ermes Torranza non si vedeva più. Parve all'amica sua che quello fosse il promesso segno sensibile, l'addio del poeta, il quale, compiuta l'opera propria, si ritraesse chetamente, si dileguasse nell'ombra, o per le condizioni misteriose della sua esistenza superiore, o, fors'anche, per effetto di un malinconico sentimento che si poteva comprendere.

— Cosa è stato?—chiese Emilio.—Cos'hai che sospiri? Bianca tornò a piegargli il viso sul petto.

that was all. But she didn't mean it that way. Did he have Torranza's letter with him? No. When had he received it? This very morning, before noon. And what did it say, exactly? It said, approximately: "On the evening of the day you receive this letter, be at Mount San Donà between ten and ten-thirty. If you see a light in the music room, if you hear someone playing and if the door is open, come in, for Bianca is waiting for you and is ready to go back to you." What was the date of the letter? The date, too! He was no longer willing to listen or to answer; surely his joy, his passion had the right, now, to take precedence over everything else. And he clasped Bianca in his arms, and smothered on her neck such an outburst of tenderness that she too was left without words. But, suddenly, a light, soft sound stirred him.

"Quiet!" she said, raising her face. She put her hands on her husband's chest and looked in the direction whence the sound had come.

On the music-rack of the piano, the ballad *Last Poetical Thought* had closed over the little picture which Bianca, not long before, had put there to hold the pages; Hermes Torranza was no longer to be seen. His friend thought that this must be the promised visible sign, the farewell of the poet, who, having finished his work, was quietly withdrawing, was vanishing into the shadow, whether because of the mysterious conditions of his supernal existence, or, perhaps, also on account of an understandably melancholy sentiment.

"What was it?" asked Emilio. "Why are you sighing?"

Bianca bowed her head on his breast again.

Renato Fucini

(1843–1921)

The Tuscan scene, with its country folk and small-town dwellers, was the subject of all of Fucini's writings, both prose and poetry. Fucini was an engineer and school-teacher, living in or near Pisa. In 1872 he published a collection of a hundred sonnets in Pisan dialect, and in later years a number of short stories, in the collections *Le Veglie di Neri* ("The Evenings of Neri," 1884), *All' Aria Aperta* ("In the Open Air," 1897) and *Nella Campagna Toscana* ("In the Tuscan Countryside," 1908).

The story *La Fonte di Pietrarsa* (from *All' Aria Aperta*) shares with Fucini's other narratives his qualities of amiability and gentle satire. It is especially significant, however, in that it symbolizes the basic problem confronting the Italy of his time—the efficient use of human and material resources. Like Pietrarsa, Italy had a wealth of untapped resources which were flowing away just out of sight and going to waste; like the Pietrarsans, the Italians were unable to agree on how to tap these desperately needed resources, and use them to improve their lot. In a situation where many Italians were sunk in degrading poverty, as was Verga's Rosso Malpelo, or in brutalized superstitions as were d'Annunzio's Radusans and Mascalicans (in *Gli Idolatri*, pp. 166–189), and as incapable of doing anything effective as were Fucini's Pietrarsans—something, in the

American phrase, "had to give." The stage was set for widespread parliamentary dissatisfaction and disillusionment with post-1870 parliamentary democracy; the result, in 1922, was the triumph of Fascism and dictatorship.

LA FONTE DI PIETRARSA

di Renato Fucini

Lo RICONOBBI da lontano. Lo riconobbi dal suo cavallino bianco, tanto fido e trottatore, e dall'arsenale di pertiche, di biffe e di altri arnesi del mestiere che lui, ingegnere del Comune, si affestellava sul barroccino tutte le volte che aveva da battere la campagna per affari della sua professione.

Quando mi fu vicino gli feci un cenno con la mano, e lui rallentò il trotto e si fermò per il saluto e per la chiacchierata indispensabile quando due persone di conoscenza s'incontrano su per i monti, in mezzo ai boschi e in luoghi solitari.

— Lei torna dalla strada nuova dell'Acquaviva? [1]

— No. Vengo da Pietrarsa [2] dove mi son trattenuto due giorni per quella benedetta fonte . . .

— Ah, a proposito! Siamo ancora a nulla?

— Sì; finalmente è tutto sistemato: livellazioni, espropriazioni, permesso della Provincia [3] . . . è fatto tutto; ho sfilato i fondamenti, ho dato gli ordini all'accollatario, e lunedì, salvo che ce lo impedisca la stagione, si mette mano al lavoro.

— E lei, ingegnere, ci crede proprio? Crede proprio sul serio che la fontana sarà fatta?

— Per bacco! Che impedimenti vuole che saltino fuori al punto nel quale siamo?

— Si vede che lei, caro ingegnere, mi scusi, veh! si vede che lei non conosce ancora che panni vestono [4] i buoni

THE FOUNTAIN OF PIETRARSA

by Renato Fucini

I RECOGNIZED him from afar. I recognized him by his little white horse, which was so faithful and such a good trotter, and by the arsenal of poles, measuring rods and other implements of his trade which he, as the engineer of the municipality, festooned around his sulky every time he had to beat about the countryside on professional business.

When he was near me, I waved to him, and he slowed his pace and stopped for the greeting and the chat which are indispensable when two acquaintances meet up in the mountains, in the middle of the forests and in lonely places.

"Are you coming back from the new Acquaviva road?"

"No. I'm coming from Pietrarsa where I've been staying for two days on account of that blessed fountain . . ."

"Ah, by the way! Are we still nowhere?"

"Yes, finally everything is arranged: levellings, appropriations, permission from the Province . . . everything is done: I have lined up the foundations, I have given the orders to the contractor, and on Monday, unless the weather prevents it, the work will be started."

"And you, engineer, do you really think it will? Do you really seriously think that the fountain will be built?"

"Good heavens! What obstacles do you expect will arise, at the point where we are now?"

"It's easy to see that you, my dear engineer . . . excuse me . . . well! . . . it's easy to see that you still don't know

villici di questi poggi remoti.

— Ma, abbia pazienza, cotesto è un pessimismo . . .

— Ebbe'; oggi siamo agli otto di marzo. Scommettiamo che fra un anno il primo mattone della fontana non è stato ancora murato.

— Le rubo la scommessa; ma scommetto.

— Che cosa scommettiamo?

— Una bella pipa di radica di scopa.

— Va bene; va bene la pipa di scopa.

— Il dì otto di marzo.

— Il dì otto di marzo. Siamo d'accordo; ma è una pipa rubata.

— Sarà quel che sarà. Dì otto di marzo.

— Pipa di radica.—

E stipulammo il contratto con una risata e una stretta di mano.

— E lei si trattiene molto quassù?

— No; forse un paio di giorni. Giovedì sera sarò di ritorno a casa. Anzi, ingegnere, lei potrebbe farmi un gran favore. Se stasera vede il mio fratello, mi faccia il piacere di dirgli che quella ricevuta, che ho cercato tanto stamani prima di partire, la troverà di certo sotto a quel libro giallo a destra della scrivania.

— Lei sarà servito puntualmente. Dunque? . . .

— Il dì otto di marzo!

— Il dì otto di marzo! A rivederci, e buona passeggiata.

— Salute, ingegnere. E si ricordi di quella ricevuta, e . . .

— E della pipa di radica!—

Dette in un gran ridere e riprese la corsa, a martinicca serrata, giù per la china tortuosa.

Allontanatosi il rumore delle ruote e il cigolìo della martinicca, cominciai a sentire lo scroscio d'una cascata d'acqua lontana. Era il famoso sbocco d'una quantità di polle ricchissime, le quali, venendo dall'alto dei poggi e scorrendo quasi alla superficie sotto il paese di Pietrarsa, facevano tutte capo in quel punto, pochi metri sotto la via, e, con un

the true character of the rustics in these out-of-the-way hills."

"But, be patient; that is a kind of pessimism . . ."

"Well, today is the eighth of March. Let's bet that in a year's time the first tile of the fountain won't yet have been laid."

"It's a steal; but I'll make the bet."

"What shall we bet?"

"A nice briar-wood pipe, of broom-plant."

"All right, let's make it a briar pipe."

"The eighth of March."

"The eighth of March. It's a bet; but it's stealing the pipe."

"That will be as it may. The eighth of March."

"A briar pipe."

And we sealed the compact with a laugh and a handshake.

"And are you staying up here for very long?"

"No; perhaps a couple of days. Thursday evening I shall be back home again. As a matter of fact, engineer, you could do me a big favor. If you see my brother this evening, please tell him that that receipt, which I looked for all this morning before I left, he can certainly find under that yellow book on the right of the desk."

"You shall be served precisely. Well, then . . . ?"

"The eighth of March!"

"The eighth of March! Good-bye, and have a good walk."

"Good-bye, engineer. And remember about that receipt, and . . ."

"And about the briar pipe!"

He gave a great burst of laughter and started off again, with his carriage brake squeezed tight, down the twisting slope.

After the noise of the wheels and the squealing of the brake had faded away in the distance, I began to hear the roar of a distant waterfall. It was the famous outlet of a number of very abundant springs, which, coming from the upper reaches of the hills and running just below the surface under the town of Pietrarsa, all came out together at that

largo getto, di lì si scaricavano sonore nel sottoposto torrente.

Lo sbocco di quelle acque era inaccessibile; il paese soffriva la sete, e il Comune deliberò, fai fai,[5] l'allacciamento delle vene superiori e la costruzione della fontana.

La deliberazione era stata accolta con suono di campane, musica e sbandierate per tutto il giorno, e gran baldoria di lumi e di fiammate, la sera.

Non c'è dubbio, pensavo; non manca altro che metter mano ai lavori. Ma fra un anno, caro ingegnere, voi pagherete, e io fumerò alla vostra bella pipa di radica di scopa.

Il paese di Pietrarsa, un piccolo borgo con quattrocento abitanti circa, si stende tutto lunga la via provinciale, senza alcuna strada traversa. Di sopra, il monte ripido; di sotto, il precipizio in fondo al quale va a frangersi la cascata. Il paesello ha tre punti che chiameremo centrali: a un capo la chiesa, all'altro un piazzaletto dove trovasi [6] l'unico albergo e la rimesse della posta; nel centro il palazzotto comunale, un caffè e le botteghe più importanti.

Naturalmente fu scelto il mezzo del paese come più comodo per tutti, e lì, un rientro di muro accanto al palazzo comunale, facilitava i lavori e si prestava ad accogliere con decoro la fontana che, con fregi barocchi e ceffi di leoni spaventosi, aveva ideato e disegnato il mio ingegnere della pipa.

Dopo un'ora di cammino, arrivato a Pietrarsa quasi a bujo, mi accorsi subito che gli eventi precipitavano e che gli affari andavano assai peggio di quello che avrei potuto supporre. Gli usci, le finestre e tutte le botteghe del centro erano chiuse; e un grosso assembramento di persone, armate di quei picchetti, di quelle biffe e di quel pali che l'ingegnere aveva piantati la mattina, dopo chi sa quante fatiche e pentimenti, urlavano sotto le finestre del sindaco.

Erano gli abitanti dei due punti estremi del paese i quali, alleati per l'occasione, protestavano di non volere la fonte

point, a few meters below the road, and, with a broad jet, emptied loudly from there down into the stream below.

The outlet of those waters was inaccessible; the town was suffering from drought, and the municipality decided repeatedly to tap the upper veins and build the fountain.

The decision had been received with ringing of bells, music and processions with banners during the whole day, and great festivities with torchlights and bonfires at night.

There's no doubt, I thought; all that's left is to set hand to the work. But a year from now, my dear engineer, you will pay and I shall be smoking on your nice briarwood pipe.

The town of Pietrarsa, a little village of around four hundred inhabitants, stretches out all along the provincial road, without any cross streets. Above is the steep mountainside; below, the steep cliff at the bottom of which the waterfall breaks. The little town has three points which we shall call central: at one end the church, at the other a little square where are located the only inn and the coach-house for the postal stage; in the center are the town hall, a café, and the most important shops.

Naturally the center of the town was chosen as being the most convenient for all, and there a recess in the wall next to the town hall made the work easy and afforded an elegant place for the fountain, conceived and designed, with baroque ornaments and ferocious lions' snouts, by my friend the engineer with the pipe.

After an hour's walk, and arriving at Pietrarsa almost at dark, I immediately noticed that the situation was developing rapidly and that matters were going considerably worse than I might have thought. The doors, the windows and all the shops in the center of town were closed; and a huge assemblage of people, armed with those pikes, those measuring-rods and those stakes which the engineer had planted in the morning, after Heaven only knows how many difficulties and changes of mind, were howling under the mayor's windows.

They were the inhabitants of the two ends of the town, who, allied for the occasion, were protesting that they did

nel centro. E i più violenti, brandendo alti i pali e le biffe,
minacciavano legnate, morte e distruzione a chi si fosse
azzardato di murare anche una pietra sola nel rientro di
muro accanto al palazzo comunale. Le donne e i ragazzi
erano i più feroci.

Il sindaco si provò tre volte a persuaderli dalla finestra;
ma la sua voce fu soffocata sotto un uragano di urli, finché
non ebbe promesso di sospendere l'incominciamento dei
lavori e di scrivere alla Prefettura.[7]

La mattina dopo, tutto era ritornato nella calma; tutti
avevano ripreso le loro faccende, e soltanto l'accollatario
della fonte girava stralunato per il paese, con una gran
pèsca in un occhio prodotta da una legnata ammollatagli,
non sa né anche [8] lui chi ringraziare, quando jersera, in quel
trambusto, si provò a dire la sua.[9]

In fin dei conti, considerata bene la cosa, i protestanti non
avevano torto. Sempre ogni cosa per comodo dei signori!
La fontana nel mezzo, eh? perché nel mezzo ci sta il sindaco,
tre assessori [10] e quel porcone del sor [11] Girolamo! Bene, eh?
I lampioni gli hanno a cavare di cima e di fondo, e piantarli
tutti davanti alla spezieria! Hanno a lastricare solamente lì,
se voglion far bene! Non gli [12] basta il vino, e vorrebbero
anche l'acqua! La fonte lì, il telegrafo lì, la farmacia lì, la
balia l'hanno voluta lì, e lì ci avrebbero a portare anche un
serpente che s'avventasse a mangiargli il core a tutti quanti
sono! Legnate! schioppettate! veleno! . . . E noi poveri
si creperà. E la chiesa non conta nulla? E il povero Gambacciani, che ha da lavare le diligenze tutti i giorni e ha
tre gubbie di muli nella stalla, dovrebbe andare fin laggiù
a pigliar l'acqua? Ma il sindaco è un galantuomo e lui,
vedrete, accomoderà ogni cosa. Speriamo!

Questi, press'a poco, i discorsi nel caffè e dal tabaccaio;
ma, alla peggio,[13] in capo a due giorni, tutti si abbonacci-

not want the fountain in the center. And the most violent, brandishing on high the stakes and the measuring-rods, were threatening blows, death and destruction to anyone who might dare to lay even a single stone in the recess in the wall next to the town hall. The women and the children were the most ferocious.

The mayor tried three times to persuade them from his window; but his voice was overwhelmed by a storm of shouts, until he had promised to postpone the beginning of the work and to write to the Prefecture.

On the following morning, everything had become calm again; all had resumed their tasks, and only the contractor for the fountain was wandering in a daze around the town, with a big bruise on one eye resulting from a blow with a stick given him by someone whom even he can't identify to thank for it, when last night, in that uproar, he had tried to have his say.

In the last analysis, if you considered the matter carefully, the objectors were not wrong. Everything was always for the convenience of the upper crust! The fountain in the middle, hey? because in the middle are the mayor, three councilmen and that big swine sor Girolamo! Nice, eh? The street-lamps have to be taken away from the top and the bottom, and all put in front of the grocer's shop! They have to pave only there, if they want to do a good job! The wine isn't enough for them; they want the water too! The fountain there, the telegraph there, the drugstore there, they insisted on having the government offices there, and there they ought also to put a serpent which would fall on them and eat the heart out of all of them! Blows! Shots! Poison! . . . And we poor people will die miserably. And the church doesn't count for anything? And poor Gambacciani, who has to wash the stage-coaches every day and has three trios of mules in the stall, should have to go all the way down there to get water? But the mayor is a gentleman, and, you'll see, he'll fix everything up. Let's hope so!

Such, approximately, was the talk in the café and at the tobacconist's shop; but, after a fashion, after two days

arono, e, quando me ne venni per tornare a casa, nessuno si sarebbe accorto che poche ore avanti s'era scatenata in paese quella po' po' di tempesta.

Intanto l'acqua della sorgente che si scaricava impetuosa giù nella profondità del dirupo, scrosciava con tanto rumore da dare perfino noia alla figliola del signor Girolamo, la quale da due mesi, Dio glielo perdoni, studiava al pianoforte il valtzer della *Traviata* per un'accademia a benefizio degli Ospizj marini.

Quando fui a metà di strada per tornarmene a casa, incontrai l'ingegnere il quale, facendo sfegatare il suo povero cavallino su per quelle salitacce, veniva verso Pietrarsa. Aveva un diavolo per capello.[14] Mi provai a rammentargli il dì otto di marzo e la pipa di radica; ma non agguantò la conia. Mi salutò, fece le viste di ridere, e scusandosi, tirò avanti per la sua strada.

Passavano i mesi. E in quel tempo io vedevo spesso alla sfuggita l'ingegnere, il quale, quando poteva farlo senza dar nell'occhio,[15] scantonava e mi scansava come un creditore molesto.

Intanto a Pietrarsa gli affari andavano di male in peggio. Il Consiglio comunale deliberò, e la Prefettura approvò, che la fontana fosse costruita sulla piazzetta delle rimesse, riconoscendo quello il luogo più adatto per il comodo della popolazione. Ma allora quelli del centro e della chiesa ripeterono le solite scenate, e tutto fu nuovamente sospeso e accomodato con una gran bastonatura all'accollatario, il quale questa volta si dovè mettere a letto e uscirne dopo un mese per andare, tutto fasciato, al *debà*.[16]

Andai per curiosità alla prima seduta del tribunale, dove trovai l'ingegnere chiamativi come testimone; e allora non potè né scantonare né scansarmi.

Era indemoniato.—Venti disegni, questi assassini! cento viaggi m'avranno fatto fare questi malfattori! e nessuno paga gli straordinari! M'hanno rovinato tutti gli strumenti, ho dovuto vendere il mi'[17] povero cavallino e son vivo per miracolo! Ma oggi mi vendico! Ma oggi mi vendico, do-

everyone calmed down, and, when I left to go back home, no one would have noticed that that slight storm had burst over the town a few hours before.

Meanwhile the water from the spring which poured impetuously down into the depths of the declivity, roared so loudly as even to disturb the daughter of sor Girolamo, who for two months, Heaven forgive her, had been practising on the pianoforte the waltz from the *Traviata* for a concert in benefit of the sailors' hostels.

When I was halfway along the road back home, I met the engineer who, working his poor little horse to death on those nasty hills, was coming up to Pietrarsa. He was in a filthy temper. I tried to remind him of the eighth of March and of the briar pipe; but he failed to appreciate the jest. He greeted me, made a show of laughing, and, excusing himself, kept on his road.

The months were passing. And in that period I often saw the engineer fleetingly, but he, whenever he could do so without being obvious about it, turned aside and avoided me like an obnoxious creditor.

Meanwhile, at Pietrarsa, matters were going from bad to worse. The Council of the municipality decided, and the Prefecture approved, that the fountain should be built on the little square by the coach-house, recognizing that as the most suitable place for the convenience of the population. But then the people of the center and the church repeated the usual scenes, and everything was postponed afresh and settled by a tremendous beating given the contractor, who this time had to go to bed, from which he got up only a month later in order to attend the hearing, all bandaged up.

I went, out of curiosity, to the first session of the court, where I found the engineer, who had been called as a witness; and then he wasn't able either to turn aside or avoid me.

He was possessed by the devil. "Twenty plans, these murderers! a hundred trips they must have made me take, these criminals! and no one pays my over-time! They have ruined all my instruments; I had to sell my poor little horse; and it's a miracle if I'm still alive! But today I'll

vessi anche rimetterci la paga, la reputazione e la pelle!
Oggi mi vendico!

Cercai di calmarlo, ma fu inutile. Smanacciando e sbattac-
chiandosi il cappello nelle ginocchia, mi lasciò per entrare
nella stanza dei testimoni, dicendomi di sull'uscio:—Lei
avrà la pipa; ma con questa canaglia oggi mi vendico!—

Come si svolgesse il processo non lo so, perché gli affari
m'impedirono di tenerci dietro; [18] ma so che ci furono tre
condannati: il sor Girolamo a quindici giorni di carcere
per ingiurie al pubblico dalla finestra; l'accollatario a
quattro settimane per eccesso di difesa, e l'ingegnere a trecento lire di multa per contravvenzione alla legge sul bollo.

— Ma perché, santo Dio!—osservò un ombrellaio ambulante, chiacchierando una sera nel caffè,—perché non vi
mettete tutti d'accordo e costruite, invece d'una sola fontana dispendiosa, tre modeste fontanelle nei tre punti
contrastati del paese?!—
La fece bona! [19]—Sperperare a quel modo i quattrini del
pubblico quando una fontana sola bastava! Eppoi perché
disonorare Pietrarsa con tre indecenti pioli di sasso quando
ci sono i mezzi per averne una di marmo coi delfini, coi
leoni e ogni cosa? Voi non siete nativo di questi posti, e vi
si compatisce.
In quel momento, la cascata, presa da un'improvvisa
onda di vento, mandò uno strepito gaio come scoppio di
risa d'una moltitudine lontana.
Anche la seconda deliberazione del Comune andò all'aria;
e dopo molti, molti mesi venne finalmente la terza. Venne,
cioè, quella buona, quella vera, quella definitiva per con-
ciliare gl'interessi di tutto il paese; una deliberazione giusta,
ponderata e distesa con mirabile chiarezza d'argomentazione
ed eleganza di forma dal consigliere Balestri; una deliberazione che, riandando scrupolosamente la storia dei fatti,
terminava inneggiando alla concordia dei popoli e alla
santa religione dei nostri padri. Fu deliberato di costruire
la fontana in faccia alla chiesa.

get my revenge! But today I'll get my revenge, even if I should have to lose my pay, my reputation and my skin in the process! Today I'll get my revenge!"

I tried to calm him down, but it was useless. Waving his hands and banging his hat on his knees, he left me to go into the witnesses' room, saying to me from the door: "You will win the pipe; but I shall have my revenge today on these rascals!"

How the trial went, I don't know, because business kept me from following it; but I know that there were three persons sentenced: sor Girolamo, to two weeks in jail for insulting the public from the window; the contractor to four weeks for excessive self-defense; and the engineer to a fine of three hundred lire for infringement of the stamp-tax law.

"But why, good Heavens!" remarked an itinerant umbrella-peddler, chatting one evening in the café, "why don't you all agree and build, instead of one expensive fountain, three modest little fountains at the three disputed points in the town?"

He caught it hot! "What, waste the public's money in that way when a single fountain would be enough? And besides, why dishonor Pietrarsa with three disgraceful columns of stone, when there are enough funds to have one of marble with dolphins, lions and everything? You are not a native of these parts, and we are sorry for you."

At that moment, the waterfall, caught by a sudden gust of wind, gave forth a merry noise like a burst of laughter from a distant crowd.

The second decision of the municipality also came to naught; and after many, many months there finally came a third. There came, that is to say, the good one, the true one, the definitive one to reconcile the interests of the whole town; a fair decision, reached after due reflection and set forth with wonderful clarity of argumentation and elegance of form by Counsellor Balestri; a decision which, after giving a scrupulous résumé of the history of the facts, ended by extolling the concord of nations and the holy religion of our fathers. It was decided to construct the

Prima che questa deliberazione tornasse al Comune col visto della Prefettura, gli abitanti del centro e quelli della piazzetta delle rimesse, s'erano già trovati d'accordo: —Se murano un mattone davanti alla chiesa, segue un macello!—

La deliberazione tornò approvata; ma nessuno si fece più vivo.[20] Il Sindaco dette le dimissioni per procurarsi la soddisfazione d'essere rieletto, e il Segretario fu lesto a mettere tutte quelle carte in uno scaffale a dormire.

Dell'accollatario non se n'è saputo più nulla. L'ingegnere ha da pensare alla sua famiglia dopo la multa che ha dovuto pagare, e ha da imporsi privazioni d'ogni genere per estinguere il debito di parecchie centinaia di lire, che gli è toccato contrarre per accomodature e per acquisto di nuovi strumenti.

Son passati due anni, e della pipa non si è più parlato. Lui sta zitto; io non ho il cuore di rammentargliela.

Intanto il paese di Pietrarsa soffre la sete. Ma nelle sere d'agosto, quando le fronde dormono raggrinzate sui rami, e le cicale stesse tacciono spossate, è un gran conforto all'arsura lo scroscio della cascata che larga e perenne, rumoreggiando si perde nelle profondità del dirupo.

fountain opposite the church.

Before this decision came back to the municipality with the approval of the Prefecture, the inhabitants of the center and those of the coach-house square were already in agreement: "If they set a single tile in front of the church, there will be a shambles!"

The decision came back approved; but nobody gave any sign of life. The Mayor resigned, to get the satisfaction of being re-elected, and the Secretary was quick to put all those papers on a shelf to lie dormant.

Of the contractor, nothing further has been heard. The engineer has to see to his family after the fine he had to pay, and he has to undergo privations of all kinds to wipe out the debt of several hundred lire which he had to incur for repairs and for the purchase of new instruments.

Two years have passed, and nothing more has been said about the pipe. He keeps quiet, and I do not have the heart to remind him of it.

Meanwhile the town of Pietrarsa is suffering from drought. But in the August evenings, when the wrinkled leaves sleep on the branches, and the very crickets are silent through exhaustion, it is a great comfort for thirst to hear the roar of the waterfall which, broad and everlasting, fades away noisily into the depths of the declivity.

Gabriele d'Annunzio

(1863–1938)

At the end of the nineteenth century, and for the first third of the twentieth, Italian literature was dominated by the flashy, superficially impressive, theatrical figure of Gabriele d'Annunzio. A native of Pescara in the Abruzzi, he began his literary career as a poet with *Primo vere* ("First Spring," 1880), followed by short stories in the *Novelle della Pescara* ("Stories of Pescara," 1886) and novels, beginning with *Il Piacere* ("Pleasure," 1890). After a series of sensational novels, especially *Il Trionfo della morte* ("The Triumph of Death," 1894), d'Annunzio passed to spectacular drama, in such plays as *La Città morta* ("The Dead City," 1898), *Francesca da Rìmini* (1901) and *La Figlia di Iòrio* ("The Daughter of Iorio," 1904). He returned to poetry in the four books of *Laudi del cielo, del mare, della terra e degli eroi* ("Praises of the Heaven, of the Sea, of the Land and of Heroes," 1903–12). In his later years, d'Annunzio played at military action as an aviator in the First World War and as a filibustering general at Fiume in 1919–21. After Fiume, d'Annunzio was treated as an idol by the Italian nationalists and made a national hero by the Fascists.

The main content of d'Annunzio's works, in both prose and poetry, is an exaltation of sensualism and sexuality, presented in brilliantly impressive language. D'Annunzio's

ideal was the quasi-Nietzschean "superman," who considers himself outside all moral laws and who seeks only the fulfillment of his own desires and pleasures without regard for their effect on others. *Gli Idolatri* (from the *Novelle della Pescara*) exemplifies d'Annunzio's strong primitivistic and sadistic bent, portraying the extreme effects of centuries-old superstitions upon the poverty-stricken, ignorant and degraded peasants of the villages of the Abruzzi. The effect of the narration is heightened by d'Annunzio's deliberately Latinizing style, in which carefully selected and often recherché vocabulary serves d'Annunzio's aims of evocative theatricality.

GLI IDOLATRI

di Gabriele d'Annunzio

I

La gran piazza sabbiosa scintillava come sparsa di pomice in polvere. Tutte le case a torno [1] imbiancate di calce parevano roventi come muraglie d'una immensa fornace che fosse ₎per estinguersi. In fondo, i pilastri della chiesa riverberavano l'irradiamento delle nuvole e si facevano roggi come di granito; le vetrate balenavano quasi contenessero lo scoppio d'un incendio interno; le figurazioni sacre prendevano un'aria viva di colori e di attitudini; tutta la mole ora, sotto lo splendore della metèora crepuscolare,[2] assumeva una più alta potenza di dominio su le case dei Radusani.[3]

Volgevano dalle strade alla piazza gruppi d'uomini e di femmine vociferando e gesticolando. In tutti gli animi il terrore superstizioso ingigantiva rapidamente; da tutte quelle fantasie incolte mille imagini terribili di castigo divino si levavano; i commenti, le contestazioni ardenti, le scongiurazioni lamentevoli, i racconti sconnessi, le preghiere, le grida si mescevano in un rumorìo cupo d'uragano imminente. Già da più giorni quei rossori sanguigni indugiavano nel cielo dopo il tramonto, invadevano la tranquillità della notte, illuminavano tragicamente i sonni delle campagne, suscitavano gli urli dei cani.

THE IDOLATERS

by Gabriele d'Annunzio

I

THE GREAT sandy square sparkled as if strewn with pow-
dered pumice stone. All the whitewashed houses around
seemed red with heat like the walls of an immense furnace
on the verge of extinction. At one end, the pillars of the
church reflected the irradiation of the clouds and became
russet as if of granite; the glazed windows flashed as though
preventing the bursting forth of an inner blaze; the holy
images took on an air alive with colors and attitudes; all
its mass now, under the glow of the aurora borealis, assumed
a loftier power of domination over the houses of the
Radusans.

Groups of men and women, vociferating and gesticulating,
were returning to the square from the streets. In all minds
superstitious terror was rapidly growing gigantic; from all
those uncultured fancies a thousand frightful images of
divine punishment were arising; comments, eager disputes,
pitiful supplications, confused narrations, prayers, cries were
mingled in a dark rumbling as of an imminent hurricane.
For a number of days that blood-red glow had remained in
the heavens after sunset, invading the peacefulness of night,
tragically illuminating the sleep of the countryside, excit-
ing the howling of dogs.

— Giacobbe! Giacobbe!—gridavano alcuni che fin allora
avevano parlato a voce bassa, innanzi alla chiesa, stretti in
torno a un pilastro del vestibolo.—Giacobbe!

Usciva dalla porta madre e si accostava agli appellanti
un uomo lungo e macilento che pareva infermo di febbre
etica, calvo su la sommità del cranio e coronato alle tempie
e alla nuca di certi lunghi capelli rossicci. I suoi piccoli
occhi cavi erano animati come dall'ardore di una passione
profonda, un po' convergenti verso la radice del naso, d'un
colore incerto. La mancanza dei due denti d'avanti nella
mascella superiore dava all'atto della sua bocca nel prof-
ferire le parole e al moto del mento aguzzo sparso di peli
una singolare apparenza di senilità faunesca. Tutto il resto
del corpo era una miserabile architettura di ossa mal celata
nei panni; e su le mani, su i polsi, sul riverso delle braccia,
sul petto la cute era piena di segni turchini, di incisioni
fatte a punta di spillo e a polvere d'indaco, in memoria de'
santuarii visitati, delle grazie ricevute, dei voti sciolti.

Come il fanatico giunse presso al gruppo del pilastro,
una confusione di domande si levò da quelli uomini ansiosi.
—Dunque? Che aveva detto Don Cònsolo?[4] Facevano
uscire soltanto il braccio d'argento? E tutto il busto non
era meglio? Quando tornava Pallura con le candele? Erano
cento libbre di cera? Soltanto cento libbre? E quando co-
minciavano le campane a suonare? Dunque? Dunque?

I clamori aumentarono in torno a Giacobbe; i più lontani si strinsero verso la chiesa; da tutte le strade la gente si
riversò su la piazza e la riempì. E Giacobbe rispondeva agli
interroganti, parlava a voce bassa, come se rivelasse segreti
terribili, come se apportasse profezie da lontano. Egli aveva
veduto nell'alto, in mezzo al sangue, una mano minacciosa,
e poi un velo nero, e poi una spada e una tromba . . .

"Racconta! Racconta!" incitavano gli altri, guardandosi
in faccia, presi da una strana avidità di ascoltare cose mera-
vigliose; mentre la favola di bocca in bocca si spandeva
rapidamente per la moltitudine assembrata.

"Giacobbe! Giacobbe!" cried some men who until then had spoken in low voices, before the church, huddled around a pillar of the vestibule. "Giacobbe!"

A tall and emaciated man who seemed stricken with hectic fever, bald on the top of his cranium and crowned at the temples and nape with a few long reddish hairs came out of the main door and approached those who called him. His small deep-set eyes were animated as if by the ardor of a profound passion; they converged somewhat towards the root of the nose, and were unidentifiable in color. The absence of the two front teeth of his upper jaw gave a singular appearance of faun-like senility to the motion of his mouth, in speaking, and to the movement of his pointed chin, covered sparsely with hairs. All the rest of his body was a wretched frame of bones ill-concealed by his clothes; and on his hands, on his wrists, on the back of his arms, and on his chest, his skin was covered with purple marks of incisions made with the point of a needle and indigo powder, in memory of the shrines he had visited, the divine favors he had received, the vows he had fulfilled.

When the fanatic came up to the group by the pillar, a confused welter of questions arose from the anxious men: "Well, then? What had Don Cònsolo said? Were they going to bring out only the silver arm? Would not the whole bust be better? When would Pallura be back with the candles? Was it a hundred pounds of wax? Only a hundred pounds? When would the bells begin to ring? Well? Well?"

The uproar grew around Giacobbe; those who were farther out pressed in towards the church; from all the streets, the people poured onto the square and filled it. And Giacobbe answered his interrogators, speaking in a low voice, as if revealing terrible secrets, as if bringing prophecies from afar. He had seen on high, in the midst of the blood, a menacing hand, and then a black veil, and then a sword and a trumpet . . .

"Tell us! Tell us!" the others urged, looking at each other, seized by a strange avidity for hearing tales of wonder, while the word spread rapidly from mouth to mouth throughout the assembled multitude.

GLI IDOLATRI

II

La gran plaga vermiglia dall'orizzonte saliva lentamente verso lo zenit, tendeva ad occupare tutta la cupola del cielo. Un vapore di fusi metalli pareva ondeggiare su i tetti delle case; e nel chiarore discendente dal crepuscolo raggi sulfurei e violetti si mescolavano con un tremolo d'iridescenza. Una lunga striscia più luminosa fuggiva verso una strada sboccante su l'argine del fiume; e s'intravedeva al fondo il fiammeggiamento delle acque tra i fusti lunghi e smilzi dei pioppetti; poi un lembo di campagna brulla, dove le vecchie torri saracene si levavano confusamente come isolotti di pietra fra le caligini. Le emanazioni affocanti del fieno mietuto si spandevano nell'aria: era a tratti come un odore di bachi putrefatti tra la frasca. Stuoli di rondini attraversavano la spazio con molto schiamazzo di stridi, trafficando dai greti del fiume alle gronde.

Nella moltitudine il mormorìo era interrotto da silenzii di aspettazione. Il nome di Pallura circolava per le bocche; impazienze irose scoppiavano qua e là. Lungo la strada del fiume non si vedeva ancora apparire il traino; le candele mancavano; Don Cònsolo indugiava per questo ad esporre le reliquie, a fare gli esorcismi; e il pericolo soprastava. Il pànico invadeva tutta quella gente ammassata come una mandra di bestie, non osante più di sollevare gli occhi al cielo. Dai petti delle femmine cominciarono a rompere i singhiozzi; e una costernazione suprema oppresse e istupidì le coscienze al suono di quel pianto.

Allora le campane finalmente squillarono. Come i bronzi stavano a poca altezza, il fremito cupo del rintocco sfiorò tutte le teste; e una specie di ululato continuo si propagava nell'aria, tra un colpo e l'altro.

— San Pantaleone! [5] San Pantaleone!
Fu un immenso grido unanime di disperati che chiedevano aiuto. Tutti in ginocchio, con le mani tese, con la faccia bianca, imploravano.

THE IDOLATERS

II

The great vermilion band rose slowly from the horizon towards the zenith and tended to occupy the entire cupola of heaven. A vapor as of molten metals seemed to hover over the roofs of the houses; and in the glow descending from the sunset, sulphur-yellow and violet rays mingled in a trembling iridescence. A long streak, more luminous, extended towards a road which came out on the bank of the river, and at its end could be glimpsed the flaming waters amongst the tall thin trunks of the poplars; beyond there was a stretch of barren countryside, from which the old Saracen towers arose confusedly like islands of stone among the mists. The suffocating emanations of the new-mown hay were spreading through the air: it was, at times, like an odor of silkworms rotting among the leaves. Flocks of sparrows flew across the space with great noise and shrieking, bustling from the edges of the river to the eaves.

In the multitude, the murmuring was interrupted by expectant silences. The name of Pallura was on all lips; angry expressions of impatience burst forth here and there. Along the road from the river there was still no sign of the cart; the candles were lacking; for this reason Don Cònsolo was delaying in exposing the relics, and in performing the exorcisms; and the danger was imminent. Panic was invading all those people massed together like a herd of beasts, no longer daring to raise their eyes to the sky. From the women's bosoms, sobs began to burst forth; and an extreme consternation oppressed and numbed men's consciences at the sound of that weeping.

Then the bells finally rang out. Since the bronze bells were at a low height, the dull vibration of their tolling seemed to graze the heads of all; and a kind of continual wailing spread through the air between one stroke and the next.

"San Pantaleone! San Pantaleone!"

It was an immense, unanimous cry from desperate people asking for aid. On their knees, with hands outstretched and faces blanched, all were imploring:

GLI IDOLATRI

— San Pantaleone!

Apparve su la porta della chiesa, in mezzo al fumo di due turiboli, Don Còsolo scintillante in una pianeta violetta a ricami d'oro. Egli teneva in alto il sacro braccio d'argento, e scongiurava l'aria gridando le parole latine:

— *Ut fidelibus tuis aeris serenitatem concedere digneris, Te rogamus, audi nos.*

L'apparizione della reliquia eccitò un delirio di tenerezza nella moltitudine. Scorrevano lagrime da tutti gli occhi; e a traverso il velo lucido delle lagrime gli occhi vedevano un miracoloso fulgore celeste emanare dalle tre dita in alto atteggiate a benedire. La figura del braccio pareva ora più grande nell'aria accesa; i raggi crepuscolari suscitavano barbagli variissimi nelle pietre preziose; il balsamo dell'incenso si spargeva rapidamente per le nari devote.

— *Te rogamus, audi nos!*

Ma, quando il braccio rientrò e le campane si arrestarono, nel momentaneo silenzio un tintinnìo prossimo di sonagli si udì, che veniva dalla strada del fiume. E avvenne allora un repentino movimento di concorso verso quella parte e molti dicevano:

— È Pallura con le candele! È Pallura che arriva! Ecco Pallura!

Il traino si avanzava scricchiolando su la ghiaia, al passo di una pesante cavalla grigia a cui il gran corno d'ottone brillava, simile a una bella mezzaluna, su la groppa. Come Giacobbe e gli altri si fecero in contro, la pacifica bestia si fermò soffiando forte dalle narici. E Giacobbe, che s'accostò primo, subito vide disteso in fondo al traino il corpo di Pallura tutto sanguinante, e si mise a urlare agitando le braccia verso la folla:

— È morto! È morto!

III

La triste novella si propagò in un baleno. La gente si accalcava in torno al traino, tendeva il collo per vedere qualche cosa, non pensava più alle minacce dell'alto, colpita dal nuovo caso inaspettato, invasa da quella natural curi-

"San Pantaleone!"

At the door of the church, amid the smoke from two thuribles, appeared Don Cònsolo, resplendent in a violet cape embroidered in gold. He held on high the holy arm of silver, and conjured the air shouting in Latin the words:

"That thou mayest deign to grant serenity of the air to thy faithful, we beg thee, hear us."

The appearance of the relic aroused a frenzy of emotion among the multitude. Tears gushed from all eyes; and through the glistening veil of tears, men's eyes saw a miraculous heavenly radiance emanate from the three fingers lifted on high in a gesture of blessing. The figure of the arm now seemed larger in the enkindled air; the rays of the sunset kindled many-colored gleams in the precious stones; the perfume of the incense spread rapidly to the nostrils of the devout.

"We beg thee, hear us!"

But, when the arm was taken back inside and the tolling ceased, in the momentary silence a tinkling of bells was heard nearby, coming from the river road. Then there was a sudden rush in that direction and many said:

"It's Pallura with the candles! Pallura is arriving! Here is Pallura!"

The cart moved forward creaking on the gravel, at the pace of a heavy gray mare whose great brass saddle-horn was shining, like a beautiful half-moon, on its back. As Giacobbe and the others went towards it, the peaceful animal stopped, snorting loudly. And Giacobbe, who went up to it first, immediately saw stretched out in the bottom of the cart the body of Pallura all covered with blood, and he started to shout, waving his arms towards the crowd:

"He is dead! He is dead!"

III

The sad news spread in a flash. People crowded around the cart, stretched their necks to see something, thinking no longer of the menace from on high, struck by the new, unexpected happening, pervaded by that ferocious inborn

osità feroce che gli uomini hanno in cospetto del sangue.
— È morto? Come è morto?

Pallura giaceva supino su le tavole, con una larga ferita in mezzo alla fronte, con un orecchio lacerato, con strappi per le braccia, nei fianchi, in una coscia. Un rivo tiepido gli colava per il cavo degli occhi giù giù sino al mento ed al collo, gli chiazzava la camicia, gli formava grumi nerastri e lucenti sul petto, su la cintola di cuoio, fin su le brache. Giacobbe stava chino sopra quel corpo; tutti gli altri a torno attendevano; una luce d'aurora illuminava i volti perplessi; e, in quel momento di silenzio, dalla riva del fiume si levava il cantico delle rane, e i pipistrelli passavano e ripassavano rasente le teste.

D'improvviso Giacobbe drizzandosi, con una gota macchiata di sangue, gridò:
— Non è morto. Respira ancora.

Un mormorìo sordo corse per la folla, e i più vicini si protesero per guardare; e l'inquietudine dei lontani cominciò a rompere in clamori. Due donne portarono un boccale d'acqua, un'altra portò qualche brandello di tela; un giovinetto offerse una zucca piena di vino. Fu lavata la faccia al ferito, fu fermato il flusso del sangue alla fronte, fu rialzato il capo. Sorsero quindi alte le voci, chiedendo le cause del fatto.—Le cento libbre di cera mancavano; appena pochi frantumi di candela rimanevano tra gli interstizi delle tavole nel fondo del traino.

I giudizii, in mezzo al sommovimento, di più in più si accendevano e s'inasprivano e cozzavano. E, come un antico odio ereditario ferveva contro il paese di Mascálico,[6] posto di contro su l'altra riva del fiume, Giacobbe disse con la voce rauca, velenosamente:
— Che i ceri sieno serviti a S. Gonselvo? [7]

Allora fu come una scintilla d'incendio. Lo spirito di chiesa si risvegliò d'un tratto in quella gente abbrutita per tanti anni nel culto cieco e feroce del suo unico idolo. Le parole del fanatico di bocca in bocca si propagarono. E, sotto il rossore tragico del crepuscolo, la moltitudine tumul-

curiosity which men have in the presence of blood.

"He is dead? How did he die?"

Pallura was lying supine on the boards, with a great wound in the middle of his forehead, with one ear lacerated, and with gashes in his arms, in his sides, in one thigh. A warm stream was pouring down through the hollows of his eyes, down, down to his chin and neck, was staining his shirt, was forming blackish and shining clots on his chest, on his leather belt and down onto his trousers. Giacobbe was bent over that body; all the others around were waiting; the light of the aurora illuminated the perplexed faces; and, in that moment of silence, from the bank of the river arose the chant of the frogs, and the bats flew back and forth just over the people's heads.

Suddenly Giacobbe straightened up, with one cheek spotted with blood, and shouted:

"He is not dead. He is still breathing."

A dull murmur ran through the crowd, and the nearest leaned forward to look; and the restlessness of those farther out began to break forth in shouts. Two women brought a jug of water, another brought a few strips of cloth; a young man offered a gourd full of wine. The wounded man's face was washed, the flow of blood from his brow was stanched, his head was raised up. Then loud voices arose, inquiring about the causes of the mishap. The hundred pounds of wax were missing; there remained only a few fragments of candles in the interstices of the boards in the bottom of the cart.

Opinions, in the midst of the commotion, were becoming more and more heated and were becoming bitter and clashing. And, since an old hereditary hatred burned against the village of Mascálico, located opposite on the other side of the river, Giacobbe said in a hoarse voice, venomously:

"Might the candles have been taken for San Gonselvo?"

This was like an incendiary spark. The spirit of religion suddenly re-awoke in those people, brutalized for so many years in the blind and ferocious worship of their only idol. The words of the fanatic were spread from mouth to mouth. And, under the tragic red glow of the twilight, the

tuante aveva apparenza d'una tribù di negri ammutinati.

Il nome del santo rompeva da tutte le gole, come un grido di guerra. I più ardenti gittavano imprecazioni contro la parte del fiume, agitando le braccia, tendendo i pugni. Poi, tutti quei volti accesi dalla collera e dalla luce, larghi e possenti, a cui i cerchi d'oro degli orecchi e il gran ciuffo della fronte davano uno strano aspetto di barbarie, tutti quei volti si tesero verso il giacente, si addolcirono di misericordia. Fu in torno al traino una sollecitudine pietosa di femmine che volevano rianimare l'agonizzante: tante mani amorevoli gli cambiarono le strisce di tela su le ferite, gli spruzzarono d'acqua la faccia, gli accostarono alle labbra bianche la zucca del vino, gli composero una specie di guanciale più molle sotto la testa.

— Pallura, povero Pallura, non rispondi?

Egli stava supino, con gli occhi chiusi, con la bocca semiaperta, con una lanugine bruna su le gote e sul mento, con una mite beltà di giovinezza ancora trasparente dai tratti tesi nella convulsione del dolore. Di sotto alla fasciatura della fronte gli colava un fil di sangue giù per la tempia; agli angoli della bocca apparivano piccole bolle di schiuma rossigna; e dalla gola gli usciva una specie di sibilo fioco, interrotto. Intorno a lui le cure, le domande, gli sguardi febbrili crescevano. La cavalla ogni tanto scoteva la testa e nitriva verso le case. Un'ansietà come d'uragano imminente pesava su tutto il paese.

S'intesero allora grida feminili verso la piazza, grida di madre, che parvero più alte in mezzo al subitaneo ammutolimento di tutte le altre voci. E una donna enorme, soffocata dall'adipe, attraversò la folla, giunse gridando presso al traino. Come ella era grave e non poteva salirvi, s'abbattè su i piedi del figlio, con parole d'amore tra i singhiozzi, con laceramenti così acuti di voce rotta e con una espressione di dolore così terribilmente bestiale che per tutti gli astanti corse un brivido e tutti rivolsero altrove la faccia.

surging multitude had the appearance of a tribe of rioting Negroes.

The name of the saint burst forth from all throats, like a war cry. Those who were most eager hurled imprecations in the direction of the river, waving their arms, shaking their fists. Then all those faces, lit up by anger and by the light, broad and powerful, to which the golden ear-rings and the long forelocks gave a strange appearance of barbarism, all those faces turned towards the prostrate man, and were softened with pity. There gathered around the cart a group of pitying, solicitous women who tried to bring life back to the dying man: so many loving hands changed the strips of cloth on his wounds, sprinkled his face with water, put the gourd of wine to his white lips, made him a kind of softer pillow under his head.

"Pallura, poor Pallura, can't you answer?"

He lay on his back, with his eyes closed, with his mouth half open, with a dark down on his cheeks and chin, with a gentle youthful beauty still shining through his features taut in the convulsion of pain. From beneath the bandages on his brow there trickled down a thin stream of blood over his temple; at the corners of his mouth appeared little bubbles of reddish foam; and from his throat issued a kind of faint, broken whistling. Around him the attentions, the questions, the feverish looks increased. The mare from time to time shook her head and whinnied towards the houses. An anxiety, as before an imminent hurricane, lay over the entire village.

Then the shrieks of a woman were heard from the direction of the square, the shrieks of a mother, which seemed all the louder in the sudden hush of all other voices. And an enormous woman, smothered in fat, passed through the crowd and came screaming up to the cart. Because she was heavy and could not mount into it, she threw herself on her son's feet, with expressions of love in the midst of her sobs, with such piercing shrieks in her broken voice and with an expression of sorrow so terrifyingly bestial that a shudder ran through all those present, and all turned their faces away.

—Zaccheo! Zaccheo! cuore mio! gioia mia!—gridava la vedova, senza finire, baciando i piedi del ferito, attraendolo a sé verso terra.

Il ferito si rimosse, torse la bocca per lo spasimo, aprì gli occhi in alto; ma certo non potè vedere, perché una specie di pellicola umida gli copriva lo sguardo. Grosse lagrime incominciarono a sgorgargli dagli angoli delle palpebre e a scorrere giù per le guance e pel collo; la bocca gli rimase torta; nel sibilo fioco della gola si sentì un vano sforzo di favella. E in torno incalzavano:

— Parla, Pallura! Chi t'ha ferito? Chi t'ha ferito? Parla! Parla!

Il moribondo aprì gli occhi un'altra volta; e come gli tenevano serrate ambo le mani, forse per quel vivo contatto di calore gli spiriti un istante gli si ridestarono, lo sguardo si illuminò. Egli ebbe su le labbra un balbettamento vago, tra la schiuma che sopravveniva più copiosa e più sanguigna. Non si capivano ancora le parole. Si udì nel silenzio la respirazione della moltitudine anelante, e gli occhi ebbero in fondo una sola fiamme, poiché tutti gli animi attendevano una parola sola.

—. . . Ma . . . Ma . . . Ma . . . scálico . . .
— Mascálico! Mascálico! urlò Giacobbe che stava chino, con l'orecchio teso, ad afferrare le sillabe fievoli da quella bocca morente.

Un fragore immenso accolse il grido. Nella moltitudine fu dapprima un mareggiamento confuso di tempesta. Poi, quando una voce soverchiante il tumulto gittò l'allarme, la moltitudine a furia si sbandò. Un pensiero solo incalzava quelli uomini, un pensiero che pareva balenato a tutte le menti in un attimo: armarsi di qualche cosa per colpire. Su tutte le coscienze instava una specie di fatalità sanguinaria, sotto il gran chiaror torvo del crepuscolo, in mezzo all'odore elettrico emanante dalla campagna ansiosa.

IV

E la falange, armata di falci, di ronche, di scuri, di zappe, di schioppi, si riunì su la piazza, dinanzi alla chiesa. E gli

"Zaccheo; Zaccheo! my heart! my jewel!" shrieked the widow, endlessly, kissing the wounded man's feet, pulling him down towards herself.

The wounded man moved, twisted his mouth in agony, opened his eyes on high; but certainly he was not able to see, because a kind of moist film covered his gaze. Great tears began to pour from the corners of his eyelids and to run down his cheeks and neck; his mouth remained twisted; in the hoarse whistling from his throat was heard a vain effort to speak. And around him they urged:

"Speak, Pallura! Who wounded you? Who wounded you? Speak! Speak!"

The dying man opened his eyes once again; and, since they were holding both his hands tight, perhaps through that contact with life and warmth his spirits re-awakened for an instant and his glance grew bright. On his lips there was a vague stammering, through the foam which was issuing more copiously and bloodier. The words were not yet understandable. In the silence could be heard the breathing of the panting multitude, and all eyes had in their depths but one flame, since all minds were waiting for but one word.

". . . Ma . . . Ma . . . Ma . . . scálico . . ."

"Mascálico! Mascálico!" howled Giacobbe, who was bending, with his ear extended, to catch the faint syllables from that dying mouth.

An immense roar greeted the shout. In the crowd there was at first a confused surge as in a storm. Then, when a voice rose above the tumult and gave the war-cry, the multitude broke up in haste. One single thought urged those men on, a thought which seemed to have flashed into all minds in an instant: to arm oneself with something to strike. Over the consciousness of all there impended a kind of sanguinary fatality, under the great sinister glow of the twilight, in the midst of the electric odor emanating from the breathless countryside.

IV

And the phalanx, armed with sickles, with billhooks, with

idolatri gridavano:

— San Pantaleone!

Don Cònsolo, atterrito dallo schiamazzo, s'era rifugiato in fondo a uno stallo, dietro l'altare. Un manipolo di fanatici, condotto da Giacobbe, penetrò nella cappella maggiore, forzò le grate di bronzo, giunse nel sotterraneo, dove il busto del santo si custodiva. Tre lampade, alimentate d'olio d'oliva, ardevano dolcemente nell'aria umida del sacrario; dietro un cristallo, l'idolo cristiano scintillava con la testa bianca in mezzo a un gran disco solare; e le pareti sparivano sotto la ricchezza dei doni.

Quando l'idolo, portato su le spalle da quattro ercoli, si mostrò alfine tra i pilastri del vestibolo, e s'irraggiò alla luce aurorale, un lungo anelito di passione corse il popolo aspettante, un fremito come d'un vento di gioia volò sopra tutte le fronti. E la colonna si mosse. E la testa enorme del santo oscillava in alto, guardando innanzi a sé dalle due orbite vuote.

Nel cielo ora, in mezzo all'ascensione eguale e cupa, a tratti passavano solchi di meteore più vive; gruppi di nuvole sottili si distaccavano dall'orlo della zona, e galleggiavano lentamente dissolvendosi. Tutto il paese di Radusa [8] appariva in dietro come un monte di cenere che covasse il fuoco; e, dinanzi, le masse della campagna si perdevano con un luccichìo indistinto. Un gran cantico di rane empiva la sonorità della solitudine.

Su la strada del fiume il traino di Pallura fece ostacolo all'incedere. Era vuoto, ma conservava tracce di sangue in più parti. Imprecazioni irose scoppiarono d'improvviso nel silenzio. Giacobbe gridò:

— Mettiamoci il santo!

E il busto fu posato su le tavole e tirato a forza di braccia nel guado. La processione di battaglia così attraversava il confine. Lungo le file correvano lampi metallici; le acque invase rompevano in sprazzi luminosi, e tutta una corrente rossa fiammeggiava fra i pioppetti, nel lontano, verso le torri quadrangolari. Mascálico si scorgeva su una piccola

axes, with mattocks, with muskets, gathered on the square, in front of the church. And the idolaters shouted:

"San Pantaleone!"

Don Cònsolo, terrified by the uproar, had taken refuge in the back of a choir stall, behind the altar. A group of fanatics, led by Giacobbe, penetrated into the main chapel, forced the bronze grill, and reached the crypt, where the bust of the saint was kept. Three lamps, fed by olive oil, were burning gently in the humid air of the sanctuary; behind a pane of glass, the Christian idol was shining with its white head in the center of a great circular halo; and the walls disappeared under the richness of the votive offerings.

When the idol, carried on the shoulders of four giants, finally appeared between the pillars of the vestibule and was irradiated by the light of the aurora, a long sigh of passion ran through the waiting populace, and a quiver as of a breath of joy passed over the brows of all. And the column moved. And the enormous head of the saint swayed on high, looking ahead out of its two empty sockets.

In the heavens now, in the midst of the dull, even rise of the aurora, more active trails of meteors passed at times; clusters of thin clouds broke off from the edge of the zone, and floated away slowly, dissolving. The whole town of Radusa appeared, in back, like a heap of ashes in which fire was smouldering; and, in front, the masses of the countryside were lost in an indistinct glimmer. A great croaking of frogs filled the sonority of the solitude.

On the river road, Pallura's cart stood in the way of their advance. It was empty, but still showed traces of blood in various places. Irate imprecations suddenly burst forth in the silence. Giacobbe shouted:

"Let us put the saint in it!"

And the bust was placed on the boards and pulled through the ford by men's arms. The battle procession thus crossed the boundary. Along the ranks ran metallic flashes; the waters, invaded, broke into luminous spray, and an entire red current flamed between the poplars, into the distance, towards the quadrangular towers. Mascálico could

altura, in mezzo agli olivi, dormente. I cani abbaiavano
qua e là, con una furiosa persistenza di risposte. La colonna,
uscita dal guado, abbandonando la via comune, avanzava
a passi rapidi per una linea diretta che tagliava i campi.
Il busto d'argento era portato di nuovo a spalle, dominava
le teste degli uomini tra il grano altissimo, odorante e tutto
stellante di lucciole vive.

D'improvviso, un pastore, che stava dentro un covile di
paglia a guardare il grano, invaso da un pazzo sbigottimento
in cospetto di tanta gente armata, si diede a fuggire su per
la costa, strillando a squarciagola:

— Aiuto! aiuto!

E gli strilli echeggiavano nell'oliveto.

Allora fu che i Radusani fecero impeto. Fra i tronchi
degli alberi, fra le canne secche, il santo di argento tra-
ballava, dava tintinni sonori agli urti dei rami, s'illuminava
di lampi vivissimi ad ogni accenno di precipizio. Dieci,
dodici, venti schioppettate grandinarono in un balenìo
vibrante, una dopo l'altra su la massa delle case. Si udirono
crepiti, poi grida; poi si udì un gran sommovimento cla-
moroso: alcune porte si aprirono, altre si chiusero; caddero
vetri in frantumi, caddero vasi di basilico, spezzati su la via.
Un fumo bianco si levava nell'aria placidamente, dietro la
corsa degli assalitori, su per l'incandescenza celeste. Tutti,
accecati, in una furia belluina, gridavano:

— A morte! a morte!

Un gruppo di idolatri si manteneva in torno a san Pantaleone. Vituperii atroci contro San Gonselvo irrompevano
tra l'agitazione delle falci e delle ronche brandite.

— Ladro! Ladro! Pezzente! Le candele! Le candele!

Altri gruppi prendevano d'assalto le porte delle case, a
colpi d'accetta. E, come le porte sgangherate e scheggiate
cadevano, i Pantaleonidi [9] saltavano nell'interno urlando,
per uccidere. Femmine seminude si rifugiavano negli angoli,
implorando pietà; si difendevano dai colpi, afferrando le
armi e tagliandosi le dita; rotolavano distese sul pavimento,
in mezzo a mucchi di coperte e di lenzuoli da cui uscivano

be seen on a small height, in the midst of the olive trees, asleep. The dogs barked here and there, with furious persistence in their replies. The column, issuing from the ford, left the main road to advance with rapid steps by a direct path that cut through the fields. The silver bust was again carried on men's shoulders; it stood out above the men's heads among the lofty grain, which was fragrant and all starry with sparkling fireflies.

Suddenly, a shepherd guarding the grain inside a hut of straw, seized with mad terror at the sight of so many armed men, took to his heels and fled up the slope, shouting at the top of his lungs:

"Help! Help!"

And the shouts echoed in the olive grove.

Then it was that the Radusans attacked. In the midst of the tree-trunks, in the midst of the dry reeds, the saint of silver tottered, rang sonorously on striking against the branches, and was illuminated by brilliant flashes every time it threatened to fall. Ten, twelve, twenty musket-shots hailed one after another in a vibrating succession of flashes against the mass of houses. Crashes were heard, then cries; then a great noisy commotion arose: some doors were opened, others were closed; panes of glass fell in fragments, vases of basil shattered on the street. A white smoke arose placidly in the air, in the wake of the attackers, up into the incandescence of the heavens. All, blinded, in a bestial fury, shouted:

"Death! Death!"

A group of idolaters kept closely around San Pantaleone. Atrocious curses against San Gonselvo burst out among the waving sickles and the brandished billhooks.

"Thief! Thief! Beggar! The candles! The candles!"

Other groups attacked the doors of houses with axe-blows. And as the doors were torn from their hinges and fell in splinters, the followers of San Pantaleone leaped inside howling, to kill. Half-naked women took refuge in corners, imploring pity; they defended themselves against blows, seizing the weapons and cutting their fingers; they rolled and stretched out on the floor, amid heaps of

le loro flosce carni nutrite di rape.

Giacobbe alto smilzo rossastro, fascio di aride ossa reso formidabile dalla passione, condottiero della strage, si arrestava ad ogni tratto per fare un largo gesto imperatorio sopra tutte le teste con una gran falce fienaia. Andava innanzi, impavido, senza cappello, nel nome di san Pantaleone. Più di trenta uomini lo seguivano. E tutti avevano la sensazione confusa e ottusa di camminare in mezzo a un incendio, sopra un terreno oscillante, sotto una vòlta ardente che fosse per crollare.

Ma da ogni parte cominciarono ad accorrere i difensori, i Mascalicesi [10] forti e neri come mulatti, sanguinarii, che si battevano con lunghi coltelli a scatto, e tiravano al ventre e alla gola, accompagnando di voci gutturali il colpo. La mischia si ritraeva a poco a poco verso la chiesa; dai tetti di due o tre case già scoppiavano le fiamme; un'orda di femmine e di fanciulli fuggiva a precipizio tra gli olivi, presa dal pànico, senza più lume negli occhi.[11]

Allora tra i maschi, senza impedimento di lagrime e di lamenti, la lotta a corpo a corpo si strinse più feroce. Sotto il cielo color di ruggine, il terreno si copriva di cadaveri. Stridevano vituperii mozzi tra i denti dei colpiti; e continuo tra i clamori persisteva il grido dei Radusani:

— Le candele! Le candele!

Ma la porta della chiesa restava sbarrata, enorme, tutta di quercia, stellante di chiodi. I Mascalicesi la difendevano contro gli urti e contro le scuri. Il santo d'argento, impassibile e bianco, oscillava nel folto della mischia, ancora sostenuto su le spalle dei quattro ercoli che sanguinavano tutti dalla testa ai piedi, non volendo cadere. Ed era nel supremo voto degli assalitori mettere l'idolo su l'altare del nemico.

Ora mentre i Mascalicesi si battevano da leoni, prodigiosamente, sul gradino di pietra, Giacobbe disparve all'improvviso, girò il fianco dell'edifizio, cercando un varco non difeso per penetrare nel sacrario. E come vide un'apertura

blankets and sheets from which protruded their flabby flesh nourished on turnips.

Giacobbe, tall, lean, reddish, a bundle of dry bones made formidable by passion, the leader of the slaughter, stopped every now and then to make a broad gesture of command over all the heads with a great sickle. He went ahead, fearless, hatless, in the name of San Pantaleone. More than thirty men followed in his train. And all had the confused, dull sensation that they were walking in the midst of a conflagration, on an unstable ground, under a burning vault that was about to collapse.

But from every direction the defenders began to hasten up, the men of Mascálico, strong and dark as mulattoes, bloodthirsty, who fought with long switch-blade knives, and struck for the belly and the throat, accompanying the blows with guttural grunts. The melee moved slowly back towards the church; from the roofs of two or three houses flames were already bursting; a horde of women and children rushed in headlong flight through the olive trees, seized by panic, blinded with terror.

Then between the men, with no hindrance from tears or laments, the hand-to-hand struggle was joined even more ferociously. Under the rust-colored heaven, the terrain was covered with corpses. Curses were shrieked and cut short between the teeth of those smitten; and continually, above the shouting, prevailed the cry of the Radusans:

"The candles! The candles!"

But the door of the church remained barred, enormous, wholly of oak, studded with nails. The men of Mascálico defended it against buffets and against axes. The silver saint, impassive and white, swayed in the thick of the melee, still held aloft on the shoulders of the four giants who were bleeding from head to foot but who refused to fall. And the supreme desire of the attackers was to place their idol on the altar of the enemy.

Now, while the men of Mascálico were fighting like lions, prodigiously, on the stone step, Giacobbe suddenly disappeared, and went around the side of the building, seeking an undefended passage to enter the sanctuary. And when

a poca altezza da terra, vi si arrampicò, vi rimase tenuto ai fianchi dall'angustia, vi si contorse, fin che non giunse a far passare il suo lungo corpo giù per lo spiraglio. Il cordiale aroma dell'incenso vaniva nel gelo notturno della casa di Dio. A tentoni nel buio, guidato dal fragore della pugna esterna, quell'uomo camminò verso la porta, inciampando nelle sedie, ferendosi alla faccia, alle mani. Rimbombava già il lavorìo furioso delle accette radusane su la durezza della quercia, quando egli cominciò con un ferro a forzare le serrature, anelante, soffocato da una violenta palpitazione di ambascia che gli diminuiva la forza, con la vista attraversata da bagliori fatui, con le ferite che gli dolevano e gli mettevano un'onda tiepida giù per la cute.

— San Pantaleone! San Pantaleone!—gridarono di fuori le voci rauche de' suoi che sentivano cedere lentamente la porta, raddoppiando gli urti e i colpi di scure. A traverso il legno giungeva lo schianto grave dei corpi che stramazzavano, il colpo secco del coltello che inchiodava là qualcuno per le reni. E pareva a Giacobbe che tutta la navata rimbombasse al battito del suo selvaggio cuore.

V

Dopo un ultimo sforzo, la porta si aprì. I Radusani si precipitarono con un immenso urlo di vittoria, passando su i corpi degli uccisi, traendo il santo d'argento all'altare. E una viva oscillazione di riverberi invase d'un tratto l'oscurità della navata, fece brillare l'oro dei candelabri, le canne dell'organo, in alto. E in quel chiaror fulvo, che or sì or no dall'incendio delle prossime case vibrava dentro, una seconda lotta si strinse. I corpi avviluppati rotolavano su i mattoni, non si distaccavano più, balzavano insieme qua e là nei divincolamenti della rabbia, urtavano e finivano sotto le panche, su i gradini delle cappelle, contro gli spigoli dei confessionali. Nella concavità raccolta della casa di Dio, il suono agghiacciante del ferro che penetra nelle carni o che scivola su le ossa, quell'unico gemito rotto dell'uomo che è colpito in una parte vitale, quello scricchiolìo che dà la

he saw an opening not high above the ground, he climbed up to it, was caught by the hips due to the narrowness, and twisted through to pass his long body down the aperture. The heady aroma of incense was dying away in the nocturnal cold of the house of God. Feeling his way in the dark, guided by the din of the fighting outside, the man went towards the door, stumbling against chairs and hurting his face and hands. The hacking of the Radusans' hatchets was already resounding furiously on the hard oak, when he began to force the locks with an iron bar, panting, stifled by a violent shortness of breath and palpitation which diminished his strength, with his range of vision crossed by imaginary flashes of fire, with his wounds hurting him and pouring a warm stream down his skin.

"San Pantaleone! San Pantaleone!" cried the voices of his men from without as they felt the door gradually give way and redoubled their buffets and their axe-blows. Through the wood came the heavy thud of bodies falling wounded, and the dry blow of the knife as it nailed someone to the spot through the loins. And to Giacobbe it seemed as if the whole nave were echoing to the beat of his savage heart.

V

After a last effort, the door opened. The Radusans rushed in with an immense shout of victory, passing over the bodies of the dead, carrying the silver saint to the altar. And brilliantly wavering reflections suddenly invaded the darkness of the nave, illuminated the gold of the candlesticks, the pipes of the organ on high. And in that tawny glow which now and again was reflected within from the burning of the nearby houses, a second battle was joined. Tightly clasped bodies rolled on the tiled floor, did not become disengaged, but bounded together hither and yon in writhings of rage, struck against the benches and rolled under them, onto the steps of the chapels, against the edges of the confessionals. In the secluded concavity of the house of God, the chilling sound of iron cutting through flesh or scraping on bone, the single broken groan of the man pierced in a vital

cassa del cranio nell'infrangersi al colpo, il ruggito di chi non vuol morire, l'ilarità atroce di chi è giunto ad uccidere, tutto distintamente si ripercoteva. E il mite odore dell'incenso vagava sul conflitto.

L'idolo d'argento non anche aveva attinto la gloria dell'altare, poiché un cerchio ostile ne precludeva l'accesso. Giacobbe si batteva con la falce, ferito in più parti, senza cedere un palmo del gradino che primo aveva conquistato. Non rimanevano se non due a sorreggere il santo. L'enorme testa bianca barcollava come ebra sul bulicame del sangue iroso. I Mascalicesi imperversavano.

Allora san Pantaleone cadde sul pavimento, dando un tintinno acuto che penetrò nel cuore di Giacobbe più a dentro che punta di coltello. Come il rosso falciatore si slanciò per rialzarlo, un gran diavolo d'uomo con un colpo di ronca stese il nemico su la schiena. Due volte questi si risollevò, e altri due colpi lo rigettarono. Il sangue gli inondava tutta la faccia e il petto e le mani; per le spalle e per le braccia le ossa gli biancicavano scoperte nei tagli profondi; ma pure egli si ostinava a riavventarsi. Inviperiti da quella feroce tenacità di vita, tre, quattro, cinque bifolchi insieme gli diedero a furia nel ventre d'onde le viscere sgorgarono. Il fanatico cadde riverso, battè la nuca sul busto d'argento, si rivoltò d'un tratto bocconi con la faccia contro il metallo, con la branche stese innanzi, con le gambe contratte. E san Pantaleone fu perduto.

part, the thud produced by the shell of the cranium shattered by a blow, the roar of one who does not want to die, the atrocious hilarity of one who has succeeded in killing—all resounded distinctly. And the mild odor of the incense hovered over the conflict.

The silver idol had not yet reached the glory of the altar, since a hostile circle blocked off access to it. Giacobbe was fighting with the sickle, although wounded in several places, without yielding an inch of the step which he had conquered earlier. Only two were left now to support the saint. The enormous head staggered as if drunk over the seething flood of wrathful gore. The men of Mascálico were fighting furiously.

Then San Pantaleone fell to the floor, giving a sharp metallic sound which pierced Giacobbe's heart more deeply than the point of a knife. As the red sickle-bearer rushed forth to lift him up again, a great devil of a man stretched his enemy on his back with a blow from a billhook. Twice Giacobbe tried to rise, and twice another blow cast him down again. Blood was inundating his whole face and chest and hands; on his shoulders and arms his bones were visible, white in the deep cuts; and even yet he persisted in returning to the fight. Infuriated by that ferocious tenacity of life, three, four, five ploughmen together struck him furiously in the belly, whence his entrails gushed forth. The fanatic fell over on his back, struck the back of his neck on the silver bust, and suddenly turned over on his stomach with his face against the metal, with his claw-like hands stretched in front of him, with his legs drawn up. And San Pantaleone was lost.

Luigi Pirandello

(1867–1936)

NEXT TO d'Annunzio, Luigi Pirandello is the best-known figure of modern Italian literature. He began as a writer of a great many short stories (*Novelle per un anno,* "Stories for a Year," so called because he originally intended to include 360 in the collection), and passed to the novel with *Il fu Mattia Pascal* ("The Late Matthew Pascal," 1904), *Uno nessuno e centomila* ("One, No One and a Hundred Thousand," 1910) and *Si gira* ("Shoot!", 1915). From the time of the First World War, Pirandello turned to the drama for the expression of his philosophical problems, and became known as one of the world's leading dramatists. His best-known plays were *Così è se vi pare* ("Right You Are," 1917), *Sei personaggi in cerca d'autore* ("Six Characters in Search of an Author," 1921), and *Enrico Quarto* ("Henry IV," 1922). Pirandello was awarded the Nobel prize for literature in 1934.

In the majority of his works, Pirandello lays emphasis on the nature and manifestations of human personality. What is an individual? Can a man, once he is thought dead, cast off his old personality and assume a new one (*Il fu Mattia Pascal*)? If a man has temporarily changed his personality through insanity, can he use his new character as a refuge from which he can come forth to complete a revenge called for by his old character (*Enrico IV*)? What

is the relation between actors' disguises on the stage and the reality of the personages they represent (*Si gira; Sei personaggi*)? Can a person's identity really be pinned down at all, in the absence of all documentation and if the person's nearest relatives give diametrically opposing accounts of the relationship (*Così è se vi pare*)? These problems were perhaps suggested to Pirandello, at least in part, by his wife's insanity; but they are also inherent in the Italian cultural situation, where the Roman law insists on absolute identity between name and person, and where a bureaucratic government makes registration in the *anàgrafe* (vital statistics bureau) and possession of an official identity card an absolute prerequisite for any sort of participation in civil existence.

The story here reproduced, *Marsina stretta,* is perhaps atypical, in that it shows little of Pirandello's preoccupation with the philosophy of personality. It will be noticed, however, that its main point lies in the way in which old Professor Gori frees himself from the constraining effect of the tight frock-coat and at the same time frees the bride and groom from the constraining effect of hypocritical social attitudes so that they are free to follow the natural bent of their own true characters.

MARSINA STRETTA

di Luigi Pirandello

Dɪ sᴏʟɪᴛᴏ il professor Gori aveva molta pazienza con la vecchia domestica, che lo serviva da circa vent'anni. Quel giorno però, per la prima volta in vita sua, gli toccava d'indossar la marsina, ed era fuori della grazia di Dio.[1]

Già il solo pensiero, che una cosa di così poco conto potesse mettere in orgasmo un animo come il suo, alieno da tutte le frivolezze e oppresso da tante gravi cure intellettuali, bastava a irritarlo. L'irritazione poi gli cresceva, considerando che con questo suo animo, potesse prestarsi a indossar quell'abito prescritto da una sciocca consuetudine per certe rappresentazioni di gala con cui la vita s'illude d'offrire a sé stessa una festa o un divertimento.

E poi, Dio mio,[2] con quel corpaccio d'ippopòtamo, di bestiaccia antidiluviana . . .

E sbuffava, il professore, e fulminava con gli occhi la domestica che, piccola e bòffice come una balla, si beava[3] alla vista del grosso padrone in quell'insolito abito di parata, senz'avvertire, la sciagurata, che mortificazione dovevano averne tutt'intorno i vecchi e onesti mobili volgari e i poveri libri nella stanzetta quasi buja e in disordine.

Quella marsina, s'intende, non l'aveva di suo, il professor Gori. La prendeva a nolo. Il commesso d'un negozio vicino glien'aveva portate su in casa una bracciata, per la scelta; e ora, con l'aria d'un compitissimo *arbiter elegantiarum*,[4] tenendo gli occhi semichiusi e sulle labbra un sorrisetto di compiacente superiorità, lo esaminava, lo faceva voltare di qua e di la,—*Pardon! Pardon!*—, e quindi concludeva,

THE TIGHT FROCK-COAT

by Luigi Pirandello

Usually Professor Gori was very patient with the old housemaid, who had been his servant for around twenty years. On that day, however, for the first time in his life, he had to put on a frock-coat, and was in a state of total rage.

Just the mere thought that a matter of so little importance could excite a mind like his, which was foreign to all frivolity and burdened by so many serious intellectual cares, was enough to irritate him. Then his irritation grew, considering that with this mind of his, he could lower himself to putting on that garb required by a foolish custom for certain gala occasions with which life deludes itself that it is indulging in a feast or an amusement.

And then, good Heavens, with that huge body like a hippopotamus, like an antediluvian monster . . .

And the professor was puffing and glaring at the housemaid, who, small and plump like a bale of cotton, was in ecstasies at the sight of her huge master in that unaccustomed parade dress, without realizing, poor thing, what mortification this must have caused to all the honest old workaday furniture around and the poor books in the little half-darkened, disordered room.

That frock-coat, of course, did not belong to Professor Gori. He was hiring it. The clerk of a nearby shop had brought up an armful to him at home, for him to choose from; and now, with the manner of a highly skilled judge of fashion, with his eyes half-closed and on his lips a little smile of complacent superiority, he was scrutinizing him, having him turn this way and that, saying *Pardon me!*

scotendo il ciuffo:

— Non va.

Il professore sbuffava ancora una volta e s'asciugava il sudore.

Ne aveva provate otto, nove, non sapeva più quante. Una più stretta dell'altra. E quel colletto in cui si sentiva impiccato! e quello sparato che gli strabuzzava, già tutto sgualcito, dal panciotto! e quella cravattina bianca inamidata e pendente, a cui ancora doveva fare il nodo, e non sapeva come!

Alla fine il commesso si compiacque di dire:

— Ecco, questa sì. Non potremmo trovar di meglio, creda pure, signore.

Il professor Gori tornò prima a fulminare [5] con uno sguardo la serva, per impedire che ripetesse:—*Dipinta! Dipinta!* [6]—; poi si guardò la marsina, in considerazione della quale, senza dubbio, quel commesso gli dava del signore: [7] poi si rivolse al commesso:

— Non ne ha più altre con sé?

— Ne ho portate su dodici, signore!

— Questa sarebbe la dodicesima?

— La dodicesima, a servirla.

— E allora va benone!

Era più stretta delle altre. Quel giovanotto, un po' risentito, concesse:

— Strettina è, ma può andare. Se volesse aver la bontà di guardarsi allo specchio . . .

— Grazie tante!—squittì il professore.—Basta lo spettacolo che sto offrendo a lei e alla mia signora serva.

Quegli, allora, pieno di dignità, inchinò appena il capo, e via, con le altre undici marsine.

— Ma è credibile?—proruppe con un gemito rabbioso il professore, provandosi ad alzar le braccia.

Si recò a guardare un profumato biglietto d'invito sul cassettone, e sbuffò di nuovo. Il convegno era per le otto, in casa della sposa, in via Milano. Venti minuti di cammino! Ed erano già le sette e un quarto.

Rientrò nella stanzetta la vecchia serva che aveva ac-

Pardon me!, and then concluding, shaking his forelock:
"It won't do."

The professor would puff once more and wipe off the sweat.

He had tried eight, nine, no telling how many. Each one tighter than the last. And that collar in which he felt strangled! and that shirt-front which was bulging, already rumpled, out of his waistcoat! and that dangling starched white tie, in which he still had to make a knot, and did not know how to!

In the end the clerk condescended to say:
"There, this one will do. We couldn't find anything better, believe me, sir."

Professor Gori first glared again at the housemaid, to keep her from repeating "Perfect! Perfect!"; then he looked at the frock-coat, on account of which, undoubtedly, the clerk was calling him "sir"; then he turned to the clerk:

"You have no others with you?"
"I brought up twelve of them, sir!"
"And this would be the twelfth?"
"The twelfth, at your service."
"Very good, then!"

It was tighter than the others. The young man, somewhat resentfully, conceded:

"It is a trifle tight, but it will be all right. If you would be so kind as to look at yourself in the mirror . . ."

"No, thank you!" yelped the professor. "I am already offering enough of a spectacle to you and to this lady, my housemaid."

The young man, then, full of dignity, scarcely nodded his head, and departed with the other eleven frock-coats.

"But can you believe it?" the professor burst out with a groan of rage, as he tried to lift his arms.

He went over to look at the perfumed invitation on the dresser, and puffed again. The time of meeting was set for eight, at the bride's home in Via Milano. A twenty-minutes' walk; and it was already a quarter past seven.

The old housemaid, who had gone to the door with the

compagnato fino alla porta il commesso.

— Zitta!—le impose subito il professore.—Provate, se vi riesce, a finir di strozzarmi con questa cravatta.

— Piano piano . . . il colletto . . . —gli raccomandò la vecchia serva. E dopo essersi forbite ben bene con un fazzoletto le mani tremicchianti, s'accinse all'impresa.

Regnò per cinque minuti il silenzio: il professore e tutta la stanza intorno parevano sospesi, come in attesa del giudizio universale.

— Fatto?

— Eh . . . —sospirò quella.

Il professor Gori scattò in piedi, urlando:

— Lasciate! Mi proverò io! Non ne posso più! [8]

Ma, appena si presentò allo specchio, diede in tali escandescenze,[9] che quella poverina si spaventò. Si fece, prima di tutto, un goffo inchino; ma, nell'inchinarsi, vedendo le due falde aprirsi e subito richiudersi, si rivoltò come un gatto che si senta qualcosa legata alla coda; e, nel rivoltarsi, *trac!,* la marsina gli si spaccò sotto un'ascella.

Diventò furibondo.

— Scucita! Scucita soltanto!—lo rassicurò subito, accorrendo, la vecchia serva.—Se la cavi, gliela ricucio!

— Ma se non ho più tempo!—urlò, esasperato, il professore.—Andrò così, per castigo! Così . . . Vuol dire che non porgerò la mano a nessuno. Lasciatemi andare!

S'annodò furiosamente la cravatta; nascose sotto il pastrano la vergogna di quell'abito; e via.

Alla fin fine, però, doveva esser contento, che diamine! Si celebrava quella mattina il matrimonio d'una sua antica allieva, a lui carissima: Cèsara Reis, la quale, per suo mezzo, con quelle nozze, otteneva il premio di tanti sacrifizi durati negli interminabili anni di scuola.

Il professor Gori, via facendo, si mise a pensare alla strana combinazione per cui quel matrimonio s'effettuava.

clerk, came back into the little room.

"Quiet!" the professor ordered her immediately. "Try, if you can, to finish the job of strangling me with this tie."

"Take it easy . . . the collar . . ." the old housemaid urged him. And after cleaning her trembling hands carefully with a handkerchief, she set about the job.

Silence prevailed for five minutes; the professor and the whole surrounding room seemed to be suspended, as if waiting for the Last Judgment.

"Finished?"

"Eh . . ." she sighed.

Professor Gori leaped to his feet, shouting:

"Stop! I'll try! I can't stand it any longer!"

But, as soon as he got in front of the mirror, he burst out in such expressions of rage, that the poor woman was terrified. First of all, he made a clumsy bow to himself; but, as he bowed, seeing the two coat-tails open and immediately close again, he turned around like a cat that feels something tied to its tail; and, as he turned around, *r-r-rip!*, the frock-coat split open under his armpit.

He was beside himself with rage.

"It's unsewed! It's just come unsewed!" the old housemaid reassured him, hurrying up immediately. "Take it off and I'll re-sew it for you!"

"But I haven't any time left!" the professor roared exasperatedly. "I shall go like this, as a punishment! Like this . . . It means I won't shake hands with anybody. Let me go!"

He furiously knotted his tie, hid the shame of that frock-coat under his top-coat, and away he went.

In the last analysis, however, he ought to have been glad, what the deuce! That morning they were holding the wedding of a former student of his, who was very dear to him: Cèsara Reis, who, through his aid, was reaping by that marriage the reward of so many sacrifices which she had made during her endless years of school.

Professor Gori, as he went along, began to think of the strange coincidence by which this marriage had come

Sì; ma come si chiamava intanto lo sposo, quel ricco signore vedovo che un giorno gli s'era presentato all'Istituto di Magistero per avere indicata da lui una istitutrice per le sue bambine?

— Grimi? Griti? No, Mitri! Ah, ecco, sì: Mitri, Mitri.

Così era nato quel matrimonio. La Reis, povera figliuola, rimasta orfana [10] a quindici anni, aveva eroicamente provveduto al mantenimento suo e della vecchia madre, lavorando un po' da sarta, un po' dando lezioni particolari; ed era riuscita a conseguire il diploma di professoressa.[11] Egli, ammirato di tanta costanza, di tanta forza d'animo, pregando, brigando, aveva potuto procacciarle un posto a Roma, nelle scuole complementari.[12] Richiesto da quel signor Griti . . .

— Griti, Griti, ecco! Si chiama Griti. Che Mitri!—gli aveva indicato la Reis. Dopo alcuni giorni se l'era veduto tornar davanti afflitto, imbarazzato. Cèsara Reis non aveva voluto accettare il posto d'istitutrice, in considerazione della sua età, del suo stato, della vecchia mamma che non poteva lasciar sola e, soprattutto, del facile malignare della gente. E chi sa con qual voce, con quale espressione gli aveva dette queste cose, la birichina!

Bella figliuola, la Reis: e di quella bellezza che a lui piaceva maggiormente: d'una bellezza a cui i diuturni dolori (non per nulla il Gori era professore d'italiano: diceva proprio così, "*i diuturni* dolori" [13]) d'una bellezza a cui i diuturni dolori avevano dato la grazia d'una soavissima mestizia, una cara e dolce nobiltà.

Certo quel signor Grimi . . .

— Ho gran paura che si chiami proprio Grimi, ora che ci penso!

Certo quel signor Grimi, fin dal primo vederla, se n'era perdutamente innamorato. Cose che càpitano, pare. E tre o quattro volte, quantunque senza speranza, era tornato a insistere, invano; alla fine, aveva pregato lui, il professor Gori, lo aveva anzi scongiurato d'interporsi, perché la signorina Reis, così bella, così modesta, così virtuosa, se

about. Yes; but what, in the meanwhile, was the name of the groom, that rich widower who, one day, had come to him at the Teachers' College to ask him to suggest a girl to tutor his daughters?

"Grimi? Griti? No, Mitri! Ah, yes, that's it: Mitri, Mitri."

That had been the origin of that marriage. Miss Reis, poor girl, had been left an orphan at fifteen years of age, and had heroically taken care of her own and her aged mother's upkeep, working a little as a seamstress, and a little by giving private lessons; and she had succeeded in getting a teacher's diploma. He, admiring such constancy and such strength of character, had, by begging and by intriguing, been able to get her a place at Rome, in the supplementary schools. When that Mr. Griti had asked him . . .

"Griti, Griti, that's it! His name is Griti. It's not Mitri at all!" . . . he had suggested Miss Reis to him. A few days later he [Griti] had come back upset and embarrassed. Cèsara Reis had not been willing to take the position as tutor, on account of her age, her rank, her old mother whom she could not leave alone, and especially people's readiness to gossip. And who knows with what tone of voice, with what expression the little rascal had said these things to him!

Beautiful, that Reis girl: and with that kind of beauty which he liked most; with a beauty on which diuturnal sorrows (not for nothing was Gori a professor of Italian: he said it just that way, "diuturnal sorrows"), with a beauty on which diuturnal sorrows had conferred the grace of a very gentle sadness, a sweet and lovable nobility.

Certainly that Mr. Grimi . . .

"I'm very much afraid that his name really is Grimi, now that I think of it!"

Certainly that Mr. Grimi, from the very first time he saw her, had fallen madly in love with her. Just one of those things, apparently. And three or four times, although without hope, he had come back and insisted, in vain; in the end, he had asked him, Professor Gori—in fact, he had begged him—to intervene, to ask Miss Reis, who was so

non l'istitutrice diventasse la seconda madre delle sue bambine. E perché no? S'era interposto, felicissimo, il professor Gori, e la Reis aveva accettato: e ora il matrimonio si celebrava, a dispetto dei parenti del signore . . . Grimi o Griti o Mitri, che vi si erano opposti accanitamente:

— E che il diavolo se li porti via tutti quanti!—concluse, sbuffando ancora una volta, il grosso professore.

Conveniva intanto recare alla sposa un mazzolino di fiori. Ella lo aveva tanto pregato perché le facesse da testimonio; ma il professore le aveva fatto notare che, in qualità di testimonio, avrebbe dovuto poi farle un regalo degno della cospicua condizione dello sposo, e non poteva: in coscienza non poteva. Bastava il sacrifizio della marsina. Ma un mazzolino, intanto, sì, ecco. E il professor Gori entrò con molta titubanza e impacciatissimo in un negozio di fiori, dove gli misero insieme un gran fascio di verdura con pochissimi fiori e molta spesa.

Pervenuto in via Milano, vide in fondo, davanti al portone in cui abitava la Reis, una frotta di curiosi. Suppose che fosse tardi; che già nell'atrio ci fossero le carrozze per il corteo nuziale, e che tutta quella genta stesse lì per assistere alla sfilata. Avanzò il passo. Ma perché tutti quei curiosi lo guardavano a quel modo? La marsina era nascosta dal soprabito. Forse . . . le falde? Si guardò dietro. No: non si vedevano. E dunque? Che era accaduto? Perché il portone era socchiuso?

Il portinajo, con aria compunta, gli domandò:
— Va su per il matrimonio, il signore?
— Sì, signore. Invitato.
— Ma . . . sa, il matrimonio non si fa più.
— Come?
— La povera signora . . . la madre . . .
— Morta?—esclamò il Gori, stupefatto, guardando il portone.
— Questa notte, improvvisamente.
Il professore restò lì, come un ceppo.

beautiful, so modest, so virtuous, to become, if not the tutor, the second mother of his girls. And why not? Professor Gori had been very glad to intervene, and Miss Reis had accepted; and now the wedding was being held, in spite of the relatives of Mr. . . . . Grimi or Griti or Mitri, who had opposed it bitterly:

"And the devil take the whole crowd of them!" concluded the fat professor, puffing once again.

In the meanwhile he had to bring the bride a little bouquet of flowers. She had begged him so insistently to serve as a witness; but the professor had pointed out to her that, as a witness, he ought then to have given her a wedding present suitable to the high social standing of the groom, and he wasn't able to; in all conscience, he wasn't able to. The sacrifice of the frock-coat was enough. But a bouquet, yes, he could. And Professor Gori went, with great hesitation and embarrassment, into a flower-shop, where they put together for him a large bunch of greenery with very few flowers and at great cost.

When he arrived at Via Milano, he saw at the end, in front of the gate of the apartment house at which Miss Reis lived, a knot of idlers. He imagined he must be late; that the carriages for the wedding procession must already be in the courtyard, and that all those people were there to watch the parade. He quickened his step. But why were all those idlers looking at him in that way? The frock-coat was hidden by the overcoat. Perhaps . . . the coat-tails? He looked in back of himself. No: they were not visible. Well, then? What had happened? Why was the gate half-closed?

The concierge, with a mournful air, asked him:

"Are you going upstairs for the wedding?"

"Yes, sir. A guest."

"But . . . you know, the wedding is off."

"What?"

"The poor lady . . . the mother . . ."

"Dead?" exclaimed Gori, in amazement, looking at the door.

"Last night, unexpectedly."

The professor stood there stock-still.

— Possibile? La madre? La signora Reis?

E volse in giro uno sguardo ai radunati, come per leggere ne' loro occhi la conferma dell'incredibile notizia. Il mazzo di fiori gli cadde di mano. Si chinò per raccattarlo, ma sentì la scucitura della marsina allargarsi sotto l'ascella, e rimase a metà. Oh Dio! la marsina . . . già! La marsina per le nozze, castigata così a comparire ora davanti alla morte. Che fare? Andar su, parato a quel modo? tornare indietro? —Raccattò il mazzo, poi, imbalordito, lo porse al portinajo.

— Mi faccia il piacere, me lo tenga lei.

Ed entrò. Si provò a salire a balzi la scala; vi riuscì per la prima branca soltanto. All'ultimo piano—maledetto pancione!—non tirava più fiato.

Introdotto nel salottino, sorprese in coloro che vi stavano radunati un certo imbarazzo, una confusione subito ripressa, come se qualcuno, al suo entrare, fosse scappato via; o come se d'un tratto si fosse troncata un'intima e animatissima conversazione.

Già impacciato per conto suo, il professor Gori si fermò poco oltre l'entrata; si guardò attorno perplesso; si sentì sperduto, quasi in mezzo a un campo nemico. Eran tutti signoroni, quelli: parenti e amici dello sposo. Quella vecchia lì era forse la madre; quelle altre due, che parevano zitellone, forse sorelle o cugine. S'inchinò goffamente. (Oh Dio, daccapo la marsina . . .) E, curvo, come tirato da dentro, volse un altro sguardo attorno, quasi per accertarsi se mai qualcuno avesse avvertito il crepito di quella maledettissima scucitura sotto l'ascella. Nessuno rispose al suo saluto, quasi che il lutto, la gravità del momento non consentissero neppure un lieve cenno del capo. Alcuni (forse intimi della famiglia) stavano costernati attorno a un signore, nel quale al Gori, guardando bene, parve di riconoscere lo sposo. Trasse un respiro di sollievo e gli s'appressò, premuroso.

— Signor Grimi . . .

THE TIGHT FROCK-COAT

"Is it possible? The mother? Mrs. Reis?"

And he glanced around the group gathered there, as if to read in their eyes the confirmation of the incredible news. The bouquet fell from his hand. He bent to pick it up, but felt the torn seam of the frock-coat grow larger under his armpit. Oh, Heavens! the frock-coat! . . . indeed! The frock-coat for the wedding, purified thus to appear now in the presence of death. What should he do? Go on up, decked out in this way? Go back?—He picked up the bouquet, then, as if dazed, handed it to the concierge.

"Do me a favor; you keep it for me."

And he entered. He tried to go up the stairs two at a time, but succeeded only for the first flight. At the top floor—curses on his fat paunch!—he was completely out of breath.

When he had been shown into the parlor, he noted in the people who were gathered there a certain embarrassment, a quickly repressed confusion, as if someone, at his entry, had hurried away, or as if an intimate and very lively conversation had suddenly been cut short.

Professor Gori, already embarrassed on his own account, stopped a little beyond the entrance; he looked around in perplexity; he felt lost, almost as if in the middle of an enemy camp. They were all very high-class people; relatives and friends of the groom. That old woman there was perhaps his mother; those two others, who seemed to be old maids, were perhaps sisters or cousins. He bowed awkwardly. (Oh Heavens, the frock-coat again . . .) And, bent over, as if pulled from within, he looked around again, as if to discover whether anyone had noticed the tearing noise of that accursed unstitched seam under the armpit. No one replied to his bow, as if the mourning and the seriousness of the occasion did not allow even a slight nod of the head. Some (perhaps close friends of the family) were standing in consternation around a gentleman, in whom Gori, on looking carefully, thought he recognized the groom. He heaved a sigh of relief and went up to him, full of concern.

"Mr. Grimi . . ."

— Migri, prego.

— Ah già, Migri . . . ci penso da un'ora, mi creda! Dicevo Grimi, Mitri, Griti . . . e non m'è venuto in mente Migri! Scusi . . . Io sono il professor Fabio Gori, si ricordera . . . quantunque ora mi veda in . . .

— Piacere, ma . . . —fece quegli, osservandolo con fredda alterigia; poi, come sovvenendosi:—Ah, Gori . . . già! lei sarebbe quello . . . sì, dico, l'autore . . . l'autore, se vogliamo, indiretto del matrimonio! Mio fratello m'ha raccontato . . .

— Come, come? scusi, lei sarebbe il fratello?

— Carlo Migri, a servirla.

— Favorirmi, grazie. Somigliantissimo, perbacco! Mi scusi, signor Gri . . . Migri già, ma . . . ma questo fulmine a ciel sereno . . . Già! Io purtroppo . . . cioè, purtroppo no: non ho da recarmelo a colpa diciamo . . . ma sì, indirettamente, per combinazione, diciamo, ho contribuito . . .

Il Migri lo interruppe con un gesto della mano, e si alzò.

— Permetta che la presenti a mia madre.

— Onoratissimo, si figuri!

Fu condotto davanti alla vecchia signora, che ingombrava con la sua enorme pinguedine mezzo canapè, vestita di nero, con una specie di cuffia pur nera sui capelli lanosi che le contornavano la faccia piatta, giallastra, quasi di cartapecora.

— Mamma, il professor Gori. Sai? quello che aveva combinato il matrimonio di Andrea.

La vecchia signora sollevò le pàlpebre gravi sonnolente, mostrando, uno più aperto e l'altro meno, gli occhi torbidi, ovati, quasi senza sguardo.

— In verità,—corresse il professore, inchinandosi questa volta con trepidante riguardo per la marsina scucita,—in verità, ecco . . . combinato no: non . . . non sarebbe la parola . . . Io, semplicemente . . .

— Voleva dare un'istitutrice alle mie nipotine,—compì la frase la vecchia signora, con voce cavernosa.—Benissimo!

"Migri, please."

"Ah yes, Migri . . . I've been thinking of it for an hour, believe me! I was saying Grimi, Mitri, Griti . . . and I didn't think of Migri! Excuse me . . . I am Professor Fabio Gori, you will remember . . . although now you see me in . . ."

"A pleasure, but . . ." the man said, looking at him with cold hauteur; then, as if remembering: "Ah, Gori . . . yes! You must be the man . . . yes, I mean, the author . . . the author, if we want to put it that way, of the marriage, indirectly! My brother has told me . . ."

"What, what? I beg your pardon, are you the brother?"

"Carlo Migri, at your service."

"Excuse me, please. You look exactly like him, by Jove! Excuse me, Mr. Gri . . . oh yes, Migri, but . . . but this bolt from the blue . . . Yes! Unfortunately I . . . that is to say, not unfortunately; I have nothing to blame myself for, shall we say . . . but yes, indirectly, by chance, shall we say, I have contributed . . ."

Migri interrupted him with a gesture, and stood up.

"Allow me to introduce you to my mother."

"I should be very much honored, of course."

He was led in front of the old lady, who filled half the sofa with her enormous bulk, dressed in black, with a kind of cap, also black, on her woolly hair that surrounded her flat, yellowish, almost parchment-like face.

"Mother, this is Professor Gori. You know? The one who had arranged Andrea's marriage."

The old lady somnolently raised her heavy eyelids, showing, with one more opened and the other less so, her muddy, egg-shaped eyes, with almost no look in them.

"As a matter of fact," the professor corrected him, bowing this time with hesitant concern for the torn frock-coat, "as a matter of fact, it is this way . . . not *arranged;* that would not . . . would not be the right word . . . I simply . . ."

". . . wanted to provide a tutor for my grandchildren," the old lady finished the sentence, with a cavernous voice.

Così difatti sarebbe stato giusto.

— Ecco, già . . . —fece il professor Gori.—Conoscendo i meriti, la modestia della signorina Reis.

— Ah, ottima figliuola, nessuno lo nega!—riconobbe subito, riabbassando le pàlpebre, la vecchia signora.—E noi, creda, siamo oggi dolentissimi . . .

— Che sciagura! Già! Così di colpo!—esclamo il Gori.

— Come se non ci fosse veramente la volontà di Dio,—concluse la vecchia signora.

Il Gori la guardò.

— Fatalità crudele . . .

Poi, guardando in giro per il salotto, domandò:

— E il signor Andrea?

Gli rispose il fratello, simulando indifferenza:

— Ma . . . non so, era qui, poco fa. Sarà andato forse a prepararsi.

— Ah!—esclamò allora il Gori, rallegrandosi improvvisamente.—Le nozze dunque si faranno lo stesso?

— No! che dice mai!—scattò la vecchia signora, stupita, offesa.—Oh Signore Iddio! Con la morta in casa? Ooh!

— Oooh!—echeggiarono, miagolando, le due zitellone con orrore.

— Prepararsi per partire,—spiegò il Migri.—Doveva partire oggi stesso con la sposa per Torino. Abbiamo le nostre cartiere lassù, a Valsangone; dove c'è tanto bisogno di lui.

— E . . . e partirà . . . così?—domandò il Gori.

— Per forza. Se non oggi, domani. L'abbiamo persuaso noi, spinto anzi, poverino. Qui, capirà, non è più prudente, né conveniente che rimanga.

— Per la ragazza . . . sola, ormai . . . —aggiunse la madre con la voce cavernosa.—Le male lingue . . .

— Eh già,—riprese il fratello.—E poi gli affari . . . Era un matrimonio . . .

"Excellent! That, in fact, would have been the right thing."

"That's it, yes . . ." said Professor Gori. "Recognizing the merits and the modesty of Miss Reis."

"Ah, an excellent girl, no one denies it," the old lady admitted immediately, lowering her eyelids. "And we, believe me, are extremely sorry today . . ."

"What a misfortune! Yes indeed! So suddenly!" exclaimed Gori.

"As if it were not really God's will," concluded the old lady.

Gori looked at her.

"A cruel stroke of fate . . ."

Then, looking around the room, he asked:

"And Mr. Andrea?"

The brother answered him, pretending indifference:

"But . . . I don't know; he was here a short time ago. Perhaps he may have gone to get ready."

"Ah!" Gori exclaimed then, suddenly cheering up. "The wedding will be held all the same, then?"

"No! What are you saying?" burst out the old woman, amazed, offended. "Good Lord in Heaven! With the dead woman in the house! O-oh!"

"O-o-o-o-oh!" yowled the two old maids, echoing her, with horror.

"To get ready to leave," Migri explained. "He was to leave today with his bride for Turin. We have our papermills up there at Valsangone, where he is needed so badly."

"And . . . and he will leave . . . like that?" Gori asked.

"Of necessity. If not today, then tomorrow. We persuaded him, in fact we urged him, poor fellow. Here, you understand, it is not prudent or suitable for him to remain any longer."

"On account of the girl . . . who is now alone . . ." the mother added with her cavernous voice. "Gossiping tongues . . ."

"Yes indeed," the brother continued. "And then, business . . . It was a marriage . . ."

— Precipitato!—proruppe una delle zitellone.

— Diciamo improvvisato,—cercò d'attenuare il Migri.—
Ora questa grave sciagura sopravviene fatalmente, come
. . . sì, per dar tempo, ecco. Un differimento s'impone . . .
per il lutto . . . e . . . E così si potrà pensare, riflettere da
una parte e dall'altra . . .

Il professor Gori rimase muto per un pezzo. L'impaccio
irritante che gli cagionava quel discorso, così tutto sospeso
in prudenti reticenze, era pur quello stesso che gli cagionava la sua marsina stretta e scucita sotto l'ascella. Scucita allo stesso modo gli sembrò quel discorso e da accogliere
con lo stesso riguardo per la scucitura segreta, col quale era
proferito. A sforzarlo un po', a non tenerlo così composto
e sospeso, con tutti i debiti riguardi, c'era pericolo che,
come la manica della marsina si sarebbe staccata, così
anche si sarebbe aperta e denudata l'ipocrisia di tutti quei
signori.

Sentì per un momento il bisogno d'astrarsi da quell'-
oppressione e anche dal fastidio che, nell'intontimento in
cui era caduto, gli dava il merlettino bianco, che orlava il
collo della casacca nera della vecchia signora. Ogni qual
volta vedeva un merlettino bianco come quello, gli si riaf-
facciava alla memoria, chi sa perché, l'immagine d'un tal
Pietro Cardella, merciaio del suo paesello lontano, afflitto
da una cisti enorme alla nuca. Gli venne di sbuffare; si
trattenne a tempo, e sospirò, come uno stupido:

— Eh già . . . povera figliuola!
Gli rispose un coro di commiserazioni per la sposa. Il
professor Gori se ne sentì all'improvviso come sferzare, e
domandò, irritatissimo:
— Dov'è? Potrei vederla?
Il Migri gl'indicò un uscio nel salottino:
— Di là, si serva . . .
E il professor Gori vi si diresse furiosamente.

"An over-hasty marriage!" one of the old maids burst forth.

"Let us say improvised," Migri said, trying to tone it down. "Now this serious misfortune has intervened as a stroke of fate, as if . . . yes, to give time, that's it. A postponement is necessary . . . on account of the mourning . . . And in that way, both parties can think the matter over . . ."

Professor Gori remained silent for a while. The irritating embarrassment that he was caused by that speech, so completely suspended in prudent reticence, was exactly the same as that which he was caused by his frock-coat, which was tight and unsewed beneath the armpit. It was unsewed in the same way that that speech seemed to him to be, and needed to be treated with the same care because of the secret disjointedness with which it had been uttered. If you forced matters a little, and did not keep it so composed and suspended, with all due concern, there was a danger that, just as the sleeve of the frock-coat would come off, so too the hypocrisy of all those high-class people would be opened up and laid bare.

He felt for a moment the need of getting away from that oppression and also from the displeasure with which, in the stupefaction into which he had fallen, he was affected by the white lace that edged the neck of the old lady's black jacket. Every time he saw a piece of white lace like that, there came to his memory, Lord only knows why, the picture of a certain Pietro Cardella, a haberdasher in his distant home town, who was afflicted with an enormous cyst on the nape of his neck. He felt like puffing; he restrained himself in time, and sighed stupidly:

"Oh yes . . . poor girl!"

In answer there arose a chorus of expressions of sympathy for the bride. Professor Gori suddenly felt as if he were lashed by this, and asked, in very great irritation:

"Where is she? Might I see her?"

Migri showed him a door in the parlor:

"In there; please go ahead . . ."

And Professor Gori went off that way in fury.

Sul lettino bianco, rigidamente stirato, il cadavere della madre, con un'enorme cuffia in capo dalle tese inamidate.

Non vide altro, in prima, il professor Gori, entrando. In preda a quell'irritazione crescente, di cui, nello stordimento e nell'impaccio, non riusciva a rendersi esatto conto, con la testa che già gli fumava,[14] anziché commuoversene, se ne sentì irritare, come per una cosa veramente assurda: stupida e crudele soperchieria della sorte che, no, perdio,[15] non si doveva a nessun costo lasciar passare!

Tutta quella rigidità della morta gli parve di parata,[16] come se quella povera vecchia si fosse stesa da sé, là, su quel letto, con quella enorme cuffia inamidata per prendersi lei, a tradimento, la festa preparata per la figliuola, e quasi quasi al professor Gori venne la tentazione di gridare:

— Su via, si alzi, mia cara vecchia signora! Non è il momento di fare scherzi di codesto genere!

Cèsara Reis stava per terra, caduta sui ginocchi; e tutta aggruppata, ora, presso il lettino su cui giaceva il cadavere della madre, non piangeva più, come sospesa in uno sbalordimento grave e vano. Tra i capelli neri, scarmigliati, aveva alcune ciocche ancora attorte dalla sera avanti in pezzetti di carta, per farsi i ricci.

Ebbene, anziché pietà, provò anche per lei quasi dispetto il professor Gori. Gli sorse prepotente il bisogno di tirarla su da terra, di scuoterla da quello sbalordimento. Non si doveva darla vinta al destino, che favoriva così iniquamente l'ipocrisia di tutti quei signori radunati nell'altra stanza! No, no: era tutto preparato, tutto pronto; quei signori là erano venuti in marsina come lui per le nozze: ebbene, bastava un atto di volontà in qualcuno; costringere quella povera fanciulla, caduta lì per terra, ad alzarsi; condurla, trascinarla, anche così mezzo sbalordita, a concludere quelle nozze per salvarla dalla rovina.

Ma stentava a sorgere in lui quell'atto di volontà, che con tanta evidenza sarebbe stato contrario alla volontà di tutti quei parenti. Come Cèsara, però, senza muovere il capo,

THE TIGHT FROCK-COAT

On the little white bed, stretched out in rigor mortis, was the body of the mother, wearing on her head a cap with starched brims.

At first Professor Gori did not see anything else as he came in. Under the influence of that growing irritation which, in his daze and annoyance he could not exactly account for, with his head already in a whirl, instead of being moved at the sight, he felt irritated at it, as if at something truly absurd: a stupidly cruel and insolent trick of fate which— no, by Jove, it should not be allowed to pass at any cost!

All that rigidity of the dead woman seemed to him a show, as if that poor old woman had of her own accord stretched herself out there, on that bed, with that enormous starched cap in order to take over for herself, by foul play, the festival prepared for her daughter; and Professor Gori was nearly tempted to shout:

"Get up, get up, my dear old lady! This is not the moment to play tricks of that kind!"

Cèsara Reis was kneeling on the floor; and all huddled, now, near the little bed on which her mother's body was lying, she was no longer weeping, but seemed suspended in a solemn and empty bewilderment. Among her disheveled black hair she had some locks still twisted up in curl-papers from the evening before.

And yet, instead of feeling pity, Professor Gori felt almost contempt for her. An imperious urge arose in him to pull her up from the floor, to shake her out of that bewilderment. She ought not to give in to destiny, which was so unfairly favoring the hypocrisy of all those upper-class people gathered in the other room! No, no; everything was all prepared, all ready; those people had come in frock-coats, as he had, for the wedding: well, all that was needed was an assertion of will-power on someone's part; to force that poor girl, who had fallen there on the floor, to get up; to lead her, drag her, even half bewildered like that, to carry through that wedding and to save her from ruin.

But that act of will-power, which would so obviously have been contrary to the wishes of all those relatives, was reluctant to arise in him. As Cèsara, however, without moving

senza batter ciglio, levò appena appena una mano ad accennar la sua mamma lì distesa, dicendogli:—"Vede, professore?"—il professore ebbe uno scatto, e:

— Sì, cara, sì!—le rispose con una concitazione quasi astiosa, che stordì la sua antica allieva.—Ma tu àlzati! Non farmi calare, perché non posso calarmi! Alzati da te! Subito, via! Su, su, fammi il piacere!

Senza volerlo, forzata da quella concitazione, la giovane si scosse dal suo abbattimento e guardò, quasi sgomenta, il professore:
— Perché?—gli chiese.
— Perché, figliuola mia . . . ma àlzati prima! ti dico che non mi posso calare, santo Dio!—le rispose il Gori.

Cèsara si alzò. Rivedendo però sul lettino il cadavere della madre, si coprì il volto con le mani e scoppiò in violenti singhiozzi. Non s'aspettava di sentirsi afferrare per le braccia e scrollare e gridare dal professore, più che mai concitato:
— No! no! no! Non piangere, ora! Abbi pazienza, figliuola! Da' ascolto a me!
Tornò a guardarlo, quasi atterrita questa volta, col pianto arrestato negli occhi, e disse:
— Ma come vuole che non pianga?
— Non devi piangere, perché non è ora di piangere, questa, per te!—tagliò corto il professore.—Tu sei rimasta sola, figliuola mia, e devi ajutarti da te! Lo capisci che devi ajutarti da te? Ora, sì, ora! Prendere tutto il tuo coraggio a due mani; stringere i denti e far quello che ti dico io!
— Che cosa, professore?
— Niente. Toglierti, prima di tutto, codesti pezzetti di carta dai capelli.
— Oh Dio,—gemette la fanciulla, sovvenendosene, e portandosi subito le mani tremanti ai capelli.
— Brava, così!—incalzò il professore.—Poi andar di là a indossare il tuo abitino di scuola; metterti il cappellino,

her head, without batting an eyelash, barely raised a hand to point to her mother stretched out there, saying to him: "You see, professor?"—the professor suddenly moved, and said:

"Yes, my dear, yes!" he answered her with an almost rancorous excitement, which amazed his former student. "But you, get up! Do not make me bend down, because I cannot bend down. Get up by yourself! Immediately, hurry! Up, up, please!"

Without wanting to, forced by that excitement, the young woman shook herself out of her dejection and looked, almost frightened, at the professor:

"Why?" she asked him.

"Because, my girl . . . but first get up! I tell you that I cannot bend down, in Heaven's name!" Gori answered her.

Cèsara got up. However, on seeing again her mother's body on the little bed, she covered her face with her hands and burst into violent sobs. She did not expect to feel herself seized by the arms and shaken and shouted at by the professor, more excited than ever:

"No! no! no! Don't weep now! Be patient, my dear girl! Listen to me!"

She looked at him again, almost terrified this time, with her tears stopped in her eyes, and said:

"But how do you expect me not to weep?"

"You must not weep, because this is not a time to weep, for you!" the professor cut her short. "You have been left alone, my dear girl, and must help yourself! Do you understand that you have to help yourself? *Now,* yes, *now!* Take all your courage in your hands; clench your teeth and do what I tell you!"

"What, professor?"

"Nothing. Take off, first of all, those pieces of paper from your hair."

"Oh, Heavens!" groaned the girl, remembering them, and immediately putting her trembling hands to her hair.

"That's right!" urged the professor. "Then go in there and put on your school dress; put on your little hat, and

e venire con me!

— Dove? che dice?

— Al Municipio, figliuola mia!

— Professore, che dice?

— Dico al Municipio, allo stato civile,[17] e poi in chiesa! Perché codesto matrimonio s'ha da fare, s'ha da fare ora stesso; o tu sei rovinata! Vedi come mi sono conciato per te? In marsina! E uno dei testimoni sarò io, come volevi tu! Lascia di qua la tua povera mamma; non pensare più a lei per un momento, non ti paja un sacrilegio! Lei stessa, la tua mamma, lo vuole! Da' ascolto a me: va a vestirti! Io dispongo tutto di là per la cerimonia: ora stesso!

— No . . . no . . . come potrei?—gridò Cèsara, ripiegandosi sul letto della madre e affondando il capo tra le braccia, disperatamente.—Impossibile, professore! Per me è finita, lo so! Egli se ne andrà, non tornerà più, mi abbandonerà . . . ma io non posso . . . non posso . . .

Il Gori non cedette; si chinò per sollevarla, per strapparla da quel letto; ma come stese le braccia, pestò rabbiosamente un piede, gridando:

— Non me ne importa niente! Farò magari da testimonio con una manica sola, ma questo matrimonio oggi si farà! Lo comprendi tu . . . guardami negli occhi!—lo comprendi, è vero? che se ti lasci scappare questo momento, tu sei perduta? Come resti, senza più il posto, senza più nessuno? Vuoi dar colpa a tua madre della tua rovina? Non sospirò [18] tanto, povera donna, questo tuo matrimonio? E vuoi ora che, per causa sua, vada a monte? [19] Che fai tu di male? Coraggio, Cèsara! Ci sono qua io: lascia a me la responsabilità di quello che fai! Va', va' a vestirti, va' a vestirsi, figliuola mia, senza perder tempo . . .

E, così dicendo, condusse la fanciulla fino all'uscio della sua cameretta, sorreggendola per le spalle. Poi riattraversò la camera mortuaria, ne serrò l'uscio, e rientrò come un guerriero nel salottino.

come with me!"

"Where? what are you saying?"

"To the City Hall, my dear girl!"

"Professor, what are you saying?"

"I say, to the City Hall, to the registry office, and then to the church! Because this marriage has to be performed, has to be performed right now; or you are ruined! Do you see what a state I am in on your account? In a frock-coat! And I shall be one of the witnesses, as you desired! Leave your poor mother here; don't think any more about her for a moment, and don't consider it a sacrilege! She herself, your mother, wants you to! Listen to me: go and get dressed! I shall arrange everything out there for the ceremony: right now!"

"No . . . no . . . how could I?" cried Cèsara, falling back again on her mother's bed and burying her head in her arms, in desperation. "It is impossible, professor! It's all up with me, I know! He will go away, will never come back, will abandon me . . . but I can't . . . I can't . . ."

Gori did not give in; he bent down to lift her up, to pull her away from that bed; but as he stretched out his arms, he angrily stamped his foot, shouting:

"I don't care in the slightest! I will even act as a witness with only one sleeve, but this wedding will be performed today! Do you understand . . . look me in the eyes! . . . you understand, don't you? that if you let this moment escape you, you are lost? How will you keep going, without your position, with no one left? Do you want to blame your mother for your ruin? Didn't the poor lady desire this marriage of yours so eagerly? And do you want it to come to nothing, on her account? What harm are you doing? Courage, Cèsara! I am here; leave to me the responsibility for what you are doing! Go, go and get dressed, go and get dressed, my girl, without losing any more time . . ."

And as he said this, he led the girl to the door of her room, supporting her by the shoulders. Then he went back through the room of death, closed the door, and went back like a warrior into the parlor.

— Non è ancora venuto lo sposo?

I parenti, gl'invitati si voltarono a guardarlo, sorpresi dal tono imperioso della voce; e il Migri domandò con simulata premura:

— Si sente male la signorina?

— Si sente benone!—gli rispose il professore guardandolo con tanti d'occhi.[20]—Anzi ho il piacere d'annunziare a lor signori che ho avuto la fortuna di persuaderla a vincersi [21] per un momento, e soffocare in sé il cordoglio. Siamo qua tutti; tutto è pronto; basterà—mi lascino dire!—basterà che uno di loro . . . lei, per esempio, sarà tanto gentile—(aggiunse, rivolgendosi a uno degli invitati)—mi farà il piacere di correre con una vettura al Municipio e di prevenire l'ufficiale dello stato civile, che . . .

Un coro di vivaci proteste interruppe a questo punto il professore. Scandalo, stupore, orrore, indignazione!

— Mi lascino spiegare!—gridò il professor Gori, che dominava tutti con la persona.—Perché questo matrimonio non si farebbe? Per il lutto della sposa, è vero? Ora, se la sposa stessa . . .

— Ma io non permetterò mai,—gridò più forte di lui, troncandogli la parola, la vecchia signora,—non permetterò mai che mio figlio . . .

— Faccia il suo dovere e una buona azione?—domandò, pronto, il Gori, compiendo lui la frase questa volta.

— Ma lei non stia a immischiarsi!—venne a dirgli, pallido e vibrante d'ira, il Migri in difesa della madre.

— Perdoni! M'immischio,—rimbeccò subito il Gori,—perché so che lei è un gentiluomo, caro signor Grimi . . .

— Migri, prego!

— Migri, Migri, e comprenderà che non è lecito né onesto sottrarsi all'estreme esigenze d'una situazione come questa. Bisogna esser più forti della sciagura che colpisce quella povera figliuola, e salvarla! Può restar sola, così, senza ajuto e senz'alcuna posizione ormai? Lo dica lei! No:

"Has the groom not come yet?"

The relatives and guests turned around to look at him, surprised by the authoritative tone of his voice; and Migri asked with pretended concern:

"Is the young lady feeling badly?"

"She is feeling excellent!" the professor answered him with a fierce glare. "On the contrary, I have the pleasure of announcing to you, ladies and gentlemen, that I have been fortunate enough to persuade her to dominate her feelings for a moment and to stifle her grief. We are all here; everything is ready; it will be enough—let me speak!—it will be enough for one of you . . . you, for example, will be so kind," he added, turning to one of the guests, "you will do me the favor of hastening in a carriage to the City Hall and of forewarning the officials of the registry office, that . . ."

A chorus of vigorous protests interrupted the professor at this point. Scandal, amazement, horror, indignation!

"Let me explain!" shouted Professor Gori, dominating all with his presence. "Why should this marriage not be performed? Because of the grief of the bride, isn't that so? Now, if the bride herself . . ."

"But I shall never permit," shouted the old lady, louder than he, interrupting him, "I shall never permit my son . . ."

". . . to do his duty and perform a good deed?" Gori quickly asked, and he was the one to finish the sentence this time.

"Just stop interfering!" Migri came up and said to him, pale and trembling with anger, in defense of his mother.

"I beg your pardon! I am interfering," Gori retorted immediately, "because I know that you are a gentleman, my dear Mr. Grimi . . ."

"Migri, please!"

"Migri, Migri, and you will understand that it is neither permissible nor honorable to refuse to meet the imperative obligations of a situation like this. We must be stronger than the misfortune which has stricken this poor girl, and save her! Can she remain alone, like this, without aid and

questo matrimonio si farà non ostante la sciagura, e non ostante . . . abbiano pazienza!

S'interruppe, infuriato e sbuffante: si cacciò una mano sotto la manica del soprabito; afferrò la manica della marsina e con uno strappo violento se la tirò fuori e la lanciò per aria. Risero tutti, senza volerlo, a quel razzo inatteso, di nuovo genere, mentre il professore, con un gran sospiro di liberazione seguitava:

— E non ostante questa manica che mi ha tormentato finora!

— Lei scherza!—riprese, ricomponendosi, il Migri.

— Nossignore: mi s'era scucita.

— Scherza! Codeste sono violenze.

— Quelle che consiglia il caso.

— O l'interesse! Le dico che non è possibile, in queste condizioni . . .

Sopravvenne per fortuna lo sposo.

— No! No! Andrea, no!—gli gridarono subito parecchie voci, di qua, di là.

Ma il Gori le sopraffece, avanzandosi verso il Migri.

— Decida lei! Mi lascino dire! Si tratta di questo: ho indotto di là la signorina Reis a farsi forza: a vincersi, considerando la gravità della situazione, in cui, caro signore, lei l'ha messa e la lascerebbe. Piacendo a lei, signor Migri, si potrebbe, senz'alcuno apparato, zitti zitti,[22] in una vettura chiusa, correre al Municipio, celebrare subito il matrimonio . . . Lei non vorrà, spero, negarsi. Ma dica, dica lei . . .

Andrea Migri, così soprappreso, guardò prima il Gori, poi gli altri, e infine rispose esitante:

— Ma . . . per me, se Cèsara vuole . . .

— Vuole! Vuole!—gridò il Gori, dominando col suo vocione le disapprovazioni degli altri.—Ecco finalmente una parola che parte dal cuore! Lei, dunque, venga, corra al Municipio, gentilissimo signore!

without any position left? You tell me! No; this wedding
will be held in spite of the calamity, and in spite of the
. . . please be patient!"

He broke off, furious and puffing; he put a hand under
the sleeve of his overcoat, grasped the sleeve of the frock-
coat and with a violent jerk pulled it out and hurled it in
the air. They all laughed, against their will, at that strange
kind of unexpected comic touch, whilst the professor,
with a great sigh of liberation, continued:

"And in spite of this sleeve which has been torturing me
until now!"

"You are joking!" Migri retorted, regaining his composure.

"No, sir; it had come unsewed."

"You are joking! Your outbursts are uncalled for."

"They are called for by the situation."

"Or by personal interest! I tell you that it is not possible,
under these conditions . . ."

Fortunately the groom arrived.

"No! No! Andrea, no!" several voices immediately called
to him, from one side and another.

But Gori overwhelmed them, advancing towards Migri.

"You decide! Let me speak! This is what is at stake: I
have induced Miss Reis in there to muster her courage; to
pull herself together, in view of the seriousness of the situation in which you, my dear sir, have placed her and would
leave her. If you are willing, Mr. Migri, we could, without
any pomp, very quietly, in a closed carriage, hasten to the
City Hall and celebrate the wedding immediately . . .
You will not, I trust, refuse. But speak, yourself . . ."

Andrea Migri, taken by surprise in this way, looked first
at Gori, then at the others, and finally answered hesitantly:

"But . . . so far as I am concerned, if Cèsara is willing . . ."

"She is willing! She is willing!" shouted Gori, over-
whelming with his loud voice the others' expressions of
disapproval. "Here, finally, is a word that comes from the
heart! You, therefore, come, kind sir, and hasten to the
City Hall!"

Prese per un braccio quell'invitato, a cui s'era rivolto la prima volta; lo accompagnò fino alla porta. Nella saletta d'ingresso vide una gran quantità di magnifiche ceste di fiori, arrivate in dono per il matrimonio, e si fece all'uscio del salotto per chiamare lo sposo e liberarlo dai parenti inviperiti, che già l'attorniavano.

— Signor Migri, signor Migri, una preghiera! Guardi . . . Quegli accorse.
— Interpretiamo il sentimento di quella poverina. Tutti questi fiori, alla morta . . . Mi ajuti!
Prese due ceste, e rientrò così nel salotto; reggendole trionfalmente, diretto alla camera mortuaria. Lo sposo lo seguiva, compunto, con altre due ceste. Fu una subitanea conversione della festa. Più d'uno accorse alla saletta, a prendere altre ceste, e a recarle in processione.

— I fiori alla morta; benissimo; i fiori alla morta!

Poco dopo, Cèsara entrò nel salotto, pallidissima, col modesto abito nero della scuola, i capelli appena ravviati, tremante dello sforzo che faceva su sé stessa per contenersi. Subito lo sposo le corse incontro, la raccolse tra le braccia, pietosamente. Tutti tacevano. Il professor Gori, con gli occhi lucenti di lagrime, pregò tre di quei signori che seguissero con lui gli sposi, per far da testimoni e s'avviarono in silenzio.
La madre, il fratello, le zitellone, gl'invitati rimasti nel salotto, ripresero subito a dar sfogo alla loro indignazione frenata per un momento, all'apparire di Cèsara. Fortuna, che la povera vecchia mamma, di là, in mezzo ai fiori, non poteva più ascoltare questa brava gente che si diceva proprio indignata per tanta irreverenza verso la morte di lei.

Ma il professor Gori, durante il tragitto, pensando a ciò che, in quel momento, certo si diceva di lui in quel salotto, rimase come intronato, e giunse al Municipio, che pareva ubriaco; [23] tanto che, non pensando più alla manica

He took by the arm that guest to whom he had spoken the first time, and went with him as far as the door. In the entrance hall he saw a great number of magnificent baskets of flowers, which had come as wedding presents, and appeared at the door of the parlor to call the groom and free him from his infuriated relatives, who were already surrounding him.

"Mr. Migri, Mr. Migri, one request! Look . . ."

Migri hastened up.

"Let us do as that poor girl would wish. All these flowers, to the dead woman . . . Help me!"

He took two baskets, and went back with them into the parlor; carrying them in triumph, he went into the room of death. The groom followed him, contritely, with two more baskets. There was an immediate change in the party. More than one person hastened to the entrance hall, to take more baskets and to carry them in a procession.

"Take the flowers to the dead woman; excellent, the flowers to the dead woman!"

Soon thereafter, Cèsara came into the parlor, very pale, in her modest black school dress, with her hair barely tidied, and trembling from the effort she was exerting to maintain her composure. Immediately the groom ran to meet her and took her in his arms with compassion. All were silent. Professor Gori, with his eyes shining with tears, requested three of the gentlemen to accompany the bride and groom with him, to serve as witnesses. They set out in silence.

The mother, the brother, the old maids and the guests who had remained in the parlor immediately began again to vent their indignation, which had been restrained for a moment on the appearance of Cèsara. It was fortunate that the poor old mother, out there in the midst of the flowers, was no longer able to hear these fine people who had been proclaiming their great indignation at such a lack of reverence on the occasion of her death.

But Professor Gori, during the trip, thought of what people must certainly, at that moment, be saying about him in that parlor, and remained in a daze so that when he arrived at the City Hall, he seemed drunk—so much so

della marsina che s'era strappata, si tolse come gli altri il soprabito.

— Professore!

— Ah già! Perbacco!—esclamò, e se lo ricacciò di furia.[24]

Finanche Cèsara ne sorrise. Ma il Gori, che s'era in certo qual modo confortato, dicendo a sé stesso che, in fin dei conti,[25] non sarebbe più tornato lì tra quella gente, non potè riderne: doveva tornarci per forza, ora, per quella manica da restituire insieme con la marsina al negoziante da cui l'aveva presa a nolo. La firma? Che firma? Ah già! sì, doveva apporre la firma come testimonio. Dove?

Sbrigata in fretta l'altra funzione in chiesa, gli sposi e i quattro testimoni rientrarono in casa.

Furono accolti con lo stesso silenzio glaciale.

Il Gori, cercando di farsi quanto più piccolo gli fosse possibile, girò lo sguardo per il salotto e, rivolgendosi a uno degli invitati, col dito su la bocca, pregò:

— Piano piano . . . Mi saprebbe dire di grazia dove sia andata a finire quella tal manica della mia marsina, che buttai all'aria poc'anzi?

E ravvolgendosela, poco dopo, entro un giornale e andandosene via quatto quatto,[26] si mise a considerare che, dopo tutto, egli doveva soltanto alla manica di quella marsina stretta la bella vittoria riportata quel giorno sul destino, perché, se quella marsina, con la manica scucita sotto l'ascella, non gli avesse suscitato tanta irritazione, egli, nella consueta ampiezza dei suoi comodi e logori abiti giornalieri, di fronte alla sciagura di quella morte improvvisa, si sarebbe abbandonato senz'altro, come un imbecille, alla commozione, a un inerte compianto della sorte infelice di quella povera fanciulla. Fuori della grazia di Dio per quella marsina stretta, aveva invece trovato, nell'irritazione, l'animo e la forza di ribellarvisi e di trionfarne.

that, no longer remembering that he had torn off the sleeve of his frock-coat, he took off his overcoat like the others.

"Professor!"

"Ah, yes! By Jove!" he exclaimed, and put it back on in a hurry.

Even Cèsara smiled at this. But Gori, who had to a certain extent consoled himself by telling himself that, after all, he wouldn't go back among those people again, could not laugh at the occurrence; now he had of necessity to go back there again, to get that sleeve and return it together with the frock-coat to the shop-keeper from whom he had rented it. The signature? What signature? Ah, yes! of course, he had to put down his signature as a witness. Where?

When the other ceremony, in church, had been quickly gotten over with, the bride and groom and the four witnesses returned home.

They were received in the same icy silence.

Gori, trying to appear as small as possible, looked around the parlor and, turning to one of the guests, with his finger on his lips, asked:

"Quietly . . . Could you please tell me what happened to that sleeve from my frock-coat, which I threw in the air a short while ago?"

And wrapping it up soon afterwards inside a newspaper and slipping away on the sly, he began to reflect that, after all, he owed his fine victory over destiny that day only to the sleeve of that tight frock-coat, because, if the frock-coat, with its sleeve that had come unstitched under his armpit, had not aroused such irritation in him, he, in the familiar roominess of his comfortable and worn-out everyday garments, would certainly have yielded, like an imbecile, to mere emotion and to inactive regret for the unhappy fate of that poor girl. In a state of total fury on account of that tight frock-coat, he had found, on the other hand, in his irritation, the courage and the strength to rebel against it and to triumph over it.

Aldo Palazzeschi

(1885–1974)

PALAZZESCHI'S REAL name was Aldo Giurlani. He was born in Florence in 1885, and, as a young man, made a name for himself as a poet and as a leading member of Filippo Marinetti's "Futurist" movement just before the First World War. Later, however, he became known chiefly as a prose writer, especially for his novels *Il còdice di Perelà* ("The Code of Perelà," 1911), *La sorelle Materassi* ("The Materassi Sisters," 1935) and *I fratelli Cùccoli* ("The Cùccoli Brothers," 1948); and for his collections of short stories *Il re bello* ("The Handsome King," 1922), *Stampe dell'Ottocento* ("Nineteenth-Century Prints," 1932) and *Il pàlio dei buffi* ("The Contest of the Queer People," 1937).

The Futurist movement had preached the dissolution of all earlier art, and its replacement by unbridled fantasy and caprice, at the whim of the individual artist, expressed by a return to pre-logical, primitive and childish forms of expression. As a literary fashion, Futurism faded after the First World War, and many of its practitioners, including Palazzeschi, returned to a more traditional type of expression, comprehensible to ordinary readers. Yet Futurism left its imprint on Palazzeschi's choice of subjects and characters and in his attitude towards them, as well as in certain violent metaphors and juxtapositions of words. Especially

in *Il pàlio dei buffi,* he shows a predilection for paradoxical situations with a humorous or wry twist, and for queer persons who, from story to story, vie with each other (whence the title "The Contest of the Queer People") in eccentric behavior and curious, unexpected reactions.

In *Bistino and the Marquis,* the situation itself, that of the ex-servants who come to lodge and support the ex-master, is of course peculiar, as is also the contrast between the characters of the incorrigibly feudal Bistino, the permanently selfish Marquis, and the skeptical, commonsensical Nunzia who is carried along unwillingly by the course of events but who ultimately uses the situation to gratify her own whims. The Marquis has eventually worked himself into a situation where, like Pirandello's Henry IV, he must play a role forever in order to live at all. There is perhaps also a bit of cultural symbolism, conscious or unconscious, in the situation. Modern Italian society has saddled itself with a useless, outworn, wasteful and ridiculously egocentric aristocracy (which, incidentally, has still persisted under the Republic), and is thereby trying to appear aristocratic to the proletarians of the rest of the world. But, in the last analysis, who is really the exploiter and who is the exploited—Bistino and Nunzia, or the Marquis? the Italian common people, or their aristocracy?

BISTINO E IL SIGNOR MARCHESE

di Aldo Palazzeschi

— Nunzia . . . sai Nunzia . . . ho visto il signor marchese.[1]

"Ah!" rispondeva la Nunzia senza voltarsi dal camino dov'era tesa a dar gli ultimi tocchi per il pranzo o la cena; e mentre una tavolina bianca, linda e lucente, apparecchiata davanti alla finestra aperta sul piccolo orto, aspettava con le braccia aperte i due commensali. La donna non dimostrava curiosità per quell'incontro, ma talora aggiungeva più condiscendente: "Che ti ha detto? che fa?" strascicando le parole in tono da non desiderare troppo certe notizie né di prestarsi a lungo per ascoltarle.

Talaltra Bistino, giungendo sulla porta di cucina spaventato e sconvolto, quasi gli mancasse il coraggio di entrare, diceva a precipizio: "Sai, l'ho visto, l'ho incontrato, gli ho parlato". Quasi non ci fosse al mondo che una persona da poter vedere, incontrare e alla quale rivolgere una parola; e che tutti gli altri non esercitassero su di lui un minimo d'interesse. "Tanto piacere" rispondeva secco la Nunzia scodinzolando fra il camino e la dispensa.

Era carino vedere quell'omone alto quasi quanto la porta, per starci sotto chinava il capo istintivamente presentendone l'architrave, nell'atteggiamento stupito di attesa, e simile a un bambino gigante seguire i movimenti che la moglie

BISTINO AND THE MARQUIS

by Aldo Palazzeschi

"Nunzia . . . you know, Nunzia . . . I saw the Marquis."

"Ah!" Nunzia would reply, without turning away from the fireplace where she was bending to put the last touches on the lunch or the dinner; and all the while a little white table, neat and shining, set in front of the window facing the little garden, was waiting with open arms for the two table companions. The woman showed no curiosity about that meeting, but sometimes she would add, more condescendingly: "What did he say to you? What is he doing?" dragging out the words in such a tone as not to desire certain news too much, nor to spend much time in listening to it.

At other times, Bistino, arriving at the kitchen door frightened and upset, as if he lacked the courage to enter, would say hurriedly: "You know, I saw him, I met him, I spoke to him." As if there were in the world only one person who could be seen, met, or spoken a word to; and as if all the others did not hold for him the slightest interest. "So glad," Nunzia would answer dryly, scuttling between the fireplace and the cupboard.

It was charming to see that big man who was almost as tall as the door (to get under it he would bow his head instinctively in anticipation of the lintel) in an astonished attitude of waiting, and like a giant child following the

eseguiva davanti al camino del quale era poco più alta,
tanto da doversi alzare sulla punta dei piedi per guardar
dentro la pentola.

Quando erano accanto, la Nunzia col suo ciuffetto dispet-
toso non arrivava alla spalla di Bistino: una coppia bene
assortita, e forse per ciò perfetta e felice.

— Ti ha chiesto qualche cosa?—aggiungeva dopo un
silenzio freddo che faceva restar fermo e a bocca aperta il
marito.

E lui, incapace di mentire alla moglie, rispondeva cauta-
mente.

— Gli ho pagato il caffè . . . il caffè . . . e una pasta.

— Aveva fame, eh?

Dopo aver pronunziato questa parola con una punta di
crudeltà, la donna dava un lungo sospiro.

— È il benefizio che producono certi incontri. Stai sicuro
che non ti renderà la cortesia.—Capiva che il marito
doveva aver fatto qualche cosa di più.

Bistino si sentiva disarmato, scoraggiato, ferito.

— Capirai . . . che cosa vuoi . . . come si fa . . .
—balbettava cercando di nascondere e di scusare l'impeto
del cuore, e di scusare insieme il signor marchese che aveva
bevuto il caffè e s'era mangiato la pasta. E forse messa in
tasca qualche liretta che il bravuomo gli aveva offerto a
titolo di grazioso prestito.

E talora la Nunzia, che voleva un gran bene al suo
Bistino, diceva una parola che dava la stura al racconto
e lui, simile ai fiumi quando rompono gli argini, la invadeva.

— Se tu vedessi . . . se tu vedessi . . .

Gli dava la stura ma non faceva che interromperlo e
ostacolargli la via.

— Chi è cagione del proprio male pianga sé stesso.—
Proclamava delle sentenze quasi leggesse nelle tavole della
legge sacra e universale; e con le quali faceva da martinicca
al marito dopo avergli dato l'aire. E quello, vero fanciullone
roseo e fresco nonostante i cinquantacinque anni, con degli
occhi celesti che sorridevano buoni e puerili, si fermava

movements which his wife made in front of the fireplace (than which she was only slightly taller, so that she had to stand on tiptoe to look inside the kettle).

When they were side by side, Nunzia with her saucy pile of hair did not come up to Bistino's shoulder: a well-assorted couple, and perhaps for that reason perfect and happy.

"Did he ask you for anything?" she would add after a cold silence which made her husband stand still and open-mouthed.

And he, incapable of lying to his wife, would answer cautiously:

"I treated him to coffee . . . coffee . . . and a pastry."

"He was hungry, eh?"

After pronouncing these words with an edge of cruelty, the woman would heave a long sigh.

"That's the profit you get from certain meetings. You can be sure that he won't return your courtesy." She understood that her husband must have done something more.

Bistino felt disarmed, discouraged, wounded.

"You see . . . what do you expect . . . what is one to do . . ." he would stammer, trying to hide and excuse the impulse of his heart, and to excuse at the same time the Marquis who had drunk the coffee and eaten the pastry. And perhaps put in his pocket a few lire that the worthy man had offered him as a friendly loan.

And sometimes Nunzia, who loved her Bistino very dearly, would say a word that would uncork the flow of narration and he, like rivers when they overflow their banks, would overwhelm her.

"If you could see . . . if you could see . . ."

She would uncork his narration, but she would only interrupt him and block his way.

"He who has caused his own woe, let him weep for himself." She would announce sententious sayings as if she were reading from the tables of sacred and universal law; with these, she would act as a brake on her husband after giving him rein. And he, a true big boy, rosy and fresh despite his fifty-five years, with blue eyes that smiled

restando con la bocca aperta. Pur dominando la donna fisicamente, si sentiva dominato nello spirito. Quell'asprezza che si rivelava unicamente quando entrava in ballo[2] il signor marchese, faceva sentire alto e chiaro i suoi princìpi di vita, la forza della virtù con la quale non si scherza. Soltanto in questo caso se la vedeva balzare davanti come una viperetta, in ogni altro non v'era moglie più docile, affezionata e tenera, ma soprattutto orgogliosa di avere a sessant'anni quel bel marito dall'aspetto gioviale, ancora forte e piacente.

* * *

Bistino non riusciva a persuadersi ch'ella non provasse compasione per una persona verso la quale lui ne provava tanta; quella pietà che i buoni cristiani devono sentire per tutte le creature, nessuna esclusa, e che lui, invece, sentiva per una sola. I suoi affetti erano due, la moglie, e il signor marchese che non riusciva a dimenticare. Ma gli[3] è che la moglie era troppo accorta e intelligente per non valutare gli svantaggi del concedere sfogo a quell'affetto e a quella compassione che nell'animo semplice di lui non l'era riuscito a vincere, e che anzi di giorno in giorno sentiva crescere.

Per modo che nella casetta dei domestici in pensione erano due divinità: una nera, il signor marchese, divenuta infernale; e la contessa, divenuta celeste. Celeste due volte possiamo aggiungere, giacché dopo essere stata per ottantasei anni un angelo sulla terra era in paradiso da cinque, e aveva lasciato un anticipo di paradiso alla cameriera fedele: quella casa pulita e perbene, un assegno di dieci lire al giorno, e tante altre cosine. Si capisce come lei potesse dare sfogo ai racconti e a tutte l'ore, e Bistino la stava a sentire come i bambini stanno a sentire la mamma quando racconta le novelle; per quanto a lui, in fondo, non glie ne[4] importasse proprio nulla della contessa che pure aveva servito dieci anni, anzi, sotto sotto l'aveva in uggia, un po' per la gelosia della moglie, ma più perché era lei che faceva sprofondare nell'inferno il suo marchese. La trovava noiosissima con tutta la sua virtù, un vero rompiscatole, ma si sarebbe

kindly and childlike, would stop with his mouth open. Even though he dominated the woman physically, he felt himself dominated in spirit. That harshness which was evident only when the Marquis was under discussion, proclaimed loudly and clearly her principles of life, the strength of virtue with which there is no joking. Only in this case did he see her leap in front of him like a little viper; in every other, there was no wife more docile, affectionate and tender, but above all proud of having, at sixty, that fine husband with the jovial appearance, still strong and attractive.

* * *

Bistino could not persuade himself that she did not feel any compassion for a person towards whom he felt so much; that pity which good Christians should feel for all creatures, none excepted, and which he, on the other hand, felt for only one. The objects of his affection were two: his wife, and the Marquis, whom he was unable to forget. But the fact is that his wife was too shrewd and intelligent not to be aware of the disadvantages of allowing expression to that affection and that compassion which, in his simple mind, he had not succeeded in overcoming, and which, on the contrary, from day to day he felt growing.

So that in the retired servants' little home there were two divinities: one black, the Marquis, who had become infernal; and the Countess, who had become celestial. Twice celestial, we might add, since after being for eighty-six years an angel on earth, she had been in Paradise for five, and had left a foretaste of Paradise to her faithful maid: that neat and respectable house, an allowance of ten lire per day, and so many other little things. It was understandable that she could give vent to her stories, and at all times too, and Bistino would listen to her as children listen to their mother when she tells stories; as for him, basically, he cared nothing at all about the Countess, whom, nevertheless, he had served for ten years; as a matter of fact, way down in his heart he disliked her, a little bit through jealousy of his wife, but more because it was she who made his Marquis be cast down into the nether regions. He found her boring

guardato bene di lasciarlo trapelare alla Nunzia che di rado, assai di rado e nei momenti di tenerezza, prestava orecchio ai suoi racconti. E lui, d'altra parte, non avrebbe trovato chi gli desse ragione. Come paragonare una donna che era stata per ottantasei anni esempio di nobiltà e saggezza, di austerità e di modestia, di carità, con un uomo divenuto a poco a poco il ricettacolo di tutti i vizi; che rimasto erede giovanissimo aveva dilapidato la propria fortuna, e fatto sparire in un batter d'occhio varie piccole eredità che la provvidenza gli aveva lasciato cadere per trattenerlo sull'orlo dell'abisso. E ora, settantenne, si trovava ridotto alla mendicità vivendo delle non laute offerte di qualche lontano parente o amico, di quelli che non gli avevano tolto il saluto e voltate le spalle, ancora disposti ad ascoltarlo pochi istanti nella via, o a leggere le sue lamentose richieste. Ridotto a chiedere in prestito cinquanta o cento lire per vedersene regalare, con sopportazione, dieci o cinque, e a mezzo di supliche umiliantissime, sussidi che non venivano mai o venivano solo in minima parte. Se poi osava spingersi fino alle soglie degli amici di un tempo, le trovava senza scampo consegnate, e discendendo a vuoto, aggrappandosi ai ricchi sostegni, sostenendosi alle monumentali balaustrate, ritrovando in quegli ambienti un brandello della perduta fierezza e dignità, borbottava ironicamente: *"ou ils sont fatigués . . . ou ils sont indisposés . . . ou ils sont malades. Il faut vraiment dire que la race décline"*. E ammesso che il caso fortunato gli facesse incontrare un vecchio amico caritatevole che con garbo gli lasciava scivolare cinquanta lire nella tasca della giacchetta, non pensava di farne tesoro o darle in acconto all'albergatore per il debito che pendeva sempre, ma chiamava un tassì, e dopo essersi fermato e fatto aspettare per un aperitivo dava l'indirizzo di una fra le migliori trattorie dove ostentando indifferenza scansava con abilità il saluto di qualche vecchio conoscente che a sua volta si domandava: "Ha fatto un'altra eredità?" E rientrando nell'albergo malfamato, d'infimo ordine, scendendo un'altra volta dal tassì, ciò che faceva montare in bestia [5] l'albergatore che gli ricordava subito e con cattiva maniera il conto da pagare, diceva a sé stesso dando le ultime lire

with all her virtues, a real bore, but he would have been very careful not to let it filter through to Nunzia that he rarely, quite rarely and in moments of tenderness, paid any attention to her stories. And he, for that matter, would not have found anyone to consider him right. How could one compare a woman who had been for eighty-six years an example of nobility and wisdom, of austerity and modesty, of charity, with a man who had become little by little a sink of all iniquities; who, having inherited it as a very young man, had squandered his own fortune, and had dissipated in the twinkling of an eye several little inheritances which Providence had let fall his way to hold him back on the edge of the abyss. And now, seventy-ish, he was reduced to beggary, living on the niggardly bounty of some distant relative or friend among those who had not rejected him and turned their backs on him and who were still willing to listen to him for a few moments in the street or to read his plaintive requests. He was reduced to asking for fifty or a hundred lire as a loan, to see himself given, with tolerance, ten or five, and, by means of most humiliating petitions, subsidies which never came or which came only in very small part. And if he dared to go to the doors of his former friends, he found them inescapably blocked, and, going downstairs empty-handed, holding onto the rich supports, supporting himself on the monumental balustrades, finding again in those surroundings a scrap of his lost pride and dignity, he would mutter ironically: "Either they are tired . . . or they are indisposed . . . or they are sick. One must really say that the race is declining." And even if a lucky chance caused him to meet some charitable old friend who would tactfully slip fifty lire into his waistcoat pocket, he did not think of setting it aside or of giving it on account to his landlord for the debt which was always hanging over him, but he would call a taxi, and after stopping and having the taxi wait while he had an apéritif, he would give the address of one of the best restaurants, where, affecting indifference, he would skilfully avoid the greeting of some old acquaintance, who would, in his turn, wonder: "Has he come into another inheritance?" And when he went

BISTINO E IL SIGNOR MARCHESE

al conducente: *"Ma vie est coûteuse mais digne"*.

Come poteva parlare di un tale arnese alla Nunzia che custodiva nel cuore la memoria di una santa donna e, come una reliquia, il suo ritratto nella bella cornice d'argento sopra il cassettone? Anche Bistino ci aveva il ritratto del marchese quando era giovane, e che bel giovane, che bel signore; ne aveva più d'uno, ma li teneva nascosti nel fondo d'un baule, mescolati a tante inutili cianfrusaglie perché non glie li trovasse la moglie. Quei rittratti doveva tenerli in fondo al baule e solamente per sé.

Quando Bistino si decise, finalmente, ad abbandonare il marchese che non aveva più una casa e viveva di espedienti, doveva avere diciotto mesi di salario ed era con le tasche vuote. Fu assunto dalla contessa in qualità di cocchiere. La contessa aveva mantenuto il cavallo fino all'ultimo dei suoi giorni, tenacemente, adducendo che non c'era bisogno di correre tanto per arrivare alla morte; e Bistino, negli ultimi tempi, per quanto avesse per i cavalli un'adorazione innata, quasi si vergognava di spasseggiar quella vecchia con un cavallo fra le macchine. Ella teneva molto alla presenza dei suoi domestici, voleva che il cocchiere e il cameriere avessero una figura decorativa, imponente. E il bel cocchiere che a quarant'anni sembrava ancora un giovinotto tanto era fresco, tanto era gagliardo, tanto il suo aspetto era sereno e virile, ferì il cuore della Nunzia che ormai si riteneva al sicuro da certe sorprese.

Nella ragazza che fino a quel giorno non sapeva che volesse dire amare, l'amore prese un'andatura bizzarra: incominciò a piangere. Di nulla nulla nascondeva il viso e piangeva dirottamente, quasi fosse una vergogna amare, quasi si vergognasse di vivere. Prima di tutto per la sua età, ma soprattutto quello che le dava un senso di disagio e di vergogna, era di amare un uomo troppo bello e alto

back to his infamous hotel, of the lowest class, on getting out
of the taxi (which would infuriate the landlord, who would
remind him immediately and rudely of his outstanding
bill), he would say to himself, giving the last lire to the
driver: "My [mode of] life is expensive, but worthy."

How could Bistino talk about such a character to Nunzia,
who kept in her heart the memory of a holy woman, and,
like a relic, her picture in the beautiful silver frame above
the chest of drawers? Bistino, too, had the picture of the
Marquis when he was young, and what a handsome young
man he was, what a fine gentleman! He had more than
one, but he kept them hidden in the bottom of a trunk, together with so much useless trash, so that his wife would
not find them. Those pictures he had to keep in the bottom
of the trunk, and for himself alone.

When Bistino had decided, finally, to leave the Marquis,
who no longer had a house and was living from hand to
mouth, he had eighteen months' salary due him and was
penniless. He was hired by the Countess as coachman. The
Countess had kept her horse until the end of her days,
tenaciously, saying that there was no need of being in such
a hurry to arrive at death; and Bistino, in recent times,
although he had an inborn adoration for horses, was almost ashamed to take that old lady out riding in a horse-
drawn carriage among the automobiles. She set great store
by her servants' appearance, and wanted her coachman
and butler to cut a decorative and imposing figure. And
the handsome coachman, who at forty still seemed a young
man because he was so fresh and vigorous and because his
appearance was so serene and manly, struck the heart of
Nunzia, who had thought that she was by then protected
against certain surprises.

With this girl, who up to that day had not known what
love meant, love took a strange turn: she began to weep.
Without any apparent reason, she would hide her face and
she would weep copiously, as if it were a shame to love, as
if she were ashamed to be alive. First of all on account of
her age, but above all what gave her a sense of discomfort
and shame, was that she, who was so little and thin, was in

un metro e ottantasei, lei così piccina e sottile, di amare quell'omone che sembrava un corazziere. Le pareva una cosa sconveniente, disonorevole. Le capitavano crisi di pianto che non riusciva a combattere.

La contessa accortasi di un turbamento nell'animo della donna, la chiamò a sé amorevolmente, e con un sorriso pieno d'indulgenze ne accolse la confessione. Al cuore non si comanda, e anche a quarantacinque anni, piccola e sottile, ci si può innamorare di un corazziere.

Parlò a Bistino con franchezza, e concluse per fissarne senza indugio le nozze. Nella sua casa non erano ammesse che le vie della legge. Bistino non se lo fece ripetere, non gli parve vero di sposare quella donnina non bella e di un'età indefinibile, ma che al cuore della contessa sentiva appoggiata bene.

Era per la contessa se avevano di proprietà quella casina di quattro stanze tutte libere, con l'orticello circondato dalle rose rampicanti, e dove Bistino si divertiva a coltivare l'insalata, i pomidori, la frutta e le verdure: "un torlo d'uovo" [6] dicevano quelli che l'andavano a vedere: "un gioiellino, una chicca". Quattro stanze piene di mobilia, una bella camera, il salotto, la cucina, e un'altra cameretta che la Nunzia teneva pronta per affittare a uno studente o a una signorina, nel caso che le rendite fossero corte per vivere. Ma le rendite bastavano, bastavano senza doversi privare di niente, ché la contessa le aveva lasciato dieci lire al giorno di pensione e prima di morire tutti i giorni tirava fuori qualcosa dalla cassetta nel tavolino da notte, o la faceva cercare a lei in quelle del cassettone: una busta, un'altra busta, un oggetto di vestiario, un oggetto di valore: "prendi, prendi Nunzia, porta via, non ti far vedere", perché i figlioli non s'accorgessero che lasciava troppe cose alla cameriera amorosa e fedele. E la Nunzia sui libretti della Cassa di Risparmio aveva venticinque anni di economie, tutto il denaro guadagnato, non aveva speso un soldo per vestirsi, della contessa le andava bene ogni cosa, era una donnina della sua corporatura, i vestiti e la biancheria, perfin le scarpe e le calze le andavano bene, e ne aveva

love with a man who was too handsome and was a meter and eighty-six centimeters tall, in love with that big man who seemed to be a cuirassier. It seemed to her to be something unfitting and dishonorable. She would have fits of weeping which she was not able to overcome.

When the Countess noticed that the woman's mind was upset, she called her to her side in a loving way, and with a smile full of indulgence she received her confession. The heart cannot be commanded, and even at forty-five, even if one is little and thin, one can fall in love with a cuirassier.

She spoke frankly to Bistino, and the upshot was that the wedding was set without delay. In her house, only legal ways were permitted. Bistino did not have to be asked twice; he could not believe that he was marrying that little woman, who was indeed homely and of an indefinable age, but who he felt had a secure position in the heart of the Countess.

It was the Countess's doing that they had as their property that little house of four rooms, all free, with a little garden surrounded by climbing roses, and in which Bistino amused himself growing lettuce, tomatoes, fruit and green vegetables: "a prize," those who came to see it would say, "a little jewel, a tidbit." Four rooms full of furniture, a fine bed-room, the living-room, the kitchen, and another little room which Nunzia kept in readiness to be rented to a student or to a young lady, in case their income was insufficient to live on. But their income was enough, quite enough without having to go without anything, for the Countess had left her ten lire per day as pension, and before dying, every day she used to pull something out of the drawer of her night table, or had her look for it in the bureau drawers: an envelope, another envelope, a piece of clothing, a valuable object: "Take it, take it, Nunzia, carry it away, don't let them see you," so that her children should not become aware that she was leaving too many things to her loving and faithful maid. And Nunzia had, in her savings bank books, the savings of twenty-five years, all the money she had earned; she had not spent a penny on clothing, for all the Countess's things fitted her well; she was a woman of the same build, and her dresses and linen, even her shoes

una scorta da poterle bastare fino a cent'anni se il Signore l'avesse lasciata vivere. La cameretta era pronta per affittare a una signorina o a uno studente ma per il momento non rappresentava una necessità, tutt'altro; le rendite erano sufficienti e la libertà della propria casa valeva più di quanto la signorina o lo studente potessero dare, si riserbava un tale rinforzo in caso di bisogno.

—Se tu vedessi . . . tu vedessi che scarpe . . . che scarpe!—Il vecchio domestico rivedeva l'armadio dov'erano scaglionate quaranta paia di scarpe:—unto, liso, senza i bottoni alla giacchetta e coi calzoni ricuciti in malo modo, deve averli rassettati da sé.

Rivedeva nella stanza di guardaroba i quattro armadi immensi, due per parte, zeppi dei vestiti e dei cappotti del padrone, per tutti i tempi e tutti i luoghi, per tutte le occasioni della sua vita d'uomo mondano, elegante: un centinaio di camicie, duecento cravatte.—Tu vedessi il colletto e la camicia . . . e i polsini, tanto sono sfilacciati sembrano con le frange, e con un dito di loia alle costure.

La donna annuiva col capo e sorrideva maro, rispondendo a ogni notizia o lasciandolo capire: "bene, bene, bene, ci ho piacere . . ."
—E lo sai dove va a dormire? In un albergo dove rimettono quelle donnine . . .
La Nunzia che seguitava a fare col capo: "bene, bene, bene, è il suo posto, ci ho piacere . . .", dava un guizzo repente:—Non ti salterà il ticchio di andarlo a trovare?

—No, macché! Ti pare . . . —rispondeva l'uomo sentendosi aggredito da quella frase.—Capirai, lo mandano via da tutte le case, non ha i soldi per pagare l'affitto. All'albergo dovrebbe pagare tre lire per notte, ma l'albergatore gli avanza trecento lire, lo tiene in uno sgabuzzino senza finestra, e la sera si deve spogliare con un pezzettino di candela, quando ce l'ha, e qualche volta niente, al buio. Il proprietario gli ha tolto la lampadina elettrica perché

and stockings fitted her well, and she had a supply sufficient to last her a hundred years if the Lord should let her live that long. The little room was ready to be rented to a young lady or a student, but for the time being it did not represent a necessity, quite the opposite; their income was sufficient and having their own house to themselves was worth more than what a young lady or a student might bring in; they were keeping this extra resource for possible need.

"If you could see . . . if you could see what shoes . . . what shoes!" The old servant recalled in his mind's eye the wardrobe in which forty pairs of shoes had been arranged in rows—"greasy, threadbare, without buttons on his coat and with his stockings mended badly; he must have mended them by himself."

He recalled in his mind's eye, in the cloak-room, the four huge wardrobes, two on each side, chock full of his master's suits and overcoats, for all seasons and all places, for all the occasions of his life as a worldly, elegant man: a hundred-odd shirts, two hundred ties. "If you could only see his collar and his shirt . . . and his cuffs, they are so frayed they seem to have fringes, and with an inch of dirt on the seams."

The woman nodded with her head and smiled bitterly, answering every report or letting it be understood: "Good, good, good, I'm glad of it . . ."

"And do you know where he goes to sleep? In a hotel where they house those women of easy virtue . . ."

Nunzia, who kept on nodding: "Good, good, good, that's the place for him, I'm glad of it," would suddenly flash forth: "You wouldn't be getting the notion of going to see him?"

"No, of course not! Do you think . . ." the man would answer, feeling as if attacked by such a question. "You understand, of course, they send him away from all the houses; he hasn't the money to pay his rent. At the hotel, he ought to pay three lire per night, but the hotel-keeper gives him an advance of three hundred lire, puts him in a tiny room without any window, and at night he has to undress by the light of a piece of candle, when he has it,

ha paura che stia sveglio nel letto a leggere il giornale.

Dimenticando per un momento quelle donnine, la Nunzia riprendeva col capo: "Bene, bene!". Bene che fosse andato a finire nel sudiciume con la gente di malaffare, bene che dovesse vivere nelle tenebre il giorno e la notte: "Bene, bene!"

* * *

Alla vita del marchese la giovinezza di Bistino era legata interamente. Era un suo contadino e lo aveva preso a quindici anni come ragazzo di scuderia. Poi, accorgendosi sempre meglio che pasta d'uomo fosse, era diventato, tutto insieme, scudiere e cameriere, uomo di fiducia, amministratore, segretario, segreto e galante. Nella vita del padrone sapeva riparare a tutto, a tutte le faccende, tutto far trovar pronto, tutto prevedere e dirigere, tutto rimediare. Aveva girato l'Europa con lui, ma in fondo non aveva visto nulla all'infuori del padrone, il padrone in tutte le nazioni europee. Del mondo conosceva un riflesso attraverso lui, i suoi gusti, le consuetudini, le idee, il suo modo di vivere, quasi fosse stato il solo e il più ragionevole: i suoi abiti, le scarpe, le sue cose. Il padrone e i cavalli. I cavalli erano quelli che ne avevano cementata l'unione; nel mondo coi suoi occhi aveva guardato soltanto i cavalli, alle passeggiate mondane, ai concorsi, alle corse rinomate. Aveva vissuto in tanti alberghi di tante città, le rivedeva tutte insieme in una giostra vertiginosa senza poter nulla fissare, nulla afferrare o di cui ricordava un particolare che a lui solo poteva aver ferito la fantasia, che lui solo era stato capace di cogliere. E parlava dei loro caratteri in una maniera così sintetica e originale da doversi chiedere come fosse costruita la sua zucca per fornire ragguagli di tal genere. Questo aveva visto. E le cameriere, in venticinque anni quante cameriere? Non sarebbe stato capace di ricordarle tutte. Si capisce che aveva finito per sposarne una, non la più bella ma la più saggia certamente, non poteva fare altra fine, e meglio di così non poteva finire.

and sometimes without anything, in the dark. The proprietor has taken away his electric light bulb because he is afraid that he will stay awake in his bed reading the paper."

Forgetting those women of easy virtue for a minute, Nunzia started to nod again: "Good, good!" Good that he should have ended up in filth with evildoers, good that he had to live in darkness day and night: "Good, good!"

* * *

Bistino's youth had been entirely linked with the life of the Marquis. He had been a peasant of his, and he had taken him at fifteen years of age as a stable boy. Then, as the Marquis had become more and more aware of the kind of man he was, he had become at the same time his stableman and valet, confidant, administrator and secretary, in private and amatory matters. In his master's life he knew how to put everything straight, take care of everything, provide everything on time, foresee and manage everything, remedy everything. He had been all over Europe with him, but in the last analysis he had seen nothing except his master himself in all the nations of Europe. Of the world, he knew a reflection through him, his tastes, his habits, his ideas, his mode of life, as if it had been the only one and the most reasonable: his clothes, his shoes, his things. His master and his horses. The horses were the thing that had held them firmly together; in the world, with his eyes he had seen only the horses, on elegant promenades, at meets, at famous races. He had lived in so many hotels in so many cities, he could see them all at the same time in a dizzying merry-go-round without being able to fix anything or grasp anything, or of which he would remember a particular which might have struck the imagination of himself alone, which he alone had been able to perceive. And he would talk about their character in such a perceptive and original way that you had to wonder how his head was built to supply him with comparisons of that kind. This was what he had seen. And the maids; in twenty-five years, how many maids? He would not have been able to remember

Se lo avesse saputo la Nunzia. Lo capiva, lo capiva anche troppo, ma non lo voleva ammettere, e soprattutto non ne voleva sentir parlare, guai a tenergliene parola, ché se lui ne avesse accennato solamente, gelosa com'era, gli si sarebbe rivoltata in furie. Il marchese era stato un donnaiolo per la pelle,[7] celeberrimo, un vero Don Giovanni;[8] le più belle donne del gran mondo, le cocottes del giorno erano state sue e, quasi fosse un quartetto predisposto, dove cadeva la padrona la cameriera cadeva di conseguenza, pareva un dovere. Bastavano due occhiate, poche parole, e cadevano come le pere quando sono mature. Bistino era stato il Don Giovanni delle cameriere, delle più belle e famose nel loro mondo quanto nel loro le padrone. O, più precisamente, il vero Don Giovanni erano state quelle che se l'erano palleggiato a volontà. Era stato anche lui un bel ragazzo, e conservando la freschezza e la serenità di uomo della campagna, era diventato un domestico elegante, irreprensibile, che sapeva cavalcare e guidare i cavalli da maestro. Faceva il bagno nell'acqua fredda tutte le mattine. Fra signore e domestico pareva un'intesa e, in fondo, un reciproco orgoglio, e una reciproca soddisfazione di maschi nel fare ciascuno, dal proprio posto, certe costatazioni che un sorriso furbo e discreto, o un colpetto di mano sulla spalla bastavano a porre in rilievo. E in quel sorriso come nel contatto della mano si nascondevano queste parole: "Come è inesauribile la vita, e come è bello vivere". Poteva Bistino dimenticare queste cose?

— Tu lo vedessi, secco, allampanato, giallo come un popone, gobbo . . . non ha più il fiato di parlare, io dico che sia malato, sembra più piccino la metà, non si riconosce, non ha una delle sue idee.

them all. Of course, he had finally married one of them, not the most beautiful but certainly the most sensible; he could have come to no other end, and he could not have ended up any better.

If Nunzia had only known! She understood, in fact she understood only too well, but she didn't want to admit it, and above all she didn't want to hear anything said about it; woe to him if he spoke to her about it, for if he had even hinted at it, she, jealous as she was, would have turned against him in a rage. The Marquis had been a woman's man from the word go, very renowned, a real Don Juan; the most beautiful women of high society and the "cocottes" of the day had been his, and, as if it had been a pre-arranged quartet, when the mistress yielded the maid fell as well; it seemed to be a duty. Two glances were enough, a few words, and they would fall like pears when they are ripe. Bistino had been the Don Juan of the maids, of those who were most beautiful and famous in their world as the mistresses in theirs. Or, more exactly, the true Don Juans had been the women who had batted him back and forth between themselves as they wished. He too had been a handsome young fellow, and, preserving the freshness and the serenity of a man of the country, he had become an elegant, irreproachable servant, who knew how to ride and drive his master's horses. He took a cold-water bath every morning. Between master and man there seemed to be an understanding, and, basically, a mutually shared pride, and a mutually shared satisfaction of men in making, each of them from his own vantage-point, certain observations which a sly and discreet smile, or a little pat on the shoulder was enough to emphasize. And in that smile, as in the contact of the hand, were hidden these words: "How inexhaustible life is, and how good it is to be alive!" Could Bistino forget these things?

"If you could only see him, dried up, gaunt, as yellow as a melon, bent over . . . he no longer has the breath to speak; I say that he is sick, he seems reduced to half his size, he is no longer recognizable, he hasn't even got one of his old ideas."

BISTINO E IL SIGNOR MARCHESE

E c'erano i malumori del marchese, i pasticci, le contrarietà: gli strozzini, le cambiali, le ipoteche, i debiti da pagare, le avventure difficili o andate alla rovescia, le impazienze, le furie violentisime. E avendo sempre Bistino alle calcagne e non avendo che lui, egli rappresentava la famiglia, tutto finiva sulle sue spalle. Bistino era felice di porgerle e capacissime. I vestiti non erano tenuti bene, le scarpe lucidate male, i cavalli non erano stati ispezionati prima d'uscire, le commissioni eseguite in modo balordo; urla e strepiti del marchese finché una scarpa o uno stivale: "pum!" gli capitavano nel groppone. Lui, invece di dolersene, amava quegli sfoghi intimi, quelle rabbie, quelle furie; sentiva in quel momento, più che in ogni altro, quello che rappresentava per il padrone, quello che era, sentiva d'essergli unito e indispensabile, più assai di quando era felice e tutto andava a vele gonfie. A chiusura di conti sentiva d'essere il solo a volergli bene, e il solo a cui il padrone volesse bene veramente. L'ira e le scenate rappresentavano l'affetto, anche le scarpe nel groppone. Infatti, non appena rasserenato, si rasserenava con facilità il marchese che attraverso la scioperataggine era d'animo generoso e nobile, diveniva espansivo, cordiale, tornava allegro, faceto, sentiva il bisogno di dimostrargli il proprio pentimento e di farsi perdonare; gli regalava del denaro, una scatola di sigarette, due cravatte, quel che gli capitava fra le mani sul momento, gli metteva una mano sulla spalla in tono amichevole, confidenziale; le furie cementavano di più il reciproco attaccamento: il cuore semplice non poteva sbagliare.

Seduto nella cucina dove la moglie preparava il pranzo o la cena, come su uno schermo l'uomo rivedeva tutte insieme queste cose, e parlava a sé stesso, non trovando adeguato riscontro al proprio sentire: "Poverino . . . le aveva proprio tutte!" Intendeva dire che tutte le passioni umane lo avevano posseduto, divorato, arso: i cavalli, il giuoco, le

BISTINO AND THE MARQUIS

And there had been the Marquis' ill-humors, the messes, the things that went wrong: the money-lenders, the promissory notes, the mortgages, the debts to be paid, the adventures which were difficult or went wrong, his expressions of impatience, his tremendous rages. And as he always had Bistino at his heels and no one but him, Bistino stood for his domestic staff and everything ended up on his shoulders. Bistino was happy to offer them, broad as they were. If the clothes had not been kept in proper condition, or the shoes had been poorly shined, or the horses had not been inspected before setting out, or errands had been carried out clumsily, there were yells and shouts from the Marquis until, bang! went a shoe or a boot on Bistino's back. He, instead of complaining, loved those intimate outbursts, those rages, those furies; he felt in that moment, more than in any other, what he symbolized for his master, what he was; he felt that he was joined to him and indispensable, considerably more so than when he [his master] was happy and everything was going ahead full sail. In the last analysis, he felt that he was the only one who loved him, and the only one whom his master really loved. His anger and rows symbolized affection, even the shoes in the small of his back. In fact, as soon as he calmed down—and the Marquis, who underneath his indolence had a generous and noble spirit, calmed down quickly—he became genial and cordial and was cheerful and witty again, and felt the need of showing Bistino that he was sorry and of begging his pardon; he would give him money, a box of cigarettes, a couple of ties, or whatever happened to be within reach at the moment, and he would put a hand on his shoulder in a friendly, confidential manner. His rages would intensify their mutual attachment; the simple heart could not be wrong.

Seated in the kitchen where his wife was preparing lunch or supper, the man would see again, as if on a screen, all these things together, and would speak to himself, finding no adequate expression for his feelings: "Poor man . . . he had absolutely all of them!" He meant that all the human passions had possessed him, devoured him, consumed him:

donne, i bagordi. Prendeva certe sbronze per le quali gli rimaneva fra le braccia tramortito, inerte, e doveva coricarlo come un lattante: "Poverino . . . le aveva tutte . . . tutte le aveva; tutte . . ." ripeteva assorto.—Poverino un corno!—rispondeva la donna per risvegliarlo.—Le aveva tutte e ora le paga tutte, a questo mondo bisogna pagare, viene il sabato, non dubitare.—Scodellava la minestra fumante e Bistino s'avvicinava alla tavola pensieroso e afflitto.—Prima o poi viene, viene, altro se viene, e c'è chi paga e chi riscuote—borbottava riportando la pentola sotto il camino:—e basta una a dover pagarne molte.

Un giorno la Nunzia scappò con una frase a cui Bistino non ebbe forza di rispondere tanto si sentì invaso dalla felicità. Non ci poteva nemmeno credere, si toccava addosso per assicurarsi d'essere sempre lui e di non sognare.

— Una di queste domeniche dobbiamo invitare a pranzo il tuo marchese. Per quel giorno gli si leva la fame, che ne deve avere la sua parte.

Appena riavuto la prese in collo e la portò in giro per tutta la casa quasi fosse stata un bimbo, un gatto o un cane, anche nell'orto la portò, dove gl'inquilini dei piani soprastanti s'affacciarono alle finestre per vedere, mentre lei si dibatteva e si agitava divincolando le gambe e ridendo convulsamente:

— Lasciami! Lasciami!—strillava,—lasciami, mi fai male! Lasciami stare.

Ma invece di posarla seguitava a correre e a ripetere:

—Accetta, vedrai, viene, lo so, sono sicuro che viene, non gli par vero di venire, lo so . . .

Sapeva di dargli una consolazione così grande che non fu capace di resistere: "Vedremo un po' quel che succede" pensava, "non cascherà il mondo per invitarlo una volta a desinare". E quando l'ebbe posata diceva:—Io dico anch'io

horses, gaming, women, riotous living. He would on occasion get so drunk that he would fall into Bistino's arms in a coma, limp, and he would have to put him to bed like a baby: "Poor man . . . he had them all . . . he had them all, all . . ." he would repeat as in a trance. "Poor man, my eye!" the woman would answer to bring him to his senses. "He had them all and now he is paying for them all; in this world, you have to pay, the day of reckoning always comes, don't doubt it." She would dish out the steaming soup and Bistino would come to the table, thoughtful and worried. "Sooner or later it comes, it comes, it certainly does come, and some people pay and some people collect what is due them," she would mutter as she put the pot back away under the fireplace again, "and one is enough so that you have to pay for a lot of them."

One day Nunzia let fall a sentence which Bistino did not have the strength to answer, because he felt so overcome with happiness. He could not even believe his ears, and he touched himself to make sure that he was still himself and was not dreaming.

"One of these Sundays we must invite your Marquis to dinner. For that day he'll be relieved of his hunger, and he must have his share of that."

As soon as he came to himself he took her up and carried her around throughout the whole house as if she had been a child, a cat or a dog; he even carried her out into the garden, where the inhabitants of the upper floors looked out of the windows to see, while she was struggling and floundering, kicking her legs and laughing convulsively:

"Let me go! Let me go!" she yelled, "Let me go, you're hurting me! Leave me alone!"

But instead of setting her down he kept on running and saying:

"He will accept, you'll see, he'll come, I know, I'm sure that he'll come, he'll be overjoyed to come, I know . . ."

She knew that she was giving him so great a consolation that she could not resist: "We'll just see what will happen," she thought, "the world won't come to an end just because we invite him once to lunch." And when Bistino had set

che viene, con quella po' po' di fetta che si rimpasta . . .

* * *

Il marchese mostrò di gradire l'invito, ma senza un sorriso; la sua bocca non era più capace di sorridere. E quella domenica all'ora fissata, si recò dall'antico domestico dove lo aspettava un pranzetto del quale approfittò parcamente. La sua fibra era scossa nel profondo, non era più che un malato e un vinto: una larva. Con molta naturalezza si mostrò riconoscente, e nella triste realtà ancora signore; tanto che gli ospiti provarono durante il pranzo una notevole delusione piuttosto che l'istintivo imbarazzo di due vecchi domestici davanti a quello che era stato il padrone.

Bistino lo guardava estatico, non credendo ai propri occhi, dimenticando di mangiare e aspettando sempre quello che non poteva venire: un segno di gioia nella faccia del vecchio pallida e affaticata, sofferente; e risvegliandosi solo per offrire un'altra cosa al signor marchese, ma che il sollecitato rifiutava con garbo e senza sorridere. Non era contento d'essere lì? Non si trovava bene? "Signor marchese, signor marchese" ripeteva Bistino fra entusiasmato e spaventato. La donna stava a vedere. Il signor marchese avrebbe preferito di non sentir pronunciare troppo spesso quel titolo così stridente nello stato attuale, ma non osava manifestarne il disappunto, mentre invece mostrava bene la soggezione del proprio abito al modo di chi per naturale pudore copre con un senso di vergogna le nudità del corpo che non vorrebbe esporre. Profondamente incuriosita al giuoco di cui non riusciva a valutare la fine, la donna li osservava tutti e due. Ora guardava il marchese: "Come t'ha conciato bene il poco cervello!" Ora guardava il marito: "Che cosa si deve vedere. Che cosa gli piace a questo zuzzerellone". E a poco a poco si sentiva presa da una vaga pietà per l'ospite e da una viva tenerezza per il marito; ma subito interrotta e cancellata dal risentimento acre, e quasi dal pentimento d'aver provato tenerezza e

her down, she said: "I too say that he'll come, with that little mouth to be fed . . ."

* * *

The Marquis showed that he appreciated the invitation, but without a smile; his mouth was no longer capable of smiling. And that Sunday, at the hour set, he went to his former servant's, where there was waiting for him a little meal of which he partook frugally. His constitution had been shaken to its depths; he was no longer anything but a sick and defeated man, an empty shell. With great naturalness he showed that he was grateful and, even in his present sad condition, still a gentleman, so much so that his hosts experienced during the meal a marked disappointment rather than the instinctive embarrassment of two old servants in the presence of the man who had been the master.

Bistino looked at him in ecstasy, not believing his own eyes, forgetting to eat and continually waiting for what could not come—a sign of happiness on the pale, wearied and suffering face of the old man—and coming out of his absorption only to offer the Marquis something further, which, on being invited, he would refuse with grace but without smiling. Was he not happy to be there? Was he not comfortable? "My lord Marquis, my lord Marquis," Bistino kept repeating, half enraptured and half frightened. The woman was observing. The Marquis would have preferred not to hear pronounced too often that title which was so discordantly at variance with his present condition, but he did not dare to show his vexation, whereas on the other hand he indeed showed uneasiness over his garb, after the fashion of a person who, out of innate modesty, covers with a sense of shame the bareness of his body which he would not like to expose to view. Deeply curious concerning this interplay, whose aim she could not fathom, the woman keep looking at both of them. Now she would look at the Marquis and think "How your lack of sense has ruined you!"; then she would look at her husband and think: "What must we see! What is it that pleases this big scatterbrain!" And gradually she felt herself overcome by a

pietà.

Dopo il pranzo i due uomini uscirono insieme; la Nunzia rimase a casa perché stanca dei preparativi che l'invito aveva richiesto, e poi perché doveva rimettere in ordine le cose; il pranzo era stato servito nel salotto, con solennità.

Una volta solo con lui, Bistino avrebbe voluto che l'antico signore si risvegliasse, si rallegrasse; lo fissava offrendogli l'anima, ma non riusciva a risvegliarlo e a farlo rallegrare. Il poveretto, sia fuori come in casa durante il pranzo, mantenne una cupa parsimonia di parole. Soprattutto Bistino avrebbe voluto portare il discorso sul passato, e cercava ogni pretesto per arrivarci: ricordava venticinque anni di vita in comune, i viaggi, le avventure, i cavalli, le donne, le sbornie . . . Ma si capiva che l'altro non era del medesimo avviso, le cose che lo avevano appassionato tanto, erano proprio quelle che non voleva ricordare, come non esistessero neppure; e si accendeva solo quando parlava del presente, delle condizioni tristissime, le angherie dell'albergatore d'infimo rango, il rifugio indecente, il cugino di Siena che sempre doveva mandare e non mandava nulla o troppo poco; quando l'aveva minacciato di farsi ricoverare nell'ospizio dei vecchi gli aveva promesso centocinquanta lire al mese per salvare la dignità del casato, e poi glie ne mandava cinquanta, o cento assai raramente, adducendo che le raccolte erano andate male. Anche un amico di Milano, ricchissimo, gli mandava di quando in quando qualche soccorso, ma erano necessarie lunghe e ripetute epistole. Gli altri facevano orecchio di mercante, gli usavano spostature, nessuno intendeva riceverlo ed ascoltarlo: *"Ou ils sont fatigués . . . ou ils sont indisposés . . . ou ils sont malades. La race décline"*. O rispondevano con offerte sproporzionate alle esigenze del vivere. Tali erano gli argomenti per cui il vecchio s'accendeva ancora, e di questi a Bistino non importava niente.

vague pity for her guest and by a strong feeling of tenderness for her husband, which, however, was immediately broken off and wiped out by bitter resentment, and almost by repentance for having felt tenderness and pity.

After dinner the two men went out together; Nunzia remained at home because she had been tired out by the preparations that the invitation had made necessary, and then because she had to put things back in shape again; the lunch had been served in the living-room, with solemnity.

Once he was alone with him, Bistino would have liked for his former master to come to life again, to cheer up; he gazed at him, offering him his soul, but he could not succeed in enlivening him and cheering him up. The poor fellow, both outdoors and at home during the meal, remained gloomily laconic. Above all, Bistino would have liked to bring the conversation around to the past, and sought every pretext to do so: he recalled twenty-five years of life in common, the trips, the adventures, the horses, the women, the sprees . . . But it was clear that the other man was not of the same opinion; the things which had formerly excited him so much were just the ones which he did not wish to remember, as if they had not even existed; and he lit up only when he talked about the present, about his miserable way of life, the meanness of the low-class hotel-keeper, his shameful lodging, his cousin in Siena who was always supposed to send him a remittance and who remitted either nothing or too little. When the Marquis had threatened to get himself committed to the old people's home, the cousin had promised him a hundred and fifty lire per month to save the family honor, and then he sent him fifty, or (very rarely) a hundred, with the excuse that the harvests had been poor. A friend of his in Milan, too, who was very rich, would send him something from time to time as a subvention, but he had to write at length and repeatedly. The others turned a deaf ear and were discourteous to him; no one had any intention of receiving him and listening to him: "Either they are tired . . . or they are indisposed . . . or they are sick. The race is declining." Or they would

BISTINO E IL SIGNOR MARCHESE

* * *

Un'altra volta i coniugi invitarono a pranzo, di domenica, il marchese. Quindi una terza, una quarta volta; finché, visto che lo si poteva invitare senza uno spostamento del costume familiare, apparecchiando in cucina come sempre, fu stabilito d'invitarlo tutte le domeniche. Una buona minestra, col brodo tirato bene, la Nunzia faceva un brodo eccellente, era quello che gradiva di più, di cui sentiva una profonda necessità e per la quale mostrava vera soddisfazione e gratitudine; dopo appariva sollevato e sazio; gli bastavano pochi bocconi di una cosa qualunque che buttava giù con lentezza, senza le voracità caratteristiche delle pance disabitate. "Questo le abbraccia lo stomaco" diceva la Nunzia con una punta d'ironia che non riusciva a vincere, mentre il poverino veramente se lo sentiva abbracciare. Altrimenti, invitandolo a mangiare di più, sfoggiava una curiosa immagine: "La bocca porta le gambe", fiera di dire una cosa spiritosa, paradossale.

Finché una domenica, con inaudita sorpresa e gioia di Bistino il signor marchese, non si sa come mai di punto in bianco incominciò a ridere: *"Ah! Ah! Ah! cochon!"* disse al vecchio servitore. "Di dove vengono quelle risate? Diventa matto?" pensava la Nunzia che s'era abituata a vederlo funebre: "è la sua fine, bisognerà chiamar gente per farlo legare". *"Ah! Ah! Ah! cochon!"* ripeteva il marchese facendo l'atto di spunzonar la pancia di Bistino che se la reggeva dal ridere.

Non era pazzia la sua ilarità inaspettata, ma scaltrezza bella e buona; e siccome Bistino rideva da crepare: "Diventano matti tutti e due", pensava la donna, "ci vorrà la gabbia del manicomio per legarli insieme".

reply with offers that were out of proportion to the demands of living. These were the topics over which the old man could still get excited, and about these Bistino cared nothing.

* * *

Once more the husband and wife invited the Marquis to dinner on Sunday; then a third time and a fourth, until, when they perceived that they could invite him without disturbing their domestic habits, and setting the table in the kitchen as usual, it was decided to invite him every Sunday. A good soup, with the broth well drawn—Nunzia made an excellent soup—was what he enjoyed most, for which he felt a deep need and for which he showed true satisfaction and gratitude; afterwards, he appeared relieved and well-fed. All he needed was a few mouthfuls of anything whatsoever, which he would consume slowly, without the voracity characteristic of uninhabited stomachs. "This will embrace your stomach," Nunzia would say, with a dash of irony which she could not succeed in overcoming, while the poor man in truth felt it embraced. Or otherwise, on inviting him to eat more, she would display a curious figure of speech: "The mouth carries the legs," proud of saying something witty and paradoxical.

Finally one Sunday, to the unprecedented surprise and joy of Bistino, the Marquis, no one knows how, all of a sudden began to laugh: "Ha, ha, ha! You swine!" he said to his old servant. "Where does that laughter come from? Is he going crazy?" thought Nunzia, who had grown accustomed to seeing him gloomy: "This is the end of him, we shall have to call someone in to have him tied up." "Ha, ha, ha! You swine!" repeated the Marquis, making as if to punch Bistino in his stomach, which he was holding for laughter.

His unexpected hilarity was not madness, but downright shrewdness, and, since Bistino was laughing fit to burst, the woman thought: "They are both going crazy, we'll have to have the cage from the madhouse and tie them both up at the same time."

Dopo di che, sollevatosi da quella prostrazione plumbea incominciò a parlare, e parlare di tutto, di tutte le cose, del più e del meno, ma del passato specialmente, i cavalli, le donne, sissignori, anche delle donne. E sempre crescendo in vivacità: *"Ah! cochon!"* ripeteva al suo vecchio cameriere. E la donna ripeteva a sé stessa: "Te lo dicevo io, ci voleva il mio brodo per risuscitare questo morto di fame".

Bistino non ci vedeva più dalla contentezza. E suggeriva, ricordava al marchese con la premura di chi deve vuotare il sacco.[9] A un certo punto lo fissava spaventato, temendo che con le proprie faccende ne spiattellasse qualcheduna delle sue, la Nunzia gli sarebbe saltata agli occhi con le unghie. Ma era bravo il marchese, bravissimo, la sapeva lunga,[10] e per quanto in catastrofe non aveva dimenticato l'arte del vivere, tanto che la donna, quando fu sola col marito finì per riconoscere: "In fondo, questi scioperati fanno ridere, quando è in valvola non è antipatico il tuo marchese". Ragione per cui venne invitato anche il giovedì. Poi tutti i giorni e infine, dopo un dibattito tutt'altro che facile, nel quale la donna alla fine dovette cedere, visto che la camera era pronta e non serviva a nessuno, e visto che il marchese col poco che mangiava non costava più di un cane, un bel giorno fu aspettato a casa di Bistino in pianta stabile. "Si proverà . . . si starà a vedere . . ." disse la Nunzia per concludere.

Vi giunse in panni di gamba e di qual genere. Né un fazzoletto, né una camicia, né un colletto, né un paio di calze. O che la roba fosse in condizioni da non superare il trasloco, o che per non insospettire il proprietario dell'albergo non avesse preso nulla; probabilmente aveva eseguito una partenza clandestina sotto gli stessi occhi dell'albergatore che gli avanzava quattrocento lire. Bisognò rifarsi da una parte, e con molta roba di Bistino per ridurlo in uno stato tollerabile.

* * *

After which, recovering from that leaden depression, he began to talk, and to talk about everything, about all things, important and unimportant, but especially about the past, the horses, the women, yes, even about the women. And growing continually more and more hilarious, he would repeat: "Ha, ha! You swine!" to his old valet. And the woman kept repeating to herself: "I told you so, it took my soup to bring this starved man back to life."

Bistino was beside himself with happiness. And he kept prompting the Marquis and reminding him with the eagerness of one who wants to hear the whole story. At a certain point he looked at him in a fright, fearing that, along with his own doings, the Marquis might let the cat out of the bag concerning some of Bistino's, and Nunzia would jump at him and scratch his eyes out. But the Marquis was clever, really clever; he knew what was what, and although he was utterly ruined he had not forgotten the art of living, so that the woman, when she was alone with her husband, had to admit finally: "After all, these good-for-nothings are amusing; when he's going strong, your Marquis is not unpleasant." For this reason he was invited on Thursdays, too: then every day, and finally, after a very difficult discussion, in which the woman eventually had to give in, seeing that the room was available and was not being used by anyone, and seeing that the Marquis ate so little that he cost no more than a dog, one fine day he was awaited at Bistino's on a permanent basis. "We'll try it out . . . we'll see . . ." said Nunzia, in concluding.

He arrived wearing everything he owned, and of what a kind it was! Not a single handkerchief, not a shirt, not a collar, not a pair of socks. Either because the stuff was in such shape that it would not have survived the move, or because, so as not to arouse the suspicions of the hotelkeeper, he had brought nothing with him; probably he had absconded under the very eyes of the hotelkeeper, to whom he owed four hundred lire. They had to start over again from scratch, and with a lot of Bistino's things, to put him in a tolerable condition again.

* * *

BISTINO E IL SIGNOR MARCHESE

Installato nella camerina luminosa e decente, al disgraziato parve di rinascere, come già la domenica alle prime cucchiaiate di quella minestra ristoratrice; ed escogitava ogni mezzo per non giuocarsi alla leggera il nuovo benessere che nulla al mondo gli avrebbe lasciato sperare. La sua educazione e la logica della vita gli avrebbero suggerito di comportarsi con tale delicatezza e un tatto così fine nelle penose circostanze, da far sentire il proprio peso meno che fosse possibile, come se non ci fosse; unico modo, insieme, di salvare presso due ex domestici benefattori l'ultimo rimasuglio della propria dignità. Ma la logica non è sempre la legge del nostro vivere anzi, il più delle volte non c'entra nemmeno per il buco della chiave, giacché esso è caratterizzato dalle illogicità più assurde.

Bistino da parte sua si addolorava che il marchese accettasse tutto senza fiatare e, con la decenza del signore caduto in disgrazia, trovasse che tutto era buono e fatto bene; e non sporgesse mai un parere, un desiderio, un ordine: "mi comandi, mi comandi, non si riguardi, non si prenda soggezione, io non ho nulla da fare", diceva Bistino offrendosi col cuore: "mi comandi signor marchese", ripeteva mortificato e offeso che l'altro non comandasse. Non riusciva a persuadersi che la persona alla quale aveva obbedito per venticinque anni si fosse dimenticata di comandare, e comandare a bacchetta come era suo costume, senza indugi o reticenze; gli pareva che di questo dovesse soffrire più di tutte le altre cose, e lo guardava deluso come a tavola le prime domeniche quando non voleva ridere e rivivere con lui tante belle memorie, parlare di un tempo e di una vita che ora gli procurava dolore. Ogni tanto s'avvicinava alla porta in ascolta quindi diceva piano, soffocando la voce: "Signor marchese, ha bisogno di niente?"

Da quel conoscitore del mondo e della vita anche nel

Once he had been installed in the bright and respectable room, the unfortunate man seemed to be born again, just as he had on that Sunday at the first spoonfuls of that health-restoring soup; and he devised every way possible not to risk lightly this new well-being which nothing in the world could have led him to hope for. His upbringing and the logic of life would have suggested to him that he behave with such delicacy and such a refinement of tact in these painful circumstances as to cause his weight to be felt as little as possible, as if he were not there; at the same time, this was the only way to save, with his two benefactors who were also former servants, the last remaining shred of his dignity. But logic is not always the law of our life; on the contrary, on most occasions it doesn't even come in through the keyhole, since our life is characterized by the most absurd illogicality.

Bistino, for his part, was grieved that the Marquis accepted everything without a word, and that, with the good manners of a well-born person who has come down in the world, he found that everything was good and well done, and never uttered an opinion, a request, an order: "I'm at your service, I'm at your service, don't be hesitant, don't be shy; I have nothing else to do," Bistino would say, offering his services with all his heart: "I'm at your service, my lord Marquis," he would repeat, shamed and offended that the other would not give him orders. He could not convince himself that the person whom he had obeyed for twenty-five years had forgotten how to give orders and to rule with an iron rod as his custom had been, without delay or reticence; Bistino thought that the Marquis must suffer from this more than everything else, and looked at him with disappointment as he had done at table on the first Sundays when the Marquis had been unwilling to laugh and to re-live with him all those beautiful memories and to talk about a time and a kind of life which now caused him sorrow. From time to time he would go up to the door and listen, and then say softly, smothering his voice: "My lord Marquis, don't you need anything?"

Like the connoisseur of the world and of life that he was,

disfacimento totale, il marchese capì che bisognava rispondere, e una mattina dalla sua camera partì una voce roca e rabbiosa, e un nome ripetuto senza tregua: "Bistino! Bistino! Bistino!" Bistino si rovesciò dal letto e corse mezzo nudo a sentire che volesse il suo antico signore; mentre la Nunzia, schizzata a sedere, stropicciandosi gli occhi si domandava impaziente: "Che gli piglia? Che vuole? Gli è venuto un accidente? Si sente male? Che maniera è questa di chiamare?"

"Bistino!" urlava il marchese; e Bistino rispondeva correndo infatuato abbottonandosi le mutande: "Eccomi, corro, pronto signor marchese".

—Che voleva?—chiese dopo prendendo partito la moglie: —Che voleva, si può sapere?

— Nulla, il vestito e le scarpe, stamani va fuori presto, fa bene con questa giornata, c'è un sole . . .

— Ah! . . . il vestito e le scarpe . . . senti senti . . . e ti chiama con quella prepotenza? Per questo ci ha svegliati e ti ha fatto alzare?

— Capirai . . . in fin dei conti è sempre un marchese, s'ha un bel dire, è abituato a comandare, poverino, non ne ha colpa, lo fa senza accorgersene, lui non se ne accorge—diceva raggiante.

— Non se ne accorge . . . perché è sempre un marchese . . . —S'erigeva gonfia di minacce:—Alla fine del salmo ci penserò io a fargliene accorgere, e dopo gli dirò che cos'è. E dirò anche quello che sei te a rispondere. Un marchese . . . Bellino, sì, bellino il tuo marchese: oggi lo fo [11] filare, gli dico di andarsene.

Bistino si buttò alle ginocchia della moglie incapace di rendersi conto riguardo al sentimento che l'animava; vedendolo apparentemente confuso e sentendolo felice interiormente; la supplicò di perdonarlo, di non mandarlo via. Ma da quel giorno nella camerina modesta e silenziosa, si fece sentire sempre più alta la voce di un padrone: "Bistino! Lesto perdio! Che fai gingillone? Polendone! Lazzerone! Stai a grattarti le natiche? Presto marmotta,

even in total ruin, the Marquis understood that he had to do something in reply, and one morning there came from his room a hoarse and angry voice, and a name repeated unceasingly: "Bistino! Bistino! Bistino!" Bistino tumbled out of bed and ran half naked to find what his old master wanted, while Nunzia jerked upright and, rubbing her eyes, wondered impatiently: "What's gotten into him? What does he want? Is he having a fit? Is he feeling bad? What manner of calling is this?"

"Bistino!" the Marquis yelled, and Bistino answered as he ran along, all excited, buttoning his underwear: "Here I am, I'm coming right away, at your service, my lord Marquis."

"What did he want?" his wife asked afterwards, taking sides: "What did he want, may one ask?"

"Nothing, his suit and shoes, this morning he's going out early, it's a good idea on a day like this; there's a sun . . ."

"Oh! . . . his suit and shoes . . . just listen to that . . . and he calls you with such arrogance! Is that why he waked us up and made you get up?"

"You see . . . after all, he's still a marquis, no matter what you say, he's accustomed to giving orders, poor man, it's not his fault, he does it without realizing, he doesn't realize," Bistino said, radiant.

"He doesn't realize . . . because he's still a marquis . . ." Nunzia rose up, swelling with threats: "When all's said and done, I'll see to making him realize, and then I'll tell him what he is. And I'll tell him also what you are when you answer. A marquis . . . A fine fellow, yes, a fine fellow, this marquis of yours; I'll chuck him out today, I'll tell him to get out of here."

Bistino cast himself at the knees of his wife, who was unable to analyze the feeling that animated him, when she saw him apparently confused but perceived that he was inwardly happy; he begged her to pardon him and not to send him away. But from that day on, in the unassuming, quiet room was heard, louder and louder, the voice of a master: "Bistino! Hurry up, for Heaven's sake! What are you doing, you loafer? You slow-poke! You lazy-bones! Are

lumacone!" Urla, comandi, rimproveri, insolenze, minacce. La Nunzia osservava il giuoco cercando di capire, ma non diceva niente. *"Je te f . . . à la porte! Vattene!"* urlava il signor marchese. Girando l'Europa Bistino non aveva imparato una parola di nessuna lingua, ma quando gridava il padrone le capiva tutte.

"Vattene? . . . Dove?" pensava la donna disorientata: "qui se uno deve andarsene sei proprio te, solamente te, caro il mio marchese, e con tutto il bagaglio che ti sei portato venendo". Non intendeva tollerare in casa sua una giostra di quella specie. Si sarebbe incaricata senza indugio di farlo marciare. Ma la faccia del marito la lasciava perplessa, le faceva rattenere quel grido di rivolta che il viso annunziava imminente. Non l'aveva visto mai così soddisfatto, così allegro, così felice. Voleva stare a vedere un altro poco come si metteva il giuoco, poi avrebbe pensato lei a dire due paroline all'ospite. Quello zuzzerellone di Bistino avrebbe avuto un bel raccomandarsi e piagnucolare.

* * *

Però con la Nunzia il marchese era un altro uomo assolutamente. Gli ordini, i rimproveri, le parolacce erano circoscritti alla sua camera con matematica precisione, e questo più ancora le dava a riflettere. Con lei era premuroso, gentile, tutto elogi e complimenti, inchini e sorrisi, finezze e galanterie, da signore autentico. Il vitto era squisito, ottimo, eccellente, lo paragonava a quello dei cuochi famosi stati nelle grandi famiglie che lei pure conosceva di nome, o di persona per averne visto i componenti presso la contessa: duchesse, principesse, marchese, fino a quello celeberrimo di Vittorio Emanuele II, che lasciò ai posteri un manuale di cucina reputatissimo. La riveriva quasi fosse ospite di una dama. E una volta in camera con Bistino, urla, scenate, insolenze, e in mezzo a quelle gridi di gioia e risate omeriche. "Ma insomma, in che mondo si vive?" pensava la Nunzia combattuta fra la ribellione e le lusinghe.

you standing there scratching your rear? Hurry up, you oaf, you snail!" Shouts, orders, scoldings, insults, threats. Nunzia observed what was going on and tried to understand, but said nothing. "I'll fire you! Get out of here!" the Marquis would shout. As they travelled around Europe, Bistino had not learned a single word in any language, but when his master shouted he understood them all.

"Get out? . . . Where to?" the woman thought in her confusion: "Here, if anybody is to get out, it ought to be you, only you, my dear Marquis, and with all the luggage you brought with you when you came." She did not intend to stand for a merry-go-round of that kind in her house; she would have taken it on herself to send him packing without delay. But her husband's face left her in perplexity, and made her restrain that cry of revolt which her face announced as imminent. She had never seen him so satisfied, so cheerful, so happy. She wanted to wait and see a little while longer how the game would go, then she was going to see about saying a word or two to their guest. It would be quite useless for that lunkhead Bistino to beg and whimper.

* * *

But with Nunzia the Marquis was a totally different man. The orders and scoldings and bad language were restricted to his room with mathematical precision, and this caused her to wonder still more. With her he was considerate, kind, full of praise and compliments, bows and smiles, expressions of refinement and delicacy, like a true gentleman. The food was exquisite, marvelous, excellent; he would compare it to that prepared by the famous cooks who had been with the great families whom even she knew by name, or in person because she had seen their members at the Countess's: duchesses, princesses, marquises, even to that very famous cook of Victor Emanuel II, who had left to posterity a highly esteemed cooking manual. He would pay his respects to her as if he were the guest of a lady of high station. But when he was in his room with Bistino, there would be shouts, rows, insults, and in their midst there would be

E parlando col marito già poneva in evidenza questa diversità: "lo fa con te perché sa di poterlo fare, con me, stai pur sicuro, non lo farebbe; con me riga diritto il signor marchese. Sa che lo può fare, si capisce, ti conosce ormai, ti conosce anche troppo e ne approfitta, guarda come si comporta con me".

Questo portava Bistino al settimo cielo, giacché se era felice che il marchese lo trattasse con l'antica confidenza e intimità, d'altra parte era felice che si comportasse da gentiluomo verso la moglie, che la rispettasse e le usasse ogni riguardo, anche perché questo serviva a paralizzarne il risentimento. "Te lo dicevo io, vedi che signore perbene, come ti considera eh? Che educazione", le ripeteva Bistino incessantemente. "Ognuno riceve il trattamento che si merita", concludeva lei rizzando la cresta, incominciando ad essere sensibile di un tale fatto e a inorgoglirsene, atteggiandosi a dignità, atteggiamento che le riusciva facile essendo vissuta al fianco di una dama irreprensibile e in margine alla società. Per concludere certe disturne il marito le rispondeva:

— Senti Nunzia, se a un tratto tu sentissi la voce della contessa che ti chiama, tu anderesti giù dalla finestra per far più presto a rispondere.

— Lo puoi dir forte, e non farei che il mio dovere.—Lo fissava minacciosa:—E vorresti mettere la contessa con questo pezzente?

— No, vedi, i denari non contano, in queste cose quello che conta è il cuore. Se anche la contessa morisse di fame tu non le daresti da mangiare?

— Me lo leverei dalla bocca per darglielo.—Veniva tutta su:—e vorresti mettere la contessa con questo scimpanzè? E poi, quando mi chiamava la contessa lo faceva con gentilezza, da persona bene educata, non gridava mica porcona,

outcries of joy and Homeric laughter. "But, after all, what sort of world is this we are living in?" Nunzia would think, torn between rebellion and flattery. And when she talked with her husband, she would make this difference clear: "He does it to you because he knows he can do it, but with me, you may be sure, he wouldn't do it; with me, my lord the Marquis walks a chalk line. He knows he can do it, of course, he knows you by now, he knows you even too well and is profiting by it; just look how he behaves with me."

This put Bistino in seventh heaven, since, if he was happy that the Marquis was treating him with his old confidence and intimacy, on the other hand he was happy that he was behaving like a gentleman to his wife, that he was respecting her and being considerate in every way, also because this served to quiet her resentment. "I told you so; do you see what a real gentleman he is, how considerate he is towards you, eh? What good breeding!" Bistino kept repeating to her incessantly. "Everyone receives the treatment he deserves," she would conclude, holding her head high, beginning to be sensitive to this state of affairs and to be proud of it, striking an attitude of dignity, an attitude which was easy for her because she had lived for forty years in contact with high society by the side of an irreproachable lady. To conclude certain disagreements, her husband would answer her:

"Listen, Nunzia, if all of a sudden you were to hear the Countess's voice calling you, you'd even jump down from the window to answer more quickly."

"You can say that out loud, and I would only be doing my duty." She would look at him threateningly: "And would you compare the Countless with this beggar?"

"No, you see, money doesn't matter, in these things what matters is the heart. If the Countess, too, were dying of hunger wouldn't you feed her?"

"I'd take the food out of my own mouth to give it to her." She would rise to her full height: ". . . but would you compare the Countess to this chimpanzee? And then, when the Countess called me, she would do so in a kindly

sudiciona, lazzerona . . .

— Sì, ma fra uomini è un'altra cosa, tu non lo puoi capire.

"Vattene!" urlava in camera il marchese: *"Je te f . . .
à la porte!* Vattene!" Bistino si rifugiava nell'orto, non
aveva il coraggio d'andar vicino alla moglie; finché un
nuovo ordine lo richiamava per fare la pace. Allora il
marchese gli metteva una mano sulla spalla e incomincia-
vano a ridere.

"Faceva la gatta morta per farsi prendere, questo furbac-
chione, ora che ci ha ficcato le gambe ha delle esigenze,
si leva la voglia di comandare, questo gran signore. Che
faccia tosta. Ci vuole la sua dose di sfacciataggine. Se lo
facesse con me si sentirebbe rispondere per le rime."

Ma il diverso contegno dell'ospite oltre che darle a riflettere la lusingava in profondità.

— Cosa vuoi, è sempre un marchese, hai un bel dire, sono
tutti uguali, ne avrò conosciuto mille, sono fatti così, sono
abituati a comandare, lui non se ne accorge.

Una mattina il marchese disse alto e netto che senza un
campanello nella camera non intendeva vivere. Si prov-
vedesse d'urgenza; non era abituato a schiantarsi le corde
della gola per chiamare il domestico.

"Il campanello? Un campanello?" . . . ripeteva la
Nunzia correndo per la casa al colmo del furore: "il campanello?" Fermandosi diventava più alta e rigida, quasi fosse
stata di legno: "un campanello?" S'inarcava come la fionda
prossima a scoccare: "il campanello per chiamare chi?"
Mentre Bistino, raggiante, era corso dall'elettricista per
farlo mettere: "Un campanello? Ma in che mondo si vive,
si può sapere?"

— Cosa vuoi, lui non se ne accorge, ma ti pare, sennò
non lo farebbe.—Rideva, Bistino, gongolando per questa
novità:—Lo fa senza accorgersene.—Non s'accorge di non
essere più un signore, voleva dire, non se ne ricorda più.
—Son tutti uguali, sono fatti così, ti pare che potesse resistere. Un signore senza campanello . . . non è una cosa

fashion, like a well-brought-up person, she certainly wouldn't call me a swine or a slattern or a slut . . ."

"Yes, but between men it's different, you can't understand."

"Get out!" the Marquis would shout in his room: "I'll fire you! Get out!" Bistino would take refuge in the garden, without daring to go near his wife, until a new order would call him back to restore peace. Then the Marquis would put a hand on his shoulder and they would start to laugh.

"He was acting the fool in order to get himself taken in, this sly rascal; now that he has gotten established he makes demands; he feels the desire to give orders, this grand nobleman. What a nerve! That was all we needed, his dose of effrontery. If he tried it on me he'd get given tit for tat."

But the twofold behavior of the guest, in addition to making her reflect, flattered her deeply.

"What do you expect, he's still a marquis, there's no use talking, they're all alike, I must have known a thousand of them, that's the way they're built, they're accustomed to giving orders, he doesn't realize it."

One morning the Marquis said flatly that he didn't intend to go on living without a bell in his room. He wanted them to get it in a hurry; he wasn't accustomed to ruining his vocal cords so as to call the servant.

"The bell? A bell?" . . . Nunzia kept repeating, running through the house at the height of fury: "The bell?" Stopping, she became more tall and rigid, as if she were of wood: "A bell?" She bent like a sling ready to shoot: "The bell to call whom?" While Bistino, all radiant, had hurried to the electrician's to have it put in: "A bell? What sort of world is this we're living in, may one ask?"

"What do you expect, he doesn't realize it, what do you think, otherwise he wouldn't do it." He was laughing, Bistino was, overjoyed at this novelty: "He does it without realizing." ("He doesn't realize that he isn't a master any more," Bistino meant, "he doesn't remember any more.") "They're all like that, that's the way they're made, do you

possibile! È gente che da quando apre gli occhi la mattina, ha il campanello in mano fino alla notte quando li richiude. Mi fa specie [12] che non l'abbia chiesto prima, che per tanto tempo sia stato senza, che sia potuto stare. Come avrà fatto? Chi sa come doveva soffrire. Un signore senza campanello non esiste, i signori il campanello ce l'hanno nel sangue.

E una volta messo il campanello la camerina funzionò alla perfezione.

"Che aspetti marmotta? Presto fannullone! Quanto ci metti a rispondere? Non lo senti il campanello, cervellone? Hai il cece nelle orecchie?"

Bistino correva gonfio dal ridere: "Non se ne accorge, poverino, non se ne ricorda più", rideva al colmo della beatitudine.

Il marchese aveva riportato la vita in quella casa dove una felicità troppo sicura e troppo uguale l'aveva resa stagnante.

E con la Nunzia a tavola, quanta galanteria, era un crescendo senza fine, un fuoco di fila di blandizie. Che raffronti lusinghieri, che argomenti aristocratici: salamelecchi, inchini. I cuochi della storia e le dame della società. La povera cucina diventava un salone abbagliante. Le duchesse, le marchese e le contesse, che la Nunzia aveva conosciuto presso la sua signora, o di cui aveva sentito parlare. Conosceva le loro storie e storielle, segreti, scandali, frittate: un repertorio inesauribile. E se non conosceva fingeva di conoscere per tener testa al marchese da persona competente, dimostrandosi all'altezza della situazione. Tutto il chiasso era circoscritto alla camera dove Bistino la mattina, svegliandosi di soprassalto alle scampanellate, correva per mettersi agli ordini del signor marchese che ogni tanto faceva le sue rimostranze e prendeva le furie. La Nunzia si voltava da un'altra parte e seguitava a dormire: "Pezzo di mammalucco, si fa anche rimpolpettare". Prestando sempre meno orecchio a quanto correva fra i due, alle urla

think he could stand it? A gentleman without a bell . . . it isn't possible! They're the sort of people who, from waking in the morning until going to sleep at night, have the bell in their hands all the time. I'm surprised that he didn't ask for it before, that he went without it for so long, that he was able to go without it. How can he have managed? Who knows how much he must have suffered? A gentleman without a bell doesn't exist; gentlemen have bells in their blood."

And once the bell had been installed, the little room worked perfectly.

"What are you waiting for, you oaf? Hurry up, you loafer? How long are you going to take to answer? Don't you hear the bell, you dullard? Have you got peas in your ears?"

Bistino would run, swelled up with laughter: "He doesn't realize, poor man, he doesn't remember any more," and he would laugh in the fullness of his bliss.

The Marquis had brought life back into that house where an excessively secure and even happiness had made it stagnant.

And with Nunzia at table, how much gallantry! It was an endless crescendo, a running fire of blandishments. What flattering comparisons, what aristocratic topics of conversation: obeisances and bows. The cooks of history and the ladies of high society. The poor kitchen became a dazzling salon. The duchesses, the marquises and the countesses, whom Nunzia had known at her mistress's, or about whom she had heard—he knew their stories and anecdotes, secrets, scandals, quarrels: an inexhaustible repertory. And if she did not know them, she made believe she knew, in order to keep pace with the Marquis like a person in the know, showing that she was up to the situation. All the uproar was restricted to the room, to which Bistino, in the morning, waking up with a start at the sound of the bell, would run to put himself at the orders of the Marquis, who, from time to time, would give him a scolding and fly into a rage. Nunzia would turn over and go back to sleep, grumbling: "Stupid blockhead, he'd even let himself be beaten to a

e ai rimproveri, come al chiasso e alle risate, quasi fossero due ragazzi che senza recar molestia fanno i loro giuochi da una parte. E una mattina: "pum!" Bistino si prese una scarpa nel groppone, finalmente! era tanto che l'aspettava.

"Bene! forte! più forte! anche quell'altra, ma è poco", ripeteva la moglie senza distrarsi dal camino dove eseguiva le proprie faccende.

* * *

Una volta questo tenore di vita divenuto normale, e la Nunzia ci aveva fatto l'abitudine, al suo spirito la bizzarra situazione fece prendere un'altra piega, opposta precisamente. Incominciò a voler uscire con loro e, con molta grazia, a pavoneggiarsi fra i due; a frequentare un caffè nel centro di Firenze, il Grande Italia in piazza Vittorio Emanuele,[13] dove contrasse alcune amicizie: un pensionato delle guardie con la moglie, un portalettere con la moglie e la figliola ch'era fidanzata ad un sergente maggiore; i poverini dovevano aspettare dieci anni prima di potersi sposare. Due signore che affittavano le camere ai pezzi grossi, alti impiegati, ufficiali superiori, stranieri ricchi . . . e che molte cose avevano imparate e potevano raccontare. Un controllore dei tranvai con la moglie e quattro figlie che tra la sfiducia e una pazienza troppo esercitata aspettavano quel partito che non poteva tornare. E a far conoscere il marchese alle nuove conoscenze: "È il marchese, sta con noi, stiamo insieme", avendo l'aria di dire: "Mettetevi sull'attenti perché siamo della gentina dimolto ma dimolto in su". E quelli che non conoscevano l'almanacco di Gotha, non sapevano neppure che esistesse, sulle prime lo sbirciavano con diffidenza, affilando il naso e consultandosi con gli occhi reciprocamente: "Sarà davvero un marchese? Un marchese vero?" Non era il caso di dire come per i brillanti: "un culo di bicchiere?" Per quanto l'avessero rimesso in ordine, la presenza del vecchio non era tale da imporre tali certezze. Ma poi, per il lustro che a tutti ne veniva di

pulp." She paid less and less attention to what went on between the two, to the shouts and scoldings, and also to the uproar and laughter, as if they were two boys playing off to one side without disturbing anyone. And one morning, "bam!" Bistino got a shoe in his back; finally! She had been expecting it for so long.

"Good! Hit him hard! Even harder! That too, but it's too little," Bistino's wife kept repeating, without turning her attention away from the fireplace where she was going about her business.

* * *

Once this way of life had become normal, and Nunzia had gotten accustomed to it, the strange situation made her mind take another tack, in exactly the opposite direction. She began to want to go out with the two of them, and, very gracefully, to strut between them; to haunt a café in the center of Florence, the "Grande Italia" in Piazza Vittorio Emanuele, where she made some friendships: a retired guardsman and his wife, a postman with his wife and their daughter who was engaged to a sergeant-major—the poor children were going to have to wait ten years before they could get married; two ladies who rented rooms to big shots, high-ranking employees, top-echelon officers, rich foreigners—and who had learned and could tell about many things; a street-car conductor, with his wife and four daughters, who, partly through distrust and partly through exercising too much patience, were still waiting for that match which was never going to come along again. And presenting the Marquis to their new friends: "This is the Marquis; he lives with us, we are together," seeming to say: "Watch out, because we folks are very, very high up in the scale." And those who did not know the Almanach de Gotha, who didn't even know it existed, would at first look askance at him, with mistrust, stroking their noses and looking at each other: "Can he really be a marquis? A real marquis?" Shouldn't they say, as of gems: "Just a piece of glass?" Even though they had put him back in good shape again, the appearance of the old man was not such as to

riflesso, impressionati da un doppio nome, e più ancora per qualche informazione circolata nel caffè, tutti finirono per credere e aspirar a quella nobile compagnia. "Non è vero, marchese? Ha sentito, marchese? Marchese che gliene pare? Che ne dice?" ripeteva la Nunzia con affabilità sostenuta, e a ogni poche parole.

E dal marchese a poco a poco, crescendo in prosopopea e faccia tosta, accennava sorvolando, o lasciava che si credesse qualcosa anche di sé; in modo da far correre la voce che se proprio non era una titolata era nobile certamente, o che almeno sua madre o la nonna lo dovevano essere. Sia l'una come l'altra, per dire la verità, avevano conosciuto un solo blasone: la falce per segar l'erba alle bestie e la zappa per preparare il campo alle patate: strumenti nobilissimi nel loro genere. Ma oramai sulla buona via questo non voleva dire. Vantava conoscenze aristocratiche, raccontava aneddoti e avventure dove entravano delle duchesse e delle contesse, come persone delle sue sfere: "Si ricorda, marchese?" Si capiva, insomma, trattarsi di un mondo elevato al quale si teneva a fare un posto sempre maggiore, e a rendere omaggio sempre crescente.

Bistino era felice e non faceva che ridere. Da perfetto domestico faceva degli inchini che potevano essere scambiati per aristocrazia millenaria da chi non è pratico di queste faccende.

In quanto al marchese, che la mattina nella sua camera doveva dare nobili scampanellate e ogni tanto prendere delle furie nobilissime, che si sarebbe risparmiate molto volentieri (senza sapere di permettersi tanto lusso, Bistino si pagava un padrone a prezzo di fallimento), non si mostrò stupito dall'arditezza della donna, nulla più lo poteva stupire, comprese anche lei e si prestò al giuoco con sollecitudine, esternando quell'avanzo della sua reale e sciagurata

make such a thing certain. But later, because of the splendor that was reflected from him onto all of them, impressed by a double name, and even more because of certain bits of information circulating in the café, they all ended up believing and aspiring to that aristocratic company. "Isn't it so, Marquis? Did you hear, Marquis? Marquis, what do you think about it? What do you say to that?" Nunzia would repeat, with unfailing amiability, and with every few words.

And, starting with the Marquis, gradually, growing in affectation and in brazenness, she would hint in passing, or let people think something about herself too, so as to start the rumor that even if she wasn't actually a titled lady, she was certainly noble, or that at least her mother or her grandmother must have been. Both of those ladies, to tell the truth, had known only one coat-of-arms: the sickle to cut hay for the animals and the hoe to get the field ready for the potatoes; instruments which, in their own kind, are very noble. But now that she was on the high road, she wasn't referring to this. She would boast of her aristocratic acquaintances, she would tell anecdotes and adventures in which there entered duchesses and countesses, as though they were of her own sphere: "Do you remember, Marquis?" It was understood, in short, that they were dealing with a lofty world for which they insisted on continually making a greater place, and giving higher and higher homage.

Bistino was happy, and did nothing but laugh. Like the perfect servant that he was, he would make bows that might be mistaken for expressions of a thousand-year-old aristocracy by people who were not in the know regarding these matters.

As for the Marquis, who every morning in his room had to ring the bell like an aristocrat and, from time to time, go into highly aristocratic rages, which he would have been very glad to get along without (without knowing that he was enjoying such luxury, Bistino was getting a master at bankruptcy clearance-sale rates), he showed no astonishment at the woman's effrontery; nothing could astonish him any more, and he understood her too and entered into the

nobiltà fra le dame del caffè.

Oramai non c'era da scegliere: da Siena venivano cinquanta lire al mese, scusse, le raccolte andavano di male in peggio, e da Milano non veniva niente perché lui si seccava a scrivere le famose epistole: per una scodella di buona minestra e un rifugio decente, bisognava fare dell'altro il marchese.

game with promptness, displaying the remnant of his real and unfortunate aristocracy among the ladies of the café.

By now, there was no choice; from Siena there came a bare fifty lire per month, the harvests were going from bad to worse, and from Milan there came nothing because he didn't want to be bothered writing his well-known letters; for a plate of good soup and a decent lodging, he had to make the other man into the Marquis.

Corrado Alvaro

(1895–1956)

Born near Reggio Calabria (at the toe of the Italian peninsula), Corrado Alvaro was one of the leading writers of mid-twentieth-century Italy. He first achieved fame with his novels, of which the most important were *L'uomo nel labirinto* ("The Man in the Labyrinth," 1926), *Vent'anni* ("Twenty Years," 1930), *L'uomo è forte* ("Man Is Strong," 1938), and especially *L'età breve* ("The Brief Age," 1947). He also published several collections of short stories, notably *Gente in Aspromonte* ("People in Aspromonte," 1930). Alvaro was remarkable among modern Italian writers for his command of clear, pure style, coupled with a remarkable sensitivity to the poetry of impressions and to nuances of character.

In *I Giocàttoli Rotti*, Alvaro presents, within the brief compass of a short story, one of the essential conflicts of modern Italy—that between old, traditional ways and a more modern approach to life. The recently restored express from Rome to Naples, on which the action of the story takes place, clearly symbolizes the new Italy of post-Second-World-War days; the old peasant woman, sunk forever in her infantile incomprehension, stands for all that the stocky man remembers from his childhood in the South of Italy and wishes to leave behind him. When he opens the door of the train, the old woman clings to the car door and to

life itself with an unreasoning and hence unfrightenable grasp. She is still alive when the train comes out of the tunnel, just as modern Italy is still saddled with its eternal *problema meridionale* ("problem of the South") after coming out of the dark days of the Second World War. Yet what can the old peasant culture bring, out of its fruitless contacts with twentieth-century life, to the children who will live in tomorrow's world, save the gadgets and toys of modern civilization, broken through hopeless incomprehension?

I GIOCATTOLI ROTTI

di Corrado Alvaro

Poco dopo la Liberazione,[1] i treni di Roma riprendevano a funzionare, fu anzi ripristinato un rapido.[2] Non era ancora come prima, ma bisogna pensare che appena qualche settimana avanti il viaggio era penoso, c'era un solo binario, e per quanto il convoglio portasse il nome di diretto,[3] si fermava di continuo, rifaceva un tratto di strada all'indietro, manovrava sui pezzi di doppio binario appena ricollocati, mentre gli operai lavoravano attorno ai ponti sostenuti da travature di legno, alle stazioni distrutte e ingombre di scheletri di vagoni.

Il rapido era pieno di gente che si contendeva i posti, che entrava dai finestrini. Faceva un caldo soffocante. L'odore della gomma e della pegamoide rendeva più disgustoso il caldo. Le liti scoppiavano da tutte le parti. Chi si era procurato il posto guardava indifferente a quella lotta, con un profondo compiacimento d'esserne fuori, o dormiva, e portava nel sonno un'espressione di disgusto e di inimicizia. Un litigio scoppiò da qualche parte, a proposito d'un segno che un tale aveva messo per occupare il posto. Aveva messo un giornale. Uno, all'apparenza studente, osservò che quello non era un segno che avesse un valore. "Che cosa vuole? Che ci metta un biglietto da mille?" chiese l'altro, un uomo con una borsa sottobraccio. L'ironia è una delle cose che i meridionali non tollerano. Lo studente reagì, i due si affrontarono, ma non accadde niente. Tutti sapevano che non

276

THE BROKEN TOYS

by Corrado Alvaro

NOT LONG after the Liberation, the trains from Rome began running again; in fact, an express was re-established. It was not yet like before, but one must keep in mind that barely a few weeks previously the trip was trying; there was only one track, and although the train was called a fast train, it was continually stopping, backing up over a stretch, shunting on sections of double track which had just been re-installed, while the workmen were laboring on the bridges held up by wooden beams, and on the stations which had been destroyed and were obstructed by skeletons of cars.

The express was full of people who were fighting for seats, who were coming in through the windows. It was suffocatingly hot. The odor of rubber and artificial leather made the heat more revolting. Quarrels were breaking out on all sides. Those who had gotten seats looked on in indifference at that struggle, with profound pleasure at being out of it; or they slept and wore in their sleep an expression of disgust and hostility. A dispute broke out somewhere, over a marker which someone had put to keep his place. He had put a newspaper. One man, a student by his appearance, remarked that that was not a valid marker. "What do you expect him to put? A thousand-lire note?" asked the other, a man with a brief-case under his arm. Irony is one of the things that South Italians will not stand for. The student reacted, the two faced up to each other,

sarebbe successo niente. I due si parlavano vicini, quasi a petto a petto, dicevano ognuno la sua frase,[4] sempre la stessa, scandita, recisa, come se recitassero insieme i versetti d'una rabbiosa orazione. Ma non successe niente. Da un'altra parte, qualcuno alimentava un nuovo litigio, offeso perché gli offrivano cinquecento lire se cedeva il suo posto. Si mise a urlare che lui avrebbe regalato mille lire. E se ne andò senza dare le mille lire, per occupare il posto d'una ragazza che aveva ceduto alle insistenze d'un intraprendente siciliano il quale assicurava che di lì a mezz'ora sarebbe partito un altro treno interamente vuoto, dove si sarebbe stati larghi, comodi, e non in quel parapiglia. Il giovane era simpatico, pieno di umore, con un'aura avventurosa e sfrontata. Cedette la ragazza, e cedette anche la donna che la accompagnava, forse sua madre; seguirono il giovane come per ascoltare il resto d'un racconto. Il giovane sapeva contraffare molti dialetti italiani, il milanese e il veneto, e assai male il toscano. Quello delle mille lire occupò uno dei due posti liberi, l'altro posto fu conteso tra un uomo di bassa statura, tarchiato, con un'ombra di grigio sul viso che faceva sospettare avesse più anni di quanti ne mostrava, e un altro, grosso, lento, prepotente, con un viso infastidito e sprezzante; portava trascuratamente nella tasca dei pantaloni un pugno di biglietti da mille fra cui cercò, sempre sprezzante, il suo biglietto di viaggio, non appena si fu seduto a quel posto. L'uomo tarchiato si arrese, e tornò indietro, nel corridoio davanti al gabinetto,[5] fitto di gente.

Da un pezzo quest'uomo non saliva su un treno, da prima della guerra, sette anni, ed egli osservava quello che si vedeva attorno attentamente. Era meridionale, il treno era pieno di meridionali, ed egli ne riconosceva il mestiere, l'occupazione, forse la professione, con l'occhio esperto di chi ha la memoria dell'esperienza. Ne riconosceva le attitudini, le virtù e i vizi, la condizione sociale, o così gli pareva. Vedeva dietro ad essi le loro case, i loro paesi, ripercorreva il cam-

but nothing happened. Everybody knew that nothing would happen. The two were near to each other as they spoke, almost face to face, each one having his say—always the same, measured, uncompromising—as if the two were reciting together the versets of a prayer of rage. But nothing happened. Somewhere else, someone was adding fuel to a new quarrel, offended because he was being offered five hundred lire if he would give up his place. He started to shout that he himself would have offered a thousand lire. And he went off without giving the thousand lire, to take the place of a girl who had yielded to the insistence of an enterprising Sicilian who was assuring her that a half hour from then another train was going to leave, entirely empty, in which they would have lots of room and would be comfortable, and not in that turmoil. The young man was attractive, full of good humor, with a venturesome and impudent manner. The girl yielded, as did the woman who was with her, perhaps her mother; they followed the young man as if to hear the rest of a story. The young man was able to imitate many Italian dialects, Milanese and Venetian, and Tuscan quite badly. The man who had talked about a thousand lire took one of the places left free, and the other place was disputed by a man of short stature, stocky, with a shadow of gray on his face which made one suspect he was older than he seemed, and another, heavy, slow, overbearing, with an expression of disgust and contempt; he carried negligently in his trousers pocket a wad of thousand-lire notes among which he looked, still contemptuously, for his ticket, as soon as he had sat down in that place. The stocky man gave up and went back out into the corridor in front of the toilet, packed with people.

This man had not traveled by train for some time, since before the war, seven years, and he noticed attentively what he saw around him. He was a South Italian; the train was full of South Italians, and he could recognize their trades, their occupations, perhaps their professions, with the expert eye of the man who has the memory of experience. He recognized their abilities, their virtues and vices, their social condition, or so it seemed to him. Behind them he saw their

mino ch'egli aveva fatto nella vita. Da molto tempo non tornava nei suoi paesi, ma si rivedeva bambino scalzo in una strada di quei paesi, si domandava quale sarebbe stata la sua sorte se fosse rimasto nei suoi paesi, a chi avrebbe somigliato fra quelli che si vedeva intorno. Ognuno di noi si porta dietro il suo passato, forse ogni momento della nostra vita è un riepilogo di quel passato, ma lo misuriamo esattamente, in un baleno, quando ci troviamo fra gente diversa, nella varietà della condizione umana che ci suggerisce l'immagine di quello che eravamo e di quello che avremmo potuto essere. Allora il passato che noi portiamo dentro di noi come qualcosa di unico, s'intirizzisce al paragone, diventa una storia minuta come tutte le altre, una questione di coincidenze, e proviamo una grande pena per noi.

Ecco, ecco un individuo cui l'uomo tarchiato doveva avere somigliato in un tempo della sua vita. Era un giovane all'apparenza studente, di quel bruno intenso di certi meridionali sul cui viso le sopracciglia nette e dense si aprono come due penne. Soltanto l'uomo tarchiato poteva distinguere, o gli pareva, che colui fosse d'una condizione modesta, ma che si fosse fatta una sommaria educazione frequentando le città e le università. Come si muoveva tra imbarazzato e distinto, con una distinzione di acquisto e un imbarazzo naturale, come si affannava a cercare un posto, a guardare fuori se qualcuno vendesse una bottiglia d'acqua; i meridionali hanno sempre sete, cercano sempre acqua, hanno del rabdomante; [6] inquieto a cercare qualche cosa, forse una donna nel corridoio, forse quel tanto di avventuroso e di nuovo che un giovane meridionale cerca sempre e non trova mai; tutto ciò l'uomo tarchiato lo sapeva bene. Lo trovava buffo, ma pure sentiva di avergli somigliato, pure era stato qualcuno come lui, con la testa piena di diritto romano, e di quelle distinzioni e di quei cavilli che dànno ai meridionali un'espressione ghiotta, un lampo di orgoglio negli occhi, come se partecipassero ai segreti di un passato. I meridionali sentono molto il passato, vi stanno come all'ombra della madre. Vi stanno come se nel mondo non ci fosse più niente da dire e tutto fosse stato detto.

houses, their towns, and he retraveled the journey he had
taken in life. For a long time he had not gone back to his
town, but he saw himself again as a barefoot boy in a street
of that town, and wondered what would have been his fate
if he had remained in his town, and whom he would have
resembled among those he saw around himself. Each one
of us carries his past with him, perhaps every moment of
our life is a recapitulation of that past, but we measure it
exactly, in a flash, when we are among people who are
different, in the variety of human conditions which suggests
to us the image of what we used to be and what we might
have been. Then the past which we carry in ourselves as
something unique is chilled at the comparison, becomes a
detailed history like all the others, a question of coinci-
dences, and we feel a great anguish for ourselves.

There, there was an individual whom the stocky man
must have resembled at one stage of his life. He was a young
man, a student by his appearance, of that intense darkness
of certain South Italians on whose faces the clearly outlined
and thick eyebrows open out like two feathers. Only the
stocky man could distinguish, or thought he could, that he
was of modest social position, but that he had gotten a
summary education living in cities and attending univer-
sities. The way he moved, half embarrassed and half distinguished, with an acquired distinction and a natural embarrassment; the way he anxiously looked for a seat and
looked out to see if anyone were selling a bottle of water
(South Italians are always thirsty, are always looking for
water; they have something of the diviner about them),
looking for something worriedly, perhaps a woman in the
corridor, perhaps that little bit of adventure and novelty
that a young South Italian is always looking for and never
finds; all this, the stocky man knew well. He found him
comical, but yet he felt that he had been like him, he had
been someone like that, with his head full of Roman law
and with those distinctions and cavils which give South
Italians an expression of avidity, a flash of pride in their
eyes, as if they were sharers of the secrets of a past. South
Italians feel the past strongly; they stand in it as in the

I GIOCATTOLI ROTTI

L'uomo tarchiato non si era accorto che proprio di faccia a lui, davanti alla porta della latrina, una donna si lamentava sommessamente. Stava seduta su un sacco gonfio, il solito sacco che riappare a certe latitudini come riappare l'asino, e si lamentava. Egli capì che quella donna diceva nel suo dialetto: "Dov'è andato? Dove se n'è andato?" Era vestita della solita veste nera che copre le madri del popolo da quelle parti, la veste nera che delinea il ventre gonfio, tutta in avanti con l'atteggiamento che si prende sotto quella veste, quello delle mani giunte sul grembo. Egli ne capiva il dialetto, e capiva che si lamentava come una chioccia senza avere la forza di reagire o di cercare, con la solitudine della chioccia che alla fine non trova altra ragione di lamentarsi che il suo stesso lamento. "Dov'è andato? Dove se n'è andato?" E colui che ella cercava era là, era suo figlio, confuso in una folla di gente tra cui ella non riusciva a distinguerlo, abituata a considerarlo come un essere unico che non si confonde fra gli altri, gli altri, nemici, strani, pieni di vizi, ladri e imbroglioni. L'uomo tarchiato era stordito di leggere in quei pensieri con tanta lucidità. Egli distingueva bene colui che ella cercava: il figlio; si aggirava con le braccia levate, come a evitare urti e contatti, si affacciava ai finestrini, cercava acqua: si sporgeva negli scompartimenti, come se ispezionasse, cercava una donna da guardare coi suoi occhi umidi sotto le sopracciglia come due penne. Certo, l'uomo tarchiato doveva averlo veduto già, ne aveva veduti tanti come lui, aveva veduto sé stesso in un altro tempo, era stato lui stesso quel tale. La donna aveva cessato di lamentarsi, come se se ne fosse dimenticata, e seduta sul sacco, con le caviglie fuori della lunga veste nera, le caviglie magre e un poco incavate in dentro, coperte della spessa calza nera di cotone, si era applicata a qualcosa che la distraeva.

shadow of a mother. They stand in it as if there were nothing more to say in the world and as if all had been said.

The stocky man had not noticed that directly facing him, in front of the toilet door, a woman was lamenting in a low voice. She was seated on a full-packed sack—the usual sack which reappears at certain latitudes just as the donkey reappears—and she was lamenting. He understood that that woman was saying in her dialect: "Where has he gone? Where has he gone to?" She was dressed in the usual black dress which covers the mothers of the common people in those regions, the black dress which outlines the swollen belly, all protruded with the posture that they take under that dress, that of the hands joined on the lap. He understood her dialect, and understood that she was lamenting like a hen, without having the strength to react or to seek, with the solitude of the hen which, in the end, finds no other reason to lament than her lament itself. "Where has he gone? Where has he gone to?" And the one she was seeking was over there, was her son, obscured among a crowd of people among whom she was not able to pick him out, accustomed as she was to considering him as a unique being who is not confused with others—others, enemies, strangers, full of vices, thieves and swindlers. The stocky man was amazed to read those thoughts with so much clarity. He could easily distinguish the one she was looking for, her son; he was going around with his arms raised, as if to avoid collisions and contacts; he was leaning out of the windows, looking for water; he was leaning into the compartments, as if he were inspecting; he was seeking for a woman to look at with his damp eyes under his eyebrows like two feathers. Certainly, the stocky man must have seen him already, he had seen so many like him; he had seen himself at another time; he himself had been that person. The woman had stopped lamenting, as if she had forgotten to, and, seated on the sack—with her ankles outside of her long black dress, her ankles which were thin and slightly hollow on the inside, covered by the thick black cotton stockings—she had turned her attention to something that was keeping her amused.

I GIOCÀTTOLI ROTTI

Era uno di quei giocàttoli che in quei giorni si vendevano attorno alla stazione, una scatola di cartone con una successione di immagini in cui era ripetuta una fuga di Fortunello [7] con un gatto nero e i gendarmi: girando una piccola manovella, le immagini si mettevano in moto, le gambe di quei personaggi pareva corressero, si moltiplicavano in un numero che non si poteva calcolare, quattro, sei, otto, e così la scena si svolgeva come al cinematografo. La donna era assorta a girare la manovella di filo di ferro, guardava diffidente i gendarmi correre, correre Fortunello, correre il gatto. Nei momenti in cui sostava tutta quella corsa, si fermavano mostrando sfumate indistintamente le quattro, le sei, le otto gambe. Poi la scena ricominciava daccapo, poi daccapo. Ella la faceva girare ostinata, domandandosi forse che divertimento ci potesse trovare il ragazzo che certo l'aspettava in paese. O forse provava il giocàttolo per gustare la gioia di quel ragazzo per assicurarsi che funzionasse bene. Finché la superficie di cellofàn che copriva la scena si staccò come una pellicola, e il giocàttolo rivelò la sua semplice ingegnosità: la pellicola era rigata, e le figure, passando e quasi impigliandosi nelle righe, acquistavano un movimento. Ella non lo capì. L'uomo tarchiato glielo avrebbe potuto spiegare, ma la guardava con una specie di acre soddisfazione, come se quel giocàttolo rappresentasse tutta la vita civile che a lei faceva tanta paura, in cui aveva paura di perdere suo figlio, il figlio che andava bramosamente cercando acqua e donne, che girava tra la folla come cercando di impastarvisi, di confondervisi. Egli avrebbe potuto spiegarglielo, ma la guardò delusa, perplessa, che insisteva a girare come se dovesse vedere ripararsi magicamente quel giocattolo, e invece la pellicola si desquamava interamente, il giocattolo era da buttare via. Allora ella si ricordò di lamentarsi: "Dov'è andato? Dove se n'è andato?" allarmata perché il treno si metteva in movimento dopo una sosta a una stazione crivellata in colpi di mitraglia. Difatti il giovane era scomparso. Ella si alzò, non resistette al movimento del treno, diede all'indietro, e l'uomo tarchiato dovette sostenerla per il braccio. Sentì quel braccio. Il braccio di sua madre, il braccio dei suoi

THE BROKEN TOYS

It was one of those toys which in those days were being sold around the station, a cardboard box with a succession of pictures in which was repeated a chase of Happy Hooligan with a black cat and the gendarmes: if one turned a little handle, the pictures were set in motion, the legs of the characters seemed to be running and were multiplied to a number which could not be calculated, four, six, eight, and in that way the scene took place as in the movies. The woman was absorbed in turning the wire handle and was looking diffidently at the gendarmes running, at Happy Hooligan running, at the cat running. In the moments when all that chasing ceased, they stopped, showing their four, six, eight legs fading off indistinctly. Then the scene started again, then again. She obstinately kept turning it, wondering perhaps what pleasure it might give the boy who certainly was expecting it in her home town. Or perhaps she was trying out the toy to savor the pleasure of that boy to make sure that it was working well. Until the surface of cellophane which covered the scene came off like a film, and the toy revealed its simple ingeniousness: the film was ruled with lines, and the figures, passing and, as it were, becoming entangled in the lines, acquiring movement. She did not understand it. The stocky man could have explained it to her, but he looked at her with a kind of bitter satisfaction, as if that toy represented all of the civilized existence which frightened her so much, in which she was afraid of losing her son, the son who was going eagerly in search of water and women, who was circulating among the crowd as if seeking to mingle with it, to become lost in it. He could have explained it to her, but he looked at her in her disappointment and perplexity, insisting on turning it as if she would see the toy repair itself by magic; on the contrary, the film came entirely apart in flakes; the toy was good only to be thrown away. Then she remembered to lament: "Where has he gone? Where has he gone to?" alarmed because the train was starting to move after a stop at a station riddled with machine-gun bullets. In fact, the young man had disappeared. She got up, but could not balance herself against the motion of the train; she stag-

ricordi, il braccio delle donne del suo paese, con quel che [8] di indefinibilmente molle e lieve. Molle come il pane fresco. Molle e lieve. Lieve come un braccio caro in cui uno risente qualche cosa di sé. Poiché si lamentava smarrita nel suo dialetto, ma senza agitarsi, già rassegnata a qualunque evento, l'uomo tarchiato le disse burbero: "Non vi preoccupate. Sarà salito in qualche altro vagone mentre il treno si muoveva."

Ella non capì certamente, ma gli credette, si rassegnò. Intuiva soltanto che c'era una spiegazione. E allora si rimise a sedere sul suo sacco, e cominciò a provare un altro giocàttolo, che raffigurava un omino di legno, sempre Fortunello, il quale comandato da una cordicella picchiava con le mani di legno su un ceppo di legno, con un rumore puerile, come forse i pupazzi del presepe odono battere l'incudine del fabro pastorello di presepe come loro, in una notte soave di Natale in cui gli atti della fatica umana diventano un gioco. Era intenta a questo lavoro quando il figlio riapparve. Ella smise il suo gioco ostinato in cui non capiva, come un gatto non capisce qualcosa che lo incuriosisce e di cui diffida, per dirgli: "Dove eri andato?" con una voce lontana di vecchio lamento. E l'uomo tarchiato la guardava, curvo su di lei come sul suo stesso passato. Con l'aria di fare un rimprovero a suo figlio, ella gli mostrò il giocàttolo rotto. Il figlio lo osservò. Irrimediabile. Aprì il sacco e lo cacciò dentro. La rassicurò con la voce imperiosa con cui si rassicura una cavalla, e riprese il suo giro inquieto pel corridoio affollato, fra le proteste della folla.

Questa era la madre. Questo era il passato come un giocàttolo smesso desquamato dalla sua superficie brillante. Ella parlò all'uomo tarchiato, accostandosi al finestrino; gli parlò come se lo conoscesse da tempo, con una confidenza naturale che offese l'uomo tarchiato. Evidentemente egli serbava qualche cosa del suo passato. Ella lo doveva sentire

gered backwards, and the stocky man had to support her by the arm. He felt that arm. The arm of his mother, the arm of his memories, the arm of the women of his home town, with that something indefinably soft and light. Soft, like fresh bread. Soft and light. Light, like a belovèd arm in which one experiences something of oneself. Since she was lamenting, bewildered, in her dialect, but without getting excited, already resigned to any outcome, the stocky man said to her brusquely: "Don't worry. He must have gotten into some other car while the train was moving."

She certainly did not understand, but she believed him and resigned herself. She only perceived intuitively that there was an explanation. And then she sat back down again on her sack, and began to try out another toy, which represented a little man of wood, still Happy Hooligan, who, governed by a string, struck with his wooden hands on a wooden block, with a childish noise, such as perhaps the puppets of the Christmas manger hear beating on the anvil of the smith, a little manger shepherd like themselves, on a gentle Christmas night in which the acts of human toil become a game. She was intent on this work when her son reappeared. She ceased her obstinate activity in which she did not understand, as a cat does not understand, something which excites one's curiosity and which one distrusts, to say to him: "Where had you gone?" with a distant voice of old lament. And the stocky man looked at her, bending over her as over his own past. With the air of reproaching her son, she showed him the broken toy. The son observed it. Irremediable. He opened the sack and shoved it inside. He reassured her with the imperious voice in which one reassures a mare, and set off again on his restless trip through the crowded corridor, among the protests of the crowd.

This was the mother. This was the past, like a discarded toy, with its shining surface flaked off. She spoke to the stocky man, approaching the window; she spoke to him as if she had known him for a long time, with a natural confidence which offended the stocky man. Evidently he still kept something of his past. She must be perceiving this

istintivamente, e si rivolgeva a lui senza esitazione, fiduciosa di lui. L'uomo tarchiato ne fu quasi offeso. Ella gli chiese con la sua voce di donna che rimane molte ore e molti giorni in silenzio, che vive sempre fra pensieri piccini, che è rimasta piccina con tutti i suoi anni: "E dove andate voi?" I viaggi, la gente che si interrogava in viaggio un tempo, gli tornarono alla mente; gli tornò alla mente Ulisse in qualche parte dei libri antichi in cui si interrogavano i viaggiatori, di dove venite, dove andate, una curiosità da gente antica che nei viaggi vedeva qualcosa di straordinario, in cui viaggiava gente singolare e avventurosa, non come ora che uno va da una città all'altra, scende dal treno, mette il piede come se fosse in casa sua riconoscendo le piazze e le strade, senza stupore.

"Vado a Napoli," egli rispose.
"Così lontano?" ella chiese.
"No, è vicino," egli disse.
"E allora, Catania,[9] dov'è? Più vicino?" chiese lei.
"No, più lontano. Veniamo da Roma."
La donna non capiva. Dovette provare un momento di vertigine, tra i due punti cardinali, nord e sud, e il treno le dovette sembrare andasse improvvisamente a ritroso. All'uomo tarchiato parve di capire così, preso anche lui da una specie di vertigine, come chi si sveglia da un sonno in una stanza sconosciuta e per un poco non riesce a orientarsi, e il mondo pare si sia rivoltato come un tavolo magico. "E Reggio?"[10] ella chiese, "è più lontano di Catania?" Egli capì che ella aveva in mente il suo viaggio di andata, e non riusciva a percepire che quello era il viaggio di ritorno, che la successione delle stazioni si rovesciava. "Avvertitemi quando saremo a Reggio," disse. Egli rispose: "Io sarò sceso prima. Ma del resto ve ne accorgerete. Dopo bisogna passare il mare, passare lo Stretto."[11] Ella cercò nella sua memoria senza trovarvi nulla. Stava affacciata al finestrino, quasi aggrappata allo sportello, in quel disorientamento in cui il suo cervello doveva aggirarsi come in un malessere. Lo provava anche l'uomo tarchiato. Forse cre-

instinctively, and turned to him without hesitation, trusting in him. The stocky man was almost offended at this. She asked him, with that voice of a woman who remains many hours and many days in silence, who always lives with little thoughts, who has remained little despite all her years: "And where are you going?" The trips and the people whom one used to interrogate on journeys in olden times, came back to his mind: he thought again of Ulysses in some part of the old books where they interrogated travelers—where do you come from, where are you going—a curiosity like that of ancient people who saw something extraordinary in trips, when unusual and venturesome people used to travel, not like now when one goes from one city to another, gets off the train and sets down his foot as if he were at home, recognizing the squares and the streets, without amazement.

"I am going to Naples," he answered.

"So far?" she asked.

"No, it is near," he said.

"And then where is Catania? Nearer?" she asked.

"No, farther. We are coming from Rome."

The woman did not understand. She must be experiencing a moment of dizziness between the two cardinal points, north and south, and the train must have seemed to her to be suddenly going backwards. The stocky man seemed to understand this, overwhelmed in his turn by a kind of dizziness, like one who wakes from sleep in an unknown room and for a short time does not succeed in getting his bearings, and the world seems to be turned around like a magic table. "And Reggio?" she asked, "is it farther than Catania?" He understood that she had in mind her outward journey, and was not able to realize that this was her return journey, and that hence the succession of stations was reversed. "Let me know when we get to Reggio," she said. He answered: "I shall have gotten off before then. But, for that matter, you will know when you are there. Afterwards, you have to pass across the sea, pass the Strait." She searched in her memory without finding anything there. She was standing looking out of the window, almost clinging

dendo di fargli piacere, elle disse: "Napoli è una bella città.
Io la vidi una volta in figura. Una bella città." Egli disse:
"Ci passeremo, potrete fermarvi, scendere dal treno." Ella
lo guardò incredula. Un pendio andava incontro a loro,
e a una tratto si mise a girare storcendo tutto un oliveto
come un battaglione in manovra. Una casupola apparve
stranamente storta a pochi metri. Ella indicò fuori un
armento per la collina e domandò: "Sono pecore?" Egli
guardò e rispose: "No, sono buoi." Ella gli credette. Stava
sempre aggrappata al finestrino, guardava il mondo come
se non lo avesse mai veduto. Non distingueva una pecora
da un bue. Dove era cresciuta? dove viveva? Si era dimenticata del figlio, era come se stando al finestrino avesse preso
una droga per dimenticare.

Una galleria si annunziò con un lungo avvertimento
della macchina, il treno vi si immerse scandendo il suo ritmo,
suscitando il tanfo d'un vecchio fumo di vecchie vaporiere.
Pareva che il treno corresse con una scarpa rotta, con un
battito alterno più forte; l'immagine che venne in mente
all'uomo tarchiato fu quella delle scarpe rotte. Lo doveva
pensare anche lei, ed egli si sentì avvolto in quei pensieri
elementari, in quella ignoranza elementare, in quella eterna
infanzia. Il vagone era piombato nel buio, non si accese
nessuna luce, un buio fragoroso. . . .

L'uomo premette col piede sulla maniglia che apriva lo
sportello.[12] Il fragore del treno, minaccioso, il vento nausea-
bondo di vecchio fumo invasero il vagone. L'uomo credette
di aver udito un grido, subito travolto dal rumore di scarpe
rotte. Egli calcolò mentalmente lo stupore di quella donna
precipitata nel vuoto. Non se ne sarebbe neppure resa
conto. Non ne sarebbe forse rimasta stupita. L'uomo si
scostò e si addossò alla parete sentendo sotto di sé il baratro.
Quando il treno uscì dalla galleria, la donna apparve aggrappata senza stupore al finestrino spalancato. Qualcuno
si mosse, accorse il figlio. La trattarono come un bambino

onto the door, in that confusion in which her brain must be whirling as in a state of malaise. The stocky man felt that way too. Perhaps thinking she would please him, she said: "Naples is a beautiful city. I saw it once in a picture. A beautiful city." He said: "We shall pass through it; you will be able to stop and get out of the train." She looked at him incredulously. A slope was coming towards them, and suddenly the line began to turn, twisting, around a whole olive grove like a battalion on maneuver. A hut appeared strangely distorted a few meters away. She pointed out to a herd on the hillside and asked: "Are they sheep?" He looked and answered: "No, they are oxen." She believed him. She was still clinging to the window, looking at the world as if she had never seen it. She could not tell a sheep from an ox. Where had she grown up? Where did she live? She had forgotten her son, and it was as if, standing at the window, she had taken a drug in order to forget.

The approach of a tunnel was announced by a long blast from the engine, and the train dived into it beating its rhythm, giving off the musty smell of old smoke from old locomotives. It seemed as if the train were running with one shoe broken, with one beat stronger than the other; the image that came to the stocky man's mind was that of the broken shoes. She must think so too, and he felt himself enveloped in those elemental thoughts, in that elemental ignorance, in that eternal childhood. The car was plunged in darkness, no light was lit, and the darkness was filled with noise. . . .

The man pushed down with his foot on the handle which opened the door. The roar of the train, menacing, and the sickening blast of old smoke rushed into the car. The man thought he heard a cry, immediately overwhelmed by the noise of broken shoes. He estimated in his mind the astonishment of that woman hurled into the void. She would not even have realized it. She perhaps would not even have been amazed by it. The man moved away and stood with his back to the wall, feeling the abyss beneath him. When the train came out of the tunnel, the woman appeared, clutching, without surprise, at the wide-open door. Someone moved;

imprudente. Ma ella non aveva capito. "Potevi morire," le disse il figlio con una voce bassa, gutturale. Ella sedette docilmente sul sacco. Riprese il suo pupazzo di legno, ne tirava il cordino, e lo guardava che picchiava picchiava. Lo avrebbe rotto prima di arrivare a casa; chissà che diavolo di paese. Avrebbe portato dei giocàttoli rotti ai suoi nipotini. I quali avrebbero avuta l'impressione di un mondo di cose rotte. . . . Delle cose nuove rotte.

her son hastened up. They treated her like an imprudent child. But she had not understood. "You might have been killed," her son said to her in a low, guttural voice. She sat down docilely on the sack. She took up again her wooden puppet, pulled its string and watched it striking; striking. She would break it before she got home: who could tell what sort of a town. She would be bringing broken toys to her grandchildren. They would get the impression of a world of things which were broken. . . . New things which were broken.

Alberto Moravia

(1907–   )

ALBERTO PÌNCHERLE (whose pen-name is Alberto Morà-via) was born in 1907. He first became famous in 1929 with his "decadent" novel *Gli Indifferenti* ("The Indifferent Ones") and has since then written a number of other novels, such as *Le Ambizioni Sbagliate* ("Disappointed Ambitions," 1935), *La Romana* ("The Woman of Rome," 1947) and *Il Conformista* ("The Conformist," 1950). He has also written a number of short stories; *Racconti Romani* ("Roman Tales," 1954), the collection from which our selection, *La Concorrenza* ("Competition"), has been taken, deals mostly with incidents in the lives of lower-class Romans.

Moravia is a continuator of one line of tradition in Italian literature, the cult of form and style to the exclusion of most other concerns. He prefers to write in a very carefully polished literary Italian, even when he puts a tale in the first person into the mouth of a Roman workman or prostitute, because, as he has said, he considers the literary language more suitable for expressing the thoughts of his characters than their native dialectal speech would be. As a result, the language of his characters is quite unrealistic and unrepresentative of the way real people would speak, even if their conversation were to be translated (as, say, Verga did) from dialect into Italian.

ALBERTO MORAVIA

Moravia's concern with literary form and with the perfection of external technique in story-telling has led him to concentrate on superficial effectiveness at the expense of psychological penetration or comprehension. The situations and types which he portrays are extremely well-drawn, and easily recognizable to anybody who has lived in Rome. Moravia normally presents only petty, contemptible people in his narratives, and when such people are sufficiently representative of widespread character-types or of important moments in Italian history (e.g., the Fascistically inclined protagonist of *The Conformist*), his portrayal is very successful. On a more everyday level of action, however, Moravia is more interested in situations than in character, and hence he rarely succeeds in making his characters live or in giving the reader an understanding of why they behave as they do. Often, Moravia gives the reader, not a character who reveals himself unconsciously in his natural speech, but one who discourses in high-flown literary language about his own psychology in the way that a man of letters might think he himself would talk if he were in the position of such a character.

Moravia's *Competition*, a story of everyday life, presents a certain type of short-sighted incomprehension and childish selfishness which some lower- and middle-class Italians manifest with regard to their economic, social and personal relationships.

LA CONCORRENZA

di Alberto Moravia

Dicono che la concorrenza è l'anima del commercio. Almeno, quando ero ragazzino, così mi assicurava mio nonno che, poveretto, per via della concorrenza era fallito due volte con una sua botteguccia di cocci e vetri. Lui la spiegava in questo modo, la legge della concorrenza: "È una legge di ferro, nessuno può sperare di sfuggirci . . . poniamo che io metta su in via dell'Anima un negozio, appunto, di stoviglie, come sarebbe a dire piatti, scodelle, tazze, bicchieri . . . poco più giù, nella stessa strada, un altro mette su un negozio eguale . . . lui mi fa la concorrenza, ossia vende le stesse stoviglie ad un prezzo minore del mio . . . la clientela passa a lui e io fallisco . . . questa è la legge della concorrenza." "Ma nonno," io rispondevo, "se tu fallisci, noialtri moriamo di fame." "Si capisce," rispondeva lui trionfante: "voi morite di fame, ma il compratore si avvantaggia." "E a me che ne importa del compratore?" "A chi lo dici . . . figurati a me . . . se dipendesse da me lo vorrei vedere scannato . . . ma, appunto, questo è il bello della legge della concorrenza: ti costringe a fare il vantaggio del compratore anche se non lo vuoi." Io concludevo: "Sarà, ma se qualcuno si mette in testa di farmi fallire, proprio apposta, io gli faccio due occhi grandi così." "Perché sei manesco e prepotente," rispondeva il nonno, "ma nel commercio la prepotenza non vale . . . ti mettono dentro e tu fallisci prima: ecco tutto . . . nel commercio non vale che la concorrenza."

COMPETITION

by Alberto Moravia

They say that competition is the life of trade. At least, when I was a little boy, that was what I was assured by my uncle, who, poor man, because of competition had failed twice with a little crockery and glassware shop he had. He used to explain the law of competition in this way: "It's an iron law, no one can hope to escape it . . . let's assume that I set up in Via dell'Anima a shop, just so, a household-ware shop, that is, for dishes, soup-plates, cups, glasses . . . a little farther down along the same street, another sets up a shop of the same kind . . . he enters into competition with me; that is to say, he sells the same utensils at a price lower than mine . . . the customers go over to him and I go bankrupt . . . that is the law of competition." "But, grandfather," I used to answer, "if you go bankrupt, we die of hunger." "Of course," he used to answer triumphantly, "you die of hunger, but the consumer benefits." "What do I care about the consumer?" "Are you telling me? . . . me, just imagine . . . if it were up to me, I'd like to see his throat cut . . . but, in fact, this is the wonderful thing about the law of competition: it forces you to benefit the consumer even if you don't want to." I would conclude: "That may be so, but if somebody takes it into their head to make me go bankrupt, on purpose, I'll glare at them like this." "Because you're quarrelsome and aggressive," my grandfather would answer, "but bullying doesn't do any good in business . . . they'll put you in

Basta, anni dopo dovevo ricordarmelo questo ragionamento sulla concorrenza. Anch'io mi ero messo nel commercio, benché più modestamente del nonno perché, nel frattempo, la famiglia era andata giù: mio padre era morto e mio nonno, mezzo paralizzato, non poteva più commerciare né fallire e stava tutto il giorno a letto. Avevo dunque ottenuto la licenza di venditore ambulante per un carrettino pieno di tutto un po': olive dolci, arance, castagne secche, fichi secchi, mandarini, noci, nocci_line americane e altra roba simile. Con questo carrettino, mi scelsi per luogo l'imboccatura del ponte che sta di fronte al traforo del Gianìcolo.[1] È un luogo frequentato, ci capitano tutti quelli che vanno e vengono da Madonna del Riposo [2] e in genere gli abitanti di Trastévere [3] e di Monteverde [4] che debbono passare per corso Vittorio.[5] Avevo calcolato bene il luogo e infatti, subito, le cose mi andarono bene. Era primavera: con le prime giornate calde, di buon mattino io mi mettevo a capo del ponte con il carrettino colmo e la sera me ne andavo che sul carrettino non erano rimasti che i cartelli dei prezzi e il copertone di incerato. La domenica, poi, con tutto quel traffico di gente che va a spasso fuori porta, avessi avuto due carrettini, non sarebbero bastati. Il commercio, insomma, prosperava; e lo dissi al nonno. Ma lui, ostinato nelle sue idee, rispose: "Per ora non si può dire . . . non hai la concorrenza e vendi come ti pare . . . aspetta."

Aveva ragione. Una mattina, ecco che un carrettino in tutto simile al mio venne a mettersi a metà del ponte. Erano in due a vendere, due donne, madre e figlia. Voglio descriverle perché sono state la causa della mia rovina e, finché campo, me le ricorderò. La madre era una contadina delle parti di Anagni,[6] e vestiva come le contadine, con la gonnella nera e lunga e uno scialletto. Aveva i capelli grigi chiusi nel fazzoletto e la faccia che ne sporgeva, tutta premurosa e falsa, sempre raggrinzata in una smorfia di sollecitudine. Quando faceva il cartoccio delle olive, oppure pesava due arance, soffiava e inarcava le ciglia come

jail and you'll go bankrupt first; that's all . . . in business, only competition counts."

Well, many years later I was to remember this discussion about competition. I too had gone into business, although more modestly than my grandfather, because in the meanwhile the family had come down in the world: my father had died and my grandfather, half paralyzed, could neither do business nor go bankrupt and stayed in bed all day. So I had gotten a peddler's license for a push-cart full of all kinds of things: sweet olives, oranges, dry chestnuts, dry figs, tangerines, walnuts, peanuts and other things like that. With this push-cart, I picked as my place the entrance to the bridge which is opposite the Janiculum tunnel. It is a crowded spot; all those who go to or come from the Madonna del Riposo pass there as well as the inhabitants of Trastevere and of Monteverde in general who have to go along Corso Vittorio. I had picked my spot well, and, in fact, immediately, my affairs prospered. It was spring: with the first warm days, early in the morning I would take up my position at the end of the bridge with my push-cart full, and in the evening I would go away with nothing left on the cart except the price-tags and the tarpaulin cover. And on Sundays, with all that traffic of people who go for walks outside the gates, even if I had had two carts, they would not have been enough. Trade, in short, was booming; and I told my grandfather so. But he was stubborn in his notions and answered: "You can't tell yet . . . you have no competition and you sell as you please . . . just wait."

He was right. One morning, here came a push-cart exactly like mine and set up shop in the middle of the bridge. There were two of them selling things, two women, mother and daughter. I want to describe them because they were the cause of my downfall, and, as long as I live, I shall remember them. The mother was a peasant woman from the Anagni region, and was dressed as peasant women are, with a long black skirt and a shawl. She had her gray hair covered with a kerchief, and her face which protruded from it was all eager and false, always wrinkled up in a grimace of solicitude. When she wrapped up the olives, or weighed

per dare a intendere che ci metteva un impegno particolare; e quindi, porgendo la merce, non mancava mai di
aggiungere qualche paroletta amabile, come: "Guarda, ti
ho capato le due arance più belle," oppure: "È più di un
etto . . . ma per te facciamo un etto, va bene?" La figlia,
lei, invece, non faceva nulla e stava lì, è la parola, per
bellezza. Perché era bella, questo lo vidi subito, sono giovanotto e le donne belle piacciono anche a me. Poteva
avere diciotto anni ma nella persona ne mostrava trenta,
tanto era sviluppata, maestosa e ben formata. Aveva il viso
bianco come il latte con un non so che di torbido, di indeciso, di schifiltoso nelle labbra carnose ma pallide e negli
occhi grigi, sempre foschi e corrucciati. Le narici le si in-
crespavano facilmente, con espressione come di schifo; e,
insomma, pareva sempre sul punto di svenire, come se fosse
stata incinta. La madre gironzolava intorno il carrettino,
tutta stracciata e vispa, i piedi in due scarpacce da uomo,
simile ad uno di quei passerotti vecchi e grossi che non
stanno mai fermi; lei, invece, vestita di una gonnella corta
e di una maglia aderente, sedeva per ore su una seggiola
facendo la calza con i ferri lunghi infilati sotto le ascelle.
Si chiamava Eunice; e a me faceva pensare all'anice, forse
per la bianchezza della carnagione, che era appunto quella
dell'anice quando ci si mette l'acqua.

Io sono alto e grosso, sempre con la barba lunga e i capelli
arruffati. I vestiti che portavo erano tutta una toppa.
Sembravo, insomma, un vagabondo o peggio. Inoltre, per
quanto cerchi di controllarmi, ho le maniere brusche e vado
in collera facilmente. La mia voce, poi, è rauca, quasi
minacciosa. Subito mi accorsi che, per la concorrenza,
questo mio aspetto mi metteva in condizioni di inferiorità.
I nostri carrettini quasi si toccavano: da una parte la
madre, con una voce di cicala, gridava: "Ma che arance
. . . che arance . . . comprate, comprate le mie arance";
dall'altra io, ritto presso il carrettino, il cappotto chiuso
sotto la gola, il berretto sugli occhi, rispondevo, con la mia

out a couple of oranges, she would puff and raise her eyebrows as if to make one believe that she were putting a special effort on it; and then, when handing over the wares, she never failed to add a few pleasant words, such as: "Look, I've chosen the two nicest oranges for you," or: "It's more than a hectogram . . . but for you, we'll call it a hectogram, O.K.?" As for the daughter, though, she did nothing and just stood there, it's exactly the right word, as an ornament. Because she was beautiful, this I saw immediately; I am a young man and I too like beautiful women. She might have been eighteen years old, but she appeared to be thirty, she was so well developed, majestic and shapely. Her face was white like milk, with an indefinable disorder, indecision, finickiness on her fleshy but pale lips and in her gray eyes which were always gloomy and vexed. She would readily wrinkle up her nostrils, with an expression as if of disgust; and, in short, she always seemed about to swoon, as if she were pregnant. Her mother would bustle about the cart, all in rags and sprightly, with her feet in two huge man-size shoes, like one of those big old sparrows that are never still; the girl, on the other hand, dressed in a short skirt and a tight-fitting sweater, would sit for hours on a chair, knitting stockings with the long knitting-needles slipped under her armpits. Her name was Eunice; and she reminded me of anise, perhaps because of the whiteness of her complexion, which was just that of anise when you put water on it.

I am tall and heavy, always unshaven and with my hair disheveled. The clothes I wore were just one large patch. I seemed, in short, to be a vagabond or even worse. Furthermore, no matter how hard I try to control myself, my manners are brusque and I get angry easily. And my voice is hoarse, almost threatening. I immediately realized that, on account of the competition, this appearance of mine put me in a disadvantageous position. Our carts were almost touching: on one side, the mother, with a voice like a cicada, would cry: "Oh, what oranges . . . what oranges . . . buy, buy my oranges"; on the other, I, standing by my cart, with my overcoat buttoned up under my throat and

vociaccia: "Arance, arance dolci, arance." La gente esitava, guardava prima me, poi la madre, finalmente guardavano la figlia e allora, specie se erano uomini, si decideva per le due donne. La madre, da vera arpia, pur pesando la merce con i soliti soffi e inarcamenti di ciglia, badava, al tempo stesso, a gridare: "Comprate, comprate," per timore che, nel frattempo, qualcuno andasse da me. La sapeva lunga [7] e, quando proprio non ce la faceva, diceva, lesta, alla figlia: "Su, Eunice, servi il signore . . . svelta." Eunice posava il lavoro, si alzava in due tempi, maestosamente, prima col petto e poi coi fianchi e serviva il cliente senza guardarlo, gli occhi bassi. Quindi, senza una parola, senza un sorriso, tornava a sedersi.

Insomma, la concorrenza: in una settimana mi soffiarono quasi tutti i compratori. Presi a odiare le due donne, specie la madre che non nascondeva la sua soddisfazione e mi lanciava un'occhiata di trionfo ogni volta che mi portava via qualche cliente indeciso. Non c'è niente di peggio in queste situazioni che perdere la testa e io, ormai, l'avevo già perduta. Diventavo ogni giorno più ispido, più brusco, più minaccioso. La barba, i vestiti rattoppati e la voce rauca facevano il resto. Gridavo: "Arance dolci" con un tono addirittura truce; e la gente, guardandomi, si spaventava e andava dritta al carrettino accanto. Un giorno, poi, la mia indole prepotente mi tradì. Un paino giovane e piccolo, in compagnia di una donna grande il doppio di lui, contemplava le mie arance e non si decideva. Io ripetevo, disgustato: "Sono belle le mie arance," e lui le tastava e tentennava il capo. Quel donnone che gli stava al braccio avrebbe potuto essere sua madre e questo lo decise. Perché lanciò un'occhiata a Eunice, bella come una statua, e allora, brutto porco, si avviò direttamente verso di lei. Io persi la pazienza e lo afferrai per un braccio dicendo: "Non le vuoi le mie arance? Preferisci quelle? Te lo dico io perché preferisci quelle: perché ci hai una donna che sem-

with my cap over my eyes, would answer, with my raucous voice: "Oranges, sweet oranges, oranges!" People would hesitate, would look first at me and then at the mother, would finally look at the daughter, and then, especially if they were men, would decide for the two women. The mother, like the real harpy she was, even while weighing the fruit with her usual puffing and raising of her eyebrows, would be careful, at the same time, to cry: "Buy, buy!" for fear lest, in the meanwhile, someone might go to my cart. She knew what was what, and, when she really couldn't do it all herself, she would quickly say to her daughter: "Get up, Eunice, help the gentleman . . . hurry!" Eunice would put her work down, would get up in two stages, majestically, first with her bosom and then with her hips, and would serve the customer without looking at him, with downcast eyes. Then, without a word, without a smile, she would sit down again.

In short, competition: within a week they took almost all my customers away from me. I began to hate the two women, particularly the mother, who did not hide her satisfaction and who would cast a glance of triumph at me every time she took some hesitant customer away from me. There is nothing worse, in situations like these, than losing your head, and by this time I had already lost mine. From day to day I became more and more shaggy, more brusque, more threatening. My beard, my patched clothes and my hoarse voice did the rest. I would cry: "Sweet oranges!" in a tone which was downright truculent; and people would look at me, be frightened, and go straight to the cart next to me. Then one day, my aggressive nature betrayed me. A fop, young and small in stature, in the company of a woman twice his size, was contemplating my oranges and could not make up his mind. I kept repeating, in disgust: "My oranges are beautiful," and he kept feeling them and shaking his head. That big woman who was on his arm might have been his mother, and this fact was decisive for him. Because he cast a glance at Eunice, who was as beautiful as a statue, and then, the dirty swine, he went directly towards her. I lost my patience and seized him by the arm,

bra un elefante e quella ragazza lì ti fa gola . . . ecco perché." Successe un pandemonio: lui che gridava: "Giù le mani o ti spacco il muso"; io che, una bottiglia in mano, rispondevo: "Provaci e vedrai"; la gente che si metteva in mezzo. Finalmente vennero le guardie e ci separarono. Ma in quell'occasione mi accorsi di due cose: prima di tutto che quel movimento di collera l'avevo avuto più per gelosia che per rabbia di concorrenza; in secondo luogo che Eunice, in quel tafferuglio, aveva, in certo modo, preso le mie parti, dicendo alle guardie che lei non aveva visto e non sapeva niente.

Insomma, mi innamorai di Eunice, o meglio mi accorsi che ero innamorato e, colto un momento che la madre non c'era, glielo dissi alla maniera mia, francamente, brutalmente. Lei non si stupì, ma si limitò a dirmi, levando gli occhi dal lavoro: "Anche tu mi piaci." Avreste dovuto vedermi. A quelle quattro parolette, acchiappai le stanghe del carrettino e via di corsa per i lungotéveri,[8] cantando a squarciagola, mentre la gente dai marciapiedi mi guardava come se fossi diventato matto. Non ero matto, ero soltanto contento. Era la prima volta che una donna mi diceva parole come quelle ed ero convinto di averla conquistata. Ma la sera stessa, all'appuntamento presso ponte Vittorio,[9] quando, dopo i soliti discorsi, tentai di prenderla per la vita e di baciarla, mi accorsi che la conquista era ancora tutta da fare. Si lasciava abbracciare e stringere un po' come una morta, le braccia penzolanti, il corpo molle, le ginocchia piegate; e se tentavo di darle un bacio, in un modo o in un altro non mi riusciva mai di incontrare le sue labbra, e il bacio andava a finire sul collo o sulla guancia. Dopo quella prima sera, ci vedemmo spesso, ma sempre con lo stesso risultato: tanto che alla fine, spazientito, le dissi: "Ma di' un po', che ci vediamo a fare?" E lei: "Sei troppo prepotente . . . con le donne bisogna essere gentili . . . fai con me come quando vendi le arance: vorresti le cose per forza." Io le dissi: "Non ti capisco, ma sono pronto a sposarti . . . poi, una volta sposati, ragioneremo." Ma lei

saying: "Don't you want my oranges? Do you prefer those? I'll tell you why you prefer those: because you have a woman who looks like an elephant and you find that girl appetizing . . . that's why." All hell broke loose: he was shouting "Hands off or I'll sock you in the puss"; I, with a bottle in my hand, was answering: "Just try it and you'll see"; people came between us. Finally the police came and separated us. But on that occasion I noticed two things: first of all, that I had had that outburst of rage more out of jealousy than out of anger at competition; in the second place, that Eunice had, in a certain way, taken my side in that scuffle, telling the police that she had seen and heard nothing.

In short, I fell in love with Eunice, or, rather, I realized that I had fallen in love, and, taking advantage of a moment when her mother was not there, I told her so after my fashion, forthrightly, brutally. She was not surprised, but confined herself to telling me, looking up from her work: "I like you, too." You ought to have seen me. At those four little words, I caught hold of the poles of the cart and rushed off along the Tiber embankment, singing at the top of my lungs, while the people on the sidewalks looked at me as if I had gone mad. I was not mad, only happy. It was the first time that a woman had said such words to me, and I was convinced that I had conquered her. But that same evening, at the rendezvous near the Vittorio bridge, when, after the usual talk, I tried to put my arm around her waist and kiss her, I realized that the conquest was still wholly unaccomplished. She would let herself be embraced and squeezed somewhat like a corpse, with her arms dangling, her body lax and her knees bent; and if I tried to give her a kiss, in one way or another I never succeeded in meeting her lips, and my kiss would end up on her neck or cheek. After that first evening, we met often, but always with the same result: so that finally, growing impatient, I said to her: "But look here, what are we meeting for?" And she: "You're too aggressive . . . with women you have to be nice . . . you act with me as you do when you sell oranges; you want to take things by force."

scosse la testa: "Per sposarsi bisogna amarsi e io non ti amo ancora . . . bisogna che a forza di gentilezza tu ti faccia amare . . . sii gentile e io ti amerò." Insomma, mi intimidí a tal punto che, ormai, non osavo più prenderla per la vita. A forza di gentilezza, eravamo diventati come fratello e sorella: sì e no [10] qualche volta le toccavo una mano. Mi pareva, è vero, che la cosa non fosse naturale; ma lei ci teneva tanto a questa gentilezza che io mi ero convinto di aver torto e di non aver mai capito nulla dell'amore.

Una di quelle sere, sebbene non avessi l'appuntamento, andai a gironzolare dalle parti di via Giulia,[11] dove lei stava di casa. Ad un vicoletto, lei mi sbucò ad un tratto sotto il naso, passandomi avanti e camminando svelta verso il lungotevere. Incuriosito, la seguii a distanza. La vidi andare dritta alla spalletta del fiume, dove c'era un uomo che sembrava aspettarla. Poi, tutto avvenne in maniera franca e spicciativa, senza alcuna gentilezza. Lei gli mise una mano sulla spalla e lui si voltò; lei gli accarezzò il viso e lui l'acchiappò per la vita; lei gli tese le labbra e lui la baciò. In un minuto, insomma, lui aveva fatto quello che io, con tutta la mia gentilezza, non ero riuscito a fare in un mese. Poi, come si girava, la luce del fanale gli cadde sul viso e lo riconobbi: era un giovanotto basso e grasso che, da ultimo, avevo visto gironzolare intorno i carrettini. Macellaio, con il negozio lì accanto, in via Giulia. Per il fisico, a petto a me, non era nulla; ma aveva la macelleria. Avevo aperto il coltello che tenevo in tasca. Lo rinchiusi, vincendomi, e me ne andai.

Il giorno dopo lasciai il carrettino nel cortile, mi alzai il bavero sul collo, mi calcai il berretto sugli occhi e mi presentai al ponte del Gianicolo, una volta tanto come compratore. Fingendo di non conoscerla, dissi alla madre:

I told her: "I don't understand you, but I'm ready to marry
you . . . then, when we're married, we'll talk." But she
shook her head: "To get married, you have to be in love,
and I don't love you yet . . . you have to make me love
you by dint of being nice . . . be nice and I'll love you."
In short, she intimidated me to such a point that henceforth
I no longer dared to put my arm around her waist. By dint
of being nice, we had become like brother and sister; occa-
sionally, perhaps, I might touch her hand. I thought, as a
matter of fact, that the situation was not natural; but she
insisted so much on this business of being nice that I was
convinced I was wrong and had never understood anything
about love.

One of those evenings, although I did not have a date
with her, I went strolling around in the region of Via Giulia,
where she lived. At the corner of an alleyway, she suddenly
came out under my nose, passing in front of me and walking
quickly towards the embankment. My curiosity was excited
and I followed her at a distance. I saw her go straight to
the river parapet, where there was a man who seemed to be
waiting for her. Then, everything happened in a forthright
and expeditious way, without any business of being nice.
She put her hand on his shoulder and he turned around;
she caressed his face and he put his arm around her waist;
she put her lips to his and he kissed her. In one minute, in
short, he had done what I, with all my nice behavior, had
not succeeded in accomplishing in a month. Then, as he
turned around, the light of the street-lamp fell on his face
and I recognized him: he was a short, fat young fellow
whom I had recently seen hanging around the carts. He was
a butcher, with his shop near there, in Via Giulia. In his
physique, compared to me, he was nothing; but he had the
butcher's shop. I had opened the knife which I kept in my
pocket. I closed it again, controlling myself, and went
away.

The next day I left the push-cart in the courtyard, pulled
up my coat-collar over my neck, pushed my cap down over
my eyes, and showed up at the Janiculum bridge as a
customer for once. Pretending not to know her, I said to

"Dammi un etto di olive, ma belle, eh," con la mia voce
più rauca e più minacciosa. Eunice che, al solito, lavorava
seduta sulla seggiola, doveva aver capito che tirava un'aria
brutta, perché mi salutò appena. Mentre la madre, senza
soffiare, anzi con sufficienza, come se mi avesse fatto la
grazia, mi pesava le olive, ecco spuntare il macellaio e
accostarsi a Eunice. Dissi alla madre: "Non rubare sul peso,
come il solito, mi raccomando." Lei, da vera strega, rispose:
"Tu, rubavi sul peso, tanto è vero che da te la gente non
ci è più venuta." Vidi il macellaio fare una carezza in capo
ad Eunice e, chinandosi, dirle qualche cosa all'orecchio;
presi il cartoccio delle olive, ne misi una in bocca e poi la
sputai proprio in faccia alla madre, e dissi: "Ahò, ma sono
marce le tue olive." Lei, arrogante, rispose: "Sei tu marcio,
brutto vagabondo." Le dissi: "Ridammi i soldi, su, non
fare storie." [12] E lei: "Macché soldi . . . vattene piuttosto."
Il macellaio, a questo punto, si avvicinò, dondolandosi sui
fianchi e domandò: "Ma che vuoi, si può sapere che vuoi?"
Risposi: "I soldi . . . queste olive sono marce"; e nello
stesso tempo gli sputai in faccia un'oliva mezza morsicata.
Subito lui mi venne sotto e mi agguantò al petto, dicendo:
"Guarda, è meglio che te ne vai." Faceva il prepotente, da
vero bullo. Io, che avevo aspettato questo momento, senza
neppure parlare mi liberai con una scossa e poi lo agguan-
tai a mia volta con una sola mano, alla gola, e lo rovesciai
indietro, sul carrettino. Intanto con l'altra mano, cercavo in
tasca il coltello. Ma per sua fortuna, il carrettino, tutto ad
un tratto, si ribaltò e lui cadde in terra tra le arance che
rotolavano d'ogni parte, mentre la gente accorreva e la
madre urlava come una ossessa. Anch'io, per lo slancio, ero
scivolato in terra. Quando mi rialzai, mi trovai di fronte a
due carabinieri. Stringevo in mano il coltello, sebbene non
avessi fatto a tempo ad aprirlo, e questo bastò. Mi arrestarono e mi portarono a Regina Coeli.[13]

Qualche mese dopo, uscii di prigione più brutto che mai,

the mother: "Give me a hectogram of olives, but nice ones, hey?" with my most raucous and threatening voice. Eunice, who, as usual, was seated on her chair working, must have understood that something nasty was in the wind, because she barely greeted me. While the mother, without puffing, in fact quite haughtily, as if she were doing me a favor, was weighing out the olives for me, here came the butcher and went up to Eunice. I said to the mother: "Don't cheat on the weight, as you usually do, please." She, like a real witch, answered: "You used to cheat on the weight, so much so that people stopped patronizing you." I saw the butcher caress Eunice's head and, bending over, say something in her ear; I took the packet of olives, put one of them in my mouth and then spat it right into the mother's face, and said: "Ugh, your olives are rotten!" She arrogantly answered: "You're rotten, you ugly vagabond!" I told her: "Give me my money back, hurry up, don't make a fuss." And she said: "What do you mean, money back . . . you get out of here." The butcher, at this point, came up, swaying his hips, and asked: "What do you want, come on now, what do you want?" I answered: "My money back . . . these olives are rotten"; and at the same time I spat a half-eaten olive into his face. Immediately he came up to me and grabbed me by the chest, saying: "Look here, you'd better get out of here." He was being aggressive, like a real bully. I had expected this moment and, without even speaking a word, freed myself with a jerk and then seized him in turn with one hand, by the throat, and hurled him backwards across the cart. In the meanwhile, with the other hand, I was feeling in my pocket for my knife. But, luckily for him, the cart suddenly overturned and he fell to the ground amidst the oranges which were rolling in every direction, while people were running up and the mother was shrieking like a madwoman. I too, because of my impetus, had slipped to the ground. When I got up again, I was facing two carabineers. I had my knife in my hand, although I had not had time to open it, and this was enough. They arrested me and took me to Regina Coeli.

A few months later, I came out of jail looking uglier than

senza soldi, senza licenza di venditore ambulante, disperato.
Il nonno, come mi vide, disse: "Sei stato vittima della concorrenza . . . ma da' retta: nel commercio, il coltello non
vale . . .vendi pure i coltelli, ma non usarli." Non gli
risposi; e siccome era una giornata di sole, me ne andai a
spasso dalle parte di via Giulia. La macelleria era aperta,
coi quarti appesi agli uncini e avvolti nella garza; e il macellaio stava in cima al banco, rosso e lustro in faccia, le
maniche rimboccate sulle braccia nude. Spaccava le bistecche
sul marmo, a colpi di mannaia. E sotto il banco, seduto su
una seggiola, intenta a far la calza, c'era Eunice. Così seppi
che si erano sposati; e lei doveva già essere incinta perché
quella calza che faceva era un calzettino rosa, piccolissimo,
proprio da lattante. Tirai avanti, guardando a tutte le
botteghe lungo la strada, nella speranza di incontrare
un'altra macelleria che facesse la concorrenza al marito di
Eunice e lo facesse fallire. Ma non c'era: nient'altro che
stagnari, falegnami, marmisti, arrotini, corniciai e roba
simile. Dove finisce via Giulia, a Ponte Sisto, [14] capii che
era inutile insistere e passai il ponte.

ever, with no money, without my peddler's license, and in despair. My grandfather, when he saw me, said: "You have been a victim of competition . . . but listen to me: in business, a knife is no use . . . sell knives, but don't use them." I did not answer him; and as it was a sunny day, I went for a walk over towards Via Giulia. The butcher's shop was open, with quarters of animals hanging on hooks and wrapped in gauze; and the butcher was standing up there behind his counter, with his face red and shiny, and with his sleeves rolled up on his bare arms. He was cutting steaks on his marble counter, with a cleaver. And down in front of the counter, seated on a chair, was Eunice, intent on knitting stockings. In that way I found out that they were married; and she must have already been pregnant, because the stocking she was making was a little pink sock, a tiny one, just the kind for a new-born baby. I kept on going, looking at all the shops along the street, in the hope of coming across another butcher's shop that would compete with Eunice's husband and make him go bankrupt. But there was none; nothing but tinsmiths, carpenters, marble-workers, knife-sharpeners, frame-makers and people like that. Where Via Giulia comes to an end, at Ponte Sisto, I understood that there was no use of hoping any longer, and I crossed the bridge.

Notes, Questionnaire,
Vocabulary

NOTES

1. One of the ten narrators, who has just told the preceding story.
2. Another of the narrators, Lauretta, who was in charge of the eighth day's amusements.
3. The narrator of this story.
4. *ingegnarsi di,* to try to.
5. = *uomo,* man.
6. *Maso = Tommaso* "Thomas".
7. = *vedèndolo,* seeing him.
8. *pòstovi,* placed there.
9. *far vista di,* to pretend to.
10. *Berlinzone,* an imaginary country.
11. *Bengodi,* an imaginary region.
12. *una oca a denaio,* a money-laying goose, i.e. one of the type that laid the golden eggs in the fable.
13. Literally, "he who took the most, had the most".
14. *hàccene = ce ne ha,* there are of them.
15. This is a proverbial rhyming expression, in which the second part has no real relation to the first, and meaning "an immense number".
16. = *deve,* must.
17. *cavelle,* Old Italian expression meaning "something, somewhat".
18. *con essoteco,* Old Italian, with you.
19. *fare il tomo,* to tumble down.
20. *tôrsene* (= *tógliersene*) *una satolla,* literally to take for oneself a gorging = to eat one's fill of it.
21. = *trova,* finds.
22. *Settignano* and *Montisci,* two towns near Florence.
23. = *ci è,* there is.
24. *Montemorello,* a hill near Florence.
25. *vatti con Dio,* a proverbial expression, literally "go with God," but here employed as a kind of intensive: "unbelievably bright."
26. = *è,* is.
27. Maso makes an accurate statement, but Calandrino interprets it as if the last *non* were pleonastic and hence meaningless.
28. The Mugnone, a small tributary of the Arno, to the northwest of Florence and at that time outside of the city walls; in the summer its bed is normally dry.

29. = *si diè*, he gave himself, he started.
30. *monistero delle donne*, literally women's monastery.
31. = *troveremo*, we shall find.
32. *grossi*, medieval silver coins of varying weight and size.
33. *di grossa pasta*, literally of coarse paste, hence not delicate or subtle (socially, intellectually).
34. = *rasciugate*, dried out.
35. *perdere il trotto per l'ambiadura*, literally to lose the trot for the gallop.
36. = *veda*, sees (present subjunctive).
37. *venturo*, coming.
38. *in sul far del dì*, at the break of day.
39. = *se lo vedeva*, he saw him [near] to himself.
40. = *no il* = *non lo*, not him.
41. = *andiàmocene*, let us go away.
42. *aprirsi*, literally the "opening", i.e. the extending or drawing back and "hauling off" of Bruno's arm.
43. *èssere tutto uno*, to be one and the same thing.
44. *monna*, a medieval Italian title for women.
45. = *vedèndolo*, seeing him.
46. *diserto*, ruined.
47. = *egli pare*, it seems.
48. Literally, without saying to us either "[go] with God or [go] with the devil".
49. = *te ne venisti*, you came away.
50. = *conciati*, bruised.
51. *con essolui*, Old Italian, with him.

MACHIAVELLI

1. A legendary king of Crete, who in ancient tradition and in Dante was imagined to be one of the judges of Hell who assigned sinners to their proper places of punishment.
2. Rhadamanthos, another legendary king of Crete and judge in Hell, renowned for the strictness and justice of his judgments.
3. Pluto, in ancient legend the ruler of Hell, and often identified in Christian legend with Satan.
4. = *fosse*, was (past subjunctive).
5. = *s'indirizzàrono*, they addressed themselves.
6. = *fóssero*, they were (past subjunctive).
7. = *sìano*, they are (present subjunctive).
8. = *si dichiarò*, it was decided.

9. = *egli,* he.
10. = *cavalli,* horses.
11. Castile, a region in the center of Spain.
12. *Ognissanti,* All Saints; a church and quarter in the western part of Florence.
13. = *potéssero,* they should be able (past subjunctive).
14. = *andàtosene,* gone (past participle).
15. Syria, a country to the east of the Mediterranean.
16. Aleppo, a Syrian city.
17. = *mostrava,* showed.
18. = *dimostrato,* demonstrated (past participle).
19. The Donati were one of the most outstanding patrician families in medieval Florence.
20. = *nondimeno,* nevertheless.
21. *dubitava,* she hesitated.
22. = *andare,* to go.
23. The Levant, the eastern end of the Mediterranean.
24. The western end of the Mediterranean. Florence was a central point in the medieval cloth trade, which involved shipping coarse woolen goods from west to east, and fine silk goods from east to west.
25. = *onórano,* they honor.
26. = *parse,* seemed (past participle, feminine plural).
27. = *eléssero,* they chose, they elected.
28. = *giuocato,* played, gamed, lost at gaming.
29. = *senza,* without.
30. *sanza essersi altrimenti assicurato,* literally "without having insured himself in any other way" than that of self-insurance.
31. *dal detto al fatto,* literally "from the word to the deed", i.e. suddenly, unexpectedly.
32. = *di nascosto,* secretly.
33. The Prato gate, on the western end of Florence.
34. = *si mìsero,* they set themselves, they began.
35. = *essendo,* being.
36. A town about two miles west of Florence and close to the Arno.
37. This *che* repeats the previous *che* "that" which precedes *se lo salvava.*
38. = *finito,* finished.
39. = *cercato,* sought.
40. *San Zanobi,* St. Zenobius, an early bishop of Florence (4th–5th centuries A.D.), renowned for his supernatural powers.
41. Naples.

42. = *ti farai,* you will have (for yourself).
43. *Lodovico,* Louis.
44. = *per l'addietro,* earlier (*addietro* = "back, behind").
45. *se ne trovavano,* there were some of them, i.e. demons.
46. = *donde,* whence, from where.
47. = *tógliere,* to take.
48. = *avremo,* we shall have.
49. Notre Dame, the great cathedral of Paris.
50. = *oltre,* in addition (to).
51. = *abbiano,* they have (present subjunctive).
52. = *rumori,* noises, din, uproar.
53. = *dìano,* they give, they attack (present subjunctive).
54. = *vèngano,* they come (present subjunctive).
55. = *pòpolo,* people, populace (as opposed to the nobility).
56. = *condotta,* led, brought.
57. = *déttero,* they gave, they attacked.
58. = *sapendo,* knowing.
59. = *tua moglie,* your wife.
60. *pensare,* literally "to think"; here, rather, "to imagine" to oneself on reflecting on the situation.
61. = *essa,* she.
62. = *volle,* wished.

BANDELLO

1. Moncalieri, a town southeast of Turin, now practically a suburb of that city.
2. Literally, "twenty-four years young".
3. = *piuttosto,* rather.
4. *tenevano del contadinesco,* literally "they had peasant-like characteristics".
5. *stanza,* here = dwelling-place.
6. A small town southwest of Moncalieri.
7. *veruno = nessuno,* no.
8. = *aiuto,* aid, help.
9. = *voglio,* I want.
10. = *egli,* it.
11. = *avrà,* she will have.
12. = *le,* to her.
13. = *vi piàcciono,* they please you.
14. = *stà bene,* it is well.
15. = *anche,* also.

NOTES

16. *con ciò sia cosa che,* an old conjunction-like phrase meaning "inasmuch as, since".
17. = *saprei,* I would know.
18. = *siete,* you are.
19. = *allora,* then, at that time.
20. = *due,* two.
21. *più accomodate* = *le più accomodate,* the most suitable.
22. *calesse,* it should be of concern, from the verb *calere,* to matter.
23. = *sarebbe,* he would be.
24. = *potè,* he was able.
25. = *con voi,* with you.
26. *guiderdone,* reward, an old word with associations of feudal loyalty and courtly love.
27. *stare sovra sé* = *stare sopra pensiero,* to be lost in thought.
28. *Monsignor(e)* was in the sixteenth century a title of courtesy, equivalent to "my lord", given to any noble person, not only to ecclesiastics.
29. = *scritti,* writings.
30. *mettersi in arnese,* to equip oneself.
31. = *doveva,* was scheduled to.
32. Rouen, the chief city of Normandy, on the Seine between Paris and Le Havre.
33. Presumably John Talbot, first earl of Shrewsbury (ca. 1380–1453), a leading English general towards the end of the Hundred Years' War.
34. = *qualcuno,* someone.
35. *solenni,* here "serious" doctors as opposed to impostors or quacks.
36. = *durante,* during.
37. *in tutto oggi,* literally "in all of today".
38. *la vostra mercè,* literally "by your grace", i.e. "thanks to you".

VERGA

1. *Malpelo,* literally "evil hair". There is a widespread folk superstition in Italy and Sicily that red hair indicates an innately evil nature.
2. *un fior di birbone,* literally "a prime example of a rascal".
3. *la bettònica* is betony, a widespread plant in Sicily and Italy; *essere conosciuto come la bettònica* = "to be very well known".

319

NOTES

4. *Monserrato*, a region of Sicily.
5. *La Carvana*, another region of Sicily.
6. *Mastro* is a dialectal form of *Maestro*, "master"; in Sicily, used as a title before a personal name.
7. *ad occhio*, literally "by eye".
8. *Bestia*, literally "beast" or "animal"; also widely used meaning "fool".
9. An *onza* was an old Sicilian gold coin.
10. *da un pezzo*, since a while, quite a while previously.
11. *Amleto*, the Italian form of *Hamlet*.
12. *comare = comadre*, godmother; in Sicily, a title given to women of the people.
13. Literally, "the beautiful bargain of Master Beast [Fool]!"
14. *Ofelia*, the Italan form of Ophelia.
15. *Non te la saresti scappata*, literally "you would not have escaped it", i.e. the danger.
16. *Avere il diavolo dalla sua*, to have the devil on one's side.
17. *ranocchio* = "frog".
18. *da più di loro*, literally "worth more than they are".
19. The passage is ambiguous in the Italian; the translation deliberately reflects this.
20. *di quelli che sembrava ci avesse messo la coda il diavolo*, literally "of those which the devil seemed to have put his tail into".
21. *che gli piangévano addosso*, literally "which were weeping on his back".
22. *La Plaja*, literally "The Beach" (from Spanish *playa* "beach").
23. *compare*, literally "godfather"; used widely in Sicily and southern Italy as a title among lower-class men, as is also *comare* "godmother" among lower-class women.
24. The *sciara* is black gravelly material formed from lava in decomposition.
25. *fare osso duro al mestiere*, to stand up under the job.
26. *più di là che di qua*, literally "more on that side than on this".
27. *Cifali*, a small town near Syracuse.

FOGAZZARO

1. The problem is whether this expression means "the Manes [ancestral spirits] of the fable" or "the fabled Manes".

320

NOTES

2. Horace ((Quintus Horatius Flaccus), the Roman poet of the Augustan Age (65–8 B.C.).
3. Venetian for "What do you expect? French poetry!" (It. *Cosa vorrà? Poesia francese*). The gentry of the Venetian region are proud of their local dialect and use it on almost all occasions when speaking among themselves.
4. *giuochi d'acqua*, fountains (Fr. *jeux d'eau*).
5. *Sior*, Venetian for *Signor(e)* "Mr., sir, lord".
6. The Euganean Hills, an isolated cluster of hills rising from the plain southwest of Padua.
7. *bezzi = quattrini*, money. A *bezzo* was an old Venetian coin.
8. *pàndoli*, a dialect term for a kind of cakes.
9. *La = Ella* (modern *Lei*), you (very formal).
10. *a fior di labbro*, lit. on the surface of her lips.
11. The *Comune* is the municipality and the government thereof.
12. *quattro*, lit. four, here used for "a few".
13. *caro lei*, lit. dear you, i.e. my dear sir.
14. *metter la testa di Farsatti*, to compare him with F.
15. *la*, here a subject pronoun referring to the situation in general.
16. *Euh!*, the conventional representation in Italian for a sound showing rejection, contempt, etc., similar to French *eu* or German *ö*.
17. *Sta a vedere*, lit. wait and see.
18. Pedrocchi's is a famous café in the center of Padua.
19. *l'ottavario dei morti*, the octave (week) of prayer for the souls of the dead, immediately after All Souls' Day (November 2).
20. *è in tavola*, lit. it (the meal) is on the table.
21. *La multa*, the fine (i.e. the excess postage charge).
22. A *palanca* was another term for a *soldo* or penny = five centesimi, equivalent at the time of this story to one American cent.
23. *leonardesca*, by Leonardo (da Vinci).
24. Stockholm (capital of Sweden).
25. *A vu*, Venetian for *a voi*, lit. (over) to you, it's your turn.
26. Carl Maria von Weber, German composer (1786–1826).

FUCINI

1. *Acquaviva*, literally "living water", is the name of an imaginary village in the Tuscan hills, chosen by Fucini to contrast with the name of Pietrarsa.

2. *Pietrarsa,* literally "burned rock", another imaginary village, whose name suggests the eternal drought which plagues it.

3. The "provinces" of Italy, of which there are ninety-two in 1960, are administrative divisions of the country corresponding roughly to the French départements.

4. *che panni vestono,* literally "what clothes they wear", i.e. what kind of character they have.

5. *fai fai,* literally "do it, do it," but meaning "repeatedly".

6. = *si trova,* is located.

7. The Prefecture is the central administrative office of an Italian province.

8. = *neanche,* not even.

9. *dire la sua,* to have his say.

10. The *assessori* are assistant judges or others who, together with the *sindaco,* form the municipal council.

11. *Sor* is a central Italian title, abbreviated from *Signor(e),* (S[ign]or).

12. = *loro,* to them.

13. *alla peggio,* at the worst, somehow or other.

14. *avere un diavolo per capello,* to be in a bad mood, in a bad temper.

15. *dar nell'occhio,* to be obvious.

16. The spelling *debà* is used here to represent the Italian pronunciation of the French word *débat,* debate, court session.

17. A Tuscan dialectal form for *mio,* my.

18. *tenerci dietro,* to keep up with it (literally, after it).

19. *Farla bona,* to "catch it hot", "stir up a hornet's nest".

20. *Farsi vivo,* to show signs of life, become active.

D'ANNUNZIO

1. *a torno* = *attorno.* D'Annunzio often separated into their component elements a number of words consisting of preposition + noun or preposition + article, as here and in *in contro* = *incontro,* toward; *su le* = *sulle,* on the; etc. He also preferred *quelli* "those", even before a vowel, to the normal form *quegli,* as in *quelli uomini* = *quegli uomini* "those men".

2. The *metèora crepuscolare* is the aurora borealis, which is very rare in Italian latitudes and hence easily the object of superstitious terror.

NOTES

3. The *Radusani*, in this story, are the Radusans or inhabitants of the imaginary town of Radusa| (see fn. 8).
4. Don Cònsolo is evidently the parish priest of Radusa. In modern Italian, the title *don* is normally given to priests, and used with either a first or a last name.
5. St. Pantaleone is the patron saint of the Radusans.
6. Mascálico is an imaginary town in the Abruzzi; its inhabitants are the hereditary enemies of the Radusans (fn. 3).
7. St. Gonselvo is the patron saint of the inhabitants of Mascálico, whom the Radusans suspect of having stolen, for their own rites of exorcism, the candles destined for the invocation to St. Pantaleone.
8. Radusa is an imaginary town in the Abruzzi.
9. *I Pantaleonidi* is a learnèd word, coined by d'Annunzio, to refer to the followers of St. Pantaleone.
10. The *Mascalicesi* are the inhabitants of Mascálico.
11. *Senza più lume negli occhi*, literally "with no light left in their eyes", i.e. blinded by terror.

PIRANDELLO

1. *Fuori della grazia di Dio*, literally, out of the grace of God (through anger).
2. *Dio mio*, literally, my God. This and similar expressions are used much more frequently and with less strength in Italian than in English.
3. *si beava*, was in a state of ecstasy.
4. *Arbiter elegantiarum* (Latin), a judge of elegance.
5. *tornò a fulminare*, literally "returned to fulminate", i.e. glared again.
6. *dipinta*, literally "as if painted", formerly said of a well-fitting suit.
7. *Dare del signore a qualcuno*, to call someone "sir".
8. *Non poterne più*, not to be able to stand something any longer.
9. *dare in escandescenze*, literally "to give = let oneself go in outbursts of anger".
10. *òrfana*, orphan, i.e. having lost either both parents or, as here, one parent (her father).
11. The terms *professore* (m.) and *professoressa* (f.) are used for teachers, not only at the college and university level, but also at lower levels in the Italian school system.
12. The *scuole complimentari* were post-elementary schools,

just above the level of the elementary grades. They have now been replaced by the *scuole medie inferiori* or junior high schools.

13. *Diuturni dolori,* literally, sorrows of long duration. Gori's choice of the adjective *diuturno* "of long duration, diuturnal" shows his fussy, pedantic insistence on elevated vocabulary and style.

14. *con la testa che già gli fumava,* literally "with his head already fuming", i.e. dizzy as if with the fumes of intoxication.

15. *perdio,* literally "by God".

16. *di parata,* on parade.

17. The *stato civile* is the registry of births, marriages and deaths. In Italy a wedding is normally performed twice: once in a civil ceremony at the City Hall, where it is officially registered in the governmental archives, and then again in a religious ceremony in church.

18. *sospirò,* literally "sighed for", i.e. desired ardently.

19. *Andare a monte,* to come to naught.

20. *Con tanti d'occhi,* literally, with so many of eyes, i.e. with a furious glare.

21. *vìncersi,* literally "to overcome herself".

22. *Zitti zitti,* literally, quietly, quietly. Note the repetition of a word (usually an adjective or adverb) for emphasis, a very frequent procedure in Italian.

23. *Che pareva ubriaco,* literally, seeming inebriated. These three words form a clause modifying *il professor Gori,* subject of *giunse.*

24. *di furia,* in a tremendous hurry.

25. *in fin dei conti,* in the last analysis, after all.

26. *quatto, quatto,* on the sly.

PALAZZESCHI

1. The use of *signor* before the title *marchese* is a way of showing special respect, which is without direct equivalent in English speech, but which we can show in writing by capitalizing the title *Marquis.*

2. *entrare in ballo,* literally "to enter into the dance", i.e. to be the topic of discussion.

3. *gli* here = *egli,* it.

4. *glie ne = gliene,* to him of it; Palazzeschi separates these two elements which are usually written together.

NOTES

5. *montare in bestia,* to become furiously angry.
6. *un torlo d'uovo,* literally "the yolk of an egg".
7. *per la pelle,* completely, thoroughly.
8. *Don Giovanni = Don Juan (Tenorio),* the legendary Spanish libertine made most famous in Mozart's opera *Don Giovanni* (1787).
9. *vuotare il sacco,* literally "to empty the sack".
10. *saperla lunga,* to "know the score".
11. *fo = faccio,* I make.
12. *mi fa specie,* it surprises me, it astonishes me.
13. Now the Piazza della Repubblica.

Alvaro

1. The Allied troops, in the Second World War, entered Rome on June 4, 1944. To judge from internal evidence, however, the Liberation referred to here is probably that of the entire country in the spring of 1945, whose official anniversary is celebrated on April 25.
2. A "ràpido" is the fastest class of train in Italy, comparable approximately to American limiteds.
3. A "diretto" is officially a "fast" train, but actually a rather slow type of express stopping at most stations of any importance.
4. *dicevano ognuno la sua frase,* literally "they were saying, each one, his own sentence".
5. The stocky man and the peasant woman are obviously standing at one end of the car; on Italian corridor coaches, the toilets are located at each end of the car, with the toilet door immediately next to the end doors of the car.
6. *Hanno del rabdomante,* literally "they have something of the [water-] diviner".
7. *Fortunello* is the Italian version of the comic-strip tramp Happy Hooligan.
8. *con quel che di indefinibilmente molle e lieve,* literally "with that something [which is] indefinably soft and light".
9. Catania is a city in Sicily, at the foot of Mount Etna, on the east coast.
10. Reggio Calabria is referred to here, a city on the toe of Italy directly opposite Messina.
11. The Strait of Messina, between Italy and Sicily; trains are ferried across this strait on large ferry-boats.
12. The doors on Italian trains open outwards; they can be

opened from the inside by a handle which is placed at the
bottom of the door, in a position to be reached (by grasping
upwards) by someone standing on the ground beside the
train. Passengers inside the train usually open the doors by
reaching out through the window and turning a handle located on the outside.

MORAVIA

1. *Il Gianìcolo* is the Janiculum, a long hill which rises
   steeply to the west of Rome and at its northern end (just
   south of St. Peter's) comes close to the Tiber river. At this
   point it is pierced by a road tunnel which carries traffic to
   the area southwest of the Vatican.
2. The *Madonna del Riposo* is a suburban region southwest of
   St. Peter's.
3. The *Trastévere* is the region "across the Tiber" from the
   center of Rome, a slum area where the oldest-established
   and most authentically local customs of Rome are still pre-
   served.
4. *Monteverde* is the region above Trastévere, south of the
   Janiculum but on the same height of land.
5. The *Corso Vittorio Emanuele* is the main street of the old
   part of Rome, between the monument to Victor Emanuel
   and the bridge leading to St. Peter's.
6. *Anagni* is a small town in the Roman *campagna,* in the
   upper reaches of the valley of the river Sacco, about 30
   miles southeast of Rome.
7. *la sapeva lunga,* she knew a thing or two, she knew the
   score, she knew what was what.
8. The *Lungotéveri* are the embankments running along
   (*lungo*) the river Tiber (*Tévere*). In each city having such
   embankments, they are named from the river along which
   they run: e.g. in Turin, they are called *Lungopò,* in Verona
   they are the *Lungàdige,* in Padua the *Lungobrenta* etc. A
   street or road running along the sea is called a *Lungomare.*
9. *Ponte Vittorio (Emanuele)* is the bridge at the northern end
   of the Corso Vittorio Emanuele (and near the northern end
   of Via Giulia) which leads across the Tiber to the Vatican.
10. *sì e no,* literally "yes and no", i.e. perhaps.
11. *Via Giulia* is a long, straight street cutting like a secant
    across that part of Rome contained within the bend of the

river Tiber, from Ponte Vittorio Emanuele on the north to
Ponte Sisto on the south.

12. *fare storie*, to raise a row, make a fuss.

13. *Regina Coeli* is the main prison of Rome.

14. *Ponte Sisto* is a bridge leading from the old part of Rome
across the Tiber into Trastévere, just at the southern end of
Via Giulia.

QUESTIONNAIRE

BOCCACCIO

1. Che tipo d'uomo era Calandrino?
2. Quali erano i suoi rapporti con Bruno e Buffalmacco?
3. Maso del Saggio perché cominciò a parlare di pietre con il suo amico?
4. Descrivete il paese di Bengodi.
5. Che cosa disse Maso del Saggio a Calandrino circa l'elitropia?
6. Dove andò Calandrino dopo di aver parlato con Maso del Saggio?
7. Calandrino e i suoi amici che cosa decisero di fare?
8. Bruno e Buffalmacco come ingannarono Calandrino nella valle del Mugnone?
9. Che cosa gettarono Bruno e Buffalmacco, e contro chi?
10. Perché i gabellieri lasciarono passare Calandrino senza dir niente?
11. Quante persone incontrò Calandrino fra la Porta a San Gallo e la casa sua?
12. Che cosa disse la moglie di Calandrino al vederlo?
13. Quale fu la risposta di Calandrino a monna Tessa?
14. A che punto sopraggiunsero Bruno e Buffalmacco?
15. Che cosa dissero Bruno e Buffalmacco a Calandrino?
16. Calandrino come spiegò le sue azioni?
17. Perché Calandrino aveva bistrattato la moglie?
18. Che ammonimento diedero Bruno e Buffalmacco a Calandrino?

MACHIAVELLI

1. Che cosa dicevano le anime dannate esser stata la cagione della loro infelicità?
2. Che cosa decisero di fare i prìncipi dell'Inferno?
3. Che cosa si comandò a Belfagor di fare?
4. Sotto quali condizioni Belfagor assunse la forma di un uomo?
5. Dove si stabilì Belfagor sulla terra: con che nome, in che città e in che quartiere?
6. Dove disse di essere stato e di aver guadagnato le sue ricchezze?
7. Di chi s'innamorò Roderigo?
8. Come si comportò la giovane, sposata che egli l'ebbe?
9. Per quali ragioni fu disperso il capitale che Roderigo aveva apportato con sé?

QUESTIONNAIRE

10. Che cosa decisero di fare i creditori di Roderigo?
11. Che cosa fece Roderigo per scappare ai suoi creditori?
12. Come fece Gianmatteo per salvare Roderigo dai suoi persecutori?
13. Che promessa fece Roderigo a Gianmatteo?
14. Come mantenne la promessa?
15. Dopo di essersi arricchito, che cosa pensava di fare Gianmatteo?
16. Come persuasero Gianmatteo ad andare in Francia?
17. Con quale punizione fu minacciato Gianmatteo, se non riuscisse a scacciare il diavolo?
18. Che risposta ebbe Gianmatteo da Roderigo quando gli parlò stavolta?
19. Che cosa disse Belfagor ai prìncipi dell'inferno, tornando dalla terra?

BANDELLO

1. Come era il carattere di Madonna Zilia?
2. Qual'era il suo atteggiamento verso il costume di baciare i forestieri?
3. Da dove veniva Monsignor Filiberto, e a che tipo di famiglia apparteneva?
4. Quale fu l'atteggiamento di Madonna Zilia verso Filiberto?
5. Quale era la riputazione degli Spoletini?
6. L'amico spoletino di Filiberto, che cosa promise di fare per far guarire quest'ultimo?
7. Lo spoletino che cosa fece per mantenere la sua promessa?
8. Che risposta ebbe Filiberto da Madonna Zilia quando le parlò?
9. Come avvenne che Filiberto fece voto di restar muto?
10. Per quanti anni doveva stare senza parlare?
11. Dove andò Filiberto dopo di essersi partito da Madonna Zilia?
12. In che modo si fece ammirare?
13. Che cosa promise il re a chi avesse fatto guarire Filiberto?
14. Con quali condizioni il re dovette modificare la sua promessa, e perchè?
15. Che cosa pensò Madonna Zilia che Filiberto avrebbe fatto, una volta liberato dal suo voto di silenzio?
16. Con che punizione fu minacciata Madonna Zilia, non avendo ottenuto i risultati che aveva sperati?
17. Come avvenne che Madonna Zilia non fu punita?

QUESTIONNAIRE

18. Che ricompenso diede il re a Monsignor Filiberto?
19. Che ricompenso diede Filiberto a Madonna Zilia?

Verga

1. Malpelo perché era chiamato così?
2. Come trattavano Malpelo a casa e nella miniera?
3. Che cosa si estraeva dalla miniera?
4. Quale era il carattere del padre di Malpelo?
5. Come morì Mastro Misciu?
6. Quando morì il padre di Malpelo, da dove fecero venire l'ingegnere?
7. Alla morte di suo padre, che cosa fece Malpelo?
8. Ranocchio chi era, e perché era stato ridotto a lavorare nella miniera?
9. Quali erano i rapporti tra Malpelo e Ranocchio?
10. Malpelo come trattava l'asino grigio?
11. Quale fu la reazione di Malpelo al vedere la scarpa di suo padre?
12. Quale fu la sorte dell'asino grigio?
13. Quale fu la sorte di Ranocchio?
14. Il fugitivo perché decise di tornare in prigione?
15. Quale fu la sorte di Malpelo?

Fogazzaro

1. Quali erano le condizioni economiche della famiglia San Donà?
2. Descrivete il carattere del Sior Beneto.
3. Descrivete la persona e il carattere di Bianca.
4. Come era andato a finire il matrimonio di Bianca, e perché?
5. Descrivete la persona e il carattere di Ermes Torranza.
6. Quali erano stati i rapporti fra Bianca e il poeta?
7. A che stagione ha luogo l'azione principale della novella?
8. Descrivete i Dalla Carretta e i loro ospiti.
9. In che modo Bianca viene a sapere della morte del suo amico?
10. Descrivete l'effetto della triste notizia su Bianca.
11. Qual'è la reazione di Bianca contro il gruppo dei Dalla Carretta?
12. Descrivete il carattere della madre di Bianca.
13. Che cosa fa Bianca, dopo di essere uscita dal gruppo?
14. Che cosa dice la lettera di Torranza?

QUESTIONNAIRE

15. Che cosa fa Bianca, dopo di aver letto la lettera?
16. Il Sior Beneto come tratta la moglie?
17. Descrivete la sala del piano.
18. Qual'è la reazione di Bianca alla musica che il poeta le ha chiesto di suonare?
19. Chi viene a trovare Bianca nella sala del piano?
20. Che cosa è stato fatto, e da chi, perché la storia si termini così?

Fucini

1. A fare che cosa l'ingegnere era stato a Pietrarsa?
2. Che cosa scommisero l'ingegnere e il suo amico?
3. Per quale ragione mancava l'acqua a Pietrarsa?
4. Dove era stato deciso dapprima di mettere la fontana?
5. Che cosa successe come risultato di questa prima decisione?
6. Quali erano le lagnanze degli abitanti degli altri quartieri?
7. Dopo la prima sommossa, dove decisero di mettere la fontana?
8. Dove decisero di metterla dopo la seconda scenata?
9. Prima della seduta del tribunale, di che cosa si lamentava l'ingegnere?
10. Che ricompenso diede il tribunale al sor Girolamo, all'accollatario e all'ingegnere?
11. Quale fu il risultato finale di tutte le deliberazioni?

D'Annunzio

1. Dove si trovano i villaggi di Radusa e di Mascálico?
2. Descrivete il fanatico Giacobbe.
3. Perché i Radusani volevano che si facesse uscire il braccio o il busto di San Pantaleone?
4. Quale era l'atteggiamento dei Radusani e dei Mascalicesi verso i loro santi patroni?
5. Pallura perché tardava a tornare con le candele?
6. In che stato era Pallura al suo ritorno?
7. Che cosa sospettarono i Radusani che fosse successo con i ceri?
8. Come era la madre di Pallura?
9. I Radusani perché attaccarono Mascálico?
10. Chi diede l'allarme ai Mascalicesi?
11. Contro chi i Radusani diressero i loro attacchi, prima di giungere alla chiesa?

QUESTIONNAIRE

12. Descrivete i Mascalicesi.
13. Che cosa volevano fare i Radusani con il busto di San Pantaleone?
14. Che cosa fece Giacobbe per far entrare i Radusani nella chiesa?
15. Quale fu la sorte di Giacobbe e di San Pantaleone?

PIRANDELLO

1. Il professor Gori perché sbuffava e s'irritava?
2. Perché era obbligato a portare la marsina?
3. Che cosa successe con la manica della marsina?
4. Che cosa trovò il professore all'arrivare a casa della signorina Reis?
5. Quale era il rapporto tra il professore e la signorina Reis?
6. Come la signorina Reis si era fidanzata con Andrea Migri?
7. Qual'era l'atteggiamento dei parenti dello sposo verso il matrimonio?
8. Descrivete la madre dello sposo.
9. In che stato era Cèsara Reis?
10. Che cosa fece il professore per incoraggiare la signorina Reis?
11. Che cosa fece il Gori per imporre ai parenti del Migri la sua volontà?
12. Che cosa successe al municipio?

PALAZZESCHI

1. All'inizio della novella, che cosa fa Nunzia?
2. Qual'è l'atteggiamento di Bistino verso il marchese? di Bistino verso Nunzia? di Nunzia verso Bistino?
3. Per chi aveva lavorato Nunzia prima di sposarsi?
4. Come Bistino e Nunzia si erano venuti a sposare?
5. Come si era rovinato il marchese?
6. Come vivono Bistino e Nunzia?
7. Il marchese come aveva trattato Bistino, e con quale risultato?
8. Qual'è l'atteggiamento di Nunzia verso il marchese?
9. Che cosa fa Bistino al sentire che Nunzia vuol invitare il marchese a pranzo?
10. Qual'è la reazione del marchese la prima volta che viene a pranzo?
11. Di che cosa si lagna il marchese?
12. Qual'è la reazione di Bistino quando il marchese si rallegra?

13. Che cosa fa il marchese per ristabilire il suo dominio su Bistino?
14. Che cosa dice Bistino a Nunzia per giustificare il contegno del marchese?
15. Quali sono le maniere del marchese verso Nunzia?
16. Nunzia permette che Bistino paragoni il marchese con la contessa, o no, e per quali ragioni?
17. Che cosa porta Bistino al colmo della beatitudine?
18. I tre dove vanno a spasso quando escono insieme?
19. Di che tipo di persone fanno la conoscenza?
20. Qual'è l'utilità di Bistino e Nunzia per il marchese? del marchese per Bistino e Nunzia?

ALVARO

1. Verso che època si svolge l'azione del racconto?
2. Da quanto tempo si era ristabilito il ràpido?
3. Quanta gente c'era nel treno?
4. Per quale ragione litigavano lo studente e l'uomo con la borsa sottobraccio?
5. L'uomo tarchiato con chi litigò dapprima?
6. Descrivete l'uomo tarchiato.
7. Descrivete il giovane osservato dall'uomo tarchiato.
8. Descrivete la vecchia seduta sul sacco.
9. Con che tipo di giocàttolo si divertiva la vecchia?
10. Come era costruito il giocàttolo?
11. Perché si lamentava la vecchia?
12. Chi venne a rassicurare la vecchia?
13. Perché la vecchia pensava che Catània fosse più vicina di Reggio?
14. Di che tipo era il secondo giocàttolo?
15. In che modo l'uomo tarchiato tentò di uccidere la vecchia?
16. Che cosa sarebbe successo anche con il secondo giocàttolo prima che la vecchia fosse tornata al suo paese?
17. Che impressione i giocàttoli avrebbero fatto sui nipotini della vecchia?

MORAVIA

1. Come definisce il nonno la legge della concorrenza?
2. Qual'è l'atteggiamento personale del nonno verso i compratori?

3. Che cosa dice il nonno sopra l'utilità della prepotenza nel commercio?
4. Che cosa vende il protagonista (la persona che narra la storia) sul suo carrettino?
5. Dove si stabilisce il protagonista?
6. Dapprima, come vanno le cose?
7. Descrivete il protagonista.
8. Descrivete le due donne che vengono a fargli concorrenza.
9. Qual'è il risultato della concorrenza tra il protagonista e le due donne, e per quale ragione?
10. Che cosa succede quando il giovane "paino" o bellimbusto si avvia verso Eunice?
11. Per quali ragioni crede il protagonista di aver attaccato briga con il giovane bellimbusto?
12. Come si sente e che cosa fa il protagonista quando Eunice gli dice che egli le piace?
13. Come riescono i tentativi del protagonista di far la corte ad Eunice?
14. Chi è l'amante di Eunice?
15. Che cosa fa il protagonista per far dispetto ad Eunice e sua madre?
16. Chi viene ad aiutare le due donne?
17. Qual'è l'èsito delle azioni del protagonista?
18. Che cosa fa dopo di essere uscito da Regina Coeli?
19. Che cosa ha causato la rovina del protagonista?

VOCABULARY

This is not a complete vocabulary, but a listing of the more unusual or more difficult words which would probably not be known after one year of Italian.

Stress is indicated wherever it does not fall on the next-to-the-last syllable. The grave accent (`) is used except for the closed *e* and *o* vowels, which are marked with the acute (´).

abbellire to embellish
abbigliamento m. garment
abbonacciare to calm down
abbondévole abundant
abbrancare to grasp, seize
abbrutire to brutalize
accadèmia f. concert
accalcarsi to crowd
accanimento m. fury
accecare to blind
accennare to make a sign
accetta f. hatchet, axe
acchiappare to seize, grab
accidènte m. mishap
acciò che in order that
accógliere to receive
accollatàrio m. contractor
accomodare to fix up
accomodato suitable
accomodatura f. repair
acconciare to fix up, take care of, make comfortable
accòrgersi (*di*) to perceive
accostarsi to go up close
acquistare to acquire
acquisto m. acquisition
addirittura downright
ad(d)ivenire to happen
addossarsi to lean against
adempiere to fulfill

àdipe f. fat
adrièto back
adunque then
affacciare to show (as at a window)
affannato out of breath
affanno m. trouble, worry
affaticarsi to strive
afferrare to grasp, seize
affestellare to festoon
affocante suffocating
affollato crowded
affondare to bury
affrettare to hurry
agghiacciante chilling
aggirarsi to turn
aggrappato clinging
agguantare to grasp, seize
agiatamente at one's ease
agio m. ease
aguzzo pointed
àire m. flight
aita f. aid, help
albèrgo m. hotel, hostel, dwelling, home
allacciamento m. linking up
allampanato emaciated, gaunt
all'analda after the fashion of Hainault (hemmed up?)
allièva f. pupil

alloggiare to lodge
allontanarsi to go away
almanco at least
altressì in the same way, likewise
ambascia f. shortness of breath
ambo both
ambulante walking, wandering
ammazzare to kill
ammiccare to wink, blink
ammirativo in amazement
ammirazione f. wonder
ammutolimento m. hush
anco also, too, still
andatura f. course, way
anelare to pant
anèlito m. sigh
angherìa f. oppression
angoscia f. anguish
animoso courageous, spirited
antipàtico repulsive
anzi che before
appagare to satisfy
appalto m. contract
appo with
arcano hidden, mysterious
arcidiàvolo m. arch-devil
arcolaio m. skein-winder
àrgine m. embankment
arnese m. implement; (worthless) fellow
arrecare to bring, cause
arrotino m. knife-sharpener
arruffato dishevelled
artificioso artful
ascella f. armpit
àspide m. asp, adder
aspro harsh
assai numerous
assediare to besiege, assail
assembramento m. assemblage
assembrare to assemble
assessore m. assistant judge
assetto m. provision, arrangement
assicurare to assure
assopirsi to become drowsy
astanti m. pl. those present

astioso rancorous
astùzia f. cleverness
attaccarsi to arise
atteggiamento m. position, attitude
atteggiarsi to take a position
attitùdine f. aptitude; attitude
attonito astonished, dazed
audace bold, daring
augùrio m. augury, omen
avemo we have
avisamento m. advice
avvantaggiarsi to be benefitted
avvedersi to become aware
avvedimento m. warning
avveduto shrewd
avvegnaché although
avvenente charming, attractive
avvenévole clever
avvenire to happen
avventurato fortunate
avviluppare to envelop, enfold
avvinchiare to entwine
avvòlgere to wrap
azzuffarsi to quarrel

bacchetta f. rod
baco m. silkworm
badare to pay attention
bagliore m. flash of fire
bagordo m. riotous feast
balbettamento m. stammering
balbettare to stammer
baldòria f. merrymaking
balenare to flash
balenìo m. succession of flashes
baleno m. flash
balìa f. authority
balordo clumsy
balzare to bound, leap
banda f. region
bandierata f. procession with banners
bandire to publish, proclaim
bando m. proclamation
bara f. bier
baratro m. abyss
barbaglio m. gleam

barcollare to stagger
barlume m. dim light
barocco over-ornamented
barroccino m. sulky
basciare to kiss
bastonatura f. beating
battilòro m. gold-beater's shop
battisòffia f. fright
battitura f. beating
battuta f. bar (of music)
bàvero m. coat-collar
beccone m. booby
beffa f. jest, trick
beffare to trick, deceive
belluino bestial
benedire to bless
berretto m. cap
bezzi m. pl. money
biancicare to shine white
biffa f. measuring-rod
bifolco m. ploughman
binàrio m. track
birbone m. rascal
birichina f. little rascal
bisaccia m. knapsack
biscia f. snake
bistecca f. steak
blasone m. coat-of-arms
boccale m. jug
bocconi face downwards
bolla f. bubble
bollo m. stamp
borbottare to mutter
bosco m. wood
botta f. blow; toad
braccio m. arm; ell
bramare to desire ardently, yearn for
bramosamente eagerly
branca f. claw
brandello m. strip, rag, scrap
brandire to brandish
brìciola f. crumb, bit
briga f. trouble, bother
brigare to intrigue
brigata f. group; household
brillante m. gem
brina f. frost

brìvido m. shiver
brontolare to grumble
brullo barren
bruttura f. filth, nastiness
buio dark
bulicame m. seething flood
bullo m. bully
bùrbero brusque, gruff
burrascoso stormy
buttare to throw

cacciare to hunt, chase, thrust
cagionare to cause
cagione f. reason
calcagno m. heel
calce f. lime
calcio m. kick
calere to matter, be important
calìgine f. mist
calvo bald
calza f. stocking
cambiale f. promissory note
cambiatore m. money-changer
càmbio m. exchange
campare to live; to save
canaglia f. rabble
canapè m. sofa
canestro m. basket
cangiare to change
canneto m. canebrake
cannuccia f. cane
canonicale canonical, pertaining to a canon
canònico m. canon (church dignitary)
càntico m. song, chant
capire to understand; to fit in
capitare to come, arrive, happen
capo m. head; chief; end
carcame m. carcass
càrcere f. jail
carèstia f. scarcity
caricare to load
càrico m. charge; burden
càrico loaded
carnagione f. complexion
carnasciale m. carnival
carrettino m. push-cart

VOCABULARY

cartapècora f. parchment
cartièra f. paper-mill
cartoccio m. wrapping up; packet
casacca f. jacket
cascata f. waterfall
caso m. case, situation
castello m. castle; fortified town
casùpola f. hut
cava f. mine
cavalcatura f. mount (horse)
cavare to take out
cavelle something, somewhat
caviglia f. ankle
cavo hollow
ceffo m. snout, face
celatamente secretly
cembanella f. clarinet
cémbolo m. cymbal
cenno m. sign
cera f. wax
cero m. wax candle
cervellone m. dullard
cesta f. basket
cheto quiet, silent
chiacchierare to chat
chiacchierata f. chat
chiarore m. glow
chiavistello m. bolt
chiazzare to stain
chicca f. piece of candy
china f. slope
chioccia f. hen
chissà who knows
ciambella f. cake
cianfrusaglie f. pl. trash
ciascheduno each one
cicala f. cicada, cricket
cicalatore m. chatterer
cigolìo m. screeching
cìngere to gird, put around
ciocca f. lock
ciotto m. (cobble)stone
circonfuso surrounding
cisti f. cyst
ciuffetto m. little tuft; pile (of hair)
ciuffo m. forelock

ciurmare to swindle
civetta f. owl
clero m. clergy
clientela f. customers
cocci m. pl. crockery
codino m. reactionary
còdolo m. handle
cógliere to pick, take
colare to pour
còllera f. anger
collòquio m. conversation
colmo full
coltello m. knife
combinare to arrange
comecché although
commesso m. clerk
comméttere to entrust
commissàrio m. official
còmodo m. comfort
còmodo comfortable
compare m. friend, crony
compatire to sympathize
compressionato complexioned
comunale municipal; county
comune m. municipality; county
conciare to ruin
conciarsi to get into a state, mess
concilio m. council
concitazione f. excitement
concorrenza f. competition
concorso f. rush
condottiero m. leader
condutta f. leadership
confortare to encourage
congedo m. leave
congiùngere to join
consuèto accustomed
cònia f. jest, joke
conquìdere to conquer, cause trouble to
considerazione f. importance
consigliare to advise
consigliere m. counsellor
consuetùdine f. custom
contadinesco peasant-like
contegno m. behavior
contestazione f. dispute
contrada f. country, region; part

338

of town

contrasto m. conflict

contravvenzione f. infringement

convenévole suitable

convenire to be fitting, necessary

convito m. banquet

convòglio m. train

copertoio m. bedcover

corazziere m. cuirassier, hussar

corbello m. basket

cordone m. string

coreggia f. belt

coricarsi to go to bed

cornamusa f. bagpipe

cornice f. eaves

corniciaio m. frame-maker

corno m. horn

corporatura f. (physical) build

corridoio m. corridor

corrucciato vexed

corsiero m. warhorse

cortile m. courtyard

coscia f. thigh

cospetto m. presence

costrìngere to force

còttimo m. piece-work

covile m. hut

cozzare to clash

credenza f. belief, trust

crepare to die, "croak"

crepuscolare of twilight

crepùscolo m. twilight

critèrio m. judgment

crivellato riddled

crollare to collapse

cruccio m. anger

cucchiaiata f. spoonful

cùffia f. cap

cullare to rock, dandle

culto m. worship

cupidigia f. greed

cùpido eager

cupo dark

cursore m. runner, courier; mail-man

cute f. skin

daccapo again

d'accordo in agreement

dado m. die (cube)

dama f. lady

damo m. lover

danaro m. money

debà = Fr. *débat,* court session

dèbito m. debt

dée it must

dèi you should

delfino m. dolphin

delusione f. disappointment

desinare to lunch

desquamarsi to flake off

dessa f. she

destarsi to awaken

destramente skillfully

dì m. day

dibàttersi to fight

difficìllimo very difficult

dilagarsi to flood, spread out

dilapidare to tear down, squander

dileguarsi to vanish

diletto belovèd

diliberare to decide

dilungarsi to go away

dimissioni f. pl. resignation

dimora f. delay

dimorare to dwell

dipintore m. painter

dipoi afterwards, then

diportarsi to carry oneself

dirupo m. declivity

disagio m. discomfort

disaventura f. misfortune

disgràzia f. misfortune, mishap

disidero m. desire, eagerness

disinore m. dishonor

dispendioso expensive

dispensare to spend

disperato m. madman

dispiegare to unfold

dissenso m. disagreement

disténdere to draw up

ditale m. thimble

doglia f. sorrow

dolersi to complain

domane tomorrow

VOCABULARY

domesticamente familiarly
domestichezza familiarity, friendship
domèstico m. friend
donde whence, whereby
donnaiòlo m. woman-chaser, woman's man
dono m. gift, boon
donzella f. damsel
dote f. dowry
dotto learnèd
drappo m. (fine) cloth
drieto behind

e' he
eb(b)ro drunk
echeggiare to echo
èdera f. ivy
ei he
el it
elitropìa f. "helitropia", an imaginary precious stone
elli he
empi(e)re to fill
epìstola f. epistle, letter
èrcole m. Hercules, giant
esàmine m. examination, study
essolui him
essortare to exhort, urge
essoteco with you
esternare to manifest, display
ètico hectic

fabbro m. smith
faccenda f. affair, business
facultà f. resource, wealth
falce f. sickle
falciatore m. sickle-bearer
falda f. coat-tail
falegname m. carpenter
fallimento m. bankruptcy
fallire to fail, go bankrupt
fallo m. error, mistake
fama f. fame; report
famiglio m. familiar, servant
fanale m. lamp
fannullone m. idler, loafer
fantasìa f. imagination

fantàstico imaginative
fantesca f. servant
farnètico m. crazy behavior
fasciare to bandage
fasciatura f. bandage
fastidiosamente irritatingly
fatica f. trouble, difficulty
fattorìa f. farm
fava f. bean
favèlla f. speech
favellare to speak
fàvola f. fable, story
fé(de) f. faith
ferita f. wound
fesso cracked
festeggiare to celebrate
fia it will be
fiammata f. blaze
fiammeggiare to flame
fiatare to breathe
fidato trusted
fìeno they will be
fièno m. hay
fiero proud; harsh, drastic
fiévole faint, weak
fìngere to pretend
fiòco faint
fionda f. slingshot
fisamente fixedly
fiso firm, hard
fitto crowded, packed
fiumicel(lo) m. little river
flébile mournful, plaintive
floscio flabby
flusso m. flow
foggia f. fashion, style
fogliame m. foliage
folto thick
forastiero m. stranger
formicolìo m. tingling
fornace f. furnace
fornire to finish
fosco gloomy
fossa f. ditch
fragore m. roar
fragoroso noisy
fràngersi to break
frantume m. fragment

340

VOCABULARY

frasca f. leaves, foliage
fraticino m. little friar, novice
fregio m. ornament
frèmito m. trembling, vibration
frettolosamente in haste
frittata f. omelet; scrape, mess
fronda f. leaf
frotta f. crowd, knot (of people)
fue was
fulgore m. radiance
fulvo tawny
fuso molten
fùssino they should be
fustagno m. fustian
fusto m. trunk (of tree)

gabbare to cheat
gagliardo vigorous, upstanding
galante gallant; amatory
galleggiare to float
gallerìa f. tunnel
garrire to gabble, scold
garza f. gauze
gastigare to punish
gelso m. mulberry-tree
gentildonna f. gentlewoman
gentile noble
gentiluomo m. gentleman, nobleman
getto m. jet
gherone m. gusset
ghiado m. sword
ghiaia f. gravel
ghiotto avid, greedy
ginestra f. broom-plant
gingillone m. loafer
ginocchioni on one's knees
giocàttolo m. toy
giornaliero everyday
giostra f. tournament; merry-go-round
giovare to be of use
girare to turn, circulate
gironzolare to move around; bustle
gittare to throw, cast, hurl
giullare m. buffoon
giùngere to arrive

gobbo hunchbacked, hunched over
godere to enjoy
gola f. throat; greed
gonfio swollen, packed full
gonna f. skirt
gonnella f. skirt
governare to govern, rule; bring up
governo m. management
gradino m. step
graffiare to scratch
gramezza f. misery
grattugiare to grate
gravare to weigh down
grembo m. lap
greto m. edge (of river)
grido m. cry, shriek
gronda f. eave
groppone m. small of the back
grossolano coarse
grumo m. clot
guai woe
guanciale m. pillow
guari hardly
guatare to look
gùbbia f. trio (of animals)
guerriero m. warrior
guidalesca f. sore
guiderdone m. reward
guizzo m. flash

hoe I have

ideare to conceive
il him
imbalordire to daze
imbiancare to whiten
imboccatura f. entrance
imbrattare to smear
imbroglione m. swindler
immischiarsi to interfere
imperciò che because
imperio m. empire
imperversare to fight furiously
impiccare to hang
imposta f. leaf (of a door)
inamidare to starch

inarcare to arch, raise
inarcarsi to bend
inasprirsi to grow harsh
incanto m. incantation
incàuto incautious
incerato m. tarpaulin
inchinarsi to bow
inchiodare to nail
inciampare to stumble
incinta pregnant
incògnito unknown
incolto uncultured
incontanente immediately
incontro m. meeting
incùdine f. anvil
indarno in vain
indebolire to weaken
indemoniato possessed by a devil
indirizzarsi to address oneself, adhere
indossare to put on
indugiare to delay, linger
indugio m. delay
infastidito disgusted
infermare to fall sick
ìnfimo very low, base
ingannare to deceive
inganno m. deceit, trickery
ingegnarsi to try
ingènuo naïve
ingigantire to grow gigantic
inginocchiarsi to kneel
ingiù downward
ingiùria f. insult
ingombro obstructed
ingordigia f. greed
iniurioso insulting
innorare to cover with gold
inquilino m. inhabitant
insino a until
inténdere to hear
intepidire to grow cold
intìngere to dip
intirizzirsi to become chilled
intronato in a stupor
inviare to send
inviperito enraged

ipoteca f. mortgage
ippocastano m. horse-chestnut
ire to go
iroso angry, wrathful
irradiamento m. irradiation
ispianare to explain
ispiare to spy out
ìspido shaggy
istiettezza f. purity
istitutrice f. tutor
istoriare to paint
ito gone
iudìzio m. judgment

laggiù down there
làgrima f. tear
lampione m. street-lamp
lanùgine f. down
lapidàrio m. lapidary, dealer in stones
larva f. ghost; mask, shell
lastricare to pave
lattante m. new-born baby
làtteo milky
lazzerone m. vagabond, lazy-bones
leggiero light; irresponsible
leggìo m. music-rack
legnata f. blow (with a stick)
lembo m. edge, strip
lentìggine f. freckle
lesto prompt, quick
letame m. manure
lettiera f. bedstead
levarsi to withdraw, desist
lezzo m. stench
libbra f. pound
licenziare to dismiss
lieve light
liscio smooth
lite f. quarrel
litigio m. quarrel
lodévole praiseworthy
lògoro worn-out
loia f. dirt, filth
loquela f. speech
luccichìo m. glimmer
lùcciola f. firefly

lucente shining
lucerna f. lamp
lumaca f. snail
lumacone m. large snail
lusinghiero flattering
lussare to dislocate
lustro shiny
lutto m. mourning

macchiare to spot
macellaio m. butcher
macellerìa f. butcher's shop
macello m. shambles
màcero bruised
macigno m. boulder
macilento emaciated
macina f. mill-stone
maestoso majestic
maestro m. teacher, tutor
maggiormente especially
maglia f. sweater
malarnese m. rascal
malfattore m. evil-doer, criminal
malgrado in spite of
malinconìa f. melancholy
malincònico melancholy
malinconoso melancholy
malo evil
malvagio wicked
mammalucco m. blockhead
mancare to fail; to die
mandarino m. tangerine
mandra f. herd
manesco quarrelsome
mànica f. sleeve
manicòmio m. madhouse
maniglia f. handle
manìpolo m. group
mannaia f. cleaver, axe
manovella f. handle
maravigliarsi be amazed
marcio rotten
marco m. promissory note
mareggiamento m. surge
marmista m. marble-worker
marmotta f. dunce, oaf
marsina f. frock-coat
martinicca f. brake

masnada f. retinue
mattone m. tile; brick
maturo ripe, well-considered, thorough
mazza f. mace
mazzolino m. bouquet
medesimamente likewise
mediante by means of
membruto limbed
mercatànzia f. merchandise
mercè f. mercy; thanks
merletto m. lace
méscere to mix, mingle
messo m. messenger
mestiere (-o) m. trade, occupation
mestìzia f. sadness
miagolare to meow, yowl
miètere to mow, reap
minaccia f. threat
minaccioso threatening
minchionerìe f. pl. nonsense
minuto detailed
mirare to look
mìschia f. mêlée
misericòrdia f. pity
mitraglia f. machine-gun bullets
mòbile m. liquid asset
modi m. pl. ways, behavior
mógliata f. your wife
mole f. mass
molesto obnoxious
molle soft
mondiglie f. pl. rubbish
monellaccio m. nasty brat
moneta f. coin
monistero m. monastery, convent
mòrdere to bite, speak sharply to
mormorìo m. murmuring
morsicare to gnaw, chew
morto dead, killed
motto m. word
multa f. fine
muraglia f. wall
murare to make a wall; to lay (tile, brick)
muricciolo m. little wall

muso m. muzzle; face
mùtolo mute

nappa f. tassel
nari f. pl. nostrils
narice f. nostril
nascoso hidden
nastro m. ribbon
nàtica f. buttock
navata f. nave
ne us
nèbbia f. fog, mist
negoziante m. shop-keeper
nemistade f. hostility
nimico m. enemy
niquitoso angry
nitrire to neigh, whinny
niuno no one
noce f. walnut
noia f. annoyance, worry
nomato named, specified
nozze f. pl. wedding
nuca f. nape of the neck
nudritore m. tutor
nuova f. news
nuovo new; strange; inexpert

occhiata f. glance
occhiello m. button-hole
oliveto m. olive-grove
ombrellaio m. umbrella-vendor
omèrico Homeric
omino m. little man
omone m. big man
orazione f. prayer
ordinare to arrange, agree, set
òrdine m. order; arrangement;
    procedure
orgoglio m. pride
orlare to edge
orlo m. edge
orto m. garden
ospìzio m. hostel
ossequi m. pl. regards
ossesso obsessed, mad
òstico repulsive
ottone m. brass

padule m. swamp
paga f. pay
paglia f. straw
paìno m. dandy, fop
palanca f. penny
palco m. (grand)stand
palesare to reveal
palleggiare to bat back and
    forth
palo m. stake
pàlpebra f. eyelid
panciotto m. waistcoat
panno m. (coarse) cloth
pantanoso swampy
paragone m. comparison
parapiglia m. turmoil
parare to decorate
parcamente sparingly, frugally
parentado m. relations
parete f. wall
pàrgolo m. child
par(i) equal, peer
partita f. departure; game
partito m. party; decision;
    (marriage) match
passata f. try
passeggiare to walk about
passeggiata f. walk, trip
pastore m. shepherd
pastrano m. overcoat
patire to suffer
pegamòide f. artificial leather
pelle f. skin
pellìcola f. film
pendìo m. slope
penoso painful
pentimento m. repentance,
    change of mind
penzolare to dangle
percepire to perceive, realize
perciocché because
pèrfido perfidious
periglioso dangerous, perilous
perseguitatore m. pursuer
pèrtica f. pole
pesare to weigh upon, trouble
pesca f. peach
pettégolo gossiping

VOCABULARY

pezzente m. beggar
piaga f. sore
piàgnere to weep
piagnucolare to whimper, snivel
pianeta f. cape
pianta f. plant
piazzaletto m. little square
picchetto m. pike
picchiare to hit, strike, tap
pìcciolo little
piè(de) m. foot
piegare to bend, yield
pilastro m. pillar
pinguèdine f. fatness
piòlo m. column
piombare to plunge
pioppo m. poplar
pipistrello m. bat
plaga f. extent, stretch
plùmbeo leaden
polendone m. slow-poke
podere m. power
poggio m. hill
polla f. spring
poltrone m. coward
pòlve(re) f. powder
pómice m. pumice
popone m. melon
popularmente with popular support
porcone m. big swine
posare to place, put down
potenza f. power
pozzo m. well; shaft
precipitare to rush headlong
prémere to press
premura f. concern
premuroso eager, solicitous
preparativo m. preparation
prepotente aggressive, overbearing, domineering
presepe m. Christmas manger
prestarsi to lend itself
presto reàdy
priego m. prayer, request
processo m. trial
proda f. edge, side
prode m. advantage

prode brave
profèzia f. prophecy
pro(f)ferire to offer; to utter
propagarsi to spread
propinquo near
proponimento m. intent
prosopopèa f. affectation
proténdersi to lean forward
prova f. test
provare to experience; to try
provigione f. stipend
pugno m. fist; blow
pungente caustic
punto not at all
puote can, is able
pupazzo m. puppet

quantunque although
quarto m. quarter
quassù up here
quatto crouched, cowering
quattrini m. pl. money
quèrcia f. oak
querela f. complaint
questi this man; the latter
quivi there, then

rabdomante m. diviner
raccattare to pick up again
raccolta f. harvest
raccomandarsi to beg, implore
ràdica f. brier-wood
radunare to collect, gather
raggrinzato wrinkled up
ragionamento m. discussion
ragionare to talk, discuss
ragunare to collect, gather
rallentare to slow down
ramingo wandering
rammentare to bring to mind
rannicchiarsi to crouch
rannuvolarsi to grow cloudy, cloud over
ranòcchio m. frog
rapa f. turnip
rappacificarsi to reconcile oneself
rasciutto dry

rasente just over
rattoppare to patch up
raunare to bring together
ravviare to tidy
ravvisare to recognize
ravvòlgere to turn over
reame m. kingdom
recare to hand, give
recarsi to go; to take
regnare to reign, rule
rena f. sand
rèndita f. income
reni f. pl. loins
repentino sudden
respirare to breathe
ressa f. crowd
retta f. attention
riandare to re-trace
riavventurarsi to rush in again, return to the fight
ribaldo base
ribaltarsi to capsize, overturn
ribrezzo m. shivering
ricacciarsi to put back on
ricambiare to reciprocate, return
ricamo m. embroidery
ricettàcolo m. receptacle, sink
ricevuta f. receipt
ricògliere to collect
ricoverare to shelter
ridestarsi to re-awaken
rientro m. recess
riepìlogo m. résumé
riguardo m. consideration
rimanente m. remainder
rimasuglio m. remnant
rimboccare to roll up
rimbombare to re-echo
rimessa f. coach-house
rimpolpettare to beat to a pulp
rimpròvero m. reproof
rincrescimento m. regret
rintocco m. tolling
riperc(u)òtersi to resound
rìpido steep
ripréndere to begin again
ripristinare to re-establish
risata f. laugh

rischiarare to light up
riserbarsi to set aside (for oneself)
riso m. laughter
risollevarsi to rise again
risparmiare to save
rispianare to explain
risponsione f. answer
ristarsi to remain
risvegliarsi to awaken
ritenere to hold back
ritrarre to profit
ritratto m. profit; picture
riverberare to reflect
rivèrbero m. wavering reflection
riversare to cast down, pour
rivo m. stream
rizzarsi to stand up, stand out
roba f. stuff, things
roco hoarse
ródere to gnaw, eat
roggio russet
rogna f. mange
romanza f. ballad
romeo m. pilgrim, traveller
romore m. noise, hue-and-cry; noise-making instrument
romoreggiare to make a noise
rompiscàtole m. bore
ronca f. billhook
róndine f. sparrow
rosicchiare to gnaw
rossiccio reddish
rossore m. red glow
rovente red-hot
rovesciare to turn over, overturn; to invert
rovina f. ruin
rovinare to ruin
rubare to steal
rùggine f. rust
ruggito m. roar
rugoso wrinkled
rumorìo m. rumbling
rùvido rough, coarse, rude

sabbioso sandy
sacramento m. oath

VOCABULARY

saggio m. proof
salamelecco m. obeisance
salita f. slope
salmo m. psalm
salotto m. living-room, drawing-room
saltare to jump
salute f. health; salvation
sanare to cure
sanguigno blood-red
sanguinare to bleed
sanità f. health
sano healthy
santitade f. holiness
sanza without
sappi know (imperative)
sarde it will be
satolla f. one's fill
sàvio wise
sàzio sated
sbalordimento m. daze
sbarazzare to rid
sbattacchiare to bang
sbigottire to frighten
sbilenco bandy-legged
sbirciare to eye, look askance at
sboccare to come out
sbocco outlet, outflow
sbòrnia f. drunken spree
sbracato trouserless
sbrigare to get out of the way, get over
sbrigarsi to hurry up
sbronza f. drunkenness
sbucare to come out
sbuffare to puff
scaffale m. shelf
scaglionare to arrange in rows
scaldare to heat
scalinata f. staircase
scaltrezza f. shrewdness
scalzo barefoot
scampanellata f. ring (of a bell)
scampo m. escape
scannare to cut the throat of
scansare to avoid
scantonare to turn aside
scapaccione m. cuff, blow

scapigliato disheveled
scaramuccia f. skirmish
scaricare to unload
scarmigliato disheveled
scarsella f. purse
scatenare to unchain, set loose
scàtola f. box
scavezzarsi to break one's neck
schiamazzo m. noise, din
schiantare to smash, ruin
schianto m. thud
schiccherare to scribble
schiena f. back
schifiltoso finicky
schioppettata f. musket-shot
schioppo m. musket
schiuma f. foam
schizzare to send out, jerk
sciagura f. misfortune
scialletto m. shawl
sciancato crippled
sciara f. black gravelly material formed of decomposing lava
scintillare to sparkle
scinto ungirded
sciocchezza f. foolishness
sciocco foolish
sciògliere to set loose; melt; keep (a vow)
scivolare to slide, scrape
scodella f. soup-plate
scodellare to dish out
scodinzolare to wag the tail; to scuttle
scommessa f. bet
scomméttere to bet
scompartimento m. compartment
scongiurare to beg, supplicate
scongiurazione f. supplication
sconnesso disconnected
sconsolato disconsolate, despairing
sconvòlgere to upset
scopa f. broom-plant
scòppio m. outburst
scoprire to discover, uncover
scordarsi to forget

scórrere to flow
scorta f. supply
scossa f. jerk
scricchiolare to creak
scricchiolìo m. creaking
scrivanìa f. desk
scrollare to shake
scrosciare to roar
scroscio m. roar
scucirsi to come unsewed
scucitura f. place which has come unsewed
scultòrio finely chiselled
scuòtere to shake
scure f. axe
scusso plain, bare
sdegno (outburst of) contempt
sdraiare to stretch out
seccare to bore
seco with himself (herself)
sècolo m. century; world
segare to saw, cut
sèggiola f. chair
seguzione f. execution
sembiante m. appearance
senno m. wisdom
sensìbile perceptible
serbare to keep
serrare to hold tight
serratura f. lock
servitù f. (expression of) service
sezzaio last
sfacciatàggine f. effrontery
sfegatare to work one's hardest
sferruzzare to knit vigorously
sferzare to whip
sfilaccicare to fray
sfilare to line up
sfiorare to graze
sfogo m. outlet, vent
sforzare to force
sfrontato impudent
sfuggire to escape
sfumato fading off; in dim outline
sgabuzzino m. closet, little room
sgangherato off its hinges; (of bones) scattered, separated

sgomberare to clear away
sgomentare to alarm, dismay
sgomento terrified
sgorgare to pour
sgualcire to rumple
sìbilo m. whistling
signoreggiare to rule over
signorone m. very high-class person
sìndaco m. mayor
singhiozzare to sob
singhiozzo m. sob
slancio m. impetus
slattare to wean
slavato insipid
smanacciare to wave one's hands
smarrirsi to get lost
smemorato out of one's mind
smeraldo m. emerald
smilzo thin
smorzato muffled
snodare to untie
sodo solid, heavy
sodotto seduced
soffiare to blow; steal
sóffio m. puff
soggiùngere to add
solco m. trail
soldano m. Sultan
soldo m. penny; (pl.) money
sollevare to raise
sommesso low, meek
sommovimento m. commotion
sonaglio m. bell
soperchierìa f. insult; mean trick
sopracciglio m. eyebrow
sopraggiùngere to arrive
soprapprèndere to take by surprise
soprassalto m. jerk, start
soprastare to be imminent
sopravvenire to arrive
sopruso m. imposition
sórgere to rise
sorso m. sip
sorte f. fate; lot (chance)
sottile clever

VOCABULARY

sotoporre to subject
sovente often
soverchiare to overcome, rise above
sovèrchio excessive
spaccare to split
spacciato done for, ruined
spada f. sword
spalancare to open wide
spalletta f. parapet
sparato m. shirt-front
spàrgere to shed, scatter
spàsimo m. agony
spasseggiare to take out riding
spasso m. walk
spavento m. fright
spaventoso ferocious, frightful
spazientirsi to grow impatient
sperienza f. experience, experiment
sperperare to waste
sperto expert
spesa f. expense
spezierìa f. grocer's shop
spianata f. esplanade
spiattellare to declare openly
spicciativo expeditious
spiegare to explain; to unfold
spillo m. pin
spiraglio m. aperture
spirare to expire, die
spiritato bewitched
spolpare to pull off the flesh
spórgere to extend, hold out
sportello m. door
spossato exhausted
spostamento m. displacement
spostatura f. misplaced behavior, discourtesy
sprazzo m. splash, spray
sprezzante contemptuous
sprofondare to sink
spruzzare to sprinkle
spuntare to appear
spunto blunt; lifeless
spunzonare to poke
sputare to spit
squillare to ring out

squittire to yelp
staccarsi to come off
stagnaro m. tinsmith
stamani this morning
stanga f. shaft
stanza f. room; dwelling
sténdere to extend, stretch out
stento m. toil
sterrare to dig
stinco m. shin
stizzoso irritable
stòrcere to twist
stòria f. story; history; fuss
stornello m. starling
stoviglie f. pl. household wares
strabuzzare to budge
stracciato in rags
stracco dead tired
strage f. slaughter
stralunato upset; with a vacant stare
stramazzare to fall heavily
strano strange, foreign
straordinari m. pl. over-time expenses
strappare to tear
strappo m. gash; pull, jerk
strascicare to drag out
straziare to torture
strèpito m. noise
stretta f. squeeze, contraction
stretto m. strait
strillare to yell, shriek
striscia f. strip
stropicciare to rub
strozzare to strangle
strozzino m. usurer
stuolo m. troop, flock
stupire to amaze, astonish
stura f. uncorking
suadere to persuade
subitàneo sudden
sudiciume m. filth
sufficienza f. haughtiness
suggello m. seal
sulfùreo sulphur-yellow
supèrbia f. pride
supplicare to beg

suscitare to arouse, kindle
suso up
susurrare to whisper
susurro m. whisper
suttilitate f. cleverness
svenire to faint, swoon
sventura f. misfortune
sventurato unfortunate

tafferuglio m. scuffle
talpa f. mole
tamburo m. drum
tanfo m. musty smell
tarchiato stocky
teco with you
tela f. cloth
téndere to stretch out
tènero tender; shaky
testè now
testimone m. witness
testimònio m. witness
tintinnìo m. tinkling
tintinno m. metallic sound
tomo m. tumble, fall
topo m. rat
toppa f. patch
tórbido disorderly
tordo m. thrush
tôrre to take
torvo sullen, grim
tosto soon, quickly
traballare to totter
trafelato out of breath; worn out
trafficare to bustle
traforo m. tunnel
tragitto m. trip
tràino m. cart
trambusto m. uproar
tramonto m. sunset
trapelare to leak out, filter through
trascuratamente negligently
trasloco m. moving
trastullarsi to enjoy oneself
trattenere to hold back, hold open
trattenersi to stay

travagliarsi to be busy, deal
travatura f. beam
traverso transverse
travicello m. beam
tregua f. truce, interruption
tribolare to cause tribulation to
tromba f. trumpet
troncare to cut off
troppo too much; very
truce truculent
tue you
turchino purple
turìbolo m. thurible
tuttavìa still

ubbìa f. superstitious belief
ubbioso superstitious
ubriaca inebriated, drunk
uccellare to mock, laugh to scorn
udire to hear
uggia f. aversion, dislike
ululato m. wailing
uncino m. hook
unguento m. ointment
uragano m. hurricane
urlare to yell, howl
urlo m. howl, shout
usanza f. custom, manners
uscio m. door, exit

vadi go
vago attractive
valente worthy
valutare to evaluate, fathom
vano m. open space
vantaggio m. advantage
varco m. passage
veggendo seeing
vegnente coming
veleno m. poison
velo m. cloth
vendetta f. revenge, vengeance
vendicare to avenge
ventura f. fortune
vergogna f. shame
vernaccia f. a kind of white wine
vertìgine f. vertigo, dizziness
vertù f. power

VOCABULARY

veruno no ... at all
véscovo m. bishop
vestiàrio m. wardrobe; clothing
vetrata f. glazed window
vetri m. pl. glassware
vicoletto m. alleyway
vigna f. vineyard
vile base, venial
villano rude, discourteous
vìllico m. rustic
virtuoso powerful, endowed with (magic) strength
vispo lively, sprightly
vita f. life; waist
vitupèrio m. curse

vivanda f. food
volenteroso eager, willing
volontade f. will
vôlta f. vault
volto m. face
vosco with you

zampa f. paw
zappa f. mattock
zeppo chock-full
zitellona f. old maid
zittire to chirp (of insects)
zitto quiet
zucca f. gourd; head
zuzzerellone m. scatter-brain

A CATALOG OF SELECTED
DOVER BOOKS
IN ALL FIELDS OF INTEREST

A CATALOG OF SELECTED DOVER
BOOKS IN ALL FIELDS OF INTEREST

CONCERNING THE SPIRITUAL IN ART, Wassily Kandinsky. Pioneering work by father of abstract art. Thoughts on color theory, nature of art. Analysis of earlier masters. 12 illustrations. 80pp. of text. 5⅜ x 8½. 23411-8

ANIMALS: 1,419 Copyright-Free Illustrations of Mammals, Birds, Fish, Insects, etc., Jim Harter (ed.). Clear wood engravings present, in extremely lifelike poses, over 1,000 species of animals. One of the most extensive pictorial sourcebooks of its kind. Captions. Index. 284pp. 9 x 12. 23766-4

CELTIC ART: The Methods of Construction, George Bain. Simple geometric techniques for making Celtic interlacements, spirals, Kells-type initials, animals, humans, etc. Over 500 illustrations. 160pp. 9 x 12. (Available in U.S. only.) 22923-8

AN ATLAS OF ANATOMY FOR ARTISTS, Fritz Schider. Most thorough reference work on art anatomy in the world. Hundreds of illustrations, including selections from works by Vesalius, Leonardo, Goya, Ingres, Michelangelo, others. 593 illustrations. 192pp. 7⅛ x 10¼. 20241-0

CELTIC HAND STROKE-BY-STROKE (Irish Half-Uncial from "The Book of Kells"): An Arthur Baker Calligraphy Manual, Arthur Baker. Complete guide to creating each letter of the alphabet in distinctive Celtic manner. Covers hand position, strokes, pens, inks, paper, more. Illustrated. 48pp. 8¼ x 11. 24336-2

EASY ORIGAMI, John Montroll. Charming collection of 32 projects (hat, cup, pelican, piano, swan, many more) specially designed for the novice origami hobbyist. Clearly illustrated easy-to-follow instructions insure that even beginning papercrafters will achieve successful results. 48pp. 8¼ x 11. 27298-2

THE COMPLETE BOOK OF BIRDHOUSE CONSTRUCTION FOR WOODWORKERS, Scott D. Campbell. Detailed instructions, illustrations, tables. Also data on bird habitat and instinct patterns. Bibliography. 3 tables. 63 illustrations in 15 figures. 48pp. 5¼ x 8½. 24407-5

BLOOMINGDALE'S ILLUSTRATED 1886 CATALOG: Fashions, Dry Goods and Housewares, Bloomingdale Brothers. Famed merchants' extremely rare catalog depicting about 1,700 products: clothing, housewares, firearms, dry goods, jewelry, more. Invaluable for dating, identifying vintage items. Also, copyright-free graphics for artists, designers. Co-published with Henry Ford Museum & Greenfield Village. 160pp. 8¼ x 11. 25780-0

HISTORIC COSTUME IN PICTURES, Braun & Schneider. Over 1,450 costumed figures in clearly detailed engravings–from dawn of civilization to end of 19th century. Captions. Many folk costumes. 256pp. 8⅜ x 11¾. 23150-X

CATALOG OF DOVER BOOKS

THE STORY OF THE TITANIC AS TOLD BY ITS SURVIVORS, Jack Winocour (ed.). What it was really like. Panic, despair, shocking inefficiency, and a little heroism. More thrilling than any fictional account. 26 illustrations. 320pp. 5⅜ x 8½.
20610-6

FAIRY AND FOLK TALES OF THE IRISH PEASANTRY, William Butler Yeats (ed.). Treasury of 64 tales from the twilight world of Celtic myth and legend: "The Soul Cages," "The Kildare Pooka," "King O'Toole and his Goose," many more. Introduction and Notes by W. B. Yeats. 352pp. 5⅜ x 8½.
26941-8

BUDDHIST MAHAYANA TEXTS, E. B. Cowell and others (eds.). Superb, accurate translations of basic documents in Mahayana Buddhism, highly important in history of religions. The Buddha-karita of Asvaghosha, Larger Sukhavativyuha, more. 448pp. 5⅜ x 8½.
25552-2

ONE TWO THREE . . . INFINITY: Facts and Speculations of Science, George Gamow. Great physicist's fascinating, readable overview of contemporary science: number theory, relativity, fourth dimension, entropy, genes, atomic structure, much more. 128 illustrations. Index. 352pp. 5⅜ x 8½.
25664-2

EXPERIMENTATION AND MEASUREMENT, W. J. Youden. Introductory manual explains laws of measurement in simple terms and offers tips for achieving accuracy and minimizing errors. Mathematics of measurement, use of instruments, experimenting with machines. 1994 edition. Foreword. Preface. Introduction. Epilogue. Selected Readings. Glossary. Index. Tables and figures. 128pp. 5⅜ x 8½.
40451-X

DALÍ ON MODERN ART: The Cuckolds of Antiquated Modern Art, Salvador Dalí. Influential painter skewers modern art and its practitioners. Outrageous evaluations of Picasso, Cézanne, Turner, more. 15 renderings of paintings discussed. 44 calligraphic decorations by Dalí. 96pp. 5⅜ x 8½. (Available in U.S. only.)
29220-7

ANTIQUE PLAYING CARDS: A Pictorial History, Henry René D'Allemagne. Over 900 elaborate, decorative images from rare playing cards (14th–20th centuries): Bacchus, death, dancing dogs, hunting scenes, royal coats of arms, players cheating, much more. 96pp. 9¼ x 12¼.
29265-7

MAKING FURNITURE MASTERPIECES: 30 Projects with Measured Drawings, Franklin H. Gottshall. Step-by-step instructions, illustrations for constructing handsome, useful pieces, among them a Sheraton desk, Chippendale chair, Spanish desk, Queen Anne table and a William and Mary dressing mirror. 224pp. 8⅛ x 11¼.
29338-6

THE FOSSIL BOOK: A Record of Prehistoric Life, Patricia V. Rich et al. Profusely illustrated definitive guide covers everything from single-celled organisms and dinosaurs to birds and mammals and the interplay between climate and man. Over 1,500 illustrations. 760pp. 7½ x 10⅛.
29371-8